Lloyd Shepherd is a former journalist and digital producer who has worked for the *Guardian*, Channel 4, the BBC and Yahoo. He lives in South London with his family.

By the same author

The English Monster
The Poisoned Island
Savage Magic

LET THE WATERS ABOVE THE HEAVENS FALL,
AND THE EARTH WILL YIELD ITS FRUIT

THE QUATERNARY RESTING
IN THE TERNARY

Printed in London by Simon & Schuster,
Printers, of Gray's Inn Road, London
A.D. 2016
Soli Deo honor et gloria

THE
DETECTIVE
AND THE *Devil*

LLOYD SHEPHERD

**SIMON &
SCHUSTER**

London · New York · Sydney · Toronto · New Delhi

A CBS COMPANY

First published in Great Britain by Simon & Schuster UK Ltd, 2016
A CBS COMPANY

1 3 5 7 9 10 8 6 4 2

Simon & Schuster UK Ltd
1st Floor
Gray's Inn Road
London WC1X 8HB

www.simonandschuster.co.uk

Simon & Schuster Australia, Sydney
Simon & Schuster India, New Delhi

A CIP catalogue record for this book
is available from the British Library

Paperback ISBN: 978-1-47113-612-2
Trade Paperback ISBN: 978-1-47113-611-5
eBook ISBN: 978-1-47113-613-9

Typeset in the UK by M Rules
Printed and bound by CPI Group (UK) Ltd, Croydon, CR0 4YY

Simon & Schuster UK Ltd are committed to sourcing paper
that is made from wood grown in sustainable forests and supports the Forest
Stewardship Council, the leading international forest certification organisation.
Our books displaying the FSC logo are printed on FSC certified paper.

Let he who does not understand either be silent,
or learn

John Dee, *Propaedeumata Aphoristica*

ST. HELENA, 1815

N.G.

James Town

Turk's Cap Bay

Old Dutch Fort

Prosperous Bay

DEADWOOD PLAIN

Longwood

The Devil's Punchbowl

Halley's Mount

Mount Actæon

Diana's Peak

Shark's Valley

Cuckhold's Point

Plantation House

Mount Pleasant

Lot

Sandy Bay

Lot's Wife

High Hill

The GATES of CHAOS

Miles

0   1   2

ACT 1

LONDON

The Universe is like a lyre which has been tuned by the most excellent Maker, and the strings of this lyre are separate Species of the universal whole. If you knew how to touch these strings with skill and make them vibrate, you could bring forth astonishing harmonies. Man himself is entirely analogous to this Universal Lyre.

John Dee, *Propaedeumata Aphoristica*

1585: JACOBUS AND THE LIBRARY

By the time the barge reached Mortlake he had a revolt on his hands. The ill-headed English fools were drunk when they climbed aboard at Deptford and were half-blind and half-mad by Putney. One of them had already gone over the side into the river. Presumably he was dead by now, floating downstream of Hammersmith. The rest of them were on the point of upending the 'whoreson Dutchman' – as they had taken to calling him – into the river to join him.

'Good fellows, fall to 't yarely,' he begged in his adopted voice, the one he thought of as 'English theatrical'. It was good enough for a Bankside theatre, in his view. Too good, perhaps, for these violent men had fallen to mocking it.

'Fall to 't *thyself*,' said one of them, and some of the others giggled. 'Thou art a droning flap-mouthed clot-pole.'

'Did you hear that in a play?' said another of them.

'Go firk thyself,' came the reply.

'Do you not see it?'

He pointed dramatically upstream. The shape of a house. It might have been the necromancer's; it might have been some

3

poor bloody widow's; it might have been Hampton Court itself. He didn't know. He didn't much care by then.

'We are arrived,' he cried, praying it was true. He was by then giving serious consideration to diving off the barge and swimming back to the other boat, the one which had followed them upstream, the one only he knew about. This lot were too stupid and too drunk to be relied upon for the task to come. His scheme was as ridiculous as his dramatic facade.

And yet the place seemed right. The tide was high up against the towpath, and the lighterman he'd paid to bring them here steered the barge alongside. Oars clattered into each other as the drunken Englishmen tried to stow them. They'd been clattering into each other all the way upriver.

Now anxiety descended on his motley crew of ne'er-do-wells, the ale-stewed anger and defiance underworked by the outline of the house jagged in the moonlight, its roof steeply pointed into the sky, more assertive even than the church tower next to it. The place was directly alongside the towpath, and was encrusted with the silhouettes of chimneys and outhouses, with none of the organising principles of a noble riverside palace.

He climbed out of the barge and onto the towpath. Not one of them followed him. He looked back and they were standing in the barge, a ragtaggle gang of frightened little boys.

'How can we be certain he's not inside?' said one of them.

'He's not inside,' he replied.

'But how can we be certain?'

'He's in Poland.'

Such was his intelligence, anyway. He had no wish to encounter a wizard this evening.

'You go in first, Dutchman.'

'Yes. Fall to 't, yarely.'

A snigger from one of them lifted the mood a little. He turned towards the house.

A year in the making. A year of planning, scheming, travelling. He'd met some interesting men this past twelvemonth. Only some of them had been European.

Now he was standing on John Dee's land, beyond the towpath, and the house looked even more odd from here than it had from the river. It was completely silent. A strange smell hung in the air, a mixture of almonds and urine. In these outhouses, it was said, were Dee's laboratories, where he boiled and burned the elements of the Earth with God-knew-what intent.

He had to persuade the Englishmen to go into the house. Hell's teeth, he had to persuade *himself* to go into the house. They were against it to a man, but he'd been careful not to pay them anything upfront. Their fee depended on their completing the job. He reminded them of this now. They looked up at the shadowy house of the wizard, and three of them left, right there and then, just climbed out of the boat and walked away from the river, towards the silhouette of the church tower, muttering about how this place was wrong, wrong, wrong, and they weren't going to be possessed by the necromancer's guardian demons just for a few shillings.

He looked at the ones who remained.

'More for you lot, then.'

They looked at each other, and then they did as they were told.

They smashed their way in, shoving the door off its hinges. They tramped into the large central hall, its ceiling high but not, thought Jacobus, as high as the roof he'd seen from outside. There were other rooms, in the eaves.

He saw books. They were everywhere, stacked vertically and horizontally, in wooden shelves and cases, their spines to the wall. There was some rationale to the layout, and he almost laughed when he realised it. The books were arranged by size.

Even to an unlettered man such as Jacobus Aakster, this seemed queer and unscholarly.

The men didn't know what they were about. This was deliberate on his part. He pointed randomly at shelves, and issued commands. *Take the books out of the boxes. Put them on the floor. Take these books from the shelves. No, not those, these ones. And these. And these.*

They removed hundreds, perhaps thousands. Some of the volumes were chained, but most were not, and those on chains were simply pulled away from the wall. He cast his net wide, walking around the central hall pointing to whatever looked likely, ignoring theology and concentrating on natural philosophy and exploration, the stuff that might prove to be useful in the real world. Who knew? Perhaps Dee had discovered a north-eastern passage to Cathay, and it was hidden inside one of these books. That would be worth something, but it would be as nothing against the secret he was really here for.

He slipped away and further into the house on his own, following staircases and corridors into smaller and smaller rooms. Somewhere inside here was Dee's private room, his *interna bibliotheca*, where he communed with angels and kept his most precious books: Agrippa's *De occulta philosophica*, the *Mystica theologica* of Dionysius the Areopagite, the manuscripts of Ramon Llull.

He found it eventually, tucked away in the eaves of the steep roof. Its small window looked out onto the dark river, and its interior had been partly denuded. There was no sign of any demonic apparatus; Dee had, presumably, packed this up and taken it to Poland with him. But there were books and manuscripts, dozens more of them. Jacobus placed his candle on a pile of volumes and settled down to hunt, the noise of the men downstairs fading away as his concentration deepened onto the task at hand. The whole night – the whole year – came down to this moment. If he didn't find it, the scheme of the merchants would fail. Not to mention his own still-secret adaptation of said scheme.

But he found it. It wasn't hidden. The merchant's spies had suggested that Dee might not have known what he had in this particular manuscript, and it was indeed given no special status, nor was it locked away – though it was in this internal room, so Dee had presumably been trying to study it. It was bound in the scrappy pages of some other manuscript; some of the more hysterical sources Jacobus had consulted had said it was bound in human skin. He smiled at the workaday reality. It was slim in comparison to the hefty tomes that surrounded him in the little room. He flicked to the title page, and read it in the flickering candlelight. The strange swirling script he found inside was as he expected it. He checked a few more pages.

The manuscript was there, and then it wasn't, because it had a new home now, deep inside a hidden pocket of his coat. He stood, and went back downstairs. The work was almost done. The boxes of books they had taken from Dee's library were carried out into the garden and down to the towpath, where they were loaded onto the barge.

'Now, fellows – enjoy yourselves,' he said, passing around their money and a few bottles of very, very strong wine he'd had ready and waiting. He went out into the garden, where the lighterman was preparing to sail the barge back downstream on the tide, out into the Estuary, where the Amsterdam merchants waited for him on their ship.

'Change of plan,' he said to the lighterman. He had dropped the English theatrical airs in favour of Dutch practical. 'There's more work to be done here. I'll follow you in a few hours. Wait for me at Deptford.'

The lighterman muttered but he was being paid to do as he

was told. Jacobus untied the ropes, and the barge moved out into the stream. He watched it go before walking back along the towpath to find the second barge tied up. It had slipped a little upstream, out of sight.

He climbed in, and Mina was there with her delicious lips and her wicked chuckle, to kiss him and fondle him and congratulate him.

A vast whoop of male laughter accompanied a sudden sound of breaking glass as one of the windows of John Dee's house burst outwards. Someone had thrown a chair through it from within. Books followed the chair into the garden, and someone lit a fire as the barge pulled away into the stream. In only minutes Dee's house was flickering with the flames from the garden as a pile of books made their own inferno.

'You have it, Jacobus?' Mina said.

'I have it, beloved,' Jacobus replied.

1815: CONSTABLE HORTON
AT THE THEATRE

Six months from that night, with the island falling away to starboard, Charles Horton would remember the Drury Lane Theatre, and he would mark it as the starting point. Enter the constable, stage left.

He would recall the noisy crowd, the slow staccato of pips being spat at his shoulders from someone behind, the musky smell of the oil lamps and candles which hung precariously in the chandeliers.

He would remember the astonishing quiet that descended as the delicious verses unwrapped themselves, the shrill mob surprised to find itself distracted. There was a wizard in the building, and he weaved a powerful spell of another's devising.

The wizard's name was Edmund Kean, a young man of wide repute, his famous face tonight transformed through greasepaint enchantment into that of an ancient sage. The latest star of the Covent Garden stage, a study in controlled intensity, his robes flowing around him in richly coloured waves, as if possessed of their own character and desires.

The part he played was of a second wizard, and so strong was the magic that this other wizard seemed to occupy the young bones and muscles and face of Kean; an older wizard, the Duke of Milan, full of his own mysterious motivation.

Rather like a dream than a reassurance.

Prospero's words were not his own, and they were not Kean's. The man whose spell this was seemed to hover in the air, the puller of the strings, the play's very own Ariel.

To have no screen between this part he played
And him he played it for.

It was Charles Horton's first Shakespeare.

He was mesmerised; in truth, he had been transported from the play's opening, as a storm rang through the theatre, loud enough to wake the magistrates of Bow Street, sending the King of Naples into the depths. Outside, the whores of Drury Lane played their own parts in their own play, their audience of men clutching pennies, snatched-at by their lusts. But here inside, there was magic afoot, savage and potent and dangerous.

From his position up in the gallery, high above the stage, Horton saw the crowd in the pit, all of them standing and watching in silence. All their petty hooliganisms had been forgotten. The Drury Lane mob was notorious, but tonight the mob was tamed. It watched Kean conjure his sea-sorrow and Ariel flame amazement, flying in on unseen mechanisms, at times invisible to every eyeball, at others heard only in the groans of the shipwrecked.

Lie there, my art.

Prospero removed his cloak from his shoulders and laid it down, emphasising its circular shape with his staff. When it settled flat upon the stage it was as round as a hole looking down through the earth and out to the other side. It was something alive, quivering with the stars and planets and comets which decorated it.

From up where he sat, high in the gods, Horton looked down into the wizard's black hole and imagined shapes moved within it, as if a portal to some other London had been opened, a London where the crackles of fairy magic were commonplace.

Or perhaps that was *this* London, and another London where no stench of magic remained was looking curiously from within, back to this dreamland in which Horton now found himself.

Music filled the vaulted air of the theatre, played on instruments hidden who-knew-where, and his wife Abigail's hand squeezed in his, gripped as it had been gripped since the opening storm. Her fingers pulsed to the rhythm of the word-music.

Masks were removed, identities were revealed, love was pledged. Horton felt the terrified awe of the boatswain, *all clapped under hatches*, his wrecked ship restored by unknown capacities. Towards Caliban he felt first horror, then disgust, then a deep and senseless pity.

And Ariel – well, Ariel he thought he understood. An instrument of greater men, trapped by obligation and unseen chains of secret knowledge he was powerless to reveal.

Yes, he thought he understood that pretty well.

The play unwound itself from the magic to return to the every day. Even Prospero noticed the sea-change.

Do not infest your mind with beating on
The strangeness of this business.

The strange business of the stage began to give way to London's grubby, incessant masque. Horton could no longer ignore the fact that the Earl of – had failed to return to his box for the second part of the play, leaving the young woman who was most definitely not his wife to weep into her fan. He saw money changing hands between two men below him, and saw the handing over of an object wrapped in ticking. He could no longer ignore the woman next to him, who smelt like a wet dog and fervently whispered *The Emperor! The Emperor!* every few minutes. He would speak to her when the play ended. If she spoke of Bonaparte, he would have to haul her to Bow Street on a charge of sedition.

And he saw the boy. He emerged at the end of the row of seats, a familiar face from Wapping. What was he doing here? Horton heard the mutterings and curses of his fellow audience members, a general mild disturbance that ended with the dog-smelling woman cursing, foully, and he felt a hand on his shoulder and warm desperate breath in his ear.

'Mr Horton, you are wanted in Wapping.'

Horton was angry beyond reckoning. But he saw it in the boy's face, terror dancing in the light from the candles which must, surely, soon burn this theatre down again.

'What is it?'

'There's been more killin's on the Highway, sir! The Monster's returned!'

The words accompanied the expiry of *The Tempest*. Prospero's magic portal closed up as Kean lifted his cloak from the stage for the last time. The theatre was once again a building, prone to fire, filled with the great and the grimy. Charles Horton was himself again, a River Police constable and a careful student of the mechanisms of murder.

He looked at the boy, and wondered if he would ever escape himself.

This thing of darkness I
Acknowledge mine.

The streets outside the theatre were frantic with carriages stuck horse-to-rear along Drury Lane, but it was only a short walk down to the river. A wherry would get them to Wapping quickly enough, and if what the boy had told them at the theatre was true, speed was essential. The boy himself had disappeared into London's shadows, as boys of his type were wont to do.

Rennie's Strand Bridge, all grey granite columns and austere arches, obstructed the view of the river as Mr and Mrs Horton walked down the hill. They took a wherry from the stairs in front of Somerset House, two insignificant insects climbing aboard a leaf.

'Can it be possible, Charles?' Abigail said, as the waterman steered them downstream through the shouting vessels. 'Has the same killer returned to the Highway?'

'A coincidence, surely,' he replied.

'But such a terrible one.'

They followed the current towards the old Bridge, shooting through its starlings like thousands before them, the wherry shuddering under the strain of the rushing river. Horton instructed the waterman to leave him at the Hermitage stairs, then to take Abigail further around the Wapping bend to the stairs just past Gun Dock. He fed coins into the waterman's outstretched palm, the money which had been squirrelled away to buy the two of them some supper at a tavern to finish off their theatrical evening. But that evening had been dislocated by whatever had taken place up above the river, up on the Highway. Whatever magic there had been in Drury Lane had been replaced by something altogether darker and older.

He climbed out and watched the wherry pull away into the

stream, his eyes fixed on Abigail as she was taken by the unseen force of the river. He felt suddenly and deeply alone. A single actor in a Gothic drama. Not even an original production; a new version of an old story. Perhaps even a sequel.

He turned and walked past the Brewhouse and then the western edge of the London Dock. Rennie's stone, again, though this time arranged into walls behind which loomed the spars of ships.

On the Highway there was some of the bustle and excitement they had encountered on Drury Lane. He saw a crowd straining to watch, clustered outside a single house. There were flickering lamps lining the crowded pavements, throwing uncertain light onto the shops and taverns and houses that gazed at each other with East End defiance.

The house was number 37. It was not quite four years since the last slaughter on the Ratcliffe Highway. Indeed, the house at number 37 was so close to that other house, and so similar to it, that Horton had imagined that it was perhaps the very same house; that the frenzy which had slaughtered Timothy Marr, his wife, his shop boy and his tiny baby had returned to coat the same walls with new blood.

This house was part of the same recent development, so it looked identical. The crowd outside looked the same, too: the same curious terror, the same sharp elbows, the same mutterings. The same hunger to get inside and feast on charnel views.

Many of the neighbouring houses had been converted into shops, though these were shuttered. One of them made its business audible enough – from inside, he could hear the squawks and screeches of various animals. A menagerie, presumably, selling pets to lonely sailors on their return home, the creatures within stirred by the crowd outside.

The front door to the little house was closed, guarded by two uniformed constables. Horton did not recognise either of them, and presumed they were from Shadwell. This suggested that he would not be welcome within. The Highway was, by custom, under the purview of the Shadwell magistrates. He was a constable of the River Police and had no immediate jurisdiction here. Such matters occupied lawyers and magistrates. They did not occupy Charles Horton overmuch. Besides, he had his own history here. His own reckoning to face.

He had stood on this street more than three years ago, outside a similarly closed house with a crowd outside. Then, the country had known little of the Ratcliffe Highway, and what it had known it had tended not to like. When the horrors of Timothy Marr's house had been revealed, the panic had washed all the way to Scotland. London had birthed a Monster.

But hadn't he killed that Monster?

He had got into the Marr house from the back, he remembered, through a gap between the houses. And there it was, to his left this time – which meant Marr's house, number 29, was just the other side of the dark passageway. He felt drawn to that place, which was still empty.

He made his way through the little crowd. The small alley between the houses was unlit, as dark as a tomb, and the memory was so strong it almost carried its own smell.

He turned right at the end of the passageway, and counted along the rear of three houses. There were already a good many men inside the house, it seemed. He could see their shapes and even hear their voices. Horton let himself in through the gate in the fence, walked across the scrubby little yard, and tried the door at the back of the house.

It was open, and he stepped inside. He saw a body lying face down in the middle of the little kitchen within and a familiar and unwelcome face looking up to greet him.

'Ah, Horton,' said Edward Markland, magistrate of the Shadwell Public Office. 'I was becoming concerned that you would not be joining us.'

The kitchen's dead occupant was lying face down on the floor. The position of the body suggested that no Shadwell constable had turned the body over, which meant there was some chance that Markland had instructed his constables not to disturb anything in the house. Horton gave silent praise to whichever malignant deity presided over this place.

If he had ordered the body to remain undisturbed, it meant that Markland had anticipated Horton's arrival, which in turn meant that the magistrate intended to let him investigate the crime. So had his own magistrate John Harriott already offered Horton's help to Markland? He had done so before. It was never a pleasant prospect. Markland only cared about one thing in the world, and that was Edward Markland.

Horton took in the kitchen, turning around to view every corner. There were no signs of struggle. The room was clean, its most impressive feature a very new-looking Bodley range in the chimney place. It looked expensive. The kitchen must have been recently used; there was a faint smell, as of almonds, hanging in the air.

He turned to the body. The dead man lay face down on the floor, his arms to his side, as if he had been standing in the normal fashion and had then suddenly crashed forward onto his face.

'I instructed my men to leave the place as it was found,' said Markland, startling Horton, who had been lost in his thoughts for some moments. 'But somebody is going to have to move these bodies soon.'

'Bodies? There are others?'

'There are two dead females in the front of the house. They await your inspection.'

'My inspection?'

'I have spoken to your magistrate, constable. You will work on this case with me.'

'Very well.'

'The bodies in the house. They are somewhat ... disturbing.'

Horton looked at Markland, properly, for the first time, and saw how pale the man was.

He looks terrified.

He turned back to look at the body in the kitchen, and stood for some moments longer, forcing his eyes to imprint the position of the body on his memory. Eventually, he turned the dead man over, and recoiled.

The face had been smashed to pieces. The body had promised no such horrors in its face-down state, and the constable attending Markland muttered an obscenity under his breath.

'Were any weapons found?' Horton asked.

'A maul,' said Markland.

'Where?'

'Upstairs. In one of the bedchambers.'

Did Markland attach any significance to that? Because Horton did.

He stood and investigated the dresser in the kitchen. There were knives in there, but they were all clean and not particularly sharp. In fact, their state was in some contrast to the immaculate kitchen, their dull edges evidence of neglect. The woman of the house was not a cook, perhaps.

He went back to the body, checked the pockets of the dark coat and the waistcoat. He tried to estimate the man's age, despite the injuries to the face. He thought him to be in his middle forties, like Horton himself. The body was lean and the clothes well tended and relatively new. The hands were soft and white. Not a dock labourer or sailor or tradesman. Horton would guess at a city clerk, but a fairly well-paid one, if the clothes and the new kitchen range were any indication.

'We have names for the dead?'

'We do. This is Benjamin Johnson. He worked as a clerk for the East India Company. His wife's name was Emma. The other female was his daughter. She is in the parlour with her mother.'

Horton stood and looked down at the body on the clean kitchen floor. A City clerk, financially comfortable in his newish house on the Highway. Apart from the wrecked face, the man could be asleep, so untouched was his body and so clean his clothes. The spotless floor suggested to Horton that there would be a maid, though she did not presumably spend her nights in the house, which was somewhat unusual. There were probably other husbands in other houses in similar postures, drunk from a night in a riverside alehouse, sleeping it off on the kitchen floor. Except someone had smashed in the face of this one.

He went to the external kitchen door. It showed no sign of being forced.

'I will inspect the other bodies and the maul. Were other weapons found anywhere else in the house?'

'No,' said Markland. He looked at Horton as if he were looking at an annoying but productive animal, one that he might decide to beat. 'Have you finished in here?'

One more sweep with the eyes. One more deep glance at the body.

'Yes. Your men may clear it.'

Markland bowed, sarcastically. Horton ignored him, and walked through the kitchen into the hallway.

There, three years before, he'd seen the body of Marr's shop boy James Gowan, lying in the doorway to the shop at the front of the house, propping the door open. And there, under the stairs, had been the worst sight of all: an infant in its cot, asleep, with a terrible ribbon of blood and skin where its throat had been slashed open. Horton breathed in and looked through the door under the stairs, but saw only a cupboard containing some basic household implements: a brush, a shovel, two wooden buckets. A smell of damp. But no death.

He heard Markland barking orders from behind him. 'Stay out of his way,' the magistrate said. 'Let him sniff around in his infernal way. Come now, out of his way, man. Get this body moved. Yes, the table. We'll keep them all back here until the coroner's taken a look.'

Dark half-seen figures of men moved around the house, the shadows of Shadwell constables, irritation flowing off them in waves towards the unwelcome interloper. He ignored them.

He opened the door at the end of the hallway. A parlour, with a front door giving out onto the street. The animal noises from the shop next door were clearly audible. A tidy and well-cared-for place, with some touches of affluence. A nice-looking clock, figurines on the mantelpiece, and underneath the mantelpiece a woman, face down in the ashy grate. In a chair by the fire, another female, a girl of indiscriminate age, had lolled back, an awful red wound across her throat. Her face, like her father's, had been smashed to pieces. Most awful of all was the smell that infested the room, a stench of burned flesh rising from the fireplace.

Disturbing, Markland had said. Horton agreed. Theatrically disturbing.

Other than the awful dead figures, there were no other signs of violence. Horton minded that, and looked at the room for several minutes in the same way he'd stared into the air of the kitchen, letting the shape of the scene settle onto his mind like a white sheet drifting down on a complicated chair. He checked the front door. Again, there was no sign of forced entry.

The woman in the fireplace could not be avoided, though he would have very much liked to. The hair on the back of her head had been burned away, leaving only charred black scalp-skin, but the fire had not burned her clothes. The clothes themselves were fairly well appointed, as the husband's had been. From above and behind, the woman seemed fat, a distinct contrast to the slim man lying dead in the kitchen, and the girlish figure of the daughter in the chair.

Horton sighed, and pulled the woman's feet, such that her head came out of the grate and fell onto the stone of the hearth. He pulled her a little further until she was lying face down on the parlour's rug, and then he turned her over.

The face was another awful thing, a starched and leathery mess of sinew, muscle and bone. One eye peered madly from within; the other had burned away. The woman's teeth leered at him, delighted by some disgusting tale he had just related. His gorge rising, he stood to find Markland standing at the door, his eyes avoiding that awful ruined visage.

'You may remove them,' Horton said, stepping back into the hall and covering his mouth, still uncertain if he would avoid vomiting. He managed to contain himself, barely.

It seemed like all the men in the house were now gathering in the kitchen, leaving the rest of the house to the curious investigator from Wapping. He turned and walked up the stairs.

There were three doors off the landing, leading to three bedrooms. One must have belonged to the master and mistress of the house, and was undisturbed. Likewise the second, a smaller room with deft feminine touches – the sanctuary of the dead daughter. And in the third, a bleak reminder of past transactions.

Markland had called this a bedchamber, but it had no bed in it, only a small bureau and a chair. The maul had been placed beneath the window, and the window looked out onto the space behind the house. He looked out there, remembering the stories of the murderers escaping from the Marr household in 1811. He'd found a maul like this in that house, in this equivalent room, leaning against a wall under a window.

I'm back, he imagined the maul saying. *Did you miss me?*

Horton tried to imagine the intelligence that had stood here before him. A Monster had indeed returned to the Ratcliffe Highway – but was he an original, or a facsimile?

From the shop next door, something growled through the wall.

1588: JACOBUS AND THE MERCHANTS

It had started with a small group of Amsterdam merchants. If you were Dutch and not English, their names would have been as familiar to you as Raleigh and Drake and Hawkyns, but they weren't as flashy as your English adventurers. These were careful fellows. Money was all they cared for, and they had as much daring as a newborn gosling. They'd come up with a daring scheme, nonetheless. They just needed someone to supply the sinew. And that was him.

They'd grown rich buying pepper and suchlike from the Portuguese and reselling it in northern Europe. But Jacobus Aakster had never met a Dutch merchant who liked working with those stunted, greedy and unreliable Lisbon dogs, and these were no different. The Dutchmen wanted a direct route to the East. They wanted to cut the Portuguese out of the trade completely.

So, being careful fellows, they sought knowledge of the Eastern spice trade. They paid for spies to be sent south, east, north and west, to gather intelligence on how the papists had been able to monopolise this trade, how their navigators had inched their way down and around the black African coast for the past 150 years. By the time they met Jacobus, the merchants were well on the way to establishing a Company with the Dutch monopoly on Eastern trade.

But that wasn't what they had wanted to talk to him about. That was the legitimate business. That was for the daylight, for formal sessions with councillors and officials. What they wanted from him was something altogether more illicit. As his own beloved Mina had put it, when he'd told her of their scheme: 'You're on your own, Jacobus. You're no more than a speculative investment to those Amsterdam crocodiles.'

This was the sum of the odd scheme: a story had reached the ears of these merchants. It related to an Englishman named John Dee, who had a house upriver from London where, it was said, he had assembled a great library of esoteric and arcane knowledge. John Dee was a man of many parts: he lectured on geometry and advised on navigation, but it was said he also talked to angels and took the shape of different animals. A sorcerer and a necromancer, was Dee, a player of secret games.

Jacobus had never been in a library, but when a certain type of fellow with a certain kind of education said the word 'library' it was like another type of fellow with a very different kind of education saying 'Spanish treasure ship'. The merchants had one of these scholarly fellows with them, a dusty old specimen who used words that didn't seem to fit into sentences that never seemed to end.

Dee's library, this university fossil had said, was known to anyone in Europe who had an interest in the learning of the ancients and the new science. It was one of the largest in the civilised world, but it had been neglected in recent years, because Dee had become obsessed with talking to angels. This new tendency had turned the English court against John Dee, so he had taken his scrying to the Holy Roman Empire. His library was thus exposed and undefended.

And in that library was a manuscript. A very particular manuscript, with a very particular purpose. The old scholar's dull eyes had glittered with young hunger when he talked of this text, as if he'd have killed for it. The manuscript, if what was said of it was true, had the capacity to change everything. To make the merchants rich beyond the dreams of Croesus.

'What's in it?' Jacobus had asked, in his simple direct way.

'The great secret,' the scholar said, unhelpfully. 'The celestial light,' he added, no more helpfully. The merchants' eyes glittered in the candlelight. When they told Jacobus the great secret, his eyes glittered as well.

These merchants had put their plan to him. The main event was still the conquest of the East, in mercantile terms, but this delicious nugget was an irresistible sideshow and merchants do not grow rich by ignoring opportunities, however obscure. Seize Dee's library – a prize worthy of any group of ambitious men, worth riches in itself, droned the scholar – and at the same time seize this secret text.

Well, all right, then. A job worthy of Jacobus Aakster's skills. A lot of money changed hands over the following year – well, a lot to him, no doubt little more than a day's household silver to these wealthy men. But it was more than enough to secure the services of an ugly mercenary named Jacobus Aakster, with an unexpectedly beautiful wife who had the morals of a snake (the wife, not him, though he was hardly an angel and John Dee would not have wished to commune with him). A fighter of other people's wars, with as little money to afford property as to afford morality. *Get the library*, they told him while their scholar looked on, glassy-eyed, *but don't let on that you've got it. And make sure you get the manuscript. Steal the one, and they won't know you've stolen the other.*

How to secretly steal a library? Well, that was the easy part. The secret was in the boxes of books which his drunken English helpmates had unloaded onto the towpath. The Englishmen had grumbled about those boxes, but the English grumbled all the time. They were only happy when they grumbled. But they did what they were told, and carried the boxes from the barge up to the sorcerer's house. A thousand books, ransacked from dozens of Dutch printers and homes and sailed over to London before being transplanted onto a barge in a dark inlet near Deptford.

They burned these worthless books, and removed the others from the library to the barge. But by that time, Jacobus Aakster had disappeared, with the thing the merchants wanted most of all in his coat and his beautiful young wife Mina Koeman alongside him.

He disappeared for three years: three years during which time certain Dutch and Flemish scholars delightedly indulged themselves on Dee's stolen library, which had been transplanted to Amsterdam. But for the merchants there was no such joy. Aakster had made off with the only volume they cared about. They were murderous in their fury.

So they were surprised when, three years later, Jacobus came back to see them. He had a proposal for them. They didn't like it very much.

They met in the back of the same tavern they'd gathered in three years before. The scholar came along with them, older and dustier than ever, and the merchants placed a few mercenaries of their own at the door, to capture Jacobus or to punish him, it didn't matter which.

'You still have the manuscript?' said one of the merchants.

'In a manner of speaking,' Jacobus replied, and the merchants looked at each other with some concern. 'The physical text has been destroyed.'

The temperature in the room, which wasn't that high to begin with, fell even further.

'We will kill you, then,' said the merchant.

'Ah, well, no. I wouldn't do that. You see, I have put the text to memory. It still exists.' Jacobus tapped the side of his head. 'In here.'

'Prove it,' the merchant said.

Jacobus began to speak.

'*Seeing there is a three-fold world, combining Elementary, Celestial, and Intellectual, and every Inferior is governed by its Superior, and receiveth the influences thereof, so that the very original, and chief Worker of all doth by Angels, the Heavens, Stars, Elements, Plants, Metals and Stones convey from himself the virtues of his Omnipotency upon us . . .*'

'Enough!' said the scholar.

'Is it the text?' asked the merchant.

'The translation is ugly, but yes – it could be the *Opera*.' The scholar looked at Jacobus as if he were one of Dee's angels. The merchant looked at him as if he wanted to kill him.

'What is it that you require?' asked the merchant.

'A ship, and some men to build a fort,' Jacobus replied. 'Give me that, and I'll make all of us rich.'

CONSTABLE HORTON
INVESTIGATES

Despite his age, despite his recent illness, despite the case being Shadwell's and not Wapping's, despite all these dreary facts, it was in John Harriott's rooms at the River Police Office that a meeting was convened the next morning. The man's force of personality was still great enough to ignore the niceties of jurisdiction.

Horton saw how irritating Edward Markland of Shadwell found this continuing reality: that John Harriott was in some unfathomable way still the senior magistrate in the area, the man to whom the press and the politicians and the populace turned at times of crisis. Harriott was old, but he was still the man who had tamed the Thames.

Yet Markland behaved himself. He would continue to do so, Horton believed, because of another truth, a peculiarly sour one. Harriott was dying. Everyone knew this to be the case. His infirmity hung in the room like the stench of rotten cabbage in the street. Markland smelled it as well as anyone. All he needed to do was exploit Harriott's most useful asset – his constable Charles Horton – and who knew what would happen at the old man's demise?

It was a warm May morning. Wapping had been awake for hours, and Charles Horton had barely slept. He was wearing the same clothes as the night before. He had returned home for a few fitful hours, lying awake alongside his sleeping wife, listening to her breathe, the memory of the awful skull beneath Mrs Johnson's burnt face vivid in his mind.

Despite the early hour there was a ticklish sense of panic out in the streets, and he could sense some of it in Harriott's impressive office, with its leather chairs and fireplace and its massive desk by the riverside window. People outside were talking of the Monster again – and in their telling, he came back, the same Monster that had dispatched the Marrs and then the Williamsons three years before. Walking past the mammoth white walls of St George's in the East the previous night, Horton had seen a group of men stamping on the cobbles of the street at the crossroads where John Williams had been interred – the Williams that the Shadwell magistrates, Markland included, had decreed was the Monster. There was no logic to it, but Horton had understood the need: to stamp on returning devils, to send them back to Hell. For a moment, he had almost joined them.

Unwin the coroner planned to hold his inquest today, upstairs at the Jolly Sailor, the same venue as for the Marr inquest. Harriott had invited Unwin to this meeting, along with the surgeon Salter, who performed the coroner's medical inspections. Harriott had asked Salter to give his preliminary view and in a calm, dispassionate way the surgeon was doing so. The bodies of the Johnsons remained in their home, for now.

'The man found in the kitchen died from injuries to his head,' Salter said. 'The older woman died when she was pushed into the fire, which must have still been alight, judging by her injuries. The younger woman died either by a cut throat or an assault with a maul, or both.'

Salter was a methodical man, Horton knew, but he was also an unimaginative one. He was reading from his notes as if he were reading from a church Bible at a family funeral. He did not draw conclusions. That was not for surgeons. They cut open, they took out or they severed, they sewed up, they moved on. Salter's was a descriptive mind, not a speculative one.

When Salter finished, Harriott cursed under his breath. Even Markland, who had seen the injuries that Salter described, looked grey.

'With your permission, sir,' Horton said to Harriott, and the magistrate nods. 'Dr Salter, the girl downstairs. Had she been interfered with in any way?'

The surgeon's face was calm, but Horton could see it in his eyes: a species of fear at the demonic intensity of these deaths. Perhaps the surgeon was not so devoid of imagination after all. Even Salter could detect the smell of older murders, drifting back across years.

'I take it you mean: had she been ravished?'

'Yes.'

'For God's sake, Horton.' This from Markland. 'Is this necessary?'

'Answer the question, doctor,' said Harriott, with a scowl towards his fellow magistrate.

'There is no way of telling,' said Salter. 'Not without a full investigation of the body. And that is impossible at the house.'

'Am I to understand, then, that you have not examined the bodies unclothed?'

'Of course not, constable. I would not do so at a private residence.'

'And how do you account for the lack of any blood?'

'I beg your pardon?'

'You have stated that you believe the causes of death to have been either physical injury or burning. Yet there was no blood in the house. The floors were clean. How do you account for such a thing?'

Salter frowned.

'I cannot account for it.'

'You would expect a great amount of blood, then?'

'Yes. I can only imagine that the killer cleaned up after himself.'

'There are not even stains.'

'No. There are not.'

Unwin broke the uncomfortable silence.

'Can I suggest that Salter brings the bodies here for a full inspection? I will postpone the inquest until then.'

'It would seem the doctor has further work to do,' growled Harriott, and Salter's face reddened. Horton did not feel sorry for him. 'We have a room that has been used for such purposes before. He can use that.'

'It is agreed?' said Unwin, still trying to rescue Salter. 'How much time will you need?'

'A day. Perhaps two,' said Salter, his voice a whisper.

'Then if we are willing, I will postpone the inquest until the day after tomorrow.'

'Very well,' said Salter, and fell silent. Harriott glared at him, then turned back to Horton.

'What do we know of the deceased?' he said.

'Very little as yet,' said Horton. 'The master of the house is ... or was ... one Benjamin Johnson. I'm told he worked as a clerk for the East India Company.'

Harriott baulked at this.

'The East India Company?'

'Yes, sir. Perhaps you could assist with dealing with the Company?'

'Assist how?' asked Markland, somewhat put out.

'I have personal history with John Company,' said Harriott, glancing down at his left leg without further comment. If Markland had bothered to read Harriott's memoirs he would have known that the magistrate's left leg had been ruined in service of the Company in India. Horton found it interesting that Markland did not know this.

'Markland, have your men interrogated the neighbours?'

'They have, Harriott. Of course.'

'And their findings?'

Markland frowned at being asked to report in this fashion, but then he consulted an elegant leather notebook. A look passed between Harriott and Horton. Edward Markland, it seemed, had taken to writing notes.

'Mrs Johnson's name was Emma, the daughter was called Jane. The neighbours say they were a pleasant enough family, the wife particularly. She seems to have been generous with her money and her time, both of which she seemed to possess in decent amounts. The mother took in some sewing, and the daughter did some work alongside her.'

'Any other family?'

'The wife has a sister, living in Putney.'

'And were there any witnesses to the events?'

'None at all. No unusual noises, no raised voices at all.'

'Though there is a menagerie next door,' said Horton, causing Markland to glance at him with irritation. 'Unusual noises are not uncommon on that street.'

Markland appeared not to have noticed the strange shop next door, and did not relish having its presence pointed out to him.

'No one seen coming or going?' asked Harriott.

'No,' said Markland, looking away from Horton.

'He was careful.'

'Assuming he worked alone,' said Horton, and Harriott looked at him.

'You think there was more than one man involved?'

'I have no idea. But there is nothing to suggest there was only one man.'

'Who discovered the bodies?' asked Unwin.

'The servant, a girl called Amy Beavis. She lives with her father over towards Whitechapel.'

'I suggest Horton goes to speak with her,' said Harriott. 'He is good with servants.'

Horton had little idea what this might mean, but nodded in any case.

'Your thoughts, Horton?' This from Markland.

'My thoughts, sir?'

'Have you developed a picture of the case?'

'By no means, Mr Markland. It is far too early for such things. I will need further time to investigate.'

'Well, time is something we do not have,' said Markland. He rose, and placed a hat on his head. 'There is a frenzy of chatter in the streets. People believe the killer of the Marrs and Williamsons has returned. Nonsense, of course – Williams is dead. But the uneducated and the idle thrive on gossip. I must return to the Shadwell office. Horton will report to me any developments. Is that agreed, Harriott?'

Harriott grunted, a noise that Horton knew could signify almost anything.

'Well, then. I will go and speak to the gentlemen of the press, and try to calm the populace. Gentlemen.'

Markland left, and Unwin made his own farewell, leaving with the silent and stone-faced surgeon. Horton and Harriott were left alone.

'He will calm the populace, will he?' grumbled Harriott. 'My word, sometimes I think Edward Markland imagines himself to be Bonaparte.'

'He certainly seems to desire an empire,' said Horton, without thinking. He looked at the magistrate, embarrassed by his revealing insubordination. Harriott smiled, though the smile was an old, ill and tired thing.

'You have made an enemy of the surgeon, constable,' said Harriott.

'So it would seem, sir.'

'Tell Markland everything,' the old magistrate said. 'But tell me first.'

Amy Beavis did not live in Whitechapel, despite what Markland had said. Her address was actually Dorset Street, a place of moderately ill repute in Spitalfields, somewhat to the north of Whitechapel and a fair walk from Wapping.

The dwellings on Dorset Street were old and dilapidated, decent houses from the last century or earlier that had declined into common lodgings, a warren of the old and sick and infirm. Horton estimated that three or four dozen of the rooms on the street would be taken by whores, another three dozen by common criminals, and perhaps the same amount by weavers from old families who had failed to ascend to anything better. Some of these people were on the street, and a desperate lot they seemed.

He found the right door and told the vicious, ancient landlord within that he must speak with Mr Beavis.

'Beavis? You'll get no benefit, speaking to Beavis,' came the mysterious reply. He was shown, with surly reluctance, to a flight of stairs which looked like a line of dominoes falling down a steep hill. He made his way upwards, gingerly.

The door on which he knocked was opened by a girl whose

face was so beautiful that it seemed to light up the gloomy place. Her hair was finely cut, her skin was clean and clear, and her eyes held none of the wrenching despair of the people he'd seen outside in the street.

'Miss Beavis?' he asked.

Her eyes widened, and she nodded, carefully.

'Miss Amy Beavis? Servant to Mrs Emma Johnson?'

Her hand came to her mouth, and she stared at him, terrified. It was answer enough.

'My name is Horton, Miss Beavis. I am a constable of Wapping. I am sent to ask you some questions about the Johnsons and their terrible fate.'

The door swung wide, and an ancient was revealed, dressed in grey underthings and swinging what looked like a poker.

'I see you! I see you!'

'Sir, please, I only . . .'

'Come at last, have you? Come at last? Where is it?'

The old man shoved past him out into the hallway, and looked up.

'Roof still there. Roof still there.'

He turned back to Horton.

'Where's your machine, Jacques? Where's your bloody machine?'

The girl was beside him now, rubbing his shoulders while he glared at Horton.

'Come now, father. Come now. This is not Jacques.'

Her voice was soft, precise, well spoken, purest silk to the East End rasp of her father.

'Not Jacques? Of course it's Jacques! He's come for me, and he's not having me.'

'Sir, my name is Horton, not . . .'

'Barbarian!'

This with a shout and a lunge, accompanied by a shriek

from the girl, but the lunge was in truth more like a fall. The poker went to the ground as the old fellow collapsed into Horton's arms. He was as light as new-baked bread, and smelled like ancient dried leaves.

'Please, sir,' the girl said. 'Please. Bring him within.'

'Bloody Jacques. Come to bloody take me away. Bloody Jacques,' muttered the old fellow, but he already seemed half-asleep.

Horton took the man under the armpits and half-dragged, half-lifted him into the room. Within, there was a bed next to a fireplace, a single armchair, a dresser with some plates and bowls upon it, a small table with a pile of books. A cheap and ancient etching hung on the wall, which must once have depicted St Paul's but was now little more than a round blur inside a fog.

'Please sir. On the bed.'

Horton took the old man over to the bed, and laid him down upon it. Once horizontal, the old man's eyes opened again, and his hands reached for Horton's throat.

'Jacques! You're not taking me in your machine! No, Jacques! I'll bloody kill ye!'

Horton felt a scratch as one crooked finger flicked over the skin of his neck, but then the man's eyes closed once again, his hands fell back and his head lolled into the foul-smelling pillow. He began to snore. The girl sat in the armchair and put her head into her hands.

'Oh, forgive him, sir! Forgive him! He is overtaken by strange fancies.'

'Pray, do not concern yourself, miss. There is no damage done. But who is this Jacques? And what is his machine?'

Her hands dropped to her lap, and she looked at her father. It was an awful look in one so young: full of the desperate love of the mother, but infected by the helpless despair of the young burdened with impossible responsibility.

'They are fancies, sir. I know not where they come from. He believes a Frenchman named Jacques is to come for him in a flying machine. When he comes, the roof will fly away, and he will be taken into the sky, leaving me behind.'

'Should he not perhaps be seen by a mad-doctor? Perhaps at Bethlem ...'

'Oh no! No, sir! Not that place!'

'It is not so bad, now it has moved to new premises.'

'You can have had no experience of madhouses, sir.'

She was wrong in that, but Horton said nothing of it.

'Miss Beavis, I wish to speak to you of the Johnsons. I understand you were a domestic servant to them.'

She looked away from her father and directly at him. She really was astonishingly beautiful. Her eyes were an Irish green, and her dark hair, worn loose this morning, had more lustre in it than anything else in this benighted building.

'What am I going to do?' She glanced at her snoring father, and then back at Horton. He might, if she'd asked just then, have offered to take her in, so gloomy was her pretty countenance.

'Miss Beavis, I understand your situation is poor. But I must seek to ...'

'They were all dead when I found them.' She spoke without looking at him; those green eyes were fixed on something not in the room, not even in the moment. Perhaps she could hear the beat of Jacques' flying machine. 'They had been away for some days. Mrs Johnson had taken to going away. She liked to rent rooms by the sea. Said it did her complexion the power of good.'

'They did not take you with them?'

'No, because Mr Johnson usually stayed in town. He worked, you see.'

'At the East India Company?'

'Yes. He worked hard, did Mr Johnson. Always bringing home files and papers and suchlike.'

'So Mrs Johnson and her daughter would take the sea air regularly?'

'Oh yes. Four or five times a year.'

'How long have you worked for them?'

'Three years. I was their first servant. Mrs Johnson said she was very proud of me. Bought me clothes. Even paid for me to have a tutor.' She looked at him directly now. 'I didn't always speak like this. Mrs Johnson said it was proper for a lady like her to have a well-spoken servant. And she wanted me to be a friend to Jane. Oh God. Jane.'

She cried.

'She was ... he had ... oh my God. Oh my God.'

Horton moved towards her and squatted on his haunches in front of her. She grasped his hand, as if it were a rope and she were floundering in the sea.

'When did Mrs Johnson leave?'

'Two weeks ago. She said Mr Johnson would be staying, but then he told me he'd decided to take some time off, and was going with her.'

'When was this?'

'Two days after she left.'

'Mr Johnson told you himself that he was going?'

'Yes. I was at the house. I was cleaning. It was the middle of the day. He came into the house, and packed a bag of clothes. He said Jane had taken sick, and he was leaving immediately. I was to keep an eye on the house, he said, and clean it every third day, prior to their return.'

'So when you visited yesterday, that was the first visit for three days? And, what, your third or fourth visit since Mr Johnson left?'

'Yes, sir. My fourth, I believe.'

'Were you concerned by Johnson's news?'

'Concerned for Jane? Yes.'

'Did Mr Johnson also seem concerned?'

'Yes. He seemed greatly disturbed.'

'Was he alone? When he visited you?'

'He was alone when he came into the house. But when I saw him to the door, another man was waiting. In a carriage.'

'Did you recognise him?'

'No.'

'Did he introduce this man?'

'No. I only caught a glimpse of him in the carriage. Then Mr Johnson climbed in, and they left.'

'Did they have any other family? Mr and Mrs Johnson?'

'Mr Johnson, no. At least, none that he ever told me of. Mrs Johnson had a sister down in Putney. She spoke of her often, but never visited, as far as I know.'

'Did Mr Johnson speak of his work?'

'No. Never.'

'Did you notice if anything was missing from the house?'

He noticed something in her eyes when he asked this, something that hadn't been there before. A different kind of fear. A watchful variety.

'No, sir. I do not believe anything was missing.'

Had she taken something from the house? She would not be the first servant girl to do so. He wondered what she had been paid by Mrs Johnson. Then he thought of her in that house, alone with the dead, terrified and upset, and despised himself for his suspicions. But those suspicions, once winked into existence, would not quite subside.

'Was anything disturbed?'

She breathed in, sharply.

'My apologies. Of course things were disturbed. I mean, in

those rooms where there was no violence. Did you notice a disturbance?'

'No, sir.'

'Did Johnson keep a safe? Anywhere he might have locked up valuables?'

'No, sir. He had a desk in his bedroom. A bureau, with a lock on it.'

'It was closed when you attended?'

'Yes, sir.'

'And the key?'

'I know not, sir.'

She looked again at her father, and seemed very small indeed in the ancient armchair. But her look seemed oddly mannered, as if intended as a distraction.

'What am I to do now, sir?'

She turned those green eyes on him. He noted, mournfully, how much those eyes and that face would be worth to a Covent Garden panderer, and feared for her.

'If I can help, I will,' he said, knowing how little the words were worth.

There was still a substantial crowd outside the Johnson house, and it would only swell. In two days the coroner would bring his inquest jury to look at the house and the bodies, just as he had done with the Marr family. They would be marched down the Highway between crowds, and it may yet prove necessary for the Bow Street magistrates to send a few uniformed patrolmen to calm the crowds with their presence. Horton knew how ceremonial such a show would be. Bow Street patrolmen did not wear uniforms other than to intimidate the public.

The Shadwell magistrates had improved one thing since the first Highway murders – there were now officers in front of the house to stop people going in to gawp. The poor dead Marrs had been laid out in their house like fish down at Billingsgate, for all and sundry to come and view. The Johnsons had, at least, been spared that posthumous humiliation.

The house in daylight was clean and peaceful. The shutters were up for the day's business on the shops either side. He could see, for the first time, that one was a fishmonger which seemed to sell mainly oysters, while on the other side of Johnson's house was that odd confection of a place with the animals, which turned out to be a kind of chandlery which also contained a menagerie of creatures for sale. A marmoset monkey sat in a cage in its window looking forlorn in an ugly green outfit. It screamed at Horton as he walked up, and there were other growls and screeches from within.

He went into both shops and asked if they had heard or seen anything suspicious on the day before the killings. Neither had. The wife of the fishmonger confirmed what Markland had said about the family, while the old Irishman who ran the chandlery-cum-menagerie said he'd argued with Mrs Johnson many times about the noise from his shop. When a carriage pulled up outside the shop, almost blocking the Highway as it dropped off even more squawking creatures, Horton imagined being the shop's neighbour. 'I don't go outside much,' said the proprietor. *I'm not surprised,* thought Horton. *You'd get the rough side of most of your neighbours' tongues.* He went to the rear of number 37, as he had the previous night.

He had to do some persuading of his own to get through the door, though he suspected the constable knew perfectly well who he was and, like so many of his fellows, resented him for what he did and how he did it.

The bodies had gone from the kitchen and the parlour – Salter must already have arranged for their transport to the Wapping office. There was still a lingering humanity to the place. Mrs Johnson had been a house-proud woman – the rugs looked like new, emphasising the total absence of any blood to stain the fabric or the wood beneath.

Flies had made themselves known. It took a minute or two for the low buzzing to become obscene, and Horton pondered opening a window to let in some air. But the only window was facing the street, where onlookers waited. They would only be persuaded to climb inside if he gave them an entrance.

So. A quiet scene, it had been: the daughter sitting in the chair, the mother . . . what? Was she in here already, or was she brought in here? The girl was tied to a chair, was killed. The mother was driven into the fire – so was she alive when her daughter was killed? Did the killer hold her face into the flame while she struggled? Did he make the daughter watch?

He went to the door into the hall. The only rooms down-stairs were the parlour and the kitchen. He stepped out into the hall, and walked upstairs. There, he went first into the smallest bedroom: that of the daughter. He checked under the bed, looked in a drawer or two, opened the wardrobe. Jane Johnson had few things, but they were all well looked after and of decent quality. She had inherited a care for things and an eye for them from her mother.

He went into the main bedroom. He had given instructions to Markland that nothing be removed from the house, but had little confidence that this will have been observed. Anything of obvious value would have been liable to being picked up by a poorly paid parish constable. In this, Shadwell's parish con-stables were no different to anyone else's.

He sat on the bed, looked around the room: the bed, the cupboard, a little set of drawers, an elegant and unexpectedly expensive dressing table.

He got up and looked at the table. It was a very fine piece of furniture, even to his untutored eye. There were bottles of per-fume upon it, and he took the most expensive-looking one and inspected it, but it said little about Mrs Johnson beyond its obvious value. Various mysterious ointments and waxy-looking substances were hidden in containers which may or may not have been made of ivory and ebony – expensive again, but all built for uses which Horton could not understand. The dressing table occupied a female world in which he was an ignorant tourist. But it seemed Markland's constables had behaved themselves; he would have expected the items on this table to have found their way into pockets by now.

The dressing table had three drawers with locks, all of which were open. In one of the locks there was a key attached to a heavy-feeling gold chain. Again, it had been left untouched. The clasp of the chain was broken, and there was a tangle of blonde hair wrapped within it. Horton opened the drawer. It was empty. He opened the other two drawers, and saw they contained an untidy collection of letters and bills.

He imagined Mrs Johnson sitting here while her husband sat in his own little office, poring over his own books and correspondence, while their daughter slept in the other bedroom.

He placed the key in his pocket and went out of the bedroom, and into the third little room. He had seen the small bureau as described by Amy Beavis on his first visit to the house. The room was as calm and tidy as everything else in this place. The desk of a City clerk, and a meticulous one at that.

He tried the lid, expecting to feel his fingernails bend against its unyielding weight. But to his surprise it opened. It was unlocked.

Within, no letters remained to be sent, or even to be read. Benjamin Johnson had not been disturbed in any work here. The desk had an end-of-day appearance, as if a careful man had tidied up his place of work after its completion. A quill lay next to an inkpot and some paper. Three books sat in an orderly pile. At the top of the pile was the first volume of the Reverend Daniel Lyons' *The Environs of London*. Beneath that sat a thin and rather old volume with a grand frontispiece written in Latin, and, perhaps, in Greek. He had neither language. The final volume was also thin, but more recently published, it would seem. It bore the title *Mathematicall Preface*, and its pages were much scribbled upon. The author of this book was given as 'Dr John Dee', a name which tickled at the edges of his memory, but did no more.

It was an eclectic set of titles. He picked the books up. They felt heavy in his hands and oddly warm, as if Johnson's reading of them had left behind some memory of itself. He noticed that pages had been torn out of one of the books, *The Environs of London*. He put the books in a satchel he had brought with him, and then turned to the final object in the room, the one he had been avoiding until now.

The maul leaned against the wall under the window, exactly where he had found it the night before. As if it were on guard. Horton picked it up in both hands, felt its malignant weight and inspected its face and handle, remembering that other maul which he himself had retrieved from number 29.

But that maul, the property of a sailor, had been old and worn. The handle of this one was shiny and new, and although its flat face was too covered in the matter which once constituted the mind of Benjamin Johnson, its pick-axe face was untouched and clean. The maul was brand new.

An unlocked drawer. A pile of books. A terrible instrument. Clean floors and walls. The stories of the house whirled round his head while he stood in front of the window holding the maul, as if he might smash his way outside.

ABIGAIL AND THE DOCTOR

The day after their aborted theatre trip, Abigail walked to St Luke's hospital at Moorfields. For three months now she had been working at the place, unpaid, as a nurse. The job was part of a careful effort to place her feet back down on the normal earth and begin her life anew.

The previous year, she had taken herself to a madhouse, Brooke House in Hackney. She had been plagued at that time by terrible dreams, and these dreams had begun to bleed into her waking hours, such that she could barely leave the rooms she shared with Charles in Lower Gun Alley in Wapping. Her mind had become an unreliable and tearaway thing, and she had been forced to mislead her husband in order to get it seen to.

She had come out of Brooke House cured, or at least it had appeared so to her. The dreams had ceased. They had been replaced, though, by a lingering discomfort with her memories of the madhouse, which were murky at best and in some instances, it appeared to her, full of queasy blanks. She went in disturbed (she avoided the word 'mad', even when thinking to herself) and she came out relatively calm. Of what happened in between she had little idea.

It was this as much as anything that had taken her to St Luke's, the great asylum formed the previous century by William Battie and intended to be a progressive and humane place for the treatment of madness. Its great rival in all matters relating to mad-doctoring was Bethlem, which had just moved to an enormous new building in Lambeth, such that these gargantuan temples to the infirmities of the mind seemed to bracket the metropolis, to pinch it between their stone fingers.

Abigail had worked as a nurse at St Thomas's before she ever met her husband, so her skills were in some demand at St Luke's, but she never asked for any money, nor was it ever offered to her. St Luke's provided her with something more valuable – an education in madness, and access to its investigators.

She watched the inmates while she cared for them, and tried to understand their lunacies: their manias, their melancholies, their hysteria. She spoke to the nurses and, when she could, she spoke to the senior doctor at the place, whose name was Drysdale, and who had taken a particular interest in this intelligent woman who worked for nothing and asked such penetrating questions about mental disorder.

He had become particularly interested when she mentioned Brooke House during one of her early visits. He knew something of the place, of its own Dr Monro and its former consulting physician, Dr Bryson.

'I have heard strange stories about the place,' Dr Drysdale had said to her.

Abigail had not heard stories, but she had imagined them.

'They say Bryson was involved in some odd investigations there. Involving mesmerism.'

'Mesmerism?' Abigail asked.

'Yes, though I cannot think why a qualified doctor would indulge in such quackery. It is said Bryson had come to believe that one might be able to guide another's thoughts using a species of mesmerism. He called it *moral projection*. Did he speak to you of it?'

'I ... I do not recall.'

'You do not recall his theories? Or you do not recall the doctor?'

This seemed an oddly penetrating question, and Abigail found herself wondering if Drysdale might help her understand things from the previous year somewhat better.

'I do not recall the theories. The doctor ... Well, I recall *a doctor*, of course. But none of his details. His face, his voice, how he treated me. None of it.'

'That is most odd. Mrs Horton, I wonder if you would indulge me.'

'In what way, doctor?'

'I would like to examine you, in the mental sense. When you are here, perhaps we could spend some time talking about Brooke House and your memories of it. I am fascinated by the odd wisps of rumour I have heard. Bryson's theories, while fantastic, do in some way overlap with some of my own ideas. You are an intelligent woman who may have experienced something unique. Might I make use of your brain, as it were?'

Drysdale had smiled when he said this, and while Abigail found his request odd, she also discovered she wanted to know more of what had happened to her. Wasn't that why she had come to St Luke's in the first place? She would learn by talking to the inmates, and Drysdale would learn by talking to her, and who could say? Perhaps they would both learn things of interest.

So she fell into a pattern of working at the hospital and being spoken to, once or twice a week, by Drysdale in his consulting rooms. They spoke of many things – of her past, of her husband, of her terrible dreams and of her oddly fractured memories of Brooke House. Some things that had happened there began to reveal themselves; other things stayed hidden. But she found her intellect reviving and her mind calming under the regular activity, like a weakened leg recovering from injury. Charles knew of her working days at St Luke's, of course, but she did not share with him those sessions with Drysdale, because she knew his concern would be painful to her.

Abigail Horton had returned from St Luke's and was reading inside the apartment, which she had freshly cleaned, when her husband returned from his work. He was still wearing the clothes he had put on the previous day for their trip to the theatre. Indeed, she smelled him first rather than saw him.

'Good afternoon, husband,' she said, looking back down to her book. 'How was the magistrate?'

He kissed her, and sniffed her hair as he often did, holding the curve of her skull in his hand, such that she wondered if he thought he could cradle the mind inside, protect it from its old disturbances. Abigail lifted one hand from her book and placed it on his forearm, with an affectionate squeeze.

'What is your book?' he asked.

She smiled.

'Ah, so you will give no answer on the magistrate. Keep it to yourself, then. It is a recent novel. By a woman named Austen.'

'Do you enjoy it?'

'I do. I like to read of clever people living in circumstances different to ours. Her world is full of wealthy soldiers and summer rain. She writes beautifully. I would like to meet her.'

'You sound besotted.'

'Besotted? No. Intrigued by another woman's voice.'

'And does Mrs Austen make dinner for her husband?'

'I would be surprised if she were married. She seems to find men oddly amusing creatures. I cannot think why. Wash yourself. You smell disgusting. I will prepare you some food instead of writing my own novel.'

She stood and went into the little kitchen and looked out of the window into the street outside while she worked. Some boys were playing an elaborate game down there, watched by a fellow puffing on a pipe. He shouted something to them and they laughed and scattered.

She went back into the parlour with a pot which she placed on the fire. She set a tray down beside his chair – a plate with bread and jam and a bowl of apples she had bought that morning. Charles sat down to eat. Abigail returned to her book, and for a few minutes there was peace and a comfortable silence.

Abigail looked up from her book, and noted that her husband was in his turn looking at her. She examined him. Abigail was widely read in matters relating to chemistry, botany and anatomy. She could, she believed, cut open his chest and take out his heart. She would hold it in her hand and watch it beating, but she would still have little idea of what it contained.

'My husband has the stench of consideration about him,' she said. 'Which means my husband is working. Even while he sits with me.'

'You are a more skilled investigator than I, wife.'

'I think not. You are a dedicated sniffer of secrets. How goes this new case?'

'It is a sad one. I do not wish to labour your peace with discussion of it.'

'You do not? Do I have no say in the matter?'

She smiled as she said it, but there was a deliberate edge to her words. She wished to talk of the case, whatever her husband thought.

'Well then. The case has some unique aspects, but the most remarkable of them is its similarity to the Marr and Williamson killings. There is a good deal of panic in the neighbourhood that the same killer has returned.'

Abigail was no longer smiling, and the mention of the Ratcliffe Highway slaughter chilled the air in the room, but she was listening closely. He continued.

'The whole family was slaughtered: father, wife, daughter. The man was in the kitchen, laid out on his front. The mother was face down in the grate. The daughter was tied to a chair, her throat cut. All the family members seem to have been attacked with a maul.'

She was distracted by the awful details. She had asked him, almost a year ago, that he share such details of his work when she requested it: 'However grim, I wish to hear it.' When he had asked why, she had said she needed to test her own mind, to ensure its hardiness. It was a fragment of the same experimental regime which had been taking her to St Luke's. It involved frequent prods at her sensibility and understanding, probing for weak spots. She knew it made Charles uncomfortable.

'Benjamin Johnson was the name of the husband and father,' Charles continued. 'He was a clerk with the East India Company. I spoke to the maidservant this morning, at her father's lodgings in Spitalfields. The maid told me Mrs Johnson and her daughter had been taking the air down in Brighton in the fortnight before their deaths. Mr Johnson had joined them there shortly after they left, saying his daughter had been taken ill.'

'His employer let him go?'

'I imagine so. I have not yet spoken to anyone at the Company.'

'John Company, they call it. Or the HEIC. H as in

Honourable. And as I hear it, taking time off in such a way could be grounds for dismissal. The Company is not renowned for its treatment of its clerks.'

'You hear a lot, wife.'

'Well, it is books that I hear it from. They speak, in their own manner. So, Johnson took some time off work, and in that time somebody killed him, his wife, and his daughter. The maidservant saw nothing?'

'No. She was told to visit the house every third day. She did so, and on one of these visits she discovered the bodies. And then, there is this.'

He took the gold chain out of his pocket, and handed it to Abigail. She held it in her cupped hands as if it were liquid that might run through her fingers.

'The wife's?'

'Yes. It locked a drawer in her dressing table. The drawer was itself empty.'

'My God, Charles, is that her hair on it?'

'Yes.'

Abigail gazed upon the gold chain and the hair wound within it.

'The clasp is broken. Like it was torn from her neck.'

'Such was my reckoning also.'

'A woman with a key around her neck. A key to an open drawer. A woman with secrets, Charles.'

'Indeed. Secrets which someone else now possesses.'

'Was she killed for these secrets?'

'That is my task to uncover.'

'Shall we keep this here?'

'Yes – I imagine you have some secret place of your own in which it will be safe.'

The remark was in somewhat bad taste, and Abigail did not respond to it. She placed the necklace in a pocket of her dress.

'Well, husband. You have been busy since leaving me at the Hermitage stairs. What next, do you think?'

'I must visit the offices of the Company. I have no experience of dealing with such institutions. I know not how it will develop.'

'Your magistrate will accompany you, surely.'

'Doubtless. He is a former Company man, after all.'

'Indeed. The Indian service.'

'You have read his memoirs.'

'As I say, husband: books tell me many things.'

'Well, then – what of these?'

He reached down to his satchel, and pulled out the three books he had taken from the house on the Highway. He passed them to her, and she looked over them.

'Hmm. I know this one' – she held up the *Environs of London* – 'but the other two are a mystery to me. This one I cannot make head nor tail of, as I have no Latin, but I know someone who perhaps can. And this one – "Dr John Dee". The name is familiar to me. At least the book is in English.'

'There are pages missing from the first book – the *Environs of London*.'

'Ah, interesting. I wonder who tore them out. I assume you wish me to consult these books? To see if they might speak to me of something or other?'

'It would be of great benefit to me.'

'Really?' She put her head on one side, like a dog weighing up its owner. 'Are you humouring me, husband?'

'By no means. These books were left in Johnson's desk.'

She looked at him, her head still on one side. Her measuring was not quite finished.

'Poor husband. It must have been an awful scene. All those slit throats. The blood must have been on everything.'

'As a matter of fact, no. There was little blood. None at all, in fact.'

Abigail frowned.

'But how can that be? A slit throat will send blood in arcs all over the place. The heart pumps it into the air through the open wound. It is a basic matter of circulation.'

'Indeed? Well, how would you explain the lack of blood?'

'Perhaps the place was cleaned after the murders.'

'Yes. But I do not know why anyone should have done that. And there would still have been marks, surely.'

'Or they were dead when their throats were cut. A stopped heart will pump no blood.'

She frowned.

'What state were the bodies in, husband? If the maidservant visited every third day, they may have been there for almost three days.'

'There was little sign of decomposition last night. More this morning; there were flies in the house then. But none last night.'

'So, the bodies were fresh. There was no blood. An obvious explanation presents itself.'

'Yes. That they were killed somewhere else, and brought back to their home to be discovered, after the blood had drained from them.'

'And brought there immediately after their deaths.'

Horton nodded at the book in Abigail's lap.

'What would Miss Austen have to say on this?'

It was a poor quip, and in the universal way of wives Abigail did not even acknowledge it.

THE EAST INDIA COMPANY

East India House dominated the corner of Leadenhall Street and Lime Street like a public school bully watching for new arrivals. The buildings around it, shabby by comparison, hunkered down. It took up two hundred feet of pavement, an ordered symmetry of columns and wide wings, topped by a pediment peopled by three gigantic figures. Horton recognised Britannia sitting on a lion, but had no idea who the other two figures were supposed to be, the one sitting astride a horse, the other on what looked like a camel.

The building was like a whale bearing down on him, its mouth open, its teeth made from fluted columns. Dark-suited men swam up its steps, throwing themselves into its maw with only papers and files to add flavour.

He knew, because his magistrate John Harriott had told him as they rode up Leadenhall Street, that this frontage was relatively new, that it masked a maze of old buildings – warehouses and stables, clerks' quarters and meeting rooms – which John Company had assembled over two hundred years. The classical front was like a fine suit on a body disfigured by age and war. An application of rouge on an old, scarred hog.

Steps went up behind the pillars to a set of wooden doors which must have taken almost as many trees to build as would a frigate. The steps were shallow but even so presented difficulty to Harriott. The old man was virtually lame in his left leg, and grimaced as he made his slow way up. Horton found himself unaccountably upset by this: the wealthy building glaring down as its old servant struggled upon its face. Harriott had given his healthy leg to John Company, but John didn't care to acknowledge the gift.

Was it possible to hate a building for its character rather than its appearance? Horton was beginning to think that it might be.

He attempted to help Harriott, but was angrily waved away. He had not wanted Harriott to come; a simple letter from him would have sufficed. But Harriott had been adamant.

Eventually the old man reached the top of the steps, and they went inside. Beyond the doors, a wide corridor stretched into the building, pierced with doors and windows and staircases. The throat of the whale, leading down into its many stomachs. Dark-suited men scurried from one place to the next, all of them carrying papers, the single ones peering at something in their documents, the groups whispering in urgent tones to each other. A frenzy of information and intelligence filled the air, the great Leviathan's body filled with these paper-carrying corpuscles with their missives from its brain to its extremities.

From somewhere within the building Horton heard a great crowd of men shouting and growing silent again, and then shouting once more, as if there were a cock-fight. He and Harriott were accosted almost immediately by a man wearing the dark clothes of a servant.

'Is there something you need assistance with?'

The sentence was elegantly formed. It said Horton and Harriott were dressed better than men of the street who might have stepped in out of the cold, but not well dressed enough for anyone in this building to immediately assume they were on Company business. Perhaps Horton was an unemployed clerk, seeking deferment, accompanied by his old father, a fat man with a lame leg and a red face.

'Fetch Mr Robert Ferguson, immediately,' said Harriott, adopting a practised tone of brusque authority for which Horton was quickly thankful. Harriott had been right to come, after all. 'I am John Harriott, the supervising magistrate of the Thames River Police Office. We are here on a criminal matter.'

The servant did not move. Harriott's introduction placed him and Horton more effectively, but this servant apparently needed more evidence before heading in to speak to whatever internal brain operated this place.

'Are there any more details? It is a busy day for us, sir. There is an indigo sale. A great many brokers and dealers are within.'

'Is that the cause of that infernal racket?'

'Yes, sir. Are there any more details?'

'There are none. Fetch Ferguson, and tell him John Harriott is here to see him. Hand him this note. Do not open it yourself.'

Harriott handed over an envelope, and the servant took it rather as if he had been handed an Eastern spider. He looked about to say something, but then thought better of it.

'I'm afraid I shall have to leave you to wait here in the corridor, sir,' he said, though his tone contained no apology. 'All our rooms are taken up with the Sale.'

'We will wait. Now go.'

The man turned and left them. Harriott pointed at some old

leather seats underneath a window which was frosted and seemed to look on some interior space rather than the world outside.

'Let us sit and wait, Horton. We may be some time.'

Various people came and went and, as Harriott had predicted, the two of them were kept waiting. Every man Horton saw seemed to be engaged in the most important business on God's earth. Benjamin Johnson had been just one of these busy men. How could Horton possibly construct a personality for a dead man who had been just one among legions of scribbling, scrabbling drones?

When somebody did arrive, he did not come from within the building. Horton saw him arriving through the gigantic street door: a man in a black frock coat with black breeches and white stockings, an expensive but conservative wig on his head. He looked like William Pitt might have done had he aged beyond his early death: thin, pale, cold, more of an intelligence on legs than a person. Horton took him for sixty years or more, and observed the stick on which he seemed to depend for balance – it was topped with a small and exquisitely done golden dog's head.

'Harriott?' the pale man said to Horton, who shook his head.

'No, sir. This is Mr Harriott.'

With some difficulty, Harriott was rising from his seat. A dark cloud had set upon his face. He seemed to have recognised the man.

'Ah. Of course. Harriott, my name is Burroughs.'

'I know who you are,' replied Harriott. The newcomer blinked his pale blue eyes, while Horton took in his clothing, which was, on closer inspection, of supremely fine quality, despite its very deliberate conservatism.

'This is most irregular, sir,' said Burroughs. 'I am led to understand that you are the magistrate of the River Police. You have no jurisdiction in this place. None whatsoever.'

'And you, sir, I recall, are among other things the alderman for this ward?'

'Indeed I am. Have we met?'

'Several times. I see I made little impression.'

Burroughs ignored this.

'You know, of course, that as alderman I also represent the magistracy and hold responsibility for criminal matters. The City preserves these responsibilities seriously.'

'Indeed. The City polices itself very carefully indeed, I find.'

'It has always been thus, sir.'

'Word reached you quickly, Burroughs.'

Harriott's disdain for the man ran through every sentence he spoke. Horton had seen this before. When the magistrate did not care for someone, he had no means to hide it.

'I have been asked to attend your meeting here, as a representative of the City magistracy,' said Burroughs.

'Asked by whom?' replied Harriott.

'I beg your pardon?'

'I mean, how did you learn of our presence so quickly? Who sent for you?'

'Nobody *sent for me*, Harriott. I am not one to be *sent for*. The Company keeps its own gang of ticket porters. One was sent to my premises on Lime Street to inform me of your descent on East India House.'

'It is fortunate for all of us that you were home.'

'My home is elsewhere. I am always to be found at my business premises on a working day.'

'I would expect nothing more of a pillar of the City such as yourself. And what is your relationship with the Company?'

'With this Company?'

'Yes. With the Honourable East India Company.'

'I am a Proprietor, sir.'

'With how many votes?'

'Am I being interrogated, Harriott?'

'No indeed. But your interest in this matter is worthy of quantification, is it not?'

'I fail to see the relevance of your question.'

'Do you? Is that the same as refusing to answer it?'

The two old men were now barely inches from each other, the one tall and frigid, looking down upon the other, who was outraged but maintained a brittle politeness.

'I hold four votes,' said Burroughs, finally.

'Indeed? An influential man within the Company, then. A highly influential man.' Harriott picked his hat up from the bench behind him. 'And as such a senior fellow, I assume you are in full knowledge of the location of our meetings with the representatives of your Company?'

'My Company?'

'My apologies. *The* Company.'

Burroughs sneered unpleasantly. It was the first expression of emotion on his face, and he looked as if a horse had just voided its bowels all over his foot. He turned without further comment, and began to walk up the corridor.

'After you, Horton,' said Harriott, as angry as Horton had ever seen him. 'Let us follow the Proprietor.'

Two men awaited them in a wood-lined room filled with exceptional furniture. One of them greeted Harriott with real warmth, explaining to the others that he and Harriott served together in India. Horton assumed this was Robert Ferguson, the man Harriott had demanded to see when they arrived. Ferguson did not introduce himself to Horton, and Harriott made no effort to introduce Horton to the room.

If this was Ferguson, the years had been kinder to him than they had to Harriott; the Company man was elegantly dressed, straight-backed and vigorous, while Harriott dropped down into a leather chair with audible relief as soon as he had shaken his former comrade's hand.

Ferguson introduced the other man in the room, a rake-thin fellow who held his hands in front of him like a country vicar.

'This is Elijah Putnam, senior clerk to our committee on private trade.'

'Private trade?' asked Horton. All eyes turned to him.

'Gentlemen, this is my senior investigating constable, Charles Horton,' said Harriott. 'He has my complete faith. You can assume he speaks for me in all things.'

No one asked why, if that was the case, Harriott had not introduced his constable sooner. And no one asked what in God's name a *senior investigating constable* was. Even Horton had never heard the words before. The eyes of the other men assessed him as if he were a bag of indigo, and then looked back to Harriott.

'We have a number of directors' committees in the Company,' said Putnam. He was a man of indeterminate age, the very model of the City clerk. His hands were held in front of him, and his head bobbed up and down as he spoke, like a nervous heron with a story to tell. 'My committee is one of them. Benjamin Johnson was a clerk working to me.'

'And what is "private trade"?' asked Horton again, aware that his questions would annoy. Their eyes shifted back to him.

'It is the trade conducted by the Company's own officers and masters, with the permission of the Company,' said Harriott, impatiently. 'Now, Ferguson – you know why we are here?'

'Of course we know. We read the newspapers. They are full of this matter this morning. A terrible business.'

'These Wapping officers are here to ask some general questions only,' said Burroughs, the alderman. Harriott scowled at him and at the word *officers*, and Burroughs spoke with a certain tightness of expression that indicated he knew he was being scowled at. 'I am happy for this to occur, but would warn Harriott that this is highly irregular. He has no jurisdiction in this area, and it is somewhat unusual for him to be accompanied by a constable who asks questions in this way.'

'We are not investigating anyone,' Horton said, and the other men looked at him once again, and then looked at Harriott. *Are you going to allow a subaltern to lead this conversation?* said their faces. Harriott glared back and said nothing. Horton took this as permission to continue. 'The murders took place in Shadwell's district, but we are cooperating with Mr Markland and his fellow magistrates.'

'Why?' The question was Burroughs's. 'Are the Shadwell constables incompetent?'

'Horton is unique,' said Harriott, speaking directly to Ferguson as if seeking an ally in the room. 'He has involved himself in several major cases, all of which have been resolved.'

'Benjamin Johnson was killed, along with his family, at some point over the last four days,' said Horton. 'The murders were intense and savage and, at first glance, motiveless.'

'Like the last Highway murders, then,' said Burroughs. 'Did you bury the wrong man, constable?'

'If you refer to John Williams, Mr Burroughs, it was the Shadwell magistrates who interrogated him. Not I. And he was never charged with the killings.'

'Then you don't believe he did it? And the killer may still be at large?'

'I said no such thing.'

'You implied it.'

'There are indeed aspects of the case which bear resemblances to the 1811 murders on the Ratcliffe Highway, as you have no doubt read in the press. We are of course seeking to ascertain whether there may be other connections. It may be, as Mr Burroughs says, that the Highway killer has returned.'

Harriott snorted at that, and was about to say something, but Horton talked over him. This did nothing to endear him to the enemies he had made in the room.

'Whoever was responsible, we need to establish why Johnson was killed. What was the motivation behind it?'

'And you think the answer to that question may lie within this building?' said Burroughs.

'Perhaps. We are simply seeking to establish whether that might be the case or not. It is, you will admit, an obvious place to look.'

'I will admit nothing, constable, and if I may, your tone is impertinent.'

'Horton is only doing his job,' said Harriott, dangerously. 'And you seem oddly determined to prevent him, sir. Is there some reason for that?'

'The Company can look after its own matters,' Burroughs said, directly to Harriott. 'If you wish to find out more about Johnson, we will do it for you.'

'It would be better if you would allow us ...' said Horton, but was interrupted by the smiling Ferguson.

'We do wish to assist you,' he said, to Horton. 'Mr Burroughs is quite understandably exercised by your presence here. We do not have many dealings with the criminal author-ities. We have our own men to act as police. We deal with matters which are of enormous sensitivity. Secrecy is essential if our operations are to be maintained. It is a matter of the national interest.'

'I fail to see how Benjamin Johnson's death impinges on the national interest,' said Harriott.

'Indeed, so do I,' said Ferguson, cheerfully. 'But we have to be careful. If I give you free rein to storm around the Company asking questions, who knows what you will discover?'

Who indeed? thought Horton.

'We shall proceed like this,' said Ferguson. 'Putnam will accompany Horton to the office in which poor Johnson worked. Horton can take a look at his desk and ask some questions of those who sat near him. In the presence of Putnam, of course. If those questions, in Putnam's judgement, veer towards matters of a commercial nature, he will inform Horton of this. Will that be acceptable?'

It was by no means acceptable to Horton, but he had to admit that it was unlikely he would have been given unfettered access to the internal functions of the Company. Harriott looked furiously at Ferguson, and seemed about to say so, but then he glanced at Horton, who nodded. Better to have some access than none at all, and talking himself into closed entities like East India House was not his magistrate's forte.

'That will be acceptable,' Harriott said.

Like a great heart beating in an unseen chamber, the noise from the indigo sale grew and then receded again as Horton followed Putnam into the depths of the gigantic building – down the whale's throat and into its gut. They passed windows which looked out on inner courtyards deep within the property, doors festooned with oddly banal titles – *Military Fund Committee, Freight Office, House Committee, Auditor's Office, Law Suits Committee* – and still they kept going. One ancient black door carried the legend *Secret Committee*, but it was a huge door with massive lettering and was clearly unembarrassed by its conspiratorial title.

It seemed impossible to be walking for so long and still to be within the same building. Left turns followed right turns through a random progression of corridors and staircases. It was as if the geometries of the City were giving way to the strange secret histories of this extraordinary Company which now, after two centuries, encompassed an Empire.

Putnam tried to make conversation as they walked, his head bobbing as they went. He was the same height as Horton, but his narrow back was bent, as if the head were too heavy for it. He seemed to have no fat on him whatsoever.

'I did not know, constable, that you were involved in the *Solander* affair.'

'You followed the case?'

'Oh, indeed. Avidly so. The Otaheite connection, you understand. I travelled to that island myself, once.'

'You were a seaman?'

'No! Not in any sense, constable. I was sent by the Company to investigate bread fruit as a possible food source for our plantations in India. I have some knowledge of horticulture. I hated sailing. I was sick for weeks.'

'It can affect people so.'

'Yes, indeed. But Otaheite! Such a place. I sometimes think of returning – but then I remember the sea voyage!'

'You found the island pleasant?'

'I found it extraordinary. I carry its mark on me still.'

'Many of the men of the *Solander* thought the same.'

'Indeed. And some of them died for it, did they not?'

Horton did not answer. They came to a plain door, a door very like all the dozens of doors they had already passed. *Committee For Private Trade* ran the legend inked onto its surface. Putnam opened the door and in they went.

The inside of the office was dismal, lit by candles and a flickering fire. It might have been May outside, but here within it was mid-February, cold and gloomy. Horton wondered if it had in fact always been mid-February in this odd little chapel to the personal trades of the Company's masters and officers. A dozen clerks sat at high desks, quills in their hands, beak-like noses bent over papers and ledgers and log-books, backs and shoulders bent not by the weight of burdens carried but by fingers following numbers across tables. These were the new monks of the modern religion of trade. They all turned to look at the three men who came through their door onto the outside world.

'Do not let us interrupt you,' said Putnam, as if the clerks were children and he was a headmaster showing round a prospective parent. 'This is a constable from the River Police Office, come to look into poor Johnson's death.'

'The River Police? But Juh-Juh-Johnson did not drown in the ruh-ruh-ruh-river,' said one of the clerks. Amidst this coterie of withered men, he was the tallest and thinnest of them all, his stammer ignored by him and by his colleagues. His eyes glittered in the light from the candle on his desk, and Horton noted how amused and intelligent those eyes seemed. There were precious few other signs of life in the room.

'To your work, Lamb,' said Putnam, and the clerk looked at him with a wider smile on his face, like a boy baiting an angry dog behind a fence.

'Certainly, Puh-Puh-Putnam,' he said. 'I shall not stand ah-ah-ah-accused of interrupting any investigation involving the fa-fa-fa-fate of my poor friend Johnson.' And with that the clerk turned back to his work, though not without the suspicion of a wink towards Horton.

'If you please, constable,' said Putnam. He led Horton to an empty desk, one of a pair – all the desks were arranged in twos. The unoccupied stool stood out like a ship without a mast.

The clerk sitting at the adjacent desk looked up expectantly as Horton and his chaperone approached, as if he were waiting for them. The desk itself was empty – no papers, no quill, and when Horton opened the lid there was nothing in the space within.

'Is this usual?' he asked.

'Is what usual?' replied Putnam.

'For the desk to be empty.'

'All the desks are emptied each night by myself,' Putnam said. 'The papers are locked in the safe.'

'So you read everything the clerks are working on?'

'By no means. There would not be sufficient hours in the day. I have a broad idea of what areas are being covered, that is all. Occasionally I will look in greater detail. If I am asked to by a superior.'

'So what was Johnson working on?'

'He and Baker here dealt with correspondence from the Company's Atlantic territories: St Helena and Tristan da Cunha. Also correspondence relating to activities on the western coasts of Africa.'

'But only matters relating to the private trade of Company officers?'

'The Company's formal dealings with the Atlantic territories are somewhat smaller than with its main holdings in India, constable. We tend to cover other areas as well, as they are too small to be dealt with by other offices.'

'What other areas might those be?'

'Stores and provisions, mainly. These territories depend on the Company for the materials of life. They are not self-sufficient in the way India is.'

Horton turned to the man sitting next to Johnson's desk.

'Baker?'

'Yes, constable.' The man was young and earnest, with a trace of Cockney about his accent, though it had been carefully smoothed down.

'You knew Johnson?'

'Yes, constable.'

'Did you communicate with him?'

'Not all that much, constable. Kept himself to himself. A fine fellow, but a shy one.'

'And you both worked on St Helena matters?'

'Yes.'

'I have a cousin who is a planter there. Just outside Georgetown.'

'Do you?'

Baker smiled.

'I do not recall there being a place named Georgetown on St Helena,' said Putnam, coldly. Baker looked at him and then looked back to Horton, who did not see the point of asking any further questions of this particular clerk.

'Putnam, may I speak to you privately?'

'Is there nothing else you wish to ask Baker?' He smiled as he said this.

'No. Nothing.'

'Then let us retire to my desk.'

'There is nowhere more private?'

Putnam looked at the clerks.

'You can assume that these men are devoid of hearing for the purposes of this visit,' he said. None of the clerks lifted their heads – even the stuttering wit kept his eyes on his work. Baker had turned his eyes down to his own desk. He picked up a quill, and looked in vain for an inkpot that wasn't there.

Putnam went to sit at his desk, a lower affair situated at the end of the room. He folded into the chair as if there were hinges at his waist and back, and indicated a chair for Horton to sit in. Horton felt like a parent of a misbehaving schoolboy who was behind on his fees.

'I understand Johnson was recently given time off,' Horton said.

Putnam's face changed, became colder and a good deal more careful, and Horton saw for the first time that he had information he was not expected to have.

'Why, ah, yes. Yes, he was.'

'Was he given many days off?'

'A week, that was all.'

'For what purpose?'

'To visit his wife and daughter. I understand they were taken ill.'

'Is the Company in the habit of being so charitable with its time?'

From one of the clerks – Lamb, perhaps – came a noise that sounded almost like a chuckle.

'It is in the gift of the chief section clerk,' said Putnam.

'Meaning yourself.'

'Yes.'

'When was Johnson expected to return?'

'I'm afraid I do not recall.'

'And yet this only happened last week.'

'Well, then, of course, he was to return this week. But then these terrible events transpired.'

Putnam looked angry.

'Well, then, my thanks to you. I shall disturb you no longer.'

'Will that be all?' asked Putnam, though his voice had adopted a newly sarcastic tone. The helpful heron-like clerk was gone. Horton wondered if he was now gazing on the true face of John Company. 'You have no further questions?'

'I certainly don't think it would be fruitful to consume any more of your time. My thanks for your cooperation.'

'Well?' asked Harriott, after they had made their way out of East India House and back into a carriage, two Jonahs escaping from their cetacean prison.

'I learned only this, sir: that they are hiding something,' said Horton. 'A new clerk had been placed next to Johnson's desk. This clerk clearly knew nothing of him or his work. They were supposed to have been working together on St Helena business, among other matters, but I mentioned a fictitious town on that island, and the clerk did not notice. Putnam, the manager, had been told not to reveal anything, but he was forced to confirm that Johnson had recently taken a week off, as Amy Beavis indicated.'

'Hmm. I fail to see the relevance of this time off.'

'As do I, at present. And I must be careful not to pursue a wild goose all the way to Leadenhall Street. But their care to cover up whatever Johnson was looking into is itself interesting. He may have been up to something.'

'Or he may simply have been involved in commercial matters they wish to remain secret. It is a private company, Horton. Secrets are its stock in trade.'

'Yes, sir. But what if those secrets lead to the deaths of its clerks?'

'Hmm. No evidence for that, now, is there?'

Harriott sounded aggrieved, and Horton could detect the man's lingering loyalty to his old employer. He decided to change the subject.

'The alderman, Burroughs. What is his trade?'

'He is one of the more powerful men in the City. A broker in gold and silver bullion; there are only two in the whole City, him and Moccatta, and Burroughs makes much play of being the only *Gentile* broker. Unfortunately, he is also one of those who police these streets. The aldermen are the justices of the City peace, and yet Burroughs acts like an advocate for the HEIC.'

'It is an odd arrangement.'

'That it is, Horton. That it is. The City aldermen are

required to have paternal relationships with London's trading firms. They know how their bread is buttered, after all. But this is worse – he is a Proprietor.'

'And what does that mean, sir?'

'It means he is a joint-stock owner, and a large one; he holds four votes at the court of proprietors, which is the most any one individual is allowed. If Johnson's death is related to East India matters, Burroughs's involvement will be damnably irritating.'

'The inquest tomorrow may raise some further lines of inquiry,' Horton said. 'Also, there were some books in Johnson's house which may relate to all this. I am looking into those. I would talk to the neighbours again, and Amy Beavis. I would also like to know more about Mrs Johnson.'

'Why?'

'I believe some items may have been taken from her dressing table. There was a lock on it, but the drawer was empty.'

Harriott frowned.

'But that might be the key to the entire case! Why have you not told me this before now?'

Horton affected embarrassment, but instead felt relief. He had turned the magistrate's attention away from the East India Company, and back onto the Johnsons. He felt in his pocket for the paper that sat folded within. On the way out of the Atlantic Office section, with Putnam hard on his heels, Horton had barrelled into one of the clerks who was trying to leave the room at the same time.

'Oh! My puh-puh-pardon, constable! I was lost in my usual drah-dreamworld.'

It had been Lamb, the stammering clerk who had spoken when they first went into the room.

Stepping back, Horton indicated the door.

'After you, Mr Lamb.'

'My thanks to you, Cuh-Constable Horton.'

Lamb exited, turning right to go further into the capacious interior of John Company's headquarters. Horton turned left, Putnam close behind.

The sharp-edged note in his pocket must have been inserted there by Lamb when they bumped into each other. He had noticed it as soon as they left the private trade committee office, and had read it surreptitiously while Harriott climbed into the carriage.

'Horton – I would speak to you of Johnson. Prospect of Whitby, tonight at 7.'

It was a random element in the story, and it promised answers to questions. Not the least of which was how an East India Company clerk had known his name.

1590: JACOBUS AT THE ISLAND

It took another couple of years, but eventually they boarded a ship and sailed south. They could have left earlier, but by now Mina was heavily pregnant for the first time, and they waited for the child to be born before taking ship. Sailing with a new-born could have been an awful experience, but the infant seemed to take the rolling world of the ocean without anxiety, as if Neptune himself rocked him to sleep.

South they sailed, and as the child slept, Jacobus taught his wife the contents of the manuscript, lest something happen to him and she had to take over the Project. They had been calling it the Project for some time now, the initial capital pregnant with conspiracy.

'Can it be true, Jacobus?' Mina asked as he coached her, and she heard the contents of the book for the first time. 'Can this miracle really take place?'

'Yes, my dear, it can be true. It *is* true.'

He said it with faith, though he could still not be sure. He had not been able to follow the instructions which had been set out in the manuscript. He needed the right environment and conditions, and he believed he had found them on the island. He had spoken to several men who had visited it, and they told him about its rocky fastness and its isolation. It seemed perfect.

But now, seeing it for the first time, he felt that certainty slip, disturbed by the high rollers of the ocean beneath him.

'My days,' said Mina, holding little Jacobus in her arms. 'It looks like a prison.'

And it did. The island was encased in walls of rock, and it stood alone in the blue-green ocean. They approached from the south, the only direction which the wind would allow, and sailed around to the north side where the only reliable landing place could be found. As they went, Jacobus caught sight of men working on one of the headlands.

'Look, my love!' he shouted, excitement conquering his dismay at the initial sight of the place. 'They are building our fort!'

He found her hand with his, and they held the baby together as the South Atlantic winds moved them around the island which was to be their home.

CONSTABLE HORTON IN
THE PROSPECT OF WHITBY

Horton arrived at the Prospect soon after six. He bought himself a pint of porter and sat down near a window looking out onto the river. With Lamb not due until seven, he had some time to himself, valuable time in which to think. His eyes rested on the ships and boats crowding the river outside. Their endless activity always settled him.

His peace was short-lived. Within minutes an unwelcome figure had made himself known. Horton, gazing out onto the Thames, had not seen his arrival, and was startled by Edward Markland's hand on his shoulder and his velvet voice in his ear.

'Constable Horton. I was told I would find you in here.'

Horton frowned. Somebody at the River Police, stirring up trouble for him, had no doubt passed on his whereabouts. Or perhaps Markland had been to his home. The man did not understand other men's boundaries.

'Mr Markland,' he said. 'I am meeting somebody here shortly in reference to the current case.'

'I am glad to hear it. This will not take long.'

Markland sat down. He took no drink; in fact he looked with some distaste at the metal tankard in front of Horton.

'Does the drinking of ale aid you in your considerations, constable?' he asked.

'I find it does. Taken in reasonable amounts.'

'Ah. And I wonder what *reasonable amounts* are, constable. I am told you are a frequent denizen of this establishment.' Markland said *establishment* with the same contempt as he might say *France*.

'It is a useful spot for meeting informants, sir.'

'Is it? Reliable informants, no doubt. Made compliant through the copious taking of alcohol.' Markland sniffed, and passed a handkerchief under his nose, as if the air of the Prospect was polluting his interior.

'Now, Horton,' he said. 'You have brought me no new information on the Johnson case today. I find this unsatisfactory. It is my understanding that you have recently visited East India House.'

'You seem very well informed, sir.'

'That may be so, constable, that may be so. Still, the question remains: why did you not report to me about your visit?'

'I was planning to come to you tomorrow, sir.'

This was a lie. Indeed, he had comfortably forgotten that he was accountable to Markland on this particular case. The man was characteristically rather indolent and had, on previous cases for which Horton had investigated for him, been happy to let the constable alone. This case, it seemed, was different. Different enough to get the Shadwell magistrate away from his usual habitat and into a smelly and grimy tavern.

'Well, we shall never know if you planned to visit me or not, shall we, constable? As it is, Mr Burroughs sent me a personal note to complain about your presence.'

'Mr Burroughs is a man of your acquaintance?'

'He is indeed. And, lest it be said that I am as miserly with my information as you are with yours, know this, constable: I am, like Burroughs, a Proprietor of the East India Company. Only with one vote, but nonetheless, I have interests.'

'You did not mention this before, sir.'

'I did not think it relevant before, constable.'

'Then I take it you will no longer be involved in this particular case?'

Markland blinked and then frowned and then smiled.

'Your reasoning, constable?'

'Your personal interests, sir. If it came to pass that there were Company matters entwined with these events . . .'

'*If it came to pass*. It will not come to pass, constable. It will certainly not.'

It was rare to see the real Markland, thought Horton, but he wondered if he was seeing him now. Ambitious. Hard-nosed. Contemptuous of his inferiors. The street-fighter in the guise of the dandy.

'You seem very, very sure of yourself, constable,' Markland said.

'I beg your pardon?'

'You forget yourself. You forget who I am. I am your superior. And, in this matter, you will take direction from me.'

'And from Mr Harriott, sir.'

'Ah, yes. Harriott.'

Markland eased back in his chair, the old comfortable smile on his smooth face. His fingers stroked each other, as if they were infatuated with themselves.

'Your magistrate, constable, is not quite the man you think he is.'

The tankard in Horton's hand felt suddenly heavy. Or perhaps it was just the air in the room thinning out, its invisible odours dropping away. Markland smiled a vinegar-thin smile.

'Harriott is financially embarrassed, constable. Acutely so. He has made certain unfortunate investments. He is an inveterate fiddler in business, as you must certainly know. He has a number of patents which he has been trusting to lift him out from this temporary difficulty. Unfortunately, none of them has performed the way he may have wanted. He has been forced to move to a meaner residence in Burr Street. And he is terribly ill.'

Horton stood up.

'Sit down, constable.'

Horton's fist clenched, and Markland saw it.

'Do me violence, constable, and see what happens. Now, I say again: sit down.'

Helplessly, Horton returned to his seat.

'I regret having to bring up the unfortunate matter of your magistrate's private affairs. But you will understand I only have your best interests at heart. Harriott is your protector. He is the man who gives you clear water within which to pilot your odd little craft. But he is not a man on whom you should rely.'

Markland leaned forward.

'I am that man, constable. I am willing to be your protector.'

'Sir, I know nothing of Mr Harriott's position, financial or otherwise.'

'You do now.'

'I shall forget what I have heard. But until Mr Harriott tells me otherwise – or until his superior does – I will continue to be loyal to him.'

'Admirable. Contemptible, as well. Contemptibly short-sighted.'

'Perhaps, sir.'

'I can have you removed from this investigation, constable.'

'I'm not at all sure you can, sir. Not if Mr Harriott wishes to pursue it.'

'It is my case, not his.'

'And that is a matter for discussion between the two of you. I, as a lowly constable, only do what my magistrate tells me to.'

'Poppycock. You are your own man, Horton. Do not underestimate my intelligence.'

Horton said nothing to that. Markland stared at him, a cat gazing at a recalcitrant mouse. Then he stood.

'You will report to me every day, Horton,' he said. 'And you will, in particular, give me a full account of any dealings you may or may not have with the Honourable East India Company. I will allow you to continue your investigations in the manner you see fit, but I will not permit you to keep Harriott more regularly informed than I. Do I make myself clear, constable?'

'Yes, sir.'

'Do not make an enemy of me, Horton,' said Markland. 'Do not embarrass me in front of my peers. Do right by me, and I shall do right by you.'

He smiled, and it was not the usual Markland smile, the welcoming grin which settled the room and made everyone feel they were in the presence of integrity and wit, for however short a time. No, this was the smile of the leopard in the tree watching the gazelle walk beneath, a smile that emphasised the teeth within.

'Why, Cuh-Cuh-Cuh-Constable Horton. I do be-be-believe you may be a little the worse for drink.'

Charles Lamb announced his arrival at Horton's table in the Prospect an hour after Markland's departure. He grinned, his face warm and friendly despite the clerical pallor, and offered to buy Horton another drink. Horton agreed, though he was already on his fourth pint of porter. He had drunk rapidly after his exchange with Markland. Lamb went away and returned with the drinks: a tankard for Horton, and a jug of gin and a cup for himself.

'Fuh-fuh-fuh-forgive me for playing the lush, constable,'

said Lamb, after downing a shocking amount of gin in a single draft. 'This in-in-infernal STAMmer only responds to drink, and we need to tuh-tuh-tuh-TALK.' He swallowed more gin, and began to talk, of general matters at first: of Bonaparte's infernal return, of the battle of Tolentino, of the latest coalition and the ambitions of Russia. Lamb spoke with creativity and power, such that Horton found himself vividly picturing the Emperor's approach towards the Low Countries, his northern march into that figurative space which England shared with the United Netherlands, the flat expanses of sea and land into which the Thames poured. The ale churned in his mind as he looked out at the ships on the river, busy in their industry and diligent, oblivious to the warlike chants from over the water.

Lamb's stammer did indeed smooth out, the jagged inter-ruptions to his speech giving way to his own personality. He was a man of Horton's age, perhaps a little younger, with a handsome, open face which was quick to take delight. Lamb watched the other people in the Prospect, which by now was crowded, with the same appetite as Horton.

'Well, constable, I must say this. It is a pleasure to make your acquaintance at last.'

'I thank you, sir,' said Horton, somewhat disturbed by this. 'You knew my name at East India House. How did that come to be?'

'Know your name? Of course I know your name! The famous Charles Horton, Wapping's lonely investigator. The *éminence grise* of crime and its detection. The man who solved the *Solander* case!'

The mention of the *Solander* murders brought Horton up short, ale or no ale. How did an East India Company clerk come to know, and what is more, to obviously care about that partic-ular case and his involvement in it? But Lamb was not yet done.

'And the Sybarites? An *unusual* case. Though not as

uncommon as the London Monster of 1811. Was John Williams really involved, constable? Or was there a darker power at work?'

Lamb's handsome, intelligent face now had hunger in it. He had seen a similar appetite in the faces of newspaper men, though Lamb's interest surely could not be for financial gain, as theirs was.

'You have me at a terrible disadvantage, Lamb,' was all Horton would say. Lamb laughed delightedly.

'Perfect! Your reputation is well earned. A man who keeps his own counsel. Coleridge will be delighted.'

'Coleridge?'

'He wanted to come to meet you, but was occupied with another obligation. But I shall report back in detail.'

'Lamb, this grows tiresome. Who are you, please, to know so much of me?'

'My name is Charles Lamb, constable. As well as clerking at the Company, I write a bit. The odd essay, the occasional tragedy, even a play for Drury Lane some years ago, though it was met with precious little fanfare. Coleridge, though. You must have heard of Coleridge.'

'The name is familiar.'

'Familiar! He is one of England's finest thinkers and poets!'

'I read little poetry. In fact, none at all.'

'No. Of course you do not. But Coleridge has heard of *you*, sir. We all have. Your name has been discussed several times among us. We find you, and your works, continually fascinating. De Quincey speaks of little else. He is preparing a monograph on the Ratcliffe Highway murders.'

Horton had no idea what to say. This man was obviously well educated and no doubt financially secure – East India House clerks were well paid and vacancies were subject to ferocious competition. Yet despite his charm he talked of

Horton as if he were a subject for study, seemingly uncon-cerned by this impertinence. Who were these poets and writers, to speak of him so?

'Mr Lamb, I thank you for your enthusiasm,' he said. 'But I swear, there is nothing particular or special about me. I am only pursuing the tasks which my magistrate lays in front of me.'

'No indeed, constable. I think there is a good deal more to you than that. And I think it right that you look into the strange death of poor Ben Johnson and his family. There is a good deal more to that than meets the eye, as well.'

'Perhaps you can enlighten me.'

'I have worked as a clerk to the private trade committee for barely a year, constable. And I do believe my presence there to be in the nature of an accident – I am not as bovine as most of the clerks who go through that office.

Lamb sipped his gin more gently, his stutter gone under the drink's earlier ministrations.

'I believe Ben discovered something. It was a day some months ago. Putnam had given him a task to complete – he wanted to calculate the market rate for cattle sold in St Helena to Indiamen on the track home, or some such triviality – and gave him certain ledgers from which to gather the information. Ben became agitated at the completion of this task.'

'Agitated? In what way?'

'Nothing dramatic. He was a phlegmatic individual. And he didn't say anything explicitly. Most people would not have noticed. It has been a time of general agitation at East India House; somebody is always worried about something.'

'Why has there been such agitation?'

'There are some who think the Company is coming to the end of its time. Two years ago a law was passed which opened trade in India to interlopers, and this has sparked much dismay. Ben told me that he had noticed another change, in recent weeks, relating to St Helena directly. It was as if the Directors expected the island to slip from their grasp. He was deluged by requests for information. St Helena is an oddity in the Company's holdings. It has never paid its way, you know; it has only ever really served as a staging post for Indiamen returning home. Its loss would, one would think, bear little weight on the Company.'

'So what did Johnson discover?'

'He did not say, explicitly. But he said he thought he knew why the Directors wanted to hold on to St Helena.'

'When was this?'

'Three months ago, initially. I tried to ask him about it again later, to speak to him about his progress. But he denied having found anything of interest at all. He grew positively heated when I raised it.'

'When was this second conversation?'

'Six weeks ago.'

The man was determined to see a story here, even if none existed. He imagined Lamb perched at his clerk's desk, bored out of his wits, his mind spinning flights of fantasy from the slenderest of threads.

'Mr Lamb, it is important that we do not see things that are not there.'

Lamb's face turned sour.

'Constable, my understanding is perfectly solid. I find your suggestion impertinent. I have told you of my suspicions, and my admiration for you. I think I have done all I can.'

Lamb drank down the remainder of his gin.

'I will take my leave of you, and my imperfect understanding will accompany me. Good night, constable.'

Horton watched the clerk's thin, long shape make its way out through the crowds in the tavern, and wondered what he had said to offend him so.

My dear Sir Jonas

*I hoped to write to you before now, but have had little to report
on the main matter of my voyage. I hoped that we might have
some clear weather when the Sun came near our Zenith, so
that I might give you an account that I had near finished the
Catalogue of the Southern Stars, which is my principal
concern; but such hath been my ill fortune, that the Horizon of
this Island is almost covered with a Cloud, which sometimes
for some weeks together hath hid the Stars from us, and when it
is clear, is of so small continuance, that we cannot take any
number of observations at once; so that now when I expected to
be returning, I have not finished above half my work.*

*Such hath been my frustrations in staring at the Skies, I
have had to turn my attentions to the Island itself, and the
People upon it. There are about four hundred Whites in the
place, almost all of them planters, and a quantity of Blacks
who are slaves. These Whites appear healthy enough, for the
climate is astonishingly mild, but the Blacks are appallingly
treated. But I do not speak of these. This day I encountered a
creature who seems neither Planter nor Slave, an ugly
Creature whom I take for a Portuguese. He has neither nose
nor ears, and one of his hands is entirely missing. I spied him
by my observatory, which he was much intrigued by. He had*

no English, and I no Portuguese, but by a sequence of attempts I concluded he could speak Dutch. When I asked him how he had come by such a tongue, he said he lived with a Dutch family on the Island. There are some such families, a holdover from when the Island's status was disputed between England and Holland.

Then he began to speak of the Island. He spoke of a time when the Island was covered in forest, though it be now as bare as one of our Moors. The Portuguese had brought goats to the Island, he said, and these had multiplied to such an extent that they destroyed much of the forest; men, too, cut down trees for firewood and for distilling alcohol, in their monstrous way. I began to realise, then, that he was describing a change which had happened over decades, and this man, despite his deformities, seemed to me no older than forty years. I asked him when he had arrived on the Island, and he gave me the date of 1516. More than one hundred and sixty years ago.

I was astonished, yet he seemed undisturbed by his Revelation. I asked him how a man could live so long, and he said only that 'it is the Island', as if this explained everything. And yet there is something about this place, something I cannot fathom or fully explain. The climate is extraordinarily beneficent. I can speak of a vicar who sailed here with me with his wife, both of whom were over fifty and childless. The wife is now pregnant with child, at an age so advanced that such a condition must seem a Miracle. I have spoken to her of it at length; indeed, certain loose Tongues have begun to wag about who the true father of her astonishing child is, such is the time I have spent with her.

I would not have this Fancy shared with your fellow Royal Society councillors, Sir Jonas. It is probably no more than the idle speculation of a man grown frustrated with his work, a man stymied by Clouds. But I cannot deny that there is something inexplicable about this Island, something alien which made me give credit to the ogre's story.

I have also detected a significant Variation in the Variation of the Magneticall Needle, if such a verbal construction be not too confusing. I have been fascinated by the way Magnetic North varies as one travels south across the ocean, and am developing a theory that these Curve-Lines of Equal Variation can be mapped, and may join each other, such that a Map of Variation might be possible covering the entire Globe.

The most interesting of these is the Line of No Variation, which I conjecture from my own observations runs in a gigantic sweep from the north-west to the south-east along the central Atlantic Ocean, joining Florida and passing through St Helena to the Icey Sea beyond. However, on this Island itself, this Line of No Variation disappears, and the Variation to Magnetic North jumps to almost 10 degrees. The effect disappears a mile off the coast, such that it is barely ever noticed by navigators, as they have no need of their Compass when they can navigate by Eye.

I have no explanation for this odd behaviour of the Magneticall Needle. It worries at me like a sore Tooth, and paints the entire Island in a fog of Mystery as thick as the real fog which obscures the peaks.

I may grow fanciful. This talk of Magnetic Variation may just be down to faulty Apparatus, and my ancient ogre just a fictive Caliban, and I a Trinculo who has drunk too much of Prospero's wine. But not all discovery is made merely by Observation. There may be more here than can meet the Observer's eye. We should send more men to St Helena, and we should not limit our Gaze to the Skies.

Yours, in continuing gratitude
HALLEY, E.

CONSTABLE HORTON AND THE BODIES

The following morning, Horton took his drink-addled head and the things he had learned to the River Police Office. Despite Markland's dire warnings, it was still to Harriott that he owed his loyalty. He reported in full to the magistrate on his meeting with Charles Lamb, rehearsing the clerk's stories of Johnson's hidden discoveries within the East India Company's ledgered innards.

'What do you know of St Helena, Horton?' asked Harriott.

'I confess very little, sir.'

'The extent of my knowledge, also. I stopped there myself, on my return from India, but saw precious little of the island. I could barely walk at the time. An extraordinary prospect, though. Like a rocky fortress alone on the ocean.'

A look familiar to Horton passed over his magistrate's face, like the shadow of a cloud on blue waters. An old seaman's look, salty with memories.

'I also spoke to Mr Markland last eve,' Horton said, carefully. 'He was much exercised with our visit to East India House. It appears that he is a Proprietor in the Company.'

The wistful expression disappeared from Harriott's face, which immediately went an old and worrying shade of red.

'A Proprietor? Markland?'

'Yes, sir. He has only one vote, which suggests he may only be in possession of a small holding . . .'

'Why, this is a disgrace! Wait a minute. You met him in the Prospect?'

'Yes, sir.'

'He found you in there?'

'Yes, sir.'

'He went to look for you! He warned you off, didn't he?'

'Yes, sir. In a manner of speaking. Or rather, he intimated that I would find things difficult if I did not immediately report any developments to him.'

'Scandalous! The Home Secretary will be informed of this.'

Horton wondered if he should add what Markland had told him about Harriott's personal circumstances: how he was ill, how he was poor. But would an outbreak of hostilities between the magistrates make his investigation easier or more difficult? Harriott had always been something of a loose cannon and this had on occasion made things more difficult than they might have been. For now, Markland was more use as an ally than an enemy.

'Sir, I wonder if we should not perhaps leave Mr Markland's revelation alone.'

'What? How so? It is a clear and flagrant breach of the essential integrity of his office.'

Horton didn't know if that were true or not; he had certainly encountered a number of magistrates for whom *integrity* was no watch-word.

'Sir, Markland knows the Company, or at least aspects of the Company which are unfamiliar to you. He may provide us access we would not otherwise achieve. And it is his case, not ours. He may simply decide to keep it to himself.'

'Not if the Home Secretary tells him not to.'

And what if the Home Secretary is himself a Proprietor? thought Horton.

'Can we perhaps wait until after the coroner's inquest, sir?' he said. 'Then we shall see what we shall see.'

'No, Horton. We cannot. This is a terrible lapse. I will not stand for it.'

Harriott turned his chair to face the window. It was his customary way of dismissing his constable.

'Salter was looking for you earlier,' the magistrate said, to the window and the river. 'He wishes to show you something.'

'He is downstairs?'

'Yes. With the bodies. In the basement.'

Horton noted how the Johnson family had lost their names. They were now 'the bodies'. Subjects for inspection, not a family of warm-blooded beings. He left Harriott to his anger, and went downstairs.

The basement was used to store bodies, inspect bodies, argue over bodies. No one had decreed it so, but it had become the unofficial morgue. Once a body has been stored in a room, it never quite leaves. Horton wondered after the first body to have been stored in there; a dead waterman, perhaps, pitched over the side of his wherry, his head knocked on the starlings of London Bridge. He had set the template, and now this little room was a laboratory of decease.

Salter was waiting for him, standing over the three bodies laid out on tables. When he saw Horton enter the room he folded the newspaper he was reading.

'Bonaparte! The man is a devil,' he said.

'Indeed,' said Horton.

Salter looked down at the bodies on the tables.

'Perhaps it is for the best, that this family departed so soon. If Bonaparte makes it to the Channel . . .'

The surgeon sighed. The last time Horton had seen him, the man had been angered by the constable's impertinence. Now, his dry old face was warmer.

'You were right, constable,' Salter said. 'I should have checked the bodies unclothed.'

Horton looked down at the table. He sniffed the air as he did so. There was something oddly reminiscent about the odour.

'Come to this side,' Salter said. He pointed to the body of Benjamin Johnson. 'The bodies are decaying rapidly. Another day, and the skin might have disintegrated entirely.' Johnson's shirt was unbuttoned to his waist. Salter peeled back the two sides of the shirt, revealing the grey expanse of the man's chest and stomach. There was a sense of movement beneath the skin, as if the dead organs were beginning to slide around each other in their decay. It sickened Horton.

'Now, constable. Can you see that?'

Salter pointed to the left-hand side of the chest, above Johnson's still heart. There was the outline of a shape there, about four inches high, and faint. Horton leaned in, smelling the horrible miasma around the body as it enveloped him, but smelling something else, that same strange smell he had detected when he came in. He peered at the shadowy image on Johnson's flesh. It depicted an odd geometric shape: a circle atop a cross, which itself sat on top of a figure three laid on its side. The circle itself was intertwined with a crescent, giving it the impression of horns. In the middle of the circle was a single dot. Horton found himself oddly repelled by it, as if it were the sigil of some kind of demon.

'A tattoo?' asked Horton.

'No. It is ink, but only on the surface of the skin.'

'Have you seen the shape before?'

'No. I had never seen anything like it. But I have since seen it twice more.'

Salter pointed to the dead woman and her daughter.

'In the same place? Above the heart?'

'Would you like to see?'

'God, by no means. Your word is sufficient for me.'

Horton reached out and touched the point on Johnson's skin where the pattern had been inked. The skin felt like death. He pulled his finger away.

'Is it possible to say when it was put there?'

'No. It is not a tattoo, as I said, so it must be fairly recent. The mark on Johnson's chest is much fainter than those on the two females.'

'So it was perhaps older?'

'Yes. Perhaps.'

'Or someone tried to wash it off, and failed. So they did not make the attempt on the other two.'

Salter looked at him as if he had performed some kind of magic trick.

'Yes. Exactly like that.'

Horton stood up, and closed Johnson's shirt himself.

'Do you smell something odd on these bodies?' he asked Salter.

'Yes, I noticed that as well. A slight odour of bitter almonds.'

That was where he remembered the smell from. It was the same smell he had detected in Johnson's kitchen. He thought it had been a cooking smell, but it seemed to emanate from the bodies themselves.

'What does all this signify, Horton?' asked the surgeon.

'At the moment, only that it signifies something,' said Horton, not looking at him. 'But that is better than nothing.'

Upstairs, he found a piece of paper and some ink and a quill, and drew the shape on Johnson's body from memory. Then, next to it, he drew the constituent parts of the shape: the upturned crescent and number three, the circle with a dot within it, the cross. He looked at it for some time, finding it strangely profane. Was it the mark of some secret society?

He folded up the piece of paper, and went to the street door of the office. He would walk home and show the picture to Abigail. Perhaps she would recognise it.

At the door, the porter handed him a letter which had been left for him. He paused on the street outside to open and read it. The letter was from Lamb, who had paid to have it delivered by hand, presumably from East India House. Horton read the message as he made his way back over the road to his home.

My dear Horton

My apologies for leaving so precipitously last night. I'm afraid that without realising it you perfectly stuck your hand into the hornets' nest that is my Mind. You cannot have known what you said, or how it would be taken, and I can only blame myself for reacting so badly to your words.

My family has suffered for many years with misapprehensions of the fancy; it is our defining curse. I am afraid I rather took to heart your suggestion that I might in some way be imagining that there was something sinister about poor Johnson's discoveries. On reflection (and now that the gin which I drank copiously and on an empty stomach has left my system) I understand that you are only doing your job. A healthy scepticism is to be applauded in one with such duties as yours. I apologise for so taking it to heart.

I have remembered something else, which may perhaps lend some credence to the strange story I told you last night. It is this: Ben came into some money last year. He said he had inherited it from his wife's family. But his wife had no family other than a sister, a woman to whom neither he nor his wife had spoken in a good number of years. There seemed to be substantial bad blood between them. Ben often talked of it.

Some time after the news of this bequest, I happened to run into Ben and his wife at a lecture being delivered by my good friend Coleridge (the poet of whom you have not heard). We spoke of this and that, and our conversation turned to walks in the countryside. Mrs Johnson had grown up by the river, she said, and she added 'at Putney, where my sister lives'.

Is Mrs Johnson's use of the present tense to describe her sister meaningful? The woman is clearly still alive. So what was the real source of the Johnsons' money? And why did poor Ben lie about it?

Forgive me if these are idle conjectures. But it would be a source of unutterable pleasure to me, and to my acquaintances, if we were able to help you in your investigations. I can be found at the address below if you would like to talk further.

I remain
Yours sincerely
Lamb, C

Horton pondered the note as he climbed the stairs to the apartment. Lamb had shared an office with Benjamin Johnson, but it seemed he also shared something with Horton's own wife, Abigail – a disorder of the understanding which could not be shaken.

It depressed him. He had imagined Abigail to be recovered, but meeting Lamb and then reading his letter forced Horton to acknowledge that the mind, once bruised by terror, could never quite be healed.

There was some breakfast waiting for him. Abigail was reading when he came in, and gave him little attention while he sat himself down and began to slowly break his fast at the little table beneath the window.

'What do you know of Charles Lamb?' he asked. Abigail put down her book.

'Husband, you are full of surprises. Why do you ask about Charles Lamb?'

'Because I met him – yesterday, and last night. He was one of the contributors to my late night return, and to my dull head today.'

Abigail seemed amused.

'Charles Lamb? The essayist and poet? He was the man you went to meet with last night?'

'So he says. I have never heard of the fellow.'

'Husband, your ignorance in such matters astonishes me.'

'You read enough for us both.'

'There is no such idea as *reading enough*, husband.'

'So, this Lamb is a talent?'

'He is a mighty talent, in my opinion. His poems are fine enough, but his prose is wonderful: clear and filled with a great heart. How on earth did you come to meet him?'

'He is a clerk at East India House. He worked with Benjamin Johnson.'

'How extraordinary.'

'He claimed, last night, that Benjamin Johnson had discovered a conspiracy at the Company, and that this might explain his death. He became upset when I said he may have imagined it.'

'Oh, Charles, what did you say?'

'Only that we can see shadows where none exist, sometimes.'

'If you had known more of him, you would not have said such a thing.'

There was great unhappiness in these words.

'He wrote to me this morning, intimating past afflictions. Do you know of them?'

'The Lambs have suffered terribly with mental disorders. Lamb himself has experienced them, but his sister has had it the worse. During one attack, she ... well, the story is a well-known one. You must remember.'

And now he *did* remember. Mary Lamb had killed her own mother during a rage brought on, it was said, by emotional disturbance. That had been almost twenty years ago, and the newspapers then had been full of the sad tale. Charles Lamb was Mary's brother? It had taken his wife – his dear wife, who had herself spent time in a madhouse only last year – to explain the hurt in Lamb's letter.

The indelicate conclusion was that Charles Lamb was as unreliable a witness as Horton had thought him. And yet this new story of Johnson's inheritance, and of the sister of Mrs Johnson, seemed plausible. It did not ring of paranoid fantasy. He thought it worthy of some investigation.

Abigail was looking at the book on her lap, though her eyes looked elsewhere. Were they remembering Brooke House at Hackney, the place she had gone to escape the world, the world he had allowed in to poison her brain?

'Stop it,' she whispered, the harsh words breaking the silence. 'Gods, I can almost *hear* your thoughts, Charles. Your infernal self-blaming. I will not have it, husband. I will not have my condition laid at your door. You are not responsible, for you do not operate me. It is an insult, to me, to have you blame yourself so.'

They had had other conversations like this. There was always poison in them, but there was fresh bitterness in Abigail's tone. It seemed to stem from this history of Lamb's. For a moment he faced the possibility that his wife hated him. But he was aware enough to slam that door shut, as if behind it were a cellar filled with waiting demons, their eyes green and bitter in the darkness.

'Abigail, I cannot help my desire to protect you.'

'No, you cannot. But you can avoid inflicting your bloody *guilt* upon me.'

He waited for her to come back to him. She always did, and she did now. A breath of air through the nose, a shake of the head: *right, enough of that, back to it!* He watched her back away from her own despair, and thought her heroic.

'Do you want to know the result of my own investigations, husband?' she said.

'If you please.'

She took a bag from the floor by her chair, and brought it over to the table at which he sat. The bag contained the books he had brought back from number 37. She laid them on the table, one by one.

'It turns out that all three books have a common denominator – this man called Dr John Dee. And this is his most famous book.' She held up the book. 'It is called *Mathematicall Preface*. It's the preface to an Elizabethan book on Euclid.'

'On what?' Horton asked.

'Euclid was a Greek mathematician,' his wife explained. 'He laid down the principles of geometry.'

'Such as?'

'Such as the fact that two parallel lines will never intersect.'

'Is that not obvious enough to make its statement unnecessary?'

She scowled at him.

'I shall not try to elucidate Dr Dee's essay to you, husband. It suffices to say that he had some very odd ideas indeed, combined with a trained mathematical mind. I understand barely a tenth of what this book says – and so, it would seem, did Benjamin Johnson. He has written copious notes and underlinings in the book. There seems no pattern to them. And that may be because John Dee himself had the most extraordinary set of beliefs. Which brings me to the second book.'

He opened the book she handed to him. It was the *Environs of London, Volume 1: The County of Surrey*. It was written by Daniel Lyson, and published at the end of the last century.

'Some twenty pages were missing from Johnson's copy,' said Abigail. 'This is another copy, from my lending library.'

'What pages were missing?'

'Part of the section on Mortlake.'

'Mortlake? The village on the Thames?'

'Yes. I know of no other village with the name, in Surrey or indeed anywhere else.'

'Hmm. Johnson was interested in Mortlake? His wife's sister lives in Putney – or lived. It is still unclear. I wonder what he was looking at.'

'He was looking for John Dee.'

Horton looked up from the book and at his wife. There was a sparkle in her eye. She'd enjoyed her academic investigation.

'The removed pages run on from a list of notable person-ages who lived and died in Mortlake,' she said. 'The missing pages contain the longest entry of all of these. The entry is for John Dee.'

'Ah.'

'Yes. And according to the account in this volume, John Dee was something of an odd collection of parts – part-sage, part-wizard. Perhaps even a spy. Certainly an astrologer and an alchemist.'

'An alchemist?'

'Men such as Dee believed that everything on earth – including men and women – were composed of four essential elements in different compounds. Alchemists explored those combinations. They sought out the perfectibility of man, believing that through study and contemplation man could become like God.'

'Do we no longer have such men?'

'No, husband, we do not. Now, we have chemists. And we understand that there are a great many more than four essential elements.'

'And this Dee was an alchemist?'

'Among other things. He does not strike one as a particularly reliable witness, and this account of Dee's life seems to be based entirely on the Doctor's own telling. He was a fellow of Trinity College, Cambridge, and his patrons included Edward VI . . .'

Horton had to struggle with his memory to even recall this monarch.

'. . . who gave him a pension and two rectories. Dee was suspected of treason by Bloody Mary . . .'

Had she been the sister of Edward? Horton thought she was.

'. . . but returned to favour under Elizabeth.'

Who *was* Mary's sister, Horton was sure. Or her cousin?

'To this point, this could be the account of any scholar under the Tudors. In 1575, the Queen visited Dee's house in Mortlake to see his library, which was a wonder of the age, the biggest private library in England. Imagine, husband! A Queen visiting a supposed Magician!'

'It seems unlikely.'

'And it is only his account. But then Dee's life took a very odd turn. Dee claimed to be able to speak to spirits via a stone – a "scrying stone" he called it – which an angel had given him. He performed what he called "incantations" with a young man named Edward Kelly. They left England in 1583 for several years, and ended up at the court of the Holy Roman Emperor, but then Dee and Kelly fell out with each other. Dee returned to England, to find his library destroyed by a mob, and his reputation in tatters.'

'Did people really imagine him to be a magician?'

'Yes,' said Abigail. 'Well, a necromancer, meaning one who communes with demons, though Dee claimed they were angels he was talking to.'

A mob and a necromancer. For a moment, Horton was taken back to Thorpe village, a village overtaken by rumours of *maleficium* in which he had spent time the previous year.

Abigail continued: 'Dee claimed that Elizabeth herself called him back to England, and he tried to claim money from her to restore his library. He said four thousand books had been taken. Four thousand books! At a time when there were scarcely a dozen printers in the land!'

'Did the Queen listen to his claim?'

'The account doesn't say. But he must have spent more than ten years living in England again before Elizabeth died. Then James took the throne, and he did not look kindly on Dee's supposed dabblings in magic. Didn't like witches, either. Dee was accused of calling up evil spirits, and died a few years later, penniless.'

'Is there any truth to all this?'

'Well, the account goes on to speculate that Dee was actually some kind of spy, and that all his talk of magic and spirits was in fact secret codes containing political intelligence. But there seems to be no evidence for that. I can't even imagine why people would have believed it. Dee claimed to have served the Queen, but it isn't at all clear how – and all these instances of Elizabeth's attention to him come from his own account. I wouldn't be surprised to find he made the whole lot of it up.'

'The story is intriguing, certainly. But I do not see its relevance.'

'Well, there is something else here. The final paragraph lists

Dee's writings, or at least those things which Dee claimed to have written, and they are astonishingly varied. He wrote about the reformation of the Gregorian calendar, geography, natural philosophy, optics, metaphysics, astronomy, astrology and what the writer of this book calls "the occult sciences". The account says Dee was asked to use the stars to predict the most propitious time for Elizabeth's coronation.'

The calendar and the secrets of the stars, all mixed together. How on earth did Dee ever tell the difference between the real and the imagined?

'But here it is, husband. I read it this morning: "He wrote an account also of his voyage to St Helena, and a treatise on the Queen's right to certain foreign countries."'

She looked up from the book.

'Didn't you tell me yesterday that the subject of Benjamin Johnson's work was the island of St Helena?'

'I did,' he said. 'The connection is interesting. And the third volume?'

'That I can make no sense of. The title seems to be in Greek, not Latin – and I have no Greek *or* Latin. It seems to consist of a set of 120 short statements or ... Husband, are you quite well?'

Horton had opened the third volume, the tattiest and oldest of the three, at the frontispiece while Abigail spoke to him, and there it was: the strange symbol that had been left on the Johnsons' chests. It was at the centre of an arch with two columns etched on the old page. Above it he saw the words *Ioannis Dee Londoninensis*, which he thought he might now be able to translate.

And on either side of the odd symbol, the initials I and D.

Ioannis Dee. John Dee.

ABIGAIL AND THE DOCTOR

She had little time to discuss the revelation of John Dee's symbol with her husband, though she could tell him that she knew Dee called it a 'monad'. Charles had to attend the inquest into the awful murders on the Highway, so she left him to his own thoughts, and went off to St Luke's to confront hers.

It took the best part of an hour to walk to Moorfields, and she took her time, enjoying the space in which to think. She had not seen Dr Drysdale during her visit of the previous day, and she wondered if she would today. She had not spoken to him for a week. The events of the last two days – the murders on the Ratcliffe Highway, the books Charles had found, her own research into them – had taken her away from herself, and that had partly explained her reaction to Charles's concern. She had felt offended that her husband thought her mind was not strong enough to cope with these disgusting deaths, but the truth was she had worried about that herself. She had discovered that she was coping well enough, and wanted to share this knowledge with the doctor.

She went looking for him when she arrived at St Luke's, the first time she had sought him out; previously, he had come to find her. But she saw on his face as she walked into his consulting rooms that there was a simple reason for their not meeting over the past week. He had not wanted to. He seemed embarrassed and somehow irritated by her arrival.

'Ah, Mrs Horton. I'm afraid I have little time to talk today.'

'Oh. Well, I shall not disturb you.'

She turned to leave, but he called her back and asked her to sit.

'My apologies, Mrs Horton. I should not simply dismiss you. We have discussed much in these rooms, and I owe you an explanation for my avoidance of you.'

Avoidance? she thought, as she sat down.

'You have heard me speak of Dr Bryson, of Brooke House?' he said.

'The physician there? Why, yes.'

'But your memories of him remain sketchy?'

'Yes, doctor. But, as I have said, my mind was much disturbed during my sojourn at Brooke House. My recollections are generally unreliable.'

'Perhaps not as unreliable as you think, Mrs Horton. You see, Dr Bryson is not all he seems to be.'

'He is not?'

'No. In fact, the story he tells is so odd that he is currently incarcerated here, at St Luke's, for investigation.'

This disturbed her. A mad-doctor driven mad by thoughts of Brooke House?

'Bryson's theories are in themselves sound,' Drysdale continued. 'I find his concept of moral projection to have some relevance, and his belief that the effect of mesmerism can be ascribed to it will, I am sure, be demonstrated one day. But his recollections of Brooke House have become . . . well, they have turned into something altogether different.'

I am not sure I wish to hear this, Abigail thought.

'Bryson has talked extensively of a woman who had an extraordinary ability – that of persuading her fellow patients to perform actions which they were reluctant to do, or which they had not themselves desired. This was the area of his work that I was interested in; this was the essence of his *moral projection* theory of mesmerism. But I must admit that I imagined the woman of whom he spoke was yourself.'

'Me?'

'Why, yes, Mrs Horton. You do have an extraordinary capacity to put people at their ease, and I have witnessed you calming the patients here at St Luke's with just a well-chosen word or phrase. I have been working for some months now under the assumption that *you* were Dr Bryson's test patient; that he was investigating your ability while he was treating you. I was seeking to talk to him of his theories without revealing that I knew you; that I had, in fact, been investigating your own mental well-being.'

It was a pure and cold violation. She gripped one hand with the other to stop both shaking. He had been *investigating* her? Dr Drysdale seemed only depressed by his revelations. He had no conception of how he was affecting her.

'However,' he continued, 'my assumption was entirely incorrect. I had not mentioned your name to Bryson during our discussions, as I wished to maintain our confidential relationship, but I fear that during a recent session with the man I blurted it out. He remembered you, of course, or claimed he did. But he said the woman he spoke of was not you. He said you knew the woman who had the peculiar abilities I wish to investigate. Her name was Maria Cranfield. Do you recall her?'

Something twitched at the back of her understanding, a sliver of memory, but it was not enough to grasp hold of, and in any case her mind was a kaleidoscope of anger and shame. She had been used under a misapprehension. Drysdale's dishonesty dismayed her.

'Dr Drysdale, I will not return to St Luke's,' she said, standing. 'I am not your test experiment. I had thought we were jointly discussing your theories, partly as a means of understanding what happened to me at Brooke House. I had thought you wanted me to contribute to your research. I see now I was only a specimen. Goodbye.'

She turned and left, still holding her hands together, desperately trying to keep her self-possession until she could find somewhere quiet and dark to weep her shame away.

CHARLES HORTON AT THE INQUEST

The venue for the coroner's inquest into the deaths of the Johnsons was the same as it had been for the death of the Marrs – upstairs at the Jolly Sailor. The atmosphere of near-hysteria that infested the streets outside was the same. A good number of the men watching the proceedings were the same – there was John Harriott, there was Edward Markland, there were Markland's fellow Shadwell magistrates, Story and Capper.

And there was Charles Horton, sat in the same place as he had been for that other inquest almost four years ago – at the back, his face hooded, unwilling to be seen, watching and listening and trying to make sense of it all, all the time wondering if these echoes of the earlier atrocity were all part of someone's deliberate plan.

He felt unhappily led by the nose, manipulated by signs, obscured by clouds of significance. Those strange symbols on the bodies of the Johnsons, tying them to the book of the Elizabethan necromancer John Dee, were the oddest remnant of all. The symbols were not accidental, just as the maul in the little bedroom was not accidental. There was a deliberation at work here, a particular consciousness.

St Helena, too – the strangely poetic and popish name of that distant island kept repeating itself. He knew *where* the island was, of course – he was a Navy man, a mutinous officer, and all Naval officers knew the shape of Britain's overseas possessions like they knew the curves of their cannon and the smell of their sail. But he had never visited the East India Company island. The Royal Navy only visited Company lands when there was trouble afoot.

These considerations were interrupted by the arrival of the jury, which was walked into the room by Unwin. The men were as pale and grim-faced as the Marr jury had been, and Horton wondered if they had also been taken to the River Police Office to view the dead bodies. If so, they had walked a good way, watched over by a fair-sized crowd which had come out to see if, as rumoured, the Monster had returned.

With the jury seated, Salter was the first to be interrogated by Unwin. He described the condition of the bodies – the damaged faces, the shattered craniums and slashed throats.

'Was there anything unusual about the bodies, other than the terrible violence?' asked Unwin.

'There were two matters of note,' said Salter. 'One was the absence of any blood at the scene of the crime, despite the terrible injuries.'

'To what do you attribute that?'

'Either the house was cleaned, or the bodies were brought there from somewhere else.'

'Already dead?'

'I cannot tell. They may have been.'

'So the cause of death may *not* have been the maul and the fire and the knife?'

'That is possible.'

'What might it have been?'

'There is no way of saying.'

'And the other unusual matter?'

'There were markings on the bodies. The same mark above the heart of each of the deceased.'

'What kind of markings?'

'A deliberate symbol, consisting of a crescent, a circle, a cross and an inverted number three.'

The audience whispered and moved in their seats, and already Horton could imagine the newspaper stories the next day. They would be full of ritual slaughter and secret symbols. He realised, with a little start, that he had had no opportunity to inform Markland of this development, and sure enough the Shadwell man was now staring at him across the room, fury in his eyes.

Neighbours were brought in as witnesses, though they had little enough to tell. No one had seen or heard anything unusual. But these men and women lived next door to a menagerie, so how unusual did a noise have to be to be noteworthy?

Amy Beavis took the stand last. Horton watched the faces of some of the jurors grow tender at her appearance, while others turned noticeably wolfish. Unwin, always something of a ham, became even more melodramatic at the appearance of Miss Beavis, leaning in towards her, passing her a kerchief when she became upset, all but stroking her.

She told the jury how she had discovered the bodies on that terrible day, how she had called for the watchman immediately. She then told the same story as she had told Horton – how Mrs Johnson and her daughter had gone to the coast, where they were later joined by Mr Johnson.

'Did you know of anyone who might wish harm on Mr Johnson?' said Unwin.

'No, sir. He was a kindly man. He always did right by me.'

'I have no doubt of that,' muttered a woman seated near Horton.

Unwin was a coroner, charged with identifying the cause of death rather than explaining it. In this case, the cause was obvious enough for the jury, and the verdict was straightforward: murder by persons unknown.

Horton tried to take his leave, but Markland had other ideas. The magistrate was shoving people out of his way to reach Horton even before the jury rose.

'I thought I made myself clear, Horton,' he began, his voice stretched by anger, the head of his cane rapping into Horton's chest for emphasis. 'Report to me, immediately, any discoveries. Was that not clear?'

'Perfectly clear, sir.'

'Then why is it I learn of this new development – these markings on their skin – at the confounded *inquest*?'

'Sir, I only found out about them myself this morning.'

'And did you come straight to me? Hmm? No, constable, you did not. You did *not*. There will be consequences, constable. There will indeed . . .'

John Harriott appeared at Markland's elbow. He was holding a note.

'Markland, a word, if you please.'

Harriott looked at Horton, and one of his eyes narrowed slightly in a motion so fleeting that it could easily have been missed. A wink, of all things.

'Not now, Harriott,' said Markland. 'I am discussing matters relating to the case with the constable, here.'

'Are you indeed? Well, there is someone else who would like to discuss the case with you.'

'Who?'

'The Home Secretary.'

Markland's face paled as he glanced at the note in Harriott's hand.

'Is that from … ?'

'Sidmouth? It is. I sent him a note this morning. This is his reply. We are to attend him immediately.'

'You had no right …'

'You can inform me of my rights or otherwise in the carriage on our way. Good day, Horton. Report to me this evening, if you please.'

And with that Harriott, who it seemed had learned to play the politician, turned away. He was followed by Markland, whose face was that of a dog chastised. Horton watched them leave and then looked for Amy, but the servant girl had gone.

Several uniformed Bow Street patrolmen were gathered outside St George's in the East, and Horton recognised one of them: William Jealous, whom he had met the previous year. A reliable young man, Horton recalled. Jealous nodded at him, and Horton nodded back, but did not stop. He had no particular wish to make small talk now. The other Runners turned to look at him. Did they feel the same mild antipathy towards him that his fellow waterman-constables in Wapping felt? He recalled, with some embarrassment, Charles Lamb's words, his description of Horton as some kind of *nonpareil*. He did not like the feeling. He wished that no one knew his name.

He was walking past the row of houses in which the Johnsons had lived – and, before them, the Marrs. There was a thicker crowd here, a motley collection of streetwalkers and barrow boys jostling with City gentlemen and West End ladies. Another East End crime, another reason to tour these benighted streets. A small boy of perhaps eight or nine years ran up to him.

'Do you know yer bein' follered, mate?' he said.

Horton looked around him.

'Who says I am?'

'Twitcher was first as noticed it, this mornin', but he's no' about now. Cripps is watchin' your 'ouse. I'm watchin' you.'

'Well, Rat, I'm obliged to you.'

He handed over tuppence. Horton had two dozen or more such boys keeping their eyes on Wapping and treating the whole thing as an enormously exciting game. Their utility was incalculable.

'Tell me more, Rat.'

'The feller was 'angin' about in Lower Gun Alley this mornin'. Twitcher pointed 'im out to me.'

'The man's description, if you please.'

The boy frowned, his dirty face crinkling in concentration.

''e's 'ard to describe.'

'Try.'

''e looks like you, constable. 'ard to place. Dark clothes. Dark hair. Tall. Pale. Wearin' a pea-coat.'

Horton's heart chilled.

'Does he have a limp?'

'Nah, nuffink like that.'

The chill lifted, a little.

'When was he last seen?'

'This mornin'. 'e followed you to the Office, and then 'e followed you from there back to your lodgin's. 'ung around a bit, then made off. Afore you came out.'

'And where did he go when he left Lower Gun Alley?'

'Dunno. We're not followin' 'im, are we?'

Horton looked around. The street was its normal frantic self, but now had an unwelcome whiff of purpose about it.

'And Cripps is watching my house just now?'

'That's right.'

'Well then, Rat. My thanks to you. Return to Lower Gun

Alley and keep common purpose with Cripps. If you see the man again, one of you run to the Office and report it.'

'Yes, constable.'

'You and Cripps meet me at the Prospect at seven.'

'Yes, constable.'

'There's good money in this for you, Rat. Do it well, and I'll see you right.'

'You always do, sir. I'll be off, then.'

'Give my regards to your mother.'

The boy frowned.

'My mother's gawn, constable. Coughed herself dead, she did.'

Horton remembered the woman – a pale, consumptive figure, barely able to work. Abigail had visited a dozen times or more. She would be heartbroken.

'Where are you living?'

'I must be off. Watch your back, constable.'

Before Horton could ask any further questions, Rat was gone.

Horton thought about following him, back towards Wapping and Lower Gun Alley. It was disturbing to think of his house being watched. If anyone were following, though, it would be him they would choose, not his wife. He looked around him, here at the point the Highway passed St Katharine's and headed towards the Tower. Was there anyone watching him? A queasy feeling, as if the gigantic creature of East India House was turning its head to look for him. He didn't doubt, for a moment, that this episode was to do with the current case.

He carried on walking, and reached Dorset Street after a half-hour. The place was as anonymously busy as any London street in the mid-afternoon, the end of the work day approaching, the night making its way towards the metropolis like a black sheet with which to cover iniquity. The dirty windows of the boarding houses looked like closed eyes, and the shops beneath them were picking through whatever trade they could take from the poor inhabitants.

Horton walked up to Amy Beavis's boarding house. It was quiet, and the door was open – in his experience, never a happy sign. Swallowing a great fear, he made his way inside.

If there were residents within, they were either sleeping or had left for the day. Or they were hiding in the rooms. A door opened at the back of the hallway, and a pair of eyes peeped out.

'Landlord!' shouted Horton, but the eyes widened and the door slammed. Horton made his way to the unreliable staircase, listening for any sound while his certainty grew that he was too late to be of any use to anyone.

On the second landing, the door to the room which Amy Beavis shared with her deranged father was shut. He walked up to it, put an ear to its pocked surface, and heard no sound from within. He tried the handle, and the door swung wide with a knowing squeak.

Beavis was seated on the one chair in the room, his hands clasped between his knees, his head lolling back as if he had fallen asleep. A cup lay on the floor at his feet, and whatever had been in it had seeped into the moth-eaten rug on the floor.

Amy lay on her back in front of the hearth, her dead eyes open to the ceiling. He looked down at her, as if he might see the face of the man who killed her imprinted on the eyes.

Jacques had come, it appeared. He had not been generous.

Whoever had done this must have left only moments before, and whatever had happened had happened as soon as Amy arrived home. The killer may even have been waiting for her, or had followed her from the inquest. There were no signs of a struggle; presumably Beavis had been here in the parlour when the killer first arrived.

But the scene was peaceful, domestic, quiet. How could that be?

Another cup stood on the mantel above the fireplace. He went over to it, saw clear liquid inside, sniffed two distinct smells – gin, and almonds.

If he hadn't stopped to speak to Rat, he might have disturbed them.

He moved around, forcing himself not to look too hard, to listen and to smell, to breathe in the room and to touch its stories. He focused on a corner of the wall and ceiling, an ugly brown-black locus, and then he remembered the etching, the ugly, faded picture of St Paul's.

It was no longer on the wall. He looked around the room for it, but it was not there. There was no square where the etching had hung – the revealed wall was as dirty and damp as the rest of the room. The etching had not hung there for long; Amy must have only just hung it. And now it was gone.

'Well, this *is* nice, innit.'

Rat stood in the Hortons' parlour, a grin on his face which could not have been any wider if he'd been standing in a drawing room at Windsor Castle. Abigail was warming a tub of water by the fire.

'He's not staying here without a wash,' she said to Horton. 'And are those the only clothes you own?' Rat, embarrassed by her tone, nodded. Every time Abigail spoke to him he blushed, and his eyes followed her adoringly round the room, like a puppy with a new and kind owner. 'You can borrow some of Charles's clothes while I wash them. They'll be much too big for you, of course, but they'll keep you warm enough.'

She went to fetch the clothes and the soap. She seemed angry and upset, and he wondered if his over-protectiveness was offending her again. He would have to ignore it. The boy grinned, his teeth white in the street-grime of his face. His cheerfulness astonished Horton, but then so much about these street boys astonished him – their resourcefulness, their enduring existence.

'Rehearse the plan to me, if you please, Rat,' he said.

'Right-o.' Rat held out his hand, and counted off each point on his filthy fingers, just as Horton had explained it to him.

'Article the First. I'm to stay 'ere in the 'ouse with Mrs Horton, unless she goes out, when I'm to accompany Her.' He pronounced *Horton* and *Her* with careful precision, emphasising the 'haitch' which was otherwise a stranger to his speech.

'Yes. At *all times*, Rat.'

'Article the Second. I see or 'ear anything suspicious – noise on the stairs, fellas 'anging round, anythin' – I'm to wave this 'an'kerchief out that window there.'

'And don't worry if whoever's watching the house sees you.'

'Correct, Constable Horton. 'Cos if they see *us*, they'll know *we* can see *them*, right?'

'Yes. And finally?'

'Article the Third. Cripps is organisin' the others to keep an eye on the alley. They sees my kerchief, they leg it round to the Police Office and fetch a constable. That it?'

Horton nodded.

'That's it. And here.'

He handed Rat a small purse.

'A shilling a day. That's enough for a week in there. Don't spend it right away.'

Rat's eyes widened.

'Seven shillin's? Seven bleedin' shillin's? By Lawd, constable, where'd you get seven shillin's?'

'From the magistrate. And he'll expect to see a good return for his money, too.'

Harriott had indeed provided the money; had initially

insisted that he send constables to watch Horton's house. But Horton has seen too many scowls, heard too many muttered insults as he'd turned down corridors to trust the safety of his wife and household to Wapping's constables. They were only river watchmen, after all, capable of little more than ticking off items landed from a ship. The boys of Wapping were more able.

Rat pulled himself up straight.

'I'll do right by your missus, constable. I swears I will.'

Abigail walked in, and Rat crumpled into adoration once more. Horton watched Abigail as she made herself busy washing and dressing the boy. She was irritated at him, but there was something else. He knew her well enough to know she would tell him what ailed her if she wished to tell him. After this morning's conversation, he did not wish to pester her with concern.

Perhaps Rat's presence would distract her. Perhaps protection could run in two directions. They had no children of their own, despite having wished for them, and they were now too old. Rat might be staying longer than just a few nights. It would be appropriate, he thought, to find a son out in the Wapping streets, even a dirty adoptive one.

Tomorrow would bring another inquest, this time into the deaths of Amy Beavis and her father. The Whitechapel magistrates would become involved. Arguments between them and Markland and Harriott were drearily inevitable. He would not attend the inquest, he decided. He'd had enough of jurisdictional niceties, even though the Home Secretary had brought Markland down a few pegs. But Sidmouth had also had words for Harriott.

'He told me to be careful,' the old magistrate had told him, sitting in his chair before the riverside window after Horton's return from Dorset Street. 'Markland's situation is a clear warning signal to us, Horton. The East India Company is as much a part of the fabric of this nation as the House of Commons. Hundreds of great men and dozens of famous women are stockholders in John Company, and thousands of ordinary men work for it. Throw a coin out of the window into the street, and chances are it will hit someone who has some dealings with the Company. Throw the same coin into the Commons, and it will strike a dozen men or more of the Company interest. We would do well to remember that.'

Would the pressure of powerful men now come to bear upon him? Had mighty wheels begun to turn, and would they crush those without influence? And was he really going to try and shield himself and his wife against such might with Wapping street boys?

'I will not be a prisoner, Charles,' said Abigail, as she scrubbed away at Rat's back.

'Not a prisoner.'

'No. Not quite. But I will go out as I wish, Charles. I *will*.'

A straight line had appeared in the middle of her brow, a straight line with which he knew not to argue.

'Perhaps you would prefer to spend the day in the Police Office?'

'Surrounded by ignorant men and empty bookshelves? Do not be so dull, husband.'

He watched her washing the street boy, saw the young white skin reappear from under the hard-earned grime of the Wapping street. Her hands rubbed soap into Rat's hair and stroked suds from his shoulders, and for a moment all was calm and all was love, and the schemes of powerful men held only invisible sway.

CONSTABLE HORTON AT PUTNEY

The next morning Horton travelled to Putney by water, on a River Police wherry piloted by his sour colleague Peach. As they journeyed upstream Peach glowered at him in his customary manner, as if Horton was responsible for placing Putney where it was and imposing on his tired arms.

Horton had last visited Putney in 1812, while investigating the murders of the crew of the *Solander*. The house he'd come to then had been a well-to-do place up near the Heath, with its own drive and garden. As Peach's wherry made its steady way past Vauxhall and Chelsea, Horton wondered about the captain's wife he'd met there and whether she was still sewing in the drawing room and looking out at the trees in her garden.

Emma Johnson's sister did not have the benefit of a garden. She lived in rooms above a tavern, close to where the timber bridge crossed the river to Fulham. Martha Fry was a short, dark-haired woman, ugly of face and with a beaten countenance. She looked as strong as a man, easily capable of knocking together heads in the saloon she worked in. From the cellar came the bangs and curses of men at work; they were installing one of the new beer machines.

'Lord, Jane was a beautiful child,' she said of her niece. 'As beautiful as the sun on the river. How could someone do that to a child such as her?'

Horton did not have an answer.

'My Lord Jesus Christ. What a terrible bloody awful thing.'

Her voice was unrefined. It had none of the reported gentility of her sister; even poor tutored Amy Beavis spoke better than Martha Fry. A man shouted from below, and she glared at the sound, as if all men were somehow implicated in the death of her sister and her niece.

'What did you know of your brother-in-law's work, Miss Fry?'

'East India Company, wasn't it? That's all I know. We wasn't that close.'

'You didn't speak with your sister often?'

'No. We didn't.'

Her upset had curdled to something sour.

'There was some discord between you?'

'Nothing as you could point to. She liked to lord it over me, did Emma.'

'Her neighbours in Wapping spoke highly of her.'

'Did they? She probably paid 'em off.'

'Paid them off?'

'Liked to have things over people. But I mustn't speak ill of the dead.'

'When did you last see her?'

'Two month ago. I . . . needed her help.'

'With what?'

'Look, has this got much to do with what happened to Jane?'

'It might. Did Mrs Johnson give you money?'

It was a gamble, but he was thinking of that expensive

necklace and that ornate dressing table. There was nothing so refined around Martha Fry.

'I asked her to lend me something. I'd lost my work and my place. It was either Emma or the street – and let me tell you, I thought about it.'

Her ugly face, which would have promised little enough on the street, turned dark at the memory.

'She was bloody delighted, wasn't she? Made out she was always willing to help me, that I only needed to ask. But I saw it in her eyes. She'd have it over me, wouldn't she?'

The woman's anger and shame were raw, and for a moment Horton pondered whether she might have killed the Johnsons herself. But her grief over her niece had been genuine.

'How much did she lend you?'

'What's that got to do with anything?'

'Was it a significant amount?'

'It was a fair bit. Not to her, though. Always had money.'

'You mean, she was rich?'

'No, I don't mean that. I mean she always had something spare. Even when we was young, she always had a tuppence or two. Uncanny it was. Never said where it came from. Had a bit for a dowry too, I remember. My poor father, bless his soul, he was humiliated by that. His own daughter, paying her way to a wedding! She loved it. Never said boo to her after that, right until the day he died. It was like he was scared of her.'

'And you've no idea where the money came from?'

'No, but look, it wasn't hundreds of guineas. Just the odd tuppence or shilling here or there. She squirrelled it away, God knows where. But she wasn't some bleeding Duchess.'

'Was she working when she married?'

'Yes. Worked in the same place as we all did. We were in service: me, Emma, our father.'

'Your mother?'

'Dead. Giving birth to me.'

'I am sorry for that.'

'It happens.'

'Where were you in service?'

'Here in Putney. At the house of old Suttle. Tea merchant, lived up near the Heath.'

'He lives there still?'

'No. He died some while back. His son moved in after him, but he died as well, two months ago, as I heard it. Found him dead out on Boxhill. Worse for drink. The son's wife's still there, though.'

'She lives in the house alone?'

'Far as I know.'

Horton rose, and put on his hat.

'My thanks to you, Miss Fry.'

Having come by river, he had no carriage to take him up to Putney Heath, but the walk was not a long one and the weather was dry. Putney High Street made its way south from the river, before climbing the hill up to the Heath.

Captain Suttle's house was surprisingly large, set back from the road within a walled garden which to Horton's untutored eye had been rather elegantly put together. He knocked, and was shown inside by a housemaid. Waiting in the drawing room, he looked at a large colour painting of a rocky island, hanging above the mantel. He recognised neither the artist, nor the island. It was a very ordinary painting.

'A Wapping constable,' said the woman who came into the drawing room to find Horton waiting there. 'A rare encounter for a Putney widow.' She was dressed in black, but her face was happy enough. She must have been in her fifties, and was plump and red-faced. Her cheery bonhomie reminded him strongly of that other Putney widow he had been thinking of, the wife of the dead Captain Hopkins.

'Mrs Suttle. My thanks to you for admitting me. My commiserations on the death of your husband. I wish to speak to you of a former employee.'

'Emma Fry?'

'Why, yes, ma'am, I do. You read the papers, then.'

'I do, constable. We widows have a good deal of time on our hands. It is a terrible business. Now, sit down, and I will pour us some tea.'

A servant came in and placed a tray on a fine-looking chinoiserie table, for which Horton expressed admiration.

'I don't care for it much myself, but my husband liked it. He said it reminded him of the East,' said Mrs Suttle, pouring the tea herself. 'I think you'll find our tea excellent, constable. It is one of the great benefits of being a Company widow.'

'I take it you are speaking of the East India Company?'

'Of course. Captain Suttle was a Company man and, indeed, a Company boy. Now, how is the tea?'

'It is excellent. My thanks to you.'

'I am delighted you like it. Now, to Emma.'

She settled back on her sofa, and Horton watched her prepare for a pleasurable gossip.

'Emma was the daughter of Francis Fry, I believe. He used to work here as a gardener. He lived in the attic with his two girls: Emma and the other one. Who was rather ugly, I recall.'

'Martha.'

'Oh yes, Martha! Poor thing. So ill-countenanced, and Emma such a pretty thing.'

He remembered that destroyed face in the guttered fire.

'Captain Suttle was positively enchanted by Emma. I grew quite jealous, I will admit!' She said this as if it were a huge joke, but there was an edge to her voice.

'Do you know how she met her husband?'

'I introduced them, of course! Poor Benjamin. He was a shy fellow, worked for the Company as a clerk. I met him at some party or other, and invited him to dinner. Did a spot of match-making, I will admit. He was besotted with Emma the first time he laid eyes on her, and I told her she could do little better for herself than marry a man with a Company position. They are much sought after, those jobs. Excellent pensions. For widows, too.'

'They were married soon after?'

'Oh, almost immediately. We laid on a little wedding break-fast here at the house. It was a beautiful ceremony, I will admit.'

'You seem to have shown enormous kindness to Mr Johnson and his new wife.'

'Well, one likes to help the younger people, doesn't one?'

'And did you maintain your acquaintance?'

'Not I, no! The Captain obviously saw Johnson at their place of work. But I saw nothing of Emma for many years. She wrote occasionally. To us.'

The *to us* was added hurriedly. She smiled, and almost winked. There was something charming but oddly gleeful about Mrs Suttle.

'Anyway, I did see Emma again. She visited us last year.'

'Here in Putney?'

'Yes. It was a weekend visit, something of a surprise. The Captain was delighted to see her. As was I,' she added quickly. 'I recall she left rather precipitously. I believe she may have said something to the Captain which angered him.'

'There was a scene?'

'Oh no, nothing like that. They were taking a walk in the garden, and when they came back in she left almost immedi-ately. Rather a cursory goodbye to myself. And now this terrible news.'

'And, of course, the news about the Captain.'

'Oh, yes. That was terrible too.'

This with a sip of tea and a mildly theatrical lift of the eyebrows.

'What happened to Captain Suttle, may I ask?'

'Well, you seem an intelligent fellow. Perhaps you could unlock the puzzle.'

'I understand he was found up on Boxhill?'

'Yes, and it was a deuced mystery. He has some family in the vicinity, but he hadn't visited them in years. He simply did not come home one night. He left for East India House in the morning, but then never returned. We became frantic with worry. It was a week later that he was discovered on Boxhill.'

'Who discovered him?'

'A shepherd. Thankfully his body had not been much troubled by beasts or such-like. We were able to open his casket at the funeral.'

'What was the cause of the Captain's death?'

He kept expecting the woman to show some upset at his questions, but she remained calm. She was grieving in appearance only; her husband's pension had left her in a good degree of comfort. Mrs Suttle was happy enough in her widow's weeds.

'He froze to death. I'm afraid there was a suspicion of drink having been taken. His clothes positively reeked of it.'

'Did he take drink often?'

'Oh, now and again. These men. You know.'

'A grim end.'

'Yes, indeed. I am bereft.'

Another sip of tea.

'Mrs Suttle, might I ask an indelicate question?'

She frowned, but nodded.

'Did Captain Suttle correspond with Emma Johnson? Did you ever discover any letters from her?'

'Constable, the question is impertinent and preposterous as well as indelicate. Of course he was not in correspondence with that woman. Why on earth would he be?'

She spat out the words *that woman*, and he could see she was lying.

'What did you say your name was?' she said, suddenly suspicious.

'Horton, ma'am.'

She frowned with concentration.

'I have heard the name Horton before, have I not? In connection with a Wapping constable.'

'I was in Putney the year before last, ma'am. Visiting Captain Hopkins.'

Her fat, comfortable face darkened as she stood, and Horton could see he had accidentally made an enemy.

'Then this interview is at an end, Constable Horton. Mrs Hopkins was a dear friend of mine.'

She rang the bell.

'The maid will show you out. Do not come here again.'

The change was so sudden that he wondered whether Mrs Suttle's friendship with Mrs Hopkins was anything more than an excuse to end a conversation that was veering towards uncomfortable matters. The maid arrived, and he walked towards the door. As he went, he nodded towards the mantelpiece.

'I was admiring your painting.'

'You were?' She had turned away from him, wanting him gone.

'It is very striking.'

'Captain Suttle painted it himself. From his own sketches.'

'It is a likeness of a real island?'

'Yes, of course. St Helena.'

'In the Atlantic? The Company island?'

'The very one.'

'When were you there?'

'I was not there, constable. My husband was. He was the assistant treasurer at St Helena for six years.'

It was almost full dark by the time he reached Lower Gun Alley. As he had predicted to Abigail, the trip to Putney had taken longer than he'd intended. Peach had waited for him all afternoon in the tavern where he had met Martha Fry, and by the time Horton returned from Mrs Suttle's, the man was drunk. The trip back downstream was alarming in the extreme, with half a dozen near collisions and no time to think clearly.

He left Peach singing to himself at Wapping Old Stairs, while he climbed back up to the street. The man's slurred voice echoed up from the riverbank, as if being pulled down by the receding tide. Wapping was quiet and watchful in the warm night air. To his left a great vessel was making its slow way into the Dock, and even the men shouting from its decks down to the quay sounded self-conscious, as if trying not to wake some giant within the Dock walls.

He passed the Police Office. He needed to report to Harriott, but first he needed to see Abigail. Turning the corner from Wapping Street he sensed, right away, that something was wrong. The apartment's windows on the first floor were open, but there was no light from inside; it was if they had been left open all day. He saw no movement within. He looked around to see if one of the Wapping street boys – Cripps, perhaps, or Twitcher – was watching the house, but there was no one about. A single shout rang out from by the Dock, followed by a peal of laughter.

He went through the street door and climbed up the stairs. There was still no noise, not even from the neighbouring flats. The door to his apartment was open, wide open, disgustingly open. He stood on the threshold and looked inside. More darkness. More silence. The smell of a guttered fire. He stepped inside, and an old board creaked like a mast punished by a gale. He stopped, and waited. Silence drifted in to replace the creak of the board.

If there was someone inside, they were in darkness. He, though, must have been framed by the dim glow from the hall-way. He stepped away from the door, into the shadows. Through the little parlour. Into the bedroom, to the right. Round the bed, down to the floor, moving his hands around in the pitch dark, terrified lest they brush against a lifeless face or an outstretched limb. Out to the parlour again. A scurrying of rats' feet in the walls. Some small glow from the street in here, enough to see the shapes of furniture. He walked around, looked around. Waited.

Nothing. No one was here.

Abigail was not here.

He turned and ran out, down the stairs, and barrelled out the street door, running straight into Cripps, who tumbled backwards with salty imprecations.

'Watch it! Bloody watch it!'

Horton put a hand down to help him up, even as he began his questions.

'Abigail! Where's Abigail?'

'Safe, constable. Safe. You don't need to snap my bleedin' arm! She's at the Office.'

Abigail had done exactly what he'd asked her to do: she had fled to the closest shelter at the first sign of something being awry. She was there now, sitting with John Harriott in his rooms, reading papers by the fire, and when Horton was shown in she stood and allowed herself to be wrapped within him. Horton glimpsed the magistrate over Abigail's shoulder and saw the old fellow smiling in an avuncular fashion. An oddly domestic scene.

'Where is Rat?' he asked.

'He is waiting downstairs,' replied Harriott. 'I will not have street urchins sitting in my office.'

'He is our ward, sir,' said Abigail, with some defiance, and Harriott's old face flushed red, whether in anger or embarrassment Horton did not care.

Abigail returned to her seat, and Horton stood behind her as she told her story. She had come home to find the house broken into. She'd been gone for only an hour, out buying some bread and meat, accompanied by Rat. When she'd returned it was almost completely dark. She did not go into the house, seeing it opened. She had just turned around and come here. With, Horton trusted, a watching but invisible honour guard of Wapping boys.

'Did they steal anything?' Harriott asked.

'I do not know, sir,' Abigail said.

'But – what of the necklace?' Horton asked.

'It is safe,' she said.

'What necklace?' said Harriott, irritably.

'Sir, I have spent the day in Putney, speaking to Emma Johnson's sister, and to the widow of a certain Captain Suttle. Mrs Johnson, her sister and their father were once in service in this Captain's household. I believe Mrs Johnson had some form of illicit correspondence with Captain Suttle, stretching back some time. Captain Suttle was recently found dead on Boxhill after having been missing for a week. I was told that Mrs Johnson always had a notable amount of ready money, even as a girl. And Captain Suttle had a connection to St Helena – he was a former assistant treasurer on the island.'

Harriott frowned in his chair, as if Horton had read him a riddle.

'Also this, sir. Whoever entered our lodgings did so to search them, not to harm my wife. I would imagine the most likely explanation is that someone was watching the house and waiting for her to leave. That suggests that whoever entered suspected we had discovered something, and wanted to know what it was. Or knew what it was, and wanted to retrieve it.'

'And have you? Discovered something, I mean?'

'Perhaps. This gold necklace holds a key. It unlocked a drawer in the dressing table in Mrs Johnson's bedchamber. That drawer was empty when I searched the house.'

'Meaning the killer emptied it?'

'That was my initial conjecture. The necklace has some blonde hair tangled within it. Mrs Johnson also had blonde hair.'

'*Ergo*, the key was hers, and whatever was in the drawer was hers.'

'Yes, sir.'

'*Ergo*, whatever she had in there she kept secret from her husband.'

'Possibly, sir. Even probably.'

'Such as correspondence with Captain Suttle.'

'Yes, sir.'

'A love affair?'

'That is possible. Mrs Suttle alluded to the possibility of inappropriate encounters in the past. As I said, I thought at first the killer must have taken the contents of that drawer. But now I wonder if Amy Beavis removed them, and was killed for it.'

'Eh? This did not come out at the inquest.'

'It is mere speculation on my part. But something was taken from the girl's home, I am sure of it. An etching had been hung on the wall, recently, which has now been removed. I wonder if Amy, on discovering the bodies, removed the key from her mistress's neck, opened the drawer and took the letters, hoping to make use of them. She may even have written to Captain Suttle's widow. I would wager that whoever killed Amy went to see her with the pretence of paying for whatever she had placed behind that etching. He offered a celebratory drink but then poisoned it, and left with whatever Amy had hidden.'

'The letters, perhaps?'

'Yes. The letters.'

'Which must, surely, have revealed a plot of some kind.'

'Such would be my estimation.'

Horton was acutely aware of Abigail's presence. She had not been in this room before now, and he was astonished to find how discountenanced he was by her being there. This was the room in which Horton and Harriott did their work. He felt himself watched and considered.

'It seems clear, does it not, sir, that there is conspiracy here?' he said to Harriott.

'Clear? Nothing about this is clear.'

'But the Company . . .'

Harriott bristled a little.

'The Company is very much like a nation unto itself: its own governance, its own army, its own rules,' he said. 'It must be expected that any encroachment from outside authorities will be resented.'

'Indeed so. But I suspect that this goes somewhat further than that. There seemed to be a determined effort to hide anything unusual that might have occurred in the private trade office.'

'And your hypothesis is that this may relate to the correspondence removed from Mrs Johnson's dresser.'

'Yes, sir. I have become convinced that the Johnsons were taken away and killed and then returned. Perhaps the killer wanted to stop Johnson investigating certain Company matters. Or perhaps he wanted information on what Mrs Johnson did or did not know. But whatever he was after, he wanted that search hidden beneath the outcry that the return of the Highway killer would spark. The maul was left for us to find, but this maul was new. I suspect its first use was in this act. It did not kill anybody. They were already dead.'

Rat sat in the chair by the fire, snoring softly to himself. His clean skin glowed orange and white in the flickering light. The parlour which had seemed darkly alien to Horton as he'd searched it for signs of violence was now cosy. That odd whiff of domesticity that had come to him in the magistrate's office had accompanied them home. The former mutineer, the former nurse, the street urchin. An odd family indeed.

'You will not apologise, Charles Horton,' Abigail said, putting her hands over his as they sat at the table by the window. A candle sputtered light into the room, and danced in the glass of the outside window.

'Your safety has been endangered by my activities,' said Horton, looking at the shadows which danced around her young-old eyes that had seen so much these past few years. 'If I had known it was so dangerous being my wife, and so unfruitful, I would never have married you.'

'Ah! I see. You married me, husband. But what if I married you?'

She sighed. There was a sadness in here tonight, one he could not quite explain.

'Charles, our story began with me tending you, did it not?'

Horton nodded. It had. She had been a nurse, he the victim of an attack. He had almost died.

'Did you woo me, husband? Did you read me poetry or sing me ballads?'

Horton shook his head. Indeed, he had not.

'No. You lay there barely talking. You were lost and lonely and terribly unhappy. But you noticed things. You noticed the other patients. You remembered the names of the doctors and the nurses. And you noticed *me*, Charles. I saw you reading my face, taking in my words, placing me in that capacious library which sits between your eyes. I began to think that you had given me a special place in that library. I know not why. And that's when I began to woo you, Charles Horton. I wanted to see where you had placed me.'

Rat snored, gently.

'I chose *you*, Charles Horton. And you were not an auspicious choice, all those years ago. You have improved, somewhat, like a good wine. And yet you persist in believing you press-ganged me from a happy life into a dangerous one. Not your choice, husband. *Mine*.'

'And yet – you are in danger.'

'We are all of us in danger, husband. You as much as anyone. Would you have me run away and hide?'

'A few days in Sheerness would . . .'

'Oh, you and Sheerness!'

She smiled, but was angry nonetheless. Brown eyes gazed at him from under blonde hair.

'You mentioned nothing of Dr Dee today, husband.'

'Indeed not. Mr Harriott does not react well to talk of wizards.'

'You do not believe Dee's life to have a bearing on the case?'

'How can it? Most likely, Johnson came across a reference to Dee's time in St Helena, and decided to investigate further.'

'Most likely.' She smiled a wicked smile. 'But – is it not intriguing?'

'I have the most unyielding sense that I am being passed

messages by whoever is behind all this. Have you discovered anything new in your reading today?'

She sighed, and he remembered how unhappy she had seemed the previous day when Rat first came, as if something unpleasant had occurred to her while he had been at his work.

'Only that I understand nothing of what these Elizabethan men believed,' she said. 'I cannot unwrap the odder parts of the *Mathematicall Preface*. I have resorted to the work of a man Dee refers to with admiration – but only because his book has been translated into English. I wish I had Latin!'

'Who was this other man?'

'He was called Henry Cornelius Agrippa. He was German, and denounced as a black magician during his lifetime. I could try and relate to you his cosmological view, but it would make as little sense to you as it does to me. He asserts truths rather than proves them – it is as if he is describing a different reality. He believes the stars and planets revolve around the Earth, and exert influence on everything here below by their rays. He thinks he can talk to angels. His life seems to be a mess of secret texts and hidden meanings and arcane symbols. He was, it seems, a profound influence on Dee. I think they both believed that man could be perfected somehow; that he could become one with God.'

'A blasphemous suggestion, no? Where did you discover all this?'

Abigail smiled, a secret expression that worried him profoundly.

'I asked certain people.'

'You should be careful, wife. We may be modern in our thinking, but such talk of dark arts may attract the wrong form of attention.'

'Oh, don't be silly, Charles. No one takes notice of one such as me talking of things like this. I am not Byron.'

Arcane symbols, Abigail had said, and he remembered the bodies in the Police Office, that strange symbol which had disturbed him so.

'You may not be Byron,' he said. 'But five people with links to each other are now dead, and I have no conception as to how they were killed, or indeed even *why* they were killed. There may be secret meanings in the works of this German, Agrippa. But there are secret meanings in the works of our own perpetrator, wife.'

She nodded at that, sadly, as if he had expressed a hidden but melancholy truth.

'Perhaps these dark arts are as dangerous as you say, husband,' she said. 'I shall return to my Bible and my lectures.'

'Is all well with you, wife?'

She looked out the window, and did not answer at first.

'I do believe so, yes,' she replied, unsatisfactorily.

CONSTABLE HORTON
LUNCHES WITH MR LAMB

The next day, Horton met with Charles Lamb at a coffee house just around the corner from East India House. He had written to Lamb the previous day to arrange the meeting, and had received a letter in reply with surprising alacrity. Lamb, it appeared, had been waiting to hear from him.

It was a little place, an adapted residence with tables and chairs in what must once have been the parlour. Lamb was sitting in a private room at the back of the place, to which Horton was led by a waiter with some display of subterfuge.

'You are worried lest you be seen with me,' said Horton as he sat down.

'In duh-duh-deed,' said Lamb, smiling happily through his stammer. 'And wuh-wuh-we are just two men among duhduh-dozens here.'

Lamb had ordered wine. He was excited. After downing an entire glass of wine, and pouring himself another, he winked at Horton.

'The suh-story is beginning to fuh-focus, constable. Last night my house was broken into.'

It was an unexpected statement, and an alarming one given the events at Horton's own home, but Lamb did not seem at all vexed by his news.

'Was anything stolen?' Horton asked.

'No. But my no-no-notebooks and ledgers were looked at. Some old stories and essays of mine is all they would have fuh-found. The contents amount only to whimsy and confusion.'

'Are you married?'

'No. I live with my sister. She, fortunately, was not at home. They may have been watching the house, waiting for her to leave.'

More eyes were watching more houses than he had thought. It was not a happy idea.

'Has anything like this ever happened before?'

'Of course not! This is obviously a direct consequence of my enquiries. Someone has noticed.'

'You have been making enquiries? Into what?'

'I have been busy, Constable Horton! On your behalf!'

'Lamb, I have no wish to . . .'

'Now, now, now, constable, enough. I have my bolt holes, you know. Southey is in the Lake District. If things become too hot, I shall make for the North.'

'But will that not cost you your position with the Company?'

'Not if I have information which can protect me, it won't.'

He pulled out a piece of paper.

'I have discovered something interesting. In your letter of yesterday, you told me this Captain Suttle had been an *assistant treasurer* in St Helena. As it happened, I had already discovered that.'

'When?'

'Just in the last day or two. I should add that I had never

heard of the position of *assistant treasurer*. It has never been mentioned in any correspondence I have seen relating to St Helena, and I believed I had seen it all. I have never heard a similar title in any of the Company's territories.'

'So, Suttle was lying?'

'No. He was not lying.'

'How do you know?'

'Because, earlier this month, the Company sent a *new* assistant treasurer to St Helena. He left on the *Arniston,* sailing from the Isle of Dogs on May the third. I found the order requisitioning a berth for a Captain Burroughs, and some related correspondence. I do believe it was hard for whoever organised this to keep things quiet – it is unusual for an Indiaman to stop in St Helena on the outward track.'

'Wait a minute – did you say Burroughs?'

'Yes.'

'The same name as Alderman Burroughs?'

'Robert Burroughs? The gold broker? Ah, I had not considered that possibility. The name is a common enough one.'

'Alderman Burroughs is a Proprietor of the Company.'

'Indeed. One of the greater ones, too.'

'Tell me, what is the role of this assistant treasurer?'

'Constable, I have no idea.' Lamb sipped from his wine again, the mouthfuls smaller now his stammer had been calmed. 'Absolutely none! The Company keeps copious records of all its personnel, and everyone has a job to do, in the service of the Company's chief aim.'

'Which is?'

'The enrichment of the Proprietors, of course.'

'But there is no account of the role of assistant treasurer?'

'There is no official record of it *whatsoever*. It is only alluded to, in passing, in other documents – ships' requisitions, property deeds and the like. As far as I can work out, Captain Suttle travelled to St Helena in 1808, and returned in 1814. He seemingly replaced a fellow called Captain Thomas Campbell. This Campbell had himself travelled out in 1801, replacing Captain Robert Fox, and the ledger says he was to take up Fox's position but doesn't mention what that position was. Fox went out in 1792, replacing Captain Stephen Jenkins, who went out in 1780. That's as far back as I've been able to go in the time, because I also wanted to see what had happened to these men.'

Lamb had written the names and dates down carefully on a single sheet of paper. He was, thought Horton, now the very model of the clerk, if a slightly inebriated one. A waiter came in with food.

'I looked back into the records of payment for these officers, Horton. It makes for interesting reading.'

Another swig of wine, and then Lamb spied the food. He wolfed down a forkful, which he swallowed with yet another swig. His manic excitement was smoothed beneath the clerical detail he had unearthed. Horton looked at the piece of paper Lamb had handed him. Names, numbers, titles and dates swirled before his eyes, like a Bath ball in which everyone was dancing to a different tune.

'The Company pays wages and pensions to all its officers, and these are all recorded,' continued Lamb. 'All these men received pensions on their return, but there is something very unusual about those pensions.'

'And what is that?'

'They were astonishingly large.'

'By what standards?'

'By any standards you care to choose. These men were rich, Horton. Such men as these are not supposed to be rich. They were militia men, essentially. They did not involve themselves in private trade. They were enriched by the Company itself.

There is no whiff of embezzlement or fraud about this matter. These men were simply paid huge sums. It is not immediately obvious in the records, for the sums are distributed across several ledgers. There has been a careful attempt to hide the payments. But if you know they are there, they can be found.'

'Could Benjamin Johnson have found them?'

'He *did* find them, Horton. Ledgers have to be signed out of the Archives. On each of the ones I looked at, the last man to sign them out was B. Johnson. I requested a list of all the ledgers Ben had signed out in the last twelve months. There are dozens and dozens of them. It will take me months to read them all. But I am starting today.'

'Lamb, you must not put yourself in any danger.'

'Do be quiet, Horton, you are not my aunt. And besides – there is one other thing. It may be my imagination running away from me – it has a tendency to do so – but I find it striking that none of these former *assistant treasurers* is receiving a pension any longer.'

'The Company has stopped paying them?'

'Yes, Horton. The Company has stopped paying them. Because they are all dead.'

He sat waiting in the same place he had waited with magistrate Harriott, inside the throat of the Leviathan. It was some days after his lunch with Charles Lamb and, once again, East India House had swallowed him up. The same clerks scurried in and out of the gigantic doors, and he tried to see into their faces, tried to calculate the odds of any of these men being paid to follow him, or Abigail, or even Charles Lamb. What was known about what he knew? Did the Company perceive him clambering about upon and within it? And how might it respond?

He didn't wait very long. Elijah Putnam appeared within

two minutes of his arrival, his heron's head nodding as he walked. Horton calculated Putnam's private trade office, deep within the guts of the building, was a good deal further than two minutes away. Perhaps the man had been waiting for him, watching as Horton showed his card to the same servant he had spoken to with Harriott?

'Constable,' said Putnam. His face was cold. The welcoming fellow from his last visit was gone forever it seemed, replaced by the careful individual he had said farewell to on the previous occasion. Putnam now reminded Horton strongly of Alderman Burroughs.

'Putnam,' he replied.

'You have questions to ask me? You left somewhat precipitously last time.'

'Certain matters have come to my attention, Putnam. Regarding the assistant treasurers of St Helena.'

Putnam smiled. He was not surprised. He knew what Horton had discovered. Horton found himself wondering where Charles Lamb was, today.

'Come with me, then, if you please,' said Putnam.

Horton looked at him, and at the crowd of clerks that flowed around them. He thought of the long corridors down to the private trade office, the anonymous doors off the corridor, the shadows and the corners.

'I think, if you please, that we should talk here,' he said. 'We have no need of a private room.'

Again, Putnam smiled.

'As you please.'

They sat down, and Horton pulled out the piece of paper Lamb had given him. Putnam looked at it, but Horton kept the face of it away from his eyes. The man might know Lamb's hand, after all – though he rather suspected the time for such niceties was past.

'What can you tell me about the position of assistant treasurer in St Helena, Putnam?'

'I can tell you nothing about it,' Putnam replied.

'Because you know nothing?'

Putnam waved his hand around him. *This place*, the gesture said.

'Then I shall be more specific. Tell me about Captain Campbell.'

'I do not recall the name.'

'Indeed? He was found in Kingston-upon-Thames, earlier this year. He had been attacked with some kind of a knife. It was around the same time another man, a Captain Suttle, was found at Boxhill. He too had been killed with a knife. Both smelled strongly of drink.'

'A tragedy,' said Putnam. 'Two tragedies, in fact.'

'Both Campbell and Suttle had held the office of assistant treasurer in St Helena.'

Putnam said nothing to that. He shrugged, and held out two open palms, silently repeating his inability to help.

'Captain Robert Fox, then. The predecessor of Captain Campbell. A St Albans man, I believe. A distant relative of Charles James Fox.'

'Ah, yes, I do recall Captain Fox.'

'You do?'

'Indeed, yes. There was something of a scandal concerning him, was there not? Something to do with indecency around children. He threw himself into the Thames, I believe. He was a Company man. But there are so many of us, the law of averages dictates that some will be wicked, does it not?'

'You have told me nothing I could not find for myself in the newspapers.'

'Well, the gentlemen of the press are very astute, are they not?'

'Captain Fox was an assistant treasurer at St Helena.'

'Indeed?'

'And what of Captain Stephen Jenkins? He served in St Helena from 1780 to 1792.'

'Before my time, constable, as you must realise.'

'Which is why, Putnam, the Company keeps records.'

'Records which you seem to have some access to, constable. Might I enquire as to how?'

'Captain Jenkins lived in a house on Manchester Street. I asked after him at the Public Office at Great Marlborough Street. One of the magistrates there remembered the case. Captain Jenkins was thrown from an upper window of his house in June 1798, with such force that his body had been impaled on the railings outside, where it remained until removed by constables. A woman was also found inside the house. It is assumed she was a whore. Her identity is unknown, as was the cause of her death; she seemed to have simply stopped breathing, and there were no marks on her body beyond those any man would expect to find on a London whore. An odd mark drawn in ink was found on her left breast, immediately above her heart. It was not a tattoo. It looked like this.'

Horton handed Putnam the piece of paper on which he had copied the symbol Salter had found on the bodies of the Johnsons. The clerk glanced at it, and just then – for a brief moment – something opened up in the clerk's face, some brief but potent mixture of surprise and anxiety which was shut down immediately like the snap of curtains on a room lit from behind.

'A macabre motif, constable,' said Putnam, handing it back, his face recomposed. 'I take it you expect me to see some significance in it? I'm afraid I do not.'

'Do you have a tattoo, Putnam?'

The question was almost certainly stupid, but Horton remembered their first meeting, when Putnam had spoken of Otaheite and how he *carried its mark on me still.*

'You mean, do I have this odd symbol tattooed on me? No, constable, I do not. And with that preposterous enquiry, I think we should draw this to a close.'

'What is the relationship between Captain Burroughs, the new assistant treasurer of St Helena, and Alderman Burroughs?'

Putnam stood up, and Horton did likewise, so that the two of them were once again pitched into the stream of clerks that ran along the corridor.

'Do you know where I live, Putnam?' asked Horton. 'Have you been in my apartment?'

The Company man's face was as unreadable as the marble floor.

'What do you make, constable?'

'What do I make?'

'In salary. What are you *paid*?'

'I am paid enough.'

'Really? I suspect that is not the case, in fact. When you begin to suspect the same, come and see me.'

The clerk turned away, and rejoined the black-suited throng, just another among hundreds of careful, calculating men.

During these days of corresponding and searching and travelling, Abigail remained under the watchful eyes of Rat and Cripps and the other street boys. Occasionally their numbers were supplemented by a Wapping constable on the orders of Harriott, who seemed determined to demonstrate his protectiveness towards Mrs Horton. But when she saw one of these men loitering around in Lower Gun Alley, Abigail was wont to open a window and yell at him until he left, to the sniggers of the boys in the shadows and the dismay of the neighbours.

These neighbours knew that something was afoot with Horton and his wife, but they had long known that Charles Horton had an unusual job – was, indeed, an unusual man – and that his wife was almost as odd. She kept a good clean house, that much could be said for her, but there were no children, and she read more books than was good for her – any learning garnered from books and not experience was, to most of the denizens of Lower Gun Alley, cause for great suspicion. Some of the women of the street had complained to Horton directly about the boys who hung around the place, and Horton pretended to hear their complaints and then ignored them. It was a fact, after all, that Lower Gun Alley was safer for everyone by being watched.

Rat's adoration for Abigail only grew as the days passed. He accompanied her everywhere, and grew quieter and cleaner and altogether more acceptable as a companion. Abigail was teaching him to read, an activity he clearly found astonishingly onerous but impossible to refuse, as it meant spending time in close proximity to and in conversation with the beloved Mrs Horton.

Abigail, for her part, admitted to finding the lad amusing, though Horton thought there was rather more to it than that. She had bought him new clothes and boots, such that Horton worried about the fate of the boy when all this was over and he had to rejoin his street mates in his fresh and clean attire. But when he pointed this out to Abigail, her face became desolate, and he knew he had opened a window she had deliberately closed. The question of Rat's future was, for her, best ignored. She enjoyed the boy while she could, even introducing him to the pleasures of the Royal Institution's Lecture Hall, which he had judged to be *wondrously mesmerisin'*.

She continued to read about John Dee, and about that strange symbol which seemed to attract new significance with every day that passed, such that Horton began to understand how secret texts and images could attract power just by their existence, by their promise of unifying explanations and underlying themes. The promises were empty, of course, at least in the realms of philosophy. But somebody had drawn those symbols. The *Monad*, Abigail said the symbol was called – and it was created by Dee.

The newspapers were full of the quotidian gossip and business of the metropolis, with one persistent drum beat which grew louder and louder as May progressed towards June: the extraordinary prospect of the wars with Napoleon recommencing. The emperor had left Elba, the little Mediterranean island which had been ceded to him by the European powers, three months before. In less than a hundred days he had reassembled his armies and reinfatuated the French with his talk of Imperial glory. The British government had pledged tens of thousands of men and tens of thousands of pounds to bring the French back to heel, and armies had been gathering, their swarms calculated in daily newspaper reports. Horton was struggling to keep the interest of his magistrate, John Harriott, who seemed to have taken Napoleon's activity as a personal outrage. Likewise the interest in the deaths of the Johnsons, and then of Amy Beavis, had sunk beneath the rising tide of a new Francophobia. Napoleon seemed almost infernal in his resistance to defeat: an emperor who could not die and would not surrender until Europe burned beneath his cloven feet.

Edward Markland, similarly, had become less interested in the case after the embarrassment of his visit to the Home Secretary. The political appeal of solving the murders had declined along with the public interest. There was no new

London Monster, or so every day without another killing suggested. The only Monster was Corsican, not English.

A few days after his encounter with Putnam at East India House, as May drew to an end and June came in, Horton received a letter at the Police Office. It was from Charles Lamb.

Horton – a note, scribbled in some urgency. I am this day to take the stage north, to spend time with my friend Southey in the Lakes. I am, I admit, running away. Last night, I was followed home, I know not by whom. I kept to the busiest streets, and made it to my door. I locked it and secured all the windows. I stayed awake all night, and made a point of keeping as many lamps and candles burning as possible. I was not disturbed, but the experience shook me. I have found nothing else on the St Helena assistant treasurers, and must now beat my retreat. My anxiety grows so great. I must find air and freedom. I cannot be Locked AWAY!

Lamb

The note had such frenzy that Horton feared a recurrence of Lamb's mental disarray. He tried to decode what it might mean, Lamb being followed in this way. Had he himself put Lamb in danger, when he had questioned Putnam in the way he had? Horton had been on high alert in its immediate aftermath, but had seen nothing suspicious. Was it just that the Company had been waiting for things to settle down? Might the danger Lamb perceived be real? He felt the force of Lamb's imagination and the shadow of his mania, projecting forbidding shapes into Horton's own mind.

There were three men standing at the bar of the Prospect. They were removing their coats, for the day was warm and inside the pub the air had become close and sticky. One of them rolled up his sleeves before returning to his pint, and Horton saw an enormous tattoo snaking up his arm – literally snaking, for the tattoo depicted a blue-skinned serpent, an evil thing that was at once ugly and beautiful. A reminder of his talk with Putnam.

He minded a man arriving in the pub, tall and out of place, his head turning as he looked for someone. It was Salter, the surgeon. He caught Horton's eye and walked over to him.

'Dr Salter,' Horton said. 'Were you looking for me?'

'I was.' Salter looked around once more, as if he feared every man in the pub might jump on him at once.

'Can I fetch you a drink?'

'No, indeed. I do not . . . partake.'

'Well, then, please do sit.'

Salter looked at the chair opposite Horton. It did not impress him, but he carefully placed himself in it nonetheless.

'I have some information,' Salter said. 'It relates to the odd smell we detected on the bodies of the Johnsons, and which you also reported at the home of Mr Beavis and his daughter.'

'Yes – the smell of bitter almonds.'

'Exactly. Well, it reminded me of something, but I've been busy and had not the chance to pursue it. I also wished to consult with an acquaintance of mine. Do you know of Dr Granville, physician in ordinary to His Highness the Duke of Clarence?'

Horton laughed, but seeing Salter frown he realised his mistake. Salter was not joking – he was honestly asking if Horton knew the physician to an HRH.

'No, Salter. I do not know Dr Granville.'

'Ah, well. Of course. Well, Dr Granville has been long interested in a substance named Prussic acid. Do you know of this, perhaps?'

'No.'

'It is a constituent part of the pigment Prussian blue. It is an unusual thing. It was first created in the last century by the Swedish chemist Scheele. He mixed Prussian blue with red precipitate of mercury and water, boiled and agitated and filtered it, then poured it over iron filings and added sulphuric acid. He then distilled a quarter part of it, and made Prussic acid with a mixture of sulphuric acid; the latter he removed using barytic water.'

Salter looked mesmerised. To Horton, he might as well have been speaking Greek.

'Four years ago, Gay-Lussac in France perfected this technique, and created the purest form of Prussic acid yet seen. He calls it *hydro-cyanic acid*. Dr Granville is interested in the medicinal properties of this substance – he believes it has great potential as a sedative, even more powerful, he says, than opium.'

'And its relevance to the current case?'

'Simply this: Prussic acid, or hydro-cyanic acid – whatever you wish to call it – has three distinct properties. One, it carries a strong smell of bitter almonds. Two, it has a very low boiling point, and is gaseous at some 20 degrees Celsius. Three, it is *extraordinarily* poisonous. I believe it may have been used in the deaths of the Johnsons and, almost certainly, in the deaths of the Beavises also.'

The information fitted, like an old key in a smooth lock, and Horton was grateful for it. But he wondered where it led him. He had suspected, of course, that the Johnsons and the Beavises had been poisoned. Did knowing the mechanism make any difference? If a door had opened, did it lead anywhere useful?

Horton finished his ale and left the Prospect of Whitby with Salter, bidding the doctor farewell out on the street and thanking him for his information. He walked to the River Police

Office, but there he was interrupted by Edward Markland, who was just leaving after a meeting with Harriott. As Markland made his customarily superior greeting, the office porter handed Horton a note. Markland watched him read the name of the sender on the envelope, and must have seen his face.

'Who is it from, Horton?' Markland asked, rudely. Horton swallowed his first impulse, which was to tell the man to mind his own business. However he had behaved these past weeks, Markland was still his superior.

'It is from Robert Brown, the librarian to Sir Joseph Banks,' Horton replied.

Markland raised his eyebrows.

'Indeed? You have an interesting correspondence, constable.'

He emphasised the word *constable*, as if reasserting a natural order. How on earth did one such as Horton come to be receiving letters from an esteemed man of learning like Robert Brown?

Horton opened the letter, desperately wishing he could be somewhere else, but he was trapped – Markland wanted to see what was in the letter, now, and he had no way of refusing him. As he read the note that feeling of loss of control deepened still further.

'And what does Mr Brown have to say to Constable Horton, hmm?'

'He requests that I attend Sir Joseph at his earliest convenience in Soho Square on an urgent matter relating to my wife.'

Markland's face showed shock, followed by a kind of scandalised amusement.

'Your *wife*, Horton? What on earth does Sir Joseph Banks have to do with your *wife*?'

'I confess I do not know. But it appears she is already there.'

MRS HORTON'S TRIP

Abigail had been trying not to think about that last encounter with the doctor at St Luke's, but every now and again the memory would intrude like a bad smell in a clean kitchen. She filled her days with Rat – reading with him, shopping with him, attending lectures with him. It was, in many ways, a very pleasurable time, and she almost imagined that she did have a son, that she and Charles were mother and father, but these happy thoughts only served to snag awful realisations: that her womb was barren, her life half-full, her mind preoccupied because it had nothing to love other than her strange, unfathomable partner.

Her visits to St Luke's had filled the spaces in which these thoughts tended to condense, but now that outlet was gone, leaving only that dirty sense of having been bitterly used by Drysdale.

She needed to be *of use*. So she decided on a trip. She walked down to the Wapping stairs with Rat in attendance, and took a wherry. It was a sunny day, and the river was as bustling as any London square or market. Voices called across the river from lighter to ship to barge, and their wherry made its way upstream following the same course her husband had taken to Putney. Abigail, though, went further. The trip would take time, but she was in no hurry, and besides, she enjoyed watching the riverbank change its character, from the crowded wharves of Wapping to the colourful splendour of the Tower and the City markets, and then the river widened out to the towers and roofs of Westminster and the fields of Chelsea. Then they were out in the country, on the same river but also on an utterly different one.

They went past Putney, under its wooden bridge, the palace at Fulham passing by on their right as they entered the great river-loop around Barnes. Curious trees leaned into the river to see their reflections as they passed, and as they approached their destination she saw a church tower and several roofs, one of them tall and steep and hard by the riverbank. The waterman tied up at some steps down to the shore, and Rat jumped out first and held out his hand for her, ceremoniously. She stepped up onto the bank.

'Will you wait?' she asked the waterman.

'It's you as is paying me, missus,' he said, and sat down in the boat. She turned, and faced John Dee's house.

It was both bigger and smaller than she'd expected. The house itself was large, but the ground on which it stood was cramped by surrounding houses, most of which looked more recent. The old house had a high roof, steeply pitched, like a country cottage though now tiled rather than thatched. On the other side of the path from the river stood a gate, and she remembered the story of Dee standing in his doorway, and speaking to Elizabeth while she sat in a boat on the river. Abigail went through the gate, as the Queen had refused to do, and here was the door, a black and ancient thing. Almost without thinking she knocked upon it, half expecting

Prospero to answer in his wizard's cloak, blinking with stars and planets.

The man who did answer was no wizard. He looked more like a surprised clerk.

'Can I help you?' he asked, suspiciously. *This place must get some strange visitors*, she thought to herself, and wondered as to its current owner.

'My apologies for disturbing you,' she said. 'I have come here from Wapping.'

'Indeed?'

'This is, I think – or rather, this *was* – the house of John Dee.'

'Yes. It was.'

His manner had not warmed. She thought carefully about what to say next. She decided on an excess of the truth.

'Sir, my husband is a constable in Wapping. He is investigating the deaths of a family there, and he discovered certain volumes pertaining to Dr Dee beside their bodies. He does not know I am here, but while he has been investigating these matters, I have been doing some investigating of my own. I have come here today as a result of my researches into Dr Dee. I know not quite why, but I have learned in my studies that it often serves the purpose to have visible display of what one is researching. Just seeing this house has given me some new understanding. To see inside it would, I think, help me even more so.'

He smiled, and she could see her decision to tell the truth had been the correct one.

'Madam, I see all sorts of individuals at this door. Most of them are mad or liars or both. You seem to be neither. Won't you come in?'

And he stepped back and away, and opened the door of Dr Dee's house. Taking hold of Rat's silent but warm hand, she stepped inside.

CONSTABLE HORTON RETURNS
TO THE ROYAL SOCIETY

It had been almost two years since his only visit to this place: 32 Soho Square. On that occasion, he had met with Robert Brown, Sir Joseph Banks's Scottish librarian. He had still never met Banks, though the man's name had been stamped on to a number of recent cases like the faded hallmark on an old gold ring. Or like the smell of bitter almonds, perhaps.

Sir Joseph's residence occupied one entire corner of Soho Square. It was a watchful place, its giant windows seeming like open eyes. A place to see and be seen in. A house for a well-connected man.

Horton was, frustratingly, not alone. Markland had insisted on accompanying him. They had gone into the River Police Office directly upon Horton's reading the letter. Given Wapping's dealings with Sir Joseph Banks in the past, Horton felt it essential that his magistrate be informed of the new development. His mind buzzed with possibilities. How could Abigail possibly be with Sir Joseph Banks, the President of the Royal Society, one of the most prestigious and powerful men in England? And, more to the current point, was Rat with her? A moment of comedy then, despite himself – the street urchin discussing taxonomy with the great natural philosopher in a Westminster library. Stranger things have happened, he thought – and, truly, stranger things had.

Harriott had of course demanded to come with him, but on suddenly standing from his chair the magistrate had experienced an alarming attack of breathlessness and dizziness, accompanied by what must have been terrible pain, for his aspect became pale and shocked and he collapsed back into his chair as if downed by a musket ball. Inevitably, Markland had offered to come instead, and Harriott had been forced to agree. Despite his attack and the deathly pallor which had descended on his face like fog, Harriott had still managed an apologetic glance towards Horton as he and Markland left the room.

In the carriage to Soho Square, Markland had been conciliatory towards Horton, overflowing with praise for the constable's previous work and mellifluously forgetful of his previous threats to both Horton and his magistrate. Horton decided to at least try and make some use of their unwelcome time together, even though his thoughts were so much on his wife.

'I wonder if you have ever heard of the position of assistant treasurer, sir?'

'At the Company?'

'Yes.'

'Oh, I don't involve myself in matters such as these, constable. I made my investment and, truth be told, all it's brought me is misery. The Company is not what it was.'

'Do the names Suttle or Jenkins or Fox mean anything to you?'

'In relation to the Company?'

'Yes.'

'No.'

'An officer has recently been despatched to St Helena as an assistant treasurer, sir. By the name of Burroughs. Would he be of the same family as Alderman Burroughs?'

Markland now looked worried.

'Now, constable, I have no conception of where this line of thinking ends up, but you should be careful with it.'

'Do you know Captain Burroughs?' Horton insisted.

Markland frowned.

'No. No, I do not. And Burroughs is hardly an uncommon name.'

'No, indeed. But the coincidence is striking. What can you tell me of the alderman?'

Markland, having been keen to talk at the start of the journey, was now as close-mouthed as a pickpocket being interrogated in a watch-house.

'He is a gold and silver broker.'

'And he lives in the City?'

'There, and at a place outside Sevenoaks in Kent.'

'A large house?'

'Very nearly a castle. Tremendously wealthy man, is Robert Burroughs.'

'You have visited this castle?'

'Aye, I have,' the magistrate said, and looked relieved as the carriage came to a halt. 'We're here.'

They stepped out and stood in front of number 32.

'Odd place,' Markland said. 'Like two or three houses conjoined.'

They were shown through the front door, and upstairs to the same room in which Horton had previously met Robert Brown. The librarian was not there, but Abigail was. So was Rat, who sat on a stool next to her like a protective dog, and glared at Markland lest he come too close.

'Husband,' Abigail said, rising and coming to him. She

noticed Markland, but initially ignored him – rather magnificently, Horton thought. 'You must have been concerned.' She held out two hands to him.

His relief made his hands shake as he took hers, and she looked at them with some concern and he wanted to kiss her, but Markland's presence was awkward.

'You are no prisoner, wife,' he said. 'But nonetheless – where in heaven's name did you go, to end up here?'

This to Rat as much as Abigail, and it was Rat who answered.

'Wasn't my idea, constable! Wasn't at all! Mrs Abigail said she wanted to take a trip to get some air, and I said we shouldn't, said you'd be angry, but ...'

'Silence, whelp,' said Markland. 'Who are you to address your betters so? What are you doing here?'

Rat looked like he had been slapped. Horton instinctively wished Markland ill. Abigail looked at the magistrate as if he had just let down his breeches.

'He works for me,' Horton told Markland, no longer able to keep the dislike out of his voice. 'He is charged with accompanying my wife to preserve her safety.'

'A misbegotten little runt like this? Really, Horton, all you had to do was ask for one of my constables.'

Horton, who would always choose a misbegotten little runt like Rat over any of Markland's constables, told Rat that he should head back to Wapping now, and wait for their return. Rat looked at Markland as if he might bite him, turned and made something of a bow towards Abigail (a gesture theatrically appropriate to his surroundings, as it must have seemed to Rat), and made his dignified way out.

'Now, Mrs Horton,' said Markland, bumptiously taking charge of the situation. 'Would you care to enlighten us as to your presence here?'

'She came here because I invited her,' said Sir Joseph Banks as he entered the room.

Sir Joseph arrived in the library on an extraordinary device, a wheeled chair which was all iron and leather, pushed by a servant who seemed unconscious of the bizarre picture he and Banks made. Horton had never seen such a thing as this chair, but he could see why it was needed. Banks was both enormous and decrepit, his bulging stomach bisected by a blue sash, one enormous golden star on his breast. His face was pale and puffy, but still possessed of the energy of an unquenchable will. Banks reminded Horton very strongly of John Harriott.

Markland wasted no time engaging with the politics of the situation.

'Sir Joseph, I am delighted to make your acquaintance.'

'And who are you, sir?'

'Edward Markland, Sir Joseph. Senior magistrate at the Shadwell Police Office.'

'So you are Horton,' said Banks, turning deliberately away from Markland. Horton suddenly felt like a moth must feel under the glass of a naturalist: examined, categorised, measured. 'I know a good deal about you, sir.' It was not a happy thought. It reminded him of Lamb's excitement at meeting him.

Banks turned his enormous head to Markland.

'Do you make a habit, sir, of accompanying men to appointments, when you have yourself not been invited?'

Markland blinked and blushed.

'Sir, I have been cooperating with Constable Horton here on our latest investigation. You may consider me his superior.'

'Harriott is still ill?' This to Horton.

'He had recovered, Sir Joseph,' said Horton. 'But he was taken ill again today. He wanted to come with me.'

'And I would have been delighted to see him. A fine man.'

He glared at Markland, pointedly. 'Sit, gentlemen, please. I, as you can see, am already doing so.'

Banks looked over at Abigail, and his face softened.

'I have been talking to your wife, Horton. She is a remarkable woman.'

Abigail blushed and looked down. Horton marvelled at her – she seemed positively enthralled, like a fishwife invited for tea with a duchess.

'She has caused something of a stir today, which is why you are here. My dear, perhaps you would explain to your husband.'

Horton noted that Banks had effectively assumed that Markland was no longer present. The magistrate sat on the edge of his chair, his hat on his knees, smiling fixedly. One might almost have felt sorry for him.

'Husband, I went to Mortlake today.'

It was a very good start to a story, Horton thought.

'You did?'

'Aye. I took Rat with me, in case of incident. We took a boat from the stairs. Upon reaching Mortlake, we made our way to Dr Dee's old house.'

'It still stands?' Horton said to Banks, who grunted an affirmative.

'It is an odd place, hard upon the river,' continued Abigail. 'I knocked upon the door, and a man answered. He was guarded in his welcome. The house receives a good many visitors. Dr Dee has quite a reputation among a certain type of person.'

'What type of person?'

Abigail looked at Sir Joseph, who nodded kindly, giving permission to continue. It was a silent exchange which perplexed Horton – as if his wife and Sir Joseph shared a new secret language. Which, he supposed, they did – a language of botany and astronomy and classification and theory. *Science*, Abigail called it.

'Credulous souls, the man said. Believers in spirits and spells and astrologers. I explained I was no such person. That I placed my faith in matters I could see with my own eyes.'

It was, Horton thought, a moderately dangerous thing to say in front of Edward Markland. It smacked of religious scepticism.

'The man said he was pleased to welcome one such as I, and he invited me in.'

'He invited you in?'

Abigail blushed. 'With Rat, yes, he did. I nearly refused, but the tale of Dr Dee has arrested my interest, and I wished to see inside. He showed me around the house, and he gave me tea. I told him who I was and who you were, and how we came across Dr Dee's story. At the end of my visit, and after we had spoken a little more of the discoveries you made at poor Johnson's house, he asked if I would come to tell Sir Joseph what I had told him. I agreed.'

'It seems an odd thing to agree to.'

This from Markland, whom Banks ignored magnificently, but Abigail could not.

'Well, sir, you know nothing of my personal interests. They tend towards the natural philosophical. To be given the chance to meet one such as Sir Joseph ... well, sir, I did not hesitate to say yes.'

Banks smiled at her, like he would smile at a particularly brilliant daughter.

'A remarkable wife, sir,' Banks said to Horton. 'I congratulate you. I will continue the story, if I may. Mrs Horton came here with the owner of Dee's house, a fellow by the name of Temple. He is an associate of mine. Not quite an employee or a colleague, and not a Fellow of the Society of which I am

President. But he keeps me informed as to the comings and goings at the residence of Dr Dee.'

'Why?'

Horton's single word was rudely expressed and took Banks aback momentarily. He was not used to being addressed in such a way.

'The Royal Society is at the service of the King, the Regent and the country, constable,' he said, as if Horton were a small lecture hall. 'We are the repository of all scientific knowledge collected in these islands. Dr Dee, who preceded our Society by almost a century, was one of the foremost scientific thinkers of his time. As such, he is of constant interest to us.'

'And for this reason, you called us here?'

'I wished to ascertain, constable, whether your investigations would feature anything regarding Dr Dee or his writings. I wished to offer my help.'

And, thought Horton, you wished to warn us. We are close to Royal Society ground, and that ground may be dangerous. There was something else here, something that had not yet been spoken of.

'Sir Joseph, can I say I do not believe the recent sad events on the Ratcliffe Highway have anything at all to do with this doctor you speak of,' said Markland, smoothly and happily, back in the conversation. 'I fear the constable's wife may have wasted your time.'

Abigail blushed, and for that alone Horton hated Markland. Banks continued to ignore him.

'Is that the case, constable?' he said.

'I do believe so,' said Horton, carefully.

'Well, then. I thank you all for coming here.'

He rang a bell and the servant who pushed him in entered.

'My dear, it was a pleasure to meet you. Please feel free to visit my library whenever you so choose.'

Abigail's delight at that filled the room, and Horton could see she had to prevent herself hugging the old bull in the wheeled chair. He rather thought the old bull would not have particularly minded.

'Constable, good day,' Banks said to Horton, and the servant wheeled him from the room. He said nothing to Markland.

As they left the house, a servant ran out into the street and handed Horton a note. He opened it and read.

'Tell Harriott I will attend him and thyself tonight in Wapping. Say nothing to that Shadwell idiot. Sir Jos—'

He folded the paper and handed it to Abigail.

'To reiterate his invitation to make use of his library,' he said to Markland, who grinned.

'I do believe the old goat has designs on your wife,' he said, oddly happy again after his difficult afternoon.

It had turned into a good night for secrets: the heavy warm air of the day was settling itself onto Wapping, the pressure almost palpable, squeezing in the shouts and laughter and shrieks of an ordinary East End twilight. Horton left Abigail and Rat in the apartment, checked the doors were locked, spoke to Cripps and another lad out in the street and warned them to be particularly watchful. He didn't know the source of this odd skittishness. The heavy air, perhaps, and the lingering ever-present danger to Abigail.

As he stepped out into Wapping Street, he looked to his right and to his left. Was that street woman watching him? Had that dock worker come out in suspiciously clean clothes? Was that shop clerk looking away somewhat too purposefully?

Yes. He decided that the man – he might have been a shop clerk or an office clerk – was doing just that. He caught a flash of face, that was all, and now the clerk was strolling away towards Wapping Pier Head and St Katharine's. Did he recognise him?

Was it perhaps the clerk who had been sitting at Johnson's desk when he'd visited East India House? Horton took a step or two to follow, and for a while his plans for the evening took him in the same direction as the clerk. The River Police Office was in the same direction as the man was heading. Outside the Office, Horton stopped and waited and watched.

The clerk continued to walk away from him, never looking back, if indeed he was ever in Wapping with malicious intent. He watched the man's back disappear into the crowds. The late spring sun sent shafts of light along the river and the brick walls of the Dock and its associated buildings, but they brought no illumination. Only confusion and that deep, enduring anxiety.

Three old men were waiting for him upstairs in the Office. Three ancient minds perusing imminent death, stocked with memories fraying at the edges. John Harriott, looking even older, was in his chair behind his desk, a slab of the river visible behind his head. Sir Joseph Banks was in his wheeled chair behind the fire, and Horton found himself wondering how Banks would have got up the stairs. Was he winched from outside?

And in the chair on the other side of the fire, an unexpected face, but one who had always been there whenever Horton's strange life intersected with the Royal Society: Aaron Graham, the senior magistrate from Bow Street, dressed as was his habit in some finery. It had been a year since Horton had last seen him, and though the clothes were just as expensive, the skin beneath them was terribly diminished.

Graham was the only one to stand when Horton stepped into the room, and tottered over to him like Beau Brummel's skeleton.

'Constable,' he said, and Horton was touched by the old man's unaffected pleasure. 'A delight to see you again.'

'Mr Graham. Mr Harriott. Sir Joseph.'

'Sit down, Horton,' said Banks, comfortable in charge even though they were in another man's office. Harriott said nothing.

A chair had been left for Horton. He sat in it, and looked at the three men: Graham and Sir Joseph lit by an oil lamp, Harriott by the dying light from the river.

'Horton, you are a man I can trust,' said Sir Joseph.

Was this a question? Or a statement? It was something of both. But was he indeed to be trusted, this Nore mutineer? Did Sir Joseph know of that part of his past? Horton looked at Graham, who smiled weakly but somehow reassuringly.

'I believe so, Sir Joseph.'

'Because what I am here to speak to you about is known by not half a dozen men in the world outside this room. You have perceived some of it, I think. Graham has told me of your involvement in recent matters. The Ratcliffe Highway murders. The *Solander* incident. Even, I am told, last year's affair with the woman from New South Wales, which I am to understand involved my librarian. All these incidents have involved the Royal Society in some way.'

'The Highway murders, sir? I was told that important men had an interest in them and in their conclusion. I was not informed that you were one of them.'

Sir Joseph looked at Graham and Harriott. Both men seemed suddenly uncomfortable, and Horton detected a strain of guilt in the room. He knew he had been used, of course. The extent to which those who had used him were aware of the reasons – that had remained obscure. He found himself staring at Harriott and for the first time in their association, the magistrate was unable to meet his eye.

Sir Joseph, having not apparently noticed the discomfiture of the magistrates, continued regardless.

'Horton, you are a constable. It is a lowly position; before this evening, I do believe I have never spoken to one such as you. You should not expect to always have been taken into confidences of greater men with wider horizons. That is the simple truth.'

Horton nodded to acknowledge this.

'And yet, here we are. Three men of some social standing narrating secrets to a mere waterman-constable. A man of little rank with a murky past.'

At least his question had been answered. Sir Joseph knew all about his personal history.

'This has come about because of your remarkable gifts, constable. I do believe that you might be able to solve a mystery which has occupied the finest minds this country has produced for over a century. I think the time is right to ask you to look at it. And I think it may have a great deal to do with the case you are currently investigating.'

Sir Joseph leaned his enormous body forward, and his mechanical chair creaked loudly.

'A fine word, *investigating*. We are similar, you and I. We pursue knowledge. We unpick secrets. We classify and we contain. The natural philosopher and the . . . the . . . *detective*. Yes. A fine coinage, I think. Detective Horton. It has a ring to it, does it not?'

Sir Joseph smiled, and though the smile was warm and in some ways delightful, it also contained teeth. The great man sat back in his chair.

'Know this, then, Detective Horton: the Royal Society has for one hundred and fifty years concerned itself with investigation and observation of the natural world. Our transactions have catalogued a world of wonders, from the nutrition of plants to the construction of palaces. Like my predecessors, I believe in evidence and I believe in proof. The proof of mine own eyes, and the proof of eyes other than mine which are to be trusted.'

The smile again.

'In this, we are the same, detective.'

Aaron Graham coughed, an ugly little rattle that sounded like death clearing its throat.

'When my Society began its work, the world contained much mystery,' continued Sir Joseph. 'When Robert Hooke produced his *Micrografia*, he drew things he saw through microscopes of his own design, and the world saw the monstrous and beautiful appearances of even the most ordinary flea through Hooke's perceptions. It was as if there were another world all around us, could we but see it. But there remain mysteries, Horton. Inexplicable matters, beyond understanding. Plants that grow at breakneck speeds, and seem to possess consciousness. Women who can bend other wills to their own. All of these things you have had some dealing with.'

Horton thought: *plants?*

'Some people call these things *magic*. I say any reality we do not yet understand will appear to be magical.'

Sir Joseph's enormous face flickered in the light from the oil lamp. He stared into the shadows at the corners of the room. As if he were confessing to a crowd that had hidden itself away. A man at the end of his road, making sense of things.

'Which brings me to St Helena.'

Harriott sighed, another rattling old sound of ominous import.

'St Helena is, as you know, a possession of the East India Company,' Sir Joseph continued. 'I have fought with all my might for years to extract the island from the Company's clutches, and yet the Company will not let it go. Many find this odd. St Helena does not pay its way. It is barely more than a staging post for ships returning from the East Indies and New South Wales. A rock holding a few planters, a good many slaves and whores, and no visible means of support. So why does the Company protect it so?'

Harriott, noticed Horton, had leaned forward in his chair. His face looked more animated than the constable had seen it in months. He was learning things, too.

'At the end of the seventeenth century, shortly after the foundation of our Society, we despatched a promising young man to St Helena to make improvements to our star charts, and to track a transit of Mercury across the sun. His name was Edmond Halley. His achievements were extraordinary, and my own life was linked to his, even though he died long before I was born. He predicted the transit of Venus in 1769, which was the cause of my own first voyage to observe it. To Otaheite.'

Harriott stared at Sir Joseph but Graham, Horton noted, was staring intently at *him*, as if to verify that he were following all this. If he were seeing how these events connected to each other; young Halley sailing south a century and a half ago, young Banks following him a century later, and now this room tonight, full of stories and secrets.

'Halley's trip was a success, but he came back with an odd story. He wrote a letter to a benefactor, in which he claimed there was something unique about St Helena. He had noticed – through *observation*, mind – that compass needles on the island deviated significantly from the North.'

'As they do in most places,' Horton said.

'Indeed they do. But Halley had started mapping magnetic variation, Horton. He had developed a theory that turned out to be entirely true – that one might draw lines between areas of similar magnetic variation, and that these lines would be constant. Some years after he travelled to St Helena, he produced a chart of these lines, which we now call *Halleian* lines.'

Horton knew the phrase, from his own knowledge of navigation. He had even seen Halley's map.

'I know of this chart, Sir Joseph.'

'Good. Then you know of the line of zero variation that passes, like a great curve, through the Atlantic.'

'Yes.'

'And you know that St Helena sits upon this line.'

'Yes. I understand your point now, Sir Joseph. Compass needles on St Helena should point directly at magnetic north, as there is no variation.'

'Indeed. And yet they do not. Sail a mile away from the island, and they do. But on the island itself, they vary by as much as ten degrees. Halley could find no reason for this. Nor, thus far, can we. But that is not the end of it, Horton. In the very same letter in which he first wrote these observations down, Halley also mentioned an encounter which is just as inexplicable.'

Sir Joseph looked back into the shadows, as if young Halley might be found there, scribbling his discovery.

'Halley met a man on St Helena; he described him as an ugly fellow, whom Halley took for a Portuguese. This man had neither nose nor ears, and one of his hands was entirely missing. He did not speak any English, but they managed to communicate in Dutch. The stranger claimed to have knowledge of the island before the arrival of the Dutch or the English, and when Halley asked when he had come to the island, the Portuguese said he had arrived there in 1516. A hundred and fifty years before Halley had met him.'

At this point, Horton expected Harriott, or at least Graham, to interject. A 150-year-old man on a distant island? Neither man said anything, and this disturbed Horton as much as the strange stories Sir Joseph was recounting.

'When Halley returned to England, he looked into the history of St Helena,' continued Sir Joseph. 'He discovered the tale of a Portuguese nobleman who had led a group of renegades during that country's wars in Goa. As punishment for his crimes, this man – his name was Fernando Lopez – had his right hand and the thumb of his left cut off, along with his nose and ears. Lopez later stowed away on a ship returning to Portugal, but asked to be let off at St Helena, which was then deserted. It was said he was left there with only a cockerel for company, and for years he was seen there by visiting Portuguese ships. How many years, we cannot say. This, Halley believed, was the creature he met on St Helena.'

Horton had no conception of what this could mean. Nothing Sir Joseph was saying made any sense to him at all. He looked at Harriott, but the old man was staring out of his riverside window. He tried Graham, who caught his eyes, and nodded. It was an awful thing, that nod. It seemed to say *I believe all this to be true*. And yet, how could it be?

A silence. A question was expected of him.

'And what does this . . . this *story* have to do with John Dee?'

'Ah. A good question, constable. One worthy of Detective Horton.'

Banks smiled. He seemed to be rather enjoying himself.

'What do you know of Dr John Dee, constable?'

The question did nothing to dilute Horton's confusion.

'Only what my wife told me from a guide book to Surrey.'

'Well, I will tell you this. He was a highly original thinker, a disciplined mathematician and geometer. He lectured on Euclid, and when he wrote about such matters he was as fine a mind as this country has produced. But then he began to be interested in other matters – matters of a more *celestial* kind, shall we say. He developed an extraordinarily detailed cosmological picture on the shaky edifice of Renaissance science – I cannot make head nor tail of it myself, it seems stuffed to the gunwales with arcane hogwash and esoterica. But there are some members of the Society who believed he was on to something; that he had stumbled across some great truth about the inner workings of our Reality. I do believe Dee made discoveries which remain hidden; discoveries which, if they came to light, might help to explain some of the strange things you and I have encountered together these past few years.'

Now, it was Graham's turn to sigh, gently and elegantly, but the sigh was cut off by yet another bitter little cough.

'Such has been Dee's reputation that the Royal Society has, since its formation, made itself the repository of his thought. The Society purchased Dee's house at Mortlake many, many years ago, and we have kept it on ever since. That is itself a great secret; if it were to become public, we would be a laughing stock. The world has moved on from John Dee. Or at least, it believes it has. Certain Fellows of the Society have worked to reassemble Dee's library. This library was the finest private collection of volumes in Elizabeth's England – perhaps the finest in Europe. But when he left the country under allegations of necromancy and witchcraft, the library was ransacked and destroyed. Dee eventually returned to England and made a claim to the Crown for compensation – he included a list of the volumes in his library. We have, essentially, recreated it.'

'Why?' said Harriott, suddenly. 'Surely much of the material in it is redundant?' He sounded angry to Horton's ears.

'Indeed, Harriott, much of it is. But it is a record of men's thought in the years immediately preceding the foundation of the Society. And as such it is of incalculable value. But that isn't the main reason. You see, many believe that certain *particular* volumes were stolen from Dee's library. Volumes containing great secrets. Dee was playing for high stakes, gentlemen. He believed that through a combination of what we now call science and what he called magic, man might ascend a kind of celestial stair. Might, in fact, move closer to God. This was the true work of the men we now call *alchemists* – to purify the spirit of man through the combination of elements, as one might make gold. To make man, essentially, immortal.'

The three old men were still in their room. Mortality stalked them all, and did not bother to hide itself.

This is madness, thought Charles Horton. It chilled him.

'Dee claimed he had visited St Helena, in one of his writings on navigation,' said Sir Joseph. 'There is no other evidence for him having gone there, but why even mention it? It was then an obscure staging post held by the Portuguese. Why would John Dee have an interest in it?'

The silence fell again. Horton did not know what to say.

'Do you believe this, Sir Joseph?' he asked, eventually. 'That Halley met a man who was centuries old?'

'I am not in the business of believing in anything,' said Sir Joseph, firmly. 'I am in the business of investigating and confirming, that is all. And I believe we are in the same business, are we not?'

Sir Joseph smiled that warm smile again, the smile which was practised and worn smooth with much use over the years.

'We can assume, can we not, that the Royal Society has itself investigated these matters?' asked Horton.

'Yes. We have sent dozens of men there over the years, both before and after Halley died. Halley left us with a simple instruction: *watch St Helena*. It is something we have tried to do over the decades, but God knows it is not straightforward. The East India Company guards its secrets carefully. I have tried to travel to St Helena myself on several occasions, but it has always been made clear to me that such a journey would not be countenanced.'

'Countenanced by whom?' said Horton.

'By the Crown.'

The three simple words spoke so much: of influence and power, of secrets and schemes. Yet Horton wondered if he quite believed Sir Joseph. Was the man not a friend of the now-mad King? Had he no influence in this matter? Horton looked at Harriott, and could see some of his own suspicions in the magistrate's face.

Sir Joseph shifted his enormous weight in his chair.

'Detective, here is the matter: the East India Company is, to all intents and purposes, the Crown on St Helena, as it is in India. And while we maintain cordial relations with the Company and its Directors, it is fair to say that in this, as in all things, we are in competition for funds, for attention from the Crown, for influence. The Company watches any undertakings by the Royal Society within its territories as if we were footpads creeping in to empty their pockets.'

This with a high degree of bitterness.

'And it may be that it will soon become impossible to ever find these secrets. I have heard of changes to how the island is to be governed. It appears that our interests have become conjoined, gentlemen. You are interested in St Helena. I am interested in St Helena. I propose, then, that I send you to St Helena.'

'But what does any of this have to do with the matter at hand?' Harriott asked.

'The matter at hand?' said Sir Joseph, and in his confusion was all the arrogance of the powerful, and their ignorance of the weak.

'The murder of Benjamin Johnson, his wife and his daughter. The murder of Amy Beavis and her father.'

Sir Joseph had no answer to that, and neither did Harriott or Graham. Charles Horton, though – he did have an answer. A symbol, a *Monad*, inked on the chests of the Johnsons. John Dee's symbol. He did not share this thought. It felt like a fragment of influence, a tiny portion of power which might, one day, serve a need.

Horton looked at the faces of the old men, one after another. In their exhausted eyes was the flickering excitement of one last game, a final mystery to be unlocked, perhaps the biggest of them all. And out there, perhaps, another Monster, stalking him, his wife, his home.

CONSTABLE HORTON IN KENT

It was a four-hour carriage ride from Wapping to the village of Seal, just outside Sevenoaks in Kent. This considerable ride was made worse by the persistent presence of Edward Markland, who spent his time saying very little but exuding a smug sense of superiority. It made for a tiresome journey, and Horton found himself staring at Markland on occasion and thinking to himself of what Sir Joseph had said to him last night.

Detective Horton. It has a ring to it, does it not?

Sir Joseph's stories of ancient seers and hidden texts had been suitably resonant with darkness descending on the river, but did they hold any root in the real world on this lovely spring morning? What did that phrase *the real world* possibly mean, when set against Sir Joseph's tales of mysteries and matters celestial? As he ignored Markland, he pondered Sir Joseph's proposal to send him to St Helena.

It was an extraordinary idea, and Harriott had said nothing of it as the strange little meeting broke up. It had been left to Graham to take Horton aside and talk to him of it, while the other two old men sat silently, not waiting for an answer. It had been more like they were waiting for death.

'Feel under no compulsion,' Graham had said, *sotto voce* and with a conspiratorial hand on Horton's arm. 'It is an astonishing thing to ask of you. But also, know this, Horton: your enemies are all around. And soon, all three of us will be gone. And what then?'

Horton pondered that question in the Kent-bound carriage. What had Graham meant, precisely? Who were his enemies? Was Markland one of them? And how did the ancient troika – Harriott, Graham and Sir Joseph – come to be his protectors?

He had not, he believed, deliberately enraged anyone in his years investigating matters for John Harriott. So it bemused him to think he may have made enemies. But then he considered Sir Joseph's strange tales, and wondered if it might be what he had *learned* that made him dangerous to certain powerful men. Not what he did or said, but what he had unearthed.

And then there were practical questions. If Harriott were to die soon, who would he work for? He saw no appetite for his unique skills among other magistrates – even Markland might baulk at making him an employee. He could be cast into penury at the quiver of a quill. And what then? A middle-aged mutineer with a single indescribable skill – that of a form of investigation that nobody seemed to know they needed. What possible future awaited him on the other side of Harriott's death? Did the world need *detectives*?

Perhaps that had been Graham's meaning. Perhaps he did not have enemies, quite – what he had was a scarcity of friends. Would there be opportunities in St Helena? Or even further afield? Might he find friends in further-flung corners?

He would have liked to discuss St Helena with Abigail today, during this long ride – but there had been no question of bringing her along on a journey such as this, however hesitant he might have been about leaving her in London. He had left early this morning and had gone to Harriott to propose this trip, and his magistrate had agreed, on one irritating condition: that he inform Edward Markland.

Markland had agreed, with resignation, to Horton's request. But he had insisted on accompanying him to the country residence of Alderman Robert Burroughs. 'A Wapping constable does not just show up on the doorstep of one such as Burroughs,' Markland had said. 'Is it really necessary to visit him unannounced?'

Horton, and Harriott, believed it was. Markland had been persuaded, and now here he was, glaring at Horton with his remorseless self-obsession, a baleful gadfly with sadly necessary powers.

Turning away from his own future, Horton tried to focus on the immediate questions relating to the immediate matter: why were the Johnsons killed? And, thus, who killed them? There was a form in the deaths, a pattern shared between those of the Johnsons and those of the former assistant treasurers of St Helena. Each death had told its own little drama; had contained its own staging. A family smashed to bits on the same street as the Marrs, four years before. A captain dead and naked on Boxhill. A captain dead and stabbed in a side alley in Kingston. A captain impaled on his own railings, a whore inside. A captain dead in the river, apparent suicide.

Salter's story, then, of this strange substance *Prussic acid* and its hugely poisonous qualities. Its stench hung over these murders, both literally and figuratively.

And then, that story of the strange marking, the one he had seen on the Johnsons, and the one found on the whore. John Dee's *Monad*. A direct link between all these deaths, and across the years – and another obscure association with St Helena, via that reference in the essay on John Dee.

Those two dull syllables: *John Dee. John Dee. John Dee.* Like a heartbeat that would not cease. And four others: *St Helena.* Again and again and again, that mysterious island rose up before him in this case. It reminded him of another four-syllable island – Otaheite – and the way that place had haunted the eyes of the sailors who had visited it. Paradise had imprinted itself upon their souls.

They pulled into the driveway of Seal Castle, the walls as high and as grand as any Horton had seen. The drive passed through a thick wood, and Horton watched closely for the shape he expected to see somewhere in the shadows. But he saw nothing. If the thing he suspected to be there was to be found, it must be behind the house, or further into the woods.

The house was as vast as Markland had said. Robert Burroughs had earned untold thousands from his gold and silver trading, and that gold and silver had been subject to a reverse alchemy, transmuting back into base elements: stone and brick and marble and glass. Seal Castle was gloriously appointed, supremely tasteful, hidden away behind its walls and within its woods. Horton thought of the unimpressive heron of a man who had appeared to them at East India House, and hoped fervently he was not at home.

Markland took a scroll from inside his coat.

'The warrant,' he proclaimed, grandly. 'It is incontestable, but it would be better were it to come from me. Particularly if Mr Burroughs is at home.' His face was grim and determined, and Horton found an unexpected shard of admiration for this conceited little fellow.

He watched Markland step down from the carriage, and walk up the enormous steps to Seal Castle's door. He knocked upon it, and a middle-aged fat man dressed in the garb of a butler opened it. Markland spoke to him, and was shown inside.

Such a house, Horton thought. One could fit the whole of Wapping inside its gardens, and Shadwell and Ratcliffe too. He found himself to be almost afraid of this building, or more precisely of what the house represented: money, power, privilege. It encapsulated all his concerns as to the future. He was afraid. He was afraid of how men who lived in such places might deal with a Nore mutineer and his wife should they lose the protection of an ill and impoverished magistrate.

The door to the house reopened, and Markland reappeared, accompanied by the fat butler. They made their way down the steps to the carriage, and Markland opened the door to speak to Horton.

'Mr Burroughs is not at home today. He travelled to London this morning.'

Perhaps they passed on the road, thought Horton.

'I have told this fellow,' continued Markland, 'that I am charged with asking him some questions, in the name of Justice. And that I have a warrant to enter this property, and to ask him and the other servants questions.'

The warrant had done its work, then – though Horton believed it would not have guaranteed entry if Robert Burroughs were here. Nonetheless, the butler was acquiescing. Markland's words must have had some effect.

'Now, Horton,' said Markland. 'Let us go inside, and get this over with.'

'That won't be necessary,' said Horton, and Markland glared at him. 'Tell me this: does Seal Castle have an ice house?' he said to the butler.

The butler frowned, and Markland took Horton's arm and whispered sharply in his ear.

'Constable, what on earth are you about?'

'Yes, sir,' said the butler. 'We have an icehouse. In the woods behind the house.'

'We need to see it. Immediately, if you please. And bring a key.'

Burroughs's icehouse was to the rear of the house. It was of recent construction, its bricks forming a near-perfect red half-sphere embedded deep into sandy soil, the pointing uniform and without cracks. A small door in the side of the sphere was secured by a heavy padlock. The icehouse was in deepest shade, on a north-facing dip beneath a thick canopy of trees, hidden from the sun like a sleeping dragon.

The fat manservant unlocked the padlock, and opened the door. He glanced at Horton, as he had done time and again, and Horton wondered if a note had already been sent into the City to inform Burroughs of the invasion of his property by unexplained investigators. What had Markland said to the servant behind that closed front door, while he waited in the carriage?

Horton was the only one to go inside, carrying an oil lamp supplied by the manservant. Inside the icehouse it was pitch dark, the only natural light coming from the little door, and he could see immediately that he was wrong. This was just an ordinary icehouse. Meat hung down from hooks on the walls, and on the floor of the icehouse were metal boxes containing bottles of liquid drifting in thick dark water. He put a finger into this liquid; it was ice-cold, and there were solid shapes within it where the water had made its mysterious transition into a solid.

A well-appointed, well-kept, well-designed icehouse.

A thought occurred to him, passing his lamp around the cramped interior. This was a rather *new* icehouse. He went back outside, blinking already, despite passing barely three minutes within.

'This icehouse was recently built?'

The butler nodded.

'Yes, sir.' He had called Horton 'sir' since their first arrival, apparently unable to place a London constable within his social taxonomy. 'At the beginning of the current century.'

'It replaced another icehouse?'

'Yes, sir.'

'Does that icehouse still exist?'

The butler frowned.

'Well, yes, sir. These things are impossible to demolish adequately, and ...'

'Where is the old icehouse?'

The man pointed through the trees.

'Just up there.'

'Take us there, if you please.'

The three of them walked down a small defile and further into the woods. It was darker, colder, altogether more forbidding within these trees, and Horton wondered why the new icehouse was not built in here – the conditions were so much more amenable to the creation of frozen water. Perhaps it was as the butler had said: these things were impossible to demolish.

And there it was: squat, black, ugly, old, an excretion from the gloomy hillside, a barren piece of snot on the face of the wood. Bigger than the new icehouse, its door an ancient piece of oak secured with another padlock, this one looking as if it had been placed there by Cromwell himself. But no – on Horton's inspection, the lock revealed fresh scratches at the point where the key had been inserted, presumably recently, and presumably in fumbling darkness lit only by a torch or a lamp. Horton could see the scene vividly – a carriage waiting on the driveway, men huddled round the door, men going inside to remove the cargo within.

But more than that, the door held a clearer message. Painted on its surface in lime was the image of Dee's Monad, untidily rendered but entirely deliberate. Beneath the Monad, a single word: *Beware*.

And hanging in the air, the bitter stench of almonds.

'The key?' he said to the butler, knowing the likely answer. The man had no key. He stared at the door in wonder. Horton looked around on the ground, and picked up two heavy rocks.

'No, sir, you may not ...' said the butler, but fell silent when Horton turned to him, a dedicated man armed with heavy stones. Horton looked at Markland, who said nothing but nodded slightly, in a way that might be denied later if it came to it.

'I would step away, sir,' Horton told Markland, and the magistrate did as he was told. The butler went with him. They stood some ten feet away.

Horton turned to the lock, and began to smash it between the two stones in his fist. It took a while. Flakes of the rock were sheared away by the impact, and the sound of metal on stone clattered through the trees, but eventually the old lock surrendered its ancient grip, and the door opened.

Immediately, the stench in the air deepened, and it was as if almond-gas filled his nostrils and his mouth. His head was suddenly in sharp pain and then, just as suddenly, his mind deadened and began to switch off, and the observing part of Horton – the part that was always active, always cataloguing and classifying – watched his body shut down, like a ship lowering its sails as the wind drops, and darkness rushed up from his feet, and he fell.

He awoke to light dappling through the carriage window, and the regular rocking of its movement. His head groaned in pain, and his skin felt numb and oddly unnatural, as if another man's flesh had replaced his own.

He leaned out of the window, and yelled up to the driver to stop. Then he climbed out, slowly, every move slashing pain between his temples.

'Where are we?' he asked the driver.

'Just coming up to Bexley.'

'How long was I unconscious?'

'Two hours or more. The magistrate ordered me to get you home and seek out a doctor.'

Two hours! He thought about heading back to that ice-house – but would the driver even take him? He had his orders from a superior.

It is gaseous at 20 degrees Celsius, Salter had said. Which meant the temperature in the icehouse must have climbed suf-ficiently to turn some of the acid into gas, and for that gas to escape when he'd opened the door. Was that right? Was that how this worked?

Standing outside the Shadwell carriage, there was a quiet moment. He imagined madness was about to descend. It would spread out from Seal Castle, the residence of Mr Robert Burroughs, alderman of the City, gold and silver broker and Proprietor of the East India Company. Less than thirty miles from where he was now standing, the London establishment was carrying on its normal day, unaware of the fuse which had been lit in a Kentish wood.

But what should he do next? He was in Kent, with a car-riage driver over whom he had no authority. Behind him, a magistrate he did not trust was responsible for the thing he had uncovered: a secret icehouse, with a now-familiar symbol on its door. He found himself asking an obvious question: why, actually, had Markland come with him at all? And what had Markland been doing in those two hours he had been uncon-scious?

He did not, he decided, need to travel back to Seal. The

presence of the icehouse was enough. It connected Robert Burroughs with the murder of the Johnsons, if what he suspected of the sequence of events turned out to be true. A great anxiety was coming down on him, just as that awful gas had enveloped him, but what was he to do? He needed to get back to Abigail. If he was right, the Company was elbow-deep in all this, and it would stop at nothing to hide its guilt.

He climbed back into the carriage, and they rode back to London. He asked the carriage driver to take him directly to Lower Gun Alley, and the driver agreed. He would check on Abigail and Rat and talk to the other boys, and then walk back to the River Police Office to share his information and his concerns with his own magistrate.

As the carriage turned into Lower Gun Alley, Horton saw a dark shape on the ground, and instantly his acid-dulled senses raced. He yelled at the driver to stop the carriage, and jumped out.

It was Cripps lying there, and he had been knocked senseless. The boy groaned. The instrument of his injury seemed to be a brick lying nearby. Horton looked at it, and then rushed into the building through the ominously open door.

Up the stairs to the first floor, and already he could hear the sound of a woman sobbing, and the flow of air was different through the landing and staircase, suggesting an open door or window. Running inside his front door, he found them in front of the fire.

Abigail was kneeling on the floor, and Rat was lying across her, his head in her lap. They were framed by the fireplace, though no flame crackled behind them. The night was too hot for that. A long dark line lay on the floor. The poker from the fire. Horton went to them, but Abigail looked up at him then.

'Give him room, husband,' she said, her sobs stopping while she spoke, her hand still repeatedly stroking the boy's forehead, which was covered in his dark blood. Abigail's fingertips were covered in it. 'For God's sake, give him room.'

He had never seen her so unhappy, so distraught, so miserable. His heart broke.

'Bloody ... 'ell,' said Rat, his voice barely audible. 'Bloody ... 'urts, that does.' He never looked at Horton. His eyes were fixed on Abigail. 'Has 'e gone, missus?'

Abigail, unable to speak, nodded.

'Did 'e 'urt you?'

Rat's aitches were draining away. Abigail shook her head.

'Well, then. That's all right, ain't it?'

Rat smiled then, and turned his head slightly to where Abigail's hand cradled his cheek. His dimming eyes looked at Horton.

'I cut 'im, sir,' he said, his voice fading like a passing rainstorm. ''E didn't get away un'armed. The skinny ape'll be walkin' with a limp for some days yet.'

How long had Rat been lying here, fighting death, waiting for Horton to return so he could pass on this message?

The boy looked at Abigail again, then closed his eyes, and smiled.

'You smell like flowers,' he said, and died.

CONSTABLE HORTON'S
LAST DAYS IN LONDON

It was almost impossible to get Abigail to leave Rat, but in the end he persuaded her that the boy's body would need to be investigated by the coroner, and that she should try and leave it just as they had found it. When he said this she looked at him like he was a stranger. Her face was full of a pale horror as she said: 'I won't come back here, husband. Ever again.' He placed a cloak over her shoulders, and they left the apartment together for the last time.

Harriott was at his desk at the River Police Office when Horton and Abigail appeared, and took action immediately, despatching a servant to warn his wife that they would have guests for a few days. Harriott had moved from a rather grand apartment in the Pier Head building to a small house on Burr Street, just upstream between the brewery and the Dock. Horton took Abigail there directly, feeling the awful slump in her shoulders and listening to her traumatised breath.

He had never known such anger.

Mrs Harriott greeted them with copious affection, swallowing Abigail up into her womanly regard and telling Horton his wife would be safe with her, she would be fed and bathed and could sleep. The house was cramped and meagre, and Horton remembered what Markland had told him about Harriott's financial situation. A maid was running a bath.

'Fetch her some clothes, constable,' said Mrs Harriott. What she meant was, *leave her to me, man, your rage is pouring off you like the smell of smoke.* So he went back to the apartment, where two fellow constables were already standing watch outside.

With Abigail gone, something had left the rooms he had once called home. He wondered if she had meant what she said: that she would not return here. Rat's poor ruined body would remain on the floor, waiting for the coroner, and Horton thought he could learn nothing from it. He did not want to look at it, in any case. He went into the kitchen.

'We came home and disturbed him,' Abigail had said, in an odd monotone as they walked down to Burr Street. 'He was in the kitchen. He was pouring something from a metal flask.'

'Did you recognise him?' he had whispered.

'No. He was tall and thin. Rat threw himself at him, they struggled and then ... Oh, God. Oh, Rat.'

The skinny ape will be walking with a limp. He remembered Putnam folding himself into his chair at the private trade office.

There was a jug of water on the counter in the kitchen, which Abigail always kept filled from the standpipe in the street outside. A smell came from this jug, and it was a smell he could identify immediately. It smelt both sweet and wooden. Something had been added to the water. He sniffed the large bucket under the kitchen counter – also filled from the standpipe. It gave off the same smell.

So, here it was. The poison that, he suspected, killed the Johnsons in that Kent icehouse, and perhaps some of those dead Company captains as well. The slinking, underhand, covert material that was the true cause of their deaths. He poured the water from the jug into the bucket. He picked Abigail's kitchen knife up out of the sink, and shoved it into his old leather belt. He picked up the bucket, carried it downstairs and into the street.

'Tell the coroner not to drink any water,' he told the constables outside. 'And let me know when he arrives.'

He walked to the River Police Office, the poisoned water swilling in the bucket, some of it falling on the ground to merge with the shit and sewage and mud down there.

He poisoned Wapping as he went, and thought how poisoned Wapping had already become, to him.

By him.

He went up to Harriott, his clothes sticking to his skin. He had been in a frenzy of movement since sitting so still and so anxious in that long carriage ride from Kent. His head still endured agonies. Harriott and his office were quiet. The knife in his belt felt like a bar of cool ice.

The magistrate looked up at Horton from a letter he was reading, and indicated the chair on the other side of his desk.

'Sit down, Charles.'

The mast of a ship moved past in the river outside, being towed by some small unseen pilot boat. Harriott never asked him to sit down. And he never called him *Charles*.

Horton carried the bucket of poison over to the chair: an appropriate cargo for one such as he, a husband whose wife was shivering in fear and dismay in a stranger's bath, her life infected by the venomous stench of her husband's work.

He could not sit down. The knife in his belt prevented it. Harriott saw him hesitate, saw his hand move to his side, made his assumptions.

'Leave the knife here, Charles.'

Horton did not immediately move.

'That is an order. Put the knife on my desk, and sit down.'

An old Naval strain in the old man's voice. Horton obeyed. He had been a lieutenant before he was a mutineer. The knife clattered onto Harriott's desk.

'The investigation is over, Charles.'

Horton heard the words, but did not understand them.

'Sir?'

'This letter is from Sidmouth. The Home Secretary. He is demanding an immediate cessation into all investigations relating to the murders of the Johnsons.'

'I do not understand.'

'If he can be found, Elijah Putnam is to be arrested forthwith and to be charged with the deaths of the Johnsons and the murder of the servant girl, and you are to present whatever evidence you may have collected.'

'What evidence is there against Putnam?' *The skinny ape*, he thought, again.

'The letter does not say.'

'The man is to be made a scapegoat?'

'It is no longer our concern. If I continue the investigation, I will be removed from office forthwith, and in any case I have been told my days here are numbered in months, not years.'

'He must have moved quickly to send a message to Westminster from Kent.'

He, meaning Markland.

'I have only just received this particular letter. Markland has turned out to be not quite the dandy we had previously taken him for. He has called for the investigation to be halted, and his call has been heeded.'

Horton's rage pulsed in the veins in his skull, while his body sought only rest. He looked at the knife, and imagined Putnam or any of his anonymous, birdlike clerks in front of him, tied and bound and defenceless.

'What did you discover in Seal?' Harriott asked.

'The Johnsons were not killed in their house. I do not believe they were even killed on the night before their discovery. I believe an icehouse was used to preserve their bodies for a period of time before they were returned to the Ratcliffe Highway. An icehouse in the grounds of Robert Burroughs's country residence.'

'Why?'

Why, why, why? Harriott's old and ill mouth sounded the syllable, and it made Horton want to scream.

'Benjamin Johnson discovered the existence of the assistant treasurers of St Helena,' he said. 'It may be that he discovered little else other than their inexplicable wealth. He must have told his wife, and she, as she had before, used the information to extract money from Sutton. This must have gone on for some time, and during that time Johnson was still digging away in the Archives. At some point, the Company became aware of his activities. Perhaps Sutton told them, or perhaps Johnson left himself exposed. Whatever the truth of it, the family was killed. They were taken to Seal, and they were poisoned by whatever substance is in that old icehouse. Then, they were returned to their home, to be found by Amy Beavis, who had been instructed to return at regular intervals. But she then endangered herself by removing letters from Mrs Johnson's drawer, letters which must have been from Sutton. Whoever killed these people must have realised what had happened, and went to see Amy, and killed her.'

'But why this elaboration? Why not simply kill the Johnsons in their own home? This trip to Seal and back – it seems preposterous.'

'To cause confusion. To mask the real killer. To make any accounts of movements impossible. To enable the real killer to be out of the country – even at sea – when the bodies were discovered.'

'At sea?'

'There is one man unaccounted for. Captain Edgar Burroughs. He is Alderman Robert Burroughs's nephew. He left for St Helena a few days before the Johnsons were found dead.'

Which means he did not kill Amy Beavis, thought Horton. *The skinny ape, again?*

'St Helena. That blasted place, again.'

'Yes, sir. Edgar Burroughs is the new assistant treasurer. Every other assistant treasurer for the past thirty-five years has died, seemingly violently. All of them lived well – too well, one might say. Their residences seemed beyond the means of men of their station. And Alderman Burroughs's house is stupendous, sir. I have not seen a house like it.'

'A financial conspiracy?'

'Embezzlement of the Company, perhaps. On a huge scale. Covered up by the office in which Putnam and Johnson worked. I do not know.'

'And then – Sir Joseph.'

'Yes. Sir Joseph.'

'It would explain this conspiracy.'

'That the Company has found the secret to immortal life on St Helena and is protecting it? Yes. That *would* explain the conspiracy. I have never heard such idiocy.'

'Remember your place, Horton.'

'My place is nowhere, sir. My place is beside my wife.'

Harriott sighed – a massive, frustrated noise – and picked up the letter.

'The Home Secretary is ceasing our work, Horton. We cannot pursue this.'

Horton said nothing. The knife still sat on Harriott's desk, full of possibility. Harriott turned his chair to face the bay window which looked out over the river.

'This has been tried before, Charles,' he said, and the recurrence of his first name brought Horton no comfort. 'Five years ago, they tried to have me dismissed for financial malfeasance. A bunch of charges were brought against me, claiming that I had skimmed money from the Police Office accounts. None of it came to anything. But they tried. Oh my, they tried.'

Horton had not known of this. It surprised him, that such activities could remain hidden.

'They gather, the rich men, Charles. They meet in corridors and whisper in their dining rooms, and they make their schemes, and with every snap of their fingers Justice is injured. They sicken me. This letter sickens me.'

It was awful, the change in Harriott. The transition from power to powerlessness. An old man receding into history before his constable's eyes.

'Markland is their man. I do not say he is corrupt. But he is a Proprietor of the Company, just like Burroughs. No doubt Sidmouth himself has a vote or two. The Company is enmeshed in the political and economic life of this country like some essential infection. It was such a glorious enterprise once, Horton. We subjugated a great continent. But we were not fighting for England. We were fighting for profit. Men died. My own leg, destroyed. In the pursuit of financial gain. And now, again, this.'

The letter twitched in his hand.

'This is how it will go now. Putnam will be arrested. He will be charged with every one of these murders. A willing judge – perhaps another Company Proprietor – will be found to lead a compliant jury, and the man who knows what really happened will hang. Or, possibly, that will be too big a risk. Putnam may say things they do not want heard. So perhaps another Putnam will be found, to sneak into his prison cell – they will put him in Coldbath Fields, the warders there are more than willing to turn a blind eye in return for a shilling or two – and this other Putnam will kill Putnam, and on and on it will go.'

Horton could feel it – the suffocating stench of influence. The unseen hand of secret conversations. Like poisoned air, invisible but filled with wicked power.

Money was power. That had been the essence of Harriott's elegy, and over the coming days Horton saw the truth of it. Money was the power to get the impossible done, and to cover its tracks.

The urgency to leave was growing. Not just to seek the truth – though his mind buzzed with it, curiosity was not sufficient cause to expose his wife to the dangers of such a voyage. No. He needed to get them out of London. His only friends with any influence were now Sir Joseph Banks and Aaron Graham, and these two old men wanted him for only one thing: to discover St Helena's secret. His old refuge, the rooms on Lower Gun Alley, was poisoned. Not with infected water, but with the spilled blood of a street boy.

Abigail listened as he described the situation, just as Harriott had outlined it the previous evening. How the schemes of the powerful were closing in around them. How the East India Company itself was embroiled in these murders, and how it seemed to him unlikely that Sidmouth, or anyone in power, would countenance damage to such a mighty arm of the State in the name of something as slippery as Justice.

He left out other, more prosaic matters and anxieties – Harriott's age, illness and growing infirmity being the chief of these. But they had spoken of such matters before. The murky future was now the terrifying present. Wapping had been a refuge for both of them for so many years, but now the squeals of masts in the winds sounded like the ungreased hinges of prison doors.

Harriott's prediction came to pass. Putnam was arrested, and interrogated first by the Shadwell magistrates, led by Edward Markland. Horton stopped visiting the Police Office, and followed the progress in the newspapers from a table at the Prospect of Whitby. He did not trust himself to be in the same room as Elijah Putnam.

After his initial interrogation at Shadwell, Putnam was taken to Coldbath Fields to await his full criminal trial at the Old Bailey. He should have been sent to Newgate, not Coldbath Fields. But it was just as Harriott had predicted. The warders at Coldbath Fields were notoriously open to bribes.

'It is time to leave, I think,' was all Abigail said when he suggested sailing to St Helena, and with that the decision was made.

There was no such thing as an immediate departure from London's docks and wharves. A ship had to be found. A captain had to be willing. A berth had to be made available – doubly difficult, when one of the passengers was a woman.

But money was a great solvent for problems, and a ready source of money had presented itself. Harriott spoke with Sir Joseph Banks, and the Royal Society made the funds available – or were they perhaps Sir Joseph's personal funds? Was this a private expedition, or an official one? Horton was considerably past caring about such matters.

Within a week a ship was found – a whaler, of all things, called the *Martha*. The coincidence of the name – shared with Emma Johnson's bitter and ugly sister – was striking. Her captain was called Wallace, a small but wide American with a face like the barnacled hull of his ship. He told Horton that Sir Joseph Banks had himself negotiated the arrangement in his rooms in Soho Square.

'He drove a bargain,' Wallace told Horton. 'No fool, that old man. But stopping at St Helena's on the southward track is an expensive and irritating business, Horton. It's costing Sir Joe a shilling or two.'

The *Martha* was at anchor in the Commercial Dock on the Surrey bank of the river. She was a Nantucket-built whaler seized by His Majesty's Navy during the 1812 War, and acquired

by a consortium of Liverpool merchants as a somewhat speculative investment – when she had been seized the barrels in her
hold were full of whale oil, and this single cargo alone had made
the investment worthwhile. Wallace had been her first mate when
she was captured; her captain had refused to stay with the ship
once she was seized, and was now back in Nantucket.

'You are not any kind of a Patriot, then?' asked Horton, and
Wallace's sea-swept face scowled at him.

'There's only one truth in this world, constable, and that's
money,' he said. 'The rest is just men seeking power over each
other.'

The *Martha* looked to Horton like a typical Cowes-built
whaler – barque-rigged, square-sterned – but he was no expert
in such vessels. Four of her whaleboats hung from davits: two
on the larboard side, one on the starboard, one at the stern.
Two more whaleboats were suspended on either side of the
cookhouse. The whaleboats – indeed, the entire ship – suggested a readiness to leave.

The captain showed her off in a workmanlike way – he was
proud of his vessel, but showed none of the sentimental affection of a Naval commander.

'A sailor, then, constable?' asked Wallace as they inspected
the ship.

'Not for many a year, captain,' Horton replied.

'Royal Navy man? Perhaps like the bastards who stole my
ship, eh?'

'What tonnage of oil will you bring back in her, captain?'

Wallace smiled a tight little smile.

'Perhaps 170 tons, constable. Around seventy whales.'

'It sounds an extraordinary amount.'

''Tis average, constable. Unlike you.'

Wallace never mentioned Horton's past again. He was being
paid enough not to, Horton imagined.

A small cabin had been set aside for Horton and Abigail in the officers' quarters at the stern of the ship, behind the mizzenmast. Between the mizzen and the main was steerage, where the ship boys and boat steerers were berthed. Then came the blubber room, as Wallace described it, the use of which Horton could only imagine. Then, before the foremast, was the forecastle, where the remainder of the crew would sleep. Beneath these areas was the hold which, for now, was filled with empty barrels.

'You are not concerned at having a woman on board?' Horton asked.

'Is she a great beauty, constable?' enquired Wallace, innocently. He showed Horton the lock he had had put on their cabin door. 'Keep her inside as much as you can,' he said. 'The men will behave.'

Every day Horton expected to read of Putnam's reaching an end of some kind inside Coldbath Fields, but then as the second week in June came around the *Times* ran a story.

NEW LONDON MONSTER ABSCONDS

COLDBATH FIELDS PRISON, CLERKENWELL: During the previous night, the clerk and suspected murderer ELIJAH PUTNAM made his escape from prison, only two days before his expected trial at the Old Bailey in the matter of the recent deaths on the RATCLIFFE HIGHWAY and in WHITECHAPEL. The means of Putnam's escape are not known, but it is suspected that one of his warders was attacked in the night by an accomplice and while he lay senseless Putnam and his unknown helpmate made their way into the night. E. Markland, magistrate at the SHADWELL Public Office, vowed that Putnam would be pursued and recaptured.

Abigail also read the story – Horton was powerless to prevent her. She slept little the following nights, such that it was a blessed relief to both of them when the message came that they were to make their way to the Surrey docks for immediate departure on the *Martha*.

So it was that three weeks after the terrible night in Lower Gun Alley, Horton and Abigail made their way over to the Commercial Dock. Horton's old friend Peach rowed them across, his face as warm as the inside of Mr Burroughs's icehouse. As they left the stairs by the Police Office, Horton looked up, and there, standing at his window looking over the river, he could spy the figure of John Harriott. He raised a hand, and the old figure in the window raised one in return. As they rowed across the river, the sun caught the glass of Harriott's window in a blaze of fire, and the old man disappeared.

On the Surrey shore, they left Peach in his wherry, and turned to watch him make his way back over the river.

'Farewell, Charon,' said Abigail, and Horton did not ask her to explain the reference.

They made their way round the riverbank to the Commercial Dock, and from there onto the *Martha*. Horton avoided the eyes of the crewmen preparing the ship as he walked his wife on board, and then into the cabin. 'So small, husband, so small!' exclaimed Abigail, and despite his urgings she refused to remain inside, whatever the captain might have said.

'This is my first voyage, husband. I will not spend it in a box.'

The *Martha* was ready for an immediate departure. Within two hours, they were being towed out of the Dock by a pilot. A pile of letters and newspapers was left by a bumboat, and Horton picked up a copy of the *Times* as Abigail stared out to the river as it glided past.

Putnam had still not been found. And Napoleon had just entered the United Netherlands.

INTERVAL: ABIGAIL AND THE WHALE

The dead whale's empty eyes reflected the clambering limbs of the cabin boy who was being lifted up to the hole that had been cut in its head.

'My God, no. It cannot be,' said Abigail.

The hairy steward laughed.

'Aye, it be true enough,' he said. 'Precious stuff left in there.'

The cabin boy was crying in terror, and some of the sailors shouted at him, shoving various blood-stained implements at his arse to force him upwards. There was blood and gore everywhere. The air stank of viscera.

The boy found himself standing on top of the decapitated whale's head, his feet slipping on the slick wet surface, and a bucket was passed up to him.

'In you go,' shouted the captain.

The boy was sobbing, but he nodded and looked once at the heavens as if seeking divine protection. And then he climbed into the whale's head.

Around the head were buckets and barrels containing the special oil – *spermaceti*, they called it – which had already been removed. Some of it was beginning to solidify in the outside air. Hanging off the larboard side of the *Martha* was the eviscerated carcass of the whale, now missing its head and most of its blubber.

Abigail had watched, awe-struck, as they stripped the blubber away. Two mates had cut a hole in the whale's side, into which they had placed a huge, ugly metal hook. Half a dozen seamen had begun turning the windlass, pulling the ropes through winches and the hook up and away from the whale. A strip of blubber was ripped from the side of the animal. Round and round the windlass went the sailors, and the strip became longer and longer, until twenty feet of thick blubber dripping with blood was hanging over the side of the ship.

The flesh was lowered into the blubber room below deck – spraying blood onto the deck as it went – and another hole was torn in the whale's skin. The same hook went in. The ugly process began again.

Finally, men had climbed onto the awful eviscerated thing carrying saws and knives, and severed the head.

Now the cabin boy was inside the head, while two seamen were poking a lance around inside the intestines of the skinned whale that still hung from the ship's side.

'Looking for ambergris,' said the steward.

Abigail had known where ambergris came from, but now, watching two ignorant men manipulating an iron lance inside the guts of a dead giant, she wondered at the women of London spraying scent onto their smooth, pampered skins, the noses of gentlemen twitching with delight at the smell which came from this obscenity.

The cabin boy's head reappeared, to her relief. The seamen barely noticed him as he clambered down with his bucket full of oil. Her heart went to him, as it did every time she saw him. He was only a little older than Rat had been.

Every day, when they woke into this lurching terror of water and whales, and Charles left the tiny cabin to fetch food to break their fast, she punched herself hard in the upper arm. There was a bruise there, a blue-black thing about the size of an oyster. Rat had put it there. She'd called out to him from the bedroom of the Lower Gun Alley apartment, and he'd come running in around the doorframe just as she'd been walking out, and his forehead had hit her square in the arm with the force of a swung cricket bat. The bruise had appeared the next day. Every day she punched it to make sure it did not go away. What would Dr Drysdale have made of that, she wondered?

This ship, the *Martha*, was profoundly ugly. It was festooned with elements which had no place on a ship. The steward's cookhouse, for one, and the large iron pots held in brickwork for another – the things looked impossibly heavy and bizarre against the wooden-and-cloth world of the ship.

The resentment towards her was oppressive. Superstitions about women bringing bad luck were as old as navigation, but she saw their wellspring in the hours after they had left Gravesend behind. A different peace had descended, a male comfort which was interrupted by only one thing: herself. She had found this both fascinating and pathetic.

From Gravesend they sailed to Plymouth, then south-west into a veil of fog and rain which belied the growing summer. Two weeks of fresh winds and occasionally astonishing squalls filled with such danger that she had thought she would run mad with the horror of it, and they were passing Portugal on the lee bow, another week and they were sailing between the island of Madeira on their starboard and the islands of Porto Santo and Desertos on their larboard, then Palma (one of the Canaries) appeared off in the distant south-west. Yet another week, and there were the islands of Bravo and Fogo, where slavers lay at anchor.

She had felt the fresh salt air, and despite the fear and the nausea she had imagined her spirits lifting as the fog and rain lifted and the sun beat down upon them and in the water around them the impossible sight of flying fish accompanied their progress. Yet every morning she punched her arm, remembered Rat, and thought of her sessions with Dr Drysdale, as if the bruise on her arm and the bruise in her head were joined.

The female mind is a delicate instrument, yet one of remarkable power, he had once said in his attractive Yorkshire accent. At the time, she had wondered what he had meant by that, but then that awful final revelation: that he thought *she* had this power of *moral projection*, as he had termed it, that *she* had therefore been the wellspring of the events inside Brooke House the previous year, events of which she had only a blurred recollection. She watched the poor cabin boy climbing out of the whale's head, and the comparison was obvious and disgusting, her head becoming the whale's, the cabin boy the doctor poking around within.

She remembered the feeling of a lamp in her hand, a lamp she had used with which to read, a lamp she had placed on the little table by the window in Lower Gun Alley. She had read countless books at that table, with that lamp: books on natural philosophy, on history, novels and poetry, geography and astronomy, her learning growing under the light of the lamp, her understanding illuminated by print and the lamp. Illuminated by whale oil.

Men were lighting fires beneath the big iron pots on the deck. Blubber was brought up from below and put into the pots. Oil began to run out of the pots into copper coolers which stood at their side. As night fell, the lights of the fires beneath the tryworks grew bright and fierce, and Abigail imagined them a devil-boat, a destroyer of lives, crewed by demons with knives and saws, glowing with hell-fire as they pulled south.

She wondered how many other whalers were currently slipping through the waves, how many other whaleboats were chasing how many other schools, and she thought of that lamp and that light and those books, and finally she went back to her little cabin and failed to sleep at all, the bruise on her arm pumping with her own blood in the oil-stenched dark.

ACT 2

ST HELENA

When any two of these three have been noted, what kind of third is to be sought can, accordingly, be known. The anatomies of these three – peculiar to them separately – are in the other two, but in a different way, celestial, terrestrial, or microcosmic. For example, I suggest to you the sun, gold, and man's hearts as objects to be considered by means of the laws of Anatomical Magic.

John Dee, *Propaedeumata Aphoristica*

1765: THE YEAR MINA BAXTER'S
MOTHER DIED

Mina didn't like the man from the Company. Taylor, her father called him, always with a splash of venom in his voice. She thought her father didn't like Taylor either. She wondered if he'd seen the way Taylor's greedy face darkened whenever he saw her, like he wished to do her damage of some kind.

When Taylor was in the house, she usually made herself scarce; she'd plead with Fernando to take her down to the bay, or to accompany her down to James Town, where she'd sit in the square and watch the people go by while Fernando hid in the hills, as was his way. She enjoyed it when the children of James Town approached her with their insidious intent, and she told them she knew the Cannibal of whom they often spoke, and they ran away shouting.

Sometimes a boy (never a girl) would stay behind, fearlessly saying he didn't believe her, and then she'd take the boy up into the hills above James Town, and Fernando would rise from the rocks and the boy would scream and run away, and she'd watch him while she laughed and held on to Fernando's only hand. She never told her mother or father about this sort of thing, and Fernando kept it to himself.

Childish games, these were. She wondered if tonight those childish games had come to an end. Taylor sat in her mother's chair, and that was enough to anger her, but she didn't say anything. Her father had told her often enough that she was to be polite to the man from the Company.

It had been ten minutes since her mother last screamed.

'How is the King?' she asked, as sweetly as she could manage. Her question seemed to shake the Company man from whatever thoughts he was thinking. He seemed very distracted, this evening. He frowned at her.

'The King? Which King do you mean, child?'

Now it was her turn to frown. Surely England only had one King? Even a lonely little girl on St Helena knew that!

'Why, King George, sir. Is there another King?'

'King George is dead, child. His grandson has replaced him.'

'Oh. How sad.' And it *was* sad. She hated to think of men dying. 'And what is the new King's name, sir?'

'King George.'

'They could not think of a new name for him, then?'

Taylor didn't answer that, and she decided that this meant he wanted to hear no further questions. She considered asking some anyway, just to annoy him.

There was still no sound from her mother's room.

Taylor stood up, and began looking along the bookshelves. He often did this when he visited, and she wondered what book he looked for. Once, he had exclaimed joyfully at finding something, only for his face to fall when he took it down and opened it. When she went to look at the book later on, the only words she saw were in Greek. She could read a little Greek and Latin – her father had been teaching her – but it was not sufficient to decipher what Taylor had found.

There was a movement at the library entrance, then. Her father appeared there. She looked into his face, and saw nothing but emptiness. Taylor stepped towards him, and the two of them went away, leaving her alone with the books and the yawning silence.

Eventually, she decided to go to bed. Sometimes she wasn't sure when the best time to go might be – she usually just waited until exhaustion pushed her bedwards, or her mother insisted. She could pretend it was whatever time she wanted it to be, if she didn't go outside. But now her bed felt like a refuge, a comforting soft shelter from the strange emptiness of feeling she felt in the air. As if something had departed.

She climbed into her bed without bothering to undress, her clothes smelling of the sand and salt of the bay where she had spent most of the day, gazing up at the endless blue sky and imagining flying up into it, away and over the endless ocean to those far parts of the world that she saw only in books and in the stories of her mother. She often dreamed of flying. It seemed the only way she would ever get off this island. Her family had been here for almost two hundred years, her father had told her, and he'd made her memorise all her forebears, even the ones named *Aakster* who spoke Dutch and had names that seemed to her to come from the Bible.

She tried to sleep, but couldn't, and waited for her mother to come to her, to kiss her cheek and read to her and sit beside her until tiredness seized her and dragged her away.

But her mother did not come. It was her father who came and sat on her bed. He didn't touch her as her mother did – didn't stroke her head or her face – and she thought about taking his hand and putting it on her head but something about the way her father sat beside her stopped her doing it. He looked at the corner of the room, and she wondered if he could see anything there.

'Your mother is dead,' he said, eventually. 'Your brother, too.'

Her brother, whom she had never met, who had only been a promise inside the blossoming girth of her mother's belly. She felt cheated by his non-arrival, even while she tried to wrestle her understanding into some grip on the words 'your mother is dead'.

'We must start work tomorrow, Mina,' he said, and now he did look at her, and she wondered when her father had become so old and so lost.

'What work, Papa?'

'Memory work, Mina. You have a very great deal to learn.'

'Learn about what?'

'About the reason we are here, my child. Now sleep well. Tomorrow, your life will not be as free as it has been heretofore.'

He did not kiss her as her mother had done, but he did shift a stray hair from across her forehead, and she thought that would have to be enough.

THE HORTONS ARRIVE AT ST HELENA

Approaching from the south (because of the winds, Abigail was told), the island gave no welcome. Brown rock cliffs rose up and behind these cliffs she could see the steep peaks of the interior. The hills were so high as to be in cloud; the whole place was crowned with mist. It was breathtakingly lonely.

Charles was making himself busy somewhere, so she had no one with whom to share the joy of arrival. At last, the prospect of land.

The ship rounded the island, and the north face came more into the view. The battered cliffs were pierced by tiny valleys, barely more than geographical filaments in the enormous walls of rock. How did such a thing come to be here? Did Neptune build a fortress for himself but then forget about it?

Atop some of the highest points on the sea-facing cliffs sat manmade enclosures of military fastness, prickly little structures that gave the island the aspect of a maritime fort, an outpost of Empire. An ocean-clapped castle.

The winds were quieter on the north side of the island, but the rollers on the sea were still large, and even a virgin voyager like Abigail could see how unapproachable the island was. There were no significant landing places at all, only the occasional tiny bay giving out from one of those needle ravines. She imagined the men who discovered this place sailing round and round, trying to find a way to approach, wondering what secrets those brown rock walls preserved.

They rounded a final point and, at last, a landing place. This, then, must be James Town. The town sat inside one of those ravines that pierced the outer rock wall of the island, carved out presumably by a river or stream, and unlike the other defiles this particular valley was just wide enough to insert a community. The ingenuity and determination of explorers struck her. The same energy that captured and cut that enormous whale built those little white houses which clustered up into the tiny valley. A great wall ran across the front of the valley, between the town and the shore, and behind it rose the tower of a church.

They anchored off a huge rock, at the top of which bristled one of those batteries. They climbed into a whaleboat which was lowered into the sea. The captain, Wallace, had joined them, though he still preferred to render her invisible. She could smell the destroyed sperm whale in the wood of the ship even now, though the carcass itself was left to sink into the ocean days before.

Inside the whaleboat the ocean rollers were more pronounced. She shrieked as one hit the boat, grabbing her husband's arm and holding onto it as they were rowed over to the wharf beneath the massive rock. The bruise on her own arm – Rat's bruise – throbbed under the effort.

She thought there must be ceremonies to perform – would they be greeted, questioned, even searched? This place was fortified, that much was clear, and their arrival had already sparked some activity along the wharf; other men in other boats were rowing out to the *Martha*, presumably to sell supplies. But Wallace ignored them, as did Charles, and this tipping boat was no place for questions.

It was almost impossible for her to get out of the boat and onto the wharf, so strong were the rollers. Charles climbed out first, turned and virtually swung her up to the wharf. She felt astonishingly uncomfortable, an ill-suited creature in this world of men, and for a moment as she lunged out of the boat she spied a man in the boat looking at her as the wind blew her skirts. She had experienced all sorts of looks and heard all sorts of mutterings during the voyage, and expected little else, but this felt more of a violation than any of them. She scowled at the man when she was safely on the wharf, and he grinned and looked away. The bitch was safely ashore, and his voyage could continue without the inconveniences of women.

Charles picked up the large ticking bag which contained their belongings. They walked along the wharf, and reached the point where the fortified wall protected the entrance to the town. A drawbridge across the channel of water between the wharf and the town entrance was guarded by two soldiers. Wallace went up to them.

'Master of the *Martha*, whaler out of London,' he said. 'Two passengers with us with business here on St Helena. I'd like to take them to the Governor.'

The soldiers nodded, pointing inside.

'Know your way?' one of them asked.

'Aye,' said Wallace, and in they went.

On the other side of the wall was a terrace running between a square and a large plain building towards which Wallace made his way. On the far side of the square was the church she had seen from the water, facing a fine-looking garden which looked over a street lined by terraced houses. The buildings were recognisably English – not unattractive but staunchly functional. The only decoration was supplied by Nature – the trees and plants in the garden opposite the church and, rising up on either side of the town and beyond it, the green-and-brown walls of St Helena.

The green lushness of the hills was a stark contrast to the brown fastnesses of the outward-facing cliffs. In the distance, along the valley, she could see a tantalising prospect of craggy peaks. The air was pleasantly warm, the only clouds those that ringed the peaks of the interior. In many ways, it felt like a pleasant English spring day, though in a part of England – the South Downs, perhaps – where the land had been squeezed by titanic hands to form steep valleys and impossible slopes.

And, Lord, it was good to be on solid ground once more.

Abigail saw Wallace glance uneasily at Charles as the three of them were about to step into the building wherein the island's Governor was to be found.

'You're both coming in?' he said, to Charles.

'Men's business, is it, captain?' she said, no longer disguising her dislike. 'Well, then. Men's business it is. I shall wait here.'

She sat herself on a bench at the entrance to the Castle. Charles seemed about to say something, but then thought better of it, and followed Wallace into the building.

There were very few people about, and all of them had looked at her at least once. Was it a rarity, then, a woman arriving by ship? There were women here, were there not? Look, there were two now: rather matronly looking ladies, carrying bags full of some goods or other. Their clothes were old and plain but clean and tidy – working women's clothes, untouched by Covent Garden fripperies. They appeared friendly enough, but perhaps where she was sitting – outside the Governor's office, like a naughty child waiting for the headmaster – put them off. Her arrival would be talked about today, behind the doors of those little houses which lined the street up into the valley.

There were a good many blacks working at one thing or another around the square, and the hunched way they held their heads caused her to think they must be slaves. There were Negroes in London, and in Wapping in particular, but they were free men, though they were often poor or ill or near-death. She had never seen slaves before.

Another group of women appeared, three of them this time, walking down the main street towards the sea wall. They glared at her, their faces tanned by the Atlantic sun but also painted with garish colours, and she realised with a lurch that they must be whores. Even here there were whores, responding to the arrival of the whaler. The women walked up to the guards at the drawbridge and touched them, rubbing the soldier's arms and laughing. Their shrill voices carried across the square, and Abigail felt an old helpless hatred at these women who had sold themselves to men's pleasure. Her sister was carried away, thus – though even Charles knew nothing of that.

He knows nothing of your meetings with Dr Drysdale either, her rebellious mind said, but she ignored it.

It was an odd but intriguing vista. Working women, slaves and whores, and outside the walls of the town men seeking to do business with the newly arrived ship. Was every British outpost like this?

She saw two boys loitering in the shadows of the church on the other side of the square. They were looking at her, and she waved to them. One of them started to walk across the square, as if he'd been waiting for such a call. As they came, Abigail noted another African working in the garden of a large house facing the church. His legs were chained together.

The braver of the two boys was brown-faced and scrawny,

but his face was far cleaner than those of similar age in London. There was no smog or oil or grease to cloud his features here, but he looked tired and, despite his sun-kissed skin, rather unwell.

'I will need two of you to help me carry this bag to a decent lodging house,' she said to him.

'I'm no porter.'

His accent was an odd amalgam of London's clipped consonants – reminding Abigail of Rat – and something more rural. Somerset, perhaps?

'I will pay you a penny for carrying my bag and for finding me lodgings.'

'You on your own, mistress? Did I not see another couple of fellows going in to the Guv'nor?'

'You did. My husband will accompany us when his business is concluded.'

The boy whistled back towards his companion, and the other boy began to make his way across. He was a good deal bigger than his friend.

'You do not stay at Mr Porteous's house, mistress?' said the boy.

'Which is that?'

'Over there.'

He indicated a large house on the other side of the square. It was the house where the chained Negro was working.

'No, I do not wish to stay there. Somewhere further into the town. Somewhere that has no slaves.'

'No slaves, miss?'

The boy frowned, struggling with the alien concept. Then he shrugged.

'You're to help me carry this,' the boy said to his large friend, whose face was puffy and uncomprehending. The large boy lifted up the bag, but upside-down, and Abigail darted forward, scared lest it open. 'Wait for it, Hippo!' said the first boy, so Hippo dropped the bag to the ground again.

'Oh, do be careful!' exclaimed Abigail. The first boy looked at her and smiled. Where the big lad was slow and stupid, this boy was clever and watchful. Rat, again, peeped out from the boy's eyes. She felt the ache of the bruise on her arm.

'Sorry about Hippo,' the boy said. 'He's a bit soft in the head. Product of an Incestuous Partnership, as my old man would have it. Now, off we go.'

Bit soft in the head. Dr Drysdale, again. *Go away now, please, doctor*, she thought.

'No, wait, please. My husband is still within.'

The boy grinned.

'Hang on, Hippo! The mistress ain't ready, yet.'

Hippo had lifted the bag with particular care, but now stood quite still holding the bag, looking into the middle distance.

She spoke to them while they waited. The first boy gave his name as Keneally, but when Abigail enquired about the provenance of such a name, he said it was his family's and that she should call him Ken. Hippo was Hippo because one of the island boys had been to Africa before coming here, and had seen a hippo, and had said the animal's broad stupid face was just like the face of the lad who now held her bag and patiently waited. Ken asked Abigail where she might want to stay, and she suggested an inn, if there was one with decent rooms.

'There's only one tavern, and there's no rooms in it,' Ken said. 'Normally, visitors take a room at someone's house.'

'The private houses?'

'Aye. Mr Porteous for example – he's got nice rooms.' He nodded to the house he had first pointed out. 'But there's your particularity regarding *slaves* to consider.'

Ken winked at her, and she was pleased to have found him. She wondered if her husband would be pleased – might he want to pay for Ken's eyes as he had paid for Rat's eyes in Wapping? It was a cold thought.

'I think Seale keeps a room,' says Ken. 'He's just up there.' He pointed up the street. 'And he keeps no slaves.'

'Then we shall go there, when my husband is finished.'

'Unusual, you arriving like that,' said Ken. 'We don't get a lot of arrivals like that.'

'How do people normally arrive?' Abigail asked.

'On the Indiamen – either on their way out, or on their way back. Passengers come with them. Any reason you didn't come on an Indiaman?'

This with a knowing smile. The boy's brain was quick – perhaps quicker than her husband might like. She ignored the question.

'Is your father a farmer?'

Ken snorted at that.

'Farm? Why bother with that? The Company supplies us with all we need.'

'But I had heard St Helena was a fine spot for farming?'

'Aye, it might have been once. But there's too many goats, too many rats, and too much money coming in on ships. Why bother breaking your back on the land?'

Ken said this smoothly, and Abigail thought she heard the authentic voice of the boy's father speaking. An idle man, no doubt, justifying his indolence to his son.

'So, what are you here for, then?' Ken asked. The boy was not sly about his questions.

'Why do you concern yourself with what I am here for?' she said.

'Oh. A mystery, is it?'

Abigail wondered, for a moment, if this boy was asking questions for someone else. She looked around the square to see if anyone was watching, before telling herself to keep such ridiculous suspicions well chained, as Dr Drysdale would no doubt advise, were he to step out into this English square on this strange island.

A noise from behind her, and her husband appeared with Wallace. He looked at the boys.

'Husband, this is Ken, and his burly companion is named Hippo, though not to his mother. Ken here will take us to a good place to stay.'

'Pleased to make your acquaintance, mister,' said Ken, somewhat regally. 'And what brings you to St Helena?'

She raised a warning eyebrow. Charles smiled in return. After weeks at sea, weeks in which they had spoken only in their cabin and he had spent a good deal of time working as a sailor while she watched and conversed with the steward, it felt like a reunion of sorts. In any case, he seemed to have guessed her meaning.

'My name is Horton, young fellow,' he said. 'And my business here is none of yours.'

Ken said nothing else as they walked along James Town's single street. The fact that they were doing so suggested that her husband's story had been believed by the Governor.

'I will be,' he had said, somewhere north of the line as they had lain in their tiny cabin aboard the *Martha,* 'a botanist.'

She had laughed little enough since Rat's death, but she laughed at that.

'A botanist? Husband, you know as little of flowers as I know of whaling ships.'

He had smiled at her.

'I have a letter from the President of the Royal Society that *says* I am a botanist, and that I am voyaging to St Helena to assess its suitability for a royal botanic garden,' he had said. 'And besides, I have a botanist with me, do I not?'

She remembered an old conversation about the naming of plants, and she wondered at how their lives had changed. The former nurse and the former Naval lieutenant, carrying a letter from the most famous scientific personage in England, pretending to be botanists.

But here they were, walking into James Town. Charles had not been arrested on the spot. Had a cat been set among the Governor's pigeons? Or were they just another pair of do-gooders from the North, come to transplant species as Bligh had once come to Otaheite?

Ken stopped them outside a plain-looking two-storey building. There was no indication that it was anything other than a normal residence. A man was sleeping on its doorstep. He snored loudly. The house could have been a crofter's summer residence: square, plain, its roof covered with what looked like a cross between brown mud and stone, dropped as if by gods from a Norfolk village onto this strange lonely island.

Its only notable feature was the man sleeping on the ground in front of its door, and the name of the house, which was painted on an old piece of wood nailed to its gate.

The man was dressed plainly, in cotton breeches and a white shirt. He wore his dark hair long and tied in a plait at his neck. There was something politely piratical about him. He could have been a sailor or a stevedore, and he snored as loudly as a pig.

The care taken in the sign was in stark contrast to the discombobulated figure snoring below it. The wood had been smoothed at the edges and corners, and the house's name was painted in careful, elegant letters: 'Castle of Otranto'.

'Delightful!' exclaimed Abigail.

'What is?' replied Charles.

'You do not recognise the reference in the name?'

'I do not.'

'*The Castle of Otranto* is a book by Horace Walpole. It is a favourite of mine.'

'Is it about natural philosophy?'

'No, of course it isn't. It is a novel.'

'Ah. A long book about things that never happened.'

Abigail glared at him.

'This is the place?' Charles said, doubtfully, to Ken.

'Aye – that's Seale, there, a-lying on the ground. He keeps a room. Now, mister. As to payment.'

Horton took out a leather purse. He fished out a shilling and handed it over. Ken gawped at it and looked back at Horton with new-found respect.

'There's more for you, lad. If you help me. Now you have friends?'

'Friends?'

'Other boys. Like Hippo here. Though perhaps with more . . . understanding.'

'Yes. There are others.'

'Well then. Keep an eye out for me, here and about James Town. There may be errands I need running.'

Ken looked at him carefully.

'Well, now,' he said. 'I'll consider it, mister. I will consider it. But you're somewhat mysterious, you are.' He put the coin in his pocket. 'We'll see, shall we? Come, Hippo.'

And with that strange little speech, the boys made their way back down into James Town.

'Your story, husband?' she said. Charles watched the boys walking away.

'My story was believed, I think.' He looked at her. 'The Governor was surprised, but Sir Joseph's letter carried weight and was well composed. I gained the impression that the Governor is expecting a great change in the island's fortunes – as if its status was shortly to be changed. How or why I do not know. But what will be will be. Our story means we have no need to creep around like footpads. This is an island. No one will escape it until a ship comes. Captain Burroughs will, I am sure, soon know of our arrival.'

'How will he respond?'

'I have no idea. We are, as it were, locked into a cage with the creature we are pursuing. So we may have to bring the game to him. Who knows? Perhaps he already has his little spies.' Another look at the boys, then Charles turned towards the house.

'Now, let us see about this Castle of yours.'

Charles knelt down and shook the man who was sleeping at the door by the shoulder.

'Hello? Hello?'

The man sat up and spluttered slightly. He smelled strongly of liquor, and as he stood Abigail saw he was hopelessly intoxicated. Turning to the door he banged on it with his fists.

'Eliza! Eliza! Let me in, I say!'

A muffled woman's voice shouted back from within the house. He turned back to Horton and Abigail.

'One kiss! One bloody kiss! And now see!'

He turned to bang on the door again. His transition from sleeping drunk to angry drunk had been sudden and violent, and Charles looked to be about to pull him away when the door opened and water was violently ejected from within, all over the man and all over Charles.

With a roar, the man plunged into the house, pursued by Charles, who grabbed for his waistcoat but could do no more than slow him down. Abigail followed them both inside.

The door gave onto a small parlour which was surprisingly dark after the bleached-white sunshine of the street. But it was also cool. A young woman in a dirty muslin dress stood in the middle of the room holding an earthenware jug, the water from which now dripped down the front of Charles and the owner of the house.

'Monstrous creature!' shouted the man. 'How dare you take occupation of my residence so?'

'I saw you! I bloody saw you!'

'It was a solitary kiss! A single solitary kiss! Can a widower not kiss a girl?'

The woman threw the jug at him, and he ducked, and Charles swerved away, and the thing smashed into the wall and was destroyed. The woman followed its trajectory, slapping the man in the face as she left, and exited without giving Charles or Abigail even a glance.

The man collapsed with a half-roared sigh into an ancient chair. He looked about to fall asleep when he noticed them.

'Who in the name of God are you?'

'My name is Horton. I am just arrived on the island. This is my wife.'

'Well, you appear to be standing in my house. Would you please make yourself scarce? And close the door behind you.'

And with that, he fell asleep.

They talked about finding another room, but Charles argued they should wait until the man awoke again. 'He spoke with the drink before,' he said. 'He may think differently. All we need is a room, and this place is pleasant enough.'

For herself, she was happy to find out more about this man and his oddly named house. To find a dwelling with such a name as the Castle of Otranto out here on the rim of the known world and not to investigate its owner would be drearily complacent.

The man slept for an hour, no more. When he woke, he saw the two of them sitting in chairs looking at him.

'Who in God's name are you?' he asked, for the second time.

'My name is Horton,' said Charles. 'We seek a room to lodge in for a fortnight, no more.'

'Didn't I tell you to clear off?'

'You told us so, yes. And yet here we are.'

The man blinked, and made as if to stand. But Abigail got up first and passed him a cupful of the clear water she'd taken from a jug in the little kitchen. She'd tasted the water – it was the coldest, sweetest liquid ever to have passed her lips. It must have made its way down from those mountains in the island's interior.

He looked at her as he took the cup, and she smiled, and despite what must be the beginnings of an enormous hangover, he smiled back, and drank with relief.

He was young, tall and well built. He needed to shave. Despite his drink and his incipient headache, he looked astonishingly healthy.

He drained the cup, closed his eyes and rubbed his forehead.

'What happened to Eliza?' he said.

'She left,' said Abigail. 'In something of a hurry.'

'Dammit. No one's secrets are truly secret on this bloody island.' He looked at her again. 'My apologies, ma'am.'

'No apology is necessary, sir.'

'One should not speak thus in front of one such as thee,' the man said, somewhat wolfishly. Despite her husband's presence in the room he seemed unembarrassed to talk so. He was a man with an easy way with women, it seemed.

'We seem to have interrupted a terrible disagreement,' she said. 'But I'm afraid the matter of a room is an urgent one to us. Can you accommodate us?'

He smiled at her, and then he frowned.

'Your name's Horton?'

'That's right,' said Charles.

'And your business on the island?'

Charles's face did not change. It was odd, watching him lie so smoothly.

'I am a botanist.'

'A what?'

Charles did not quite know what to say to that, so Abigail replied for him.

'My husband is an associate of the Royal Society, sir. He is an investigator of plant species and their uses and habitats.'

The man smiled at her.

'And what, pray tell, good lady, is the *Royal Society*?'

For a moment, she did not know how to answer. The Society was such a part of her life in London that the question seemed extraordinary, as if he had asked her *what is the Thames?* But then, why should a young man on the far side of the world know anything of the Royal Society?

'It is a society appointed by the Crown to pursue natural philosophy and investigation,' she said, smoothly. 'For the benefit of King, country and mankind.'

'Indeed? Then I am blessed by the presence of its representatives, am I not?'

'Blessed, sir? I think not. We will have you classified and registered before the sun goes down.'

The man sat back in his chair smiling and rubbing the stubble on his cheek. Then he stood and went towards the kitchen. Before he got there, he turned to Charles.

'Your wife is handsome and clever. There must be something about you. You may stay in my house.'

He went into the kitchen. Charles looked suddenly angry.

'His tone is insulting,' Charles said.

'He meant no disrespect.'

'One does not make so free with remarks about a man's wife in London.'

'He is not from London. We shall seek to adapt ourselves, as any creatures must when in a new environment.'

The man came back from the kitchen. 'My name is Abigail,

sir,' she said. 'Now, you have our names. Might we have yours?'

He looked at her while she spoke, and she saw that this man was a consumer of women as well as a charmer of them. His eyes twinkled with the crackle of male energy. She found herself liking him enormously. So refreshing, this lack of manners.

'My name is Seale, ma'am. Robert Francis Seale. I am the assistant storekeeper here, with the rank of Captain.'

'And you are an admirer of Mr Horace Walpole?' said Abigail.

'Not I, madam.'

'Your house has rather a striking name, Captain Seale.'

'Yes, but it is not mine. My wife must have been an admirer of this Mr Walpole. I confess to not having read his works. I never did understand the reference.'

'Forgive me, but your wife is deceased?'

'Yes. She fell ill, soon after we were wed. Her name was Harriet.'

It was an odd little echo, the name Harriet. A reminder of Wapping, so many thousands of miles away, where John Harriott might already be dead.

Stop it, she told herself, dismayed by the way her mind ran along such dark rails.

'You have always lived on the island?'

'My family has been here for some five generations. I was sent to school in England when my father died.'

'To what part of England?'

'Marlow. I chiefly remember the cold and the rain. I came back here eight years ago. I do my work, I drink my drink, and since I lost poor Harriet I make as free as I possibly can. It is a lonely life, but not a terrible one.'

'You know the island well?'

'Better than anyone! I have these past eight years been

charting it extensively; I have my own little boat to explore the shores. You won't find better maps than mine, Horton. I could show you some likely places for growing weeds.'

They made small idle chatter as the night came down, and grew comfortable with each other. Money was exchanged, and as the evening aged Abigail found herself cooking a meal for the two men, who talked in the parlour. It felt good to her to be cooking again, after so many weeks and months of travelling, of eating poor food prepared by a steward who had cared little for taste. Making something fresh and tasty was a positive pleasure.

Outside the window, it was night on the island. When she looked into the glass and saw her face reflected, there came a single moment of fear. Might someone be looking in at her, even now? Might she move her face forward and look into the glass and see the eyes of someone looking back at her – the same someone who wanted her dead back in London? The same someone who had smashed in Rat's poor face with the poker from her own fire?

Her husband laughed in the Castle's parlour. Quite suddenly, his laugh was not a happy sound.

1773: THE YEAR MINA BAXTER'S FATHER DIED

Her father was angry with her, but here at the foot of Halley's Mount she could forget that and feel the warm grass on her bare back, the sunlight on her blushing face and the hot, *hot* skin of the man who had just made love to her.

The sky was so blue and so endless. Once again she imagined floating up into that sky, up and away from St Helena, this beautiful island prison in which she was trapped by obligation and custom. It had been the cause of her latest disagreement with her father. She wanted to leave the island – not forever, just to see England, to spend some of the money which she knew was hers by right. But her father had said she was too young for such a trip – that she was needed here, in any case.

Perhaps she could escape with this man beside her, into the cold North. Or would he take her up into the sky, in one of those balloons she had read about and had even thought of building? The two of them floating to England on the incessant bloody wind.

His name was John Burroughs, and he was a captain in the island militia. His body was as thick and squat as one of the giant tortoises that lived on the island, his hair was as red as Company wine, his hands as hard as ship wood and as gentle as the silk which was her only hobby.

'That was nice,' she said, looking round at him lying naked on the ground.

'Nice?' John said, and running her eyes down his body she noticed that he was already thinking about taking her again. 'That was more than nice, Mina. I don't know what you've been reading, but whatever it is you should read some more of it.'

She reached for him with her hand, and he moaned delightfully, and although the sun was still high and the grass was still warm, she was no longer thinking about those things.

It was falling dark by the time she walked back to the old Dutch fort, leaving John to walk alone down to James Town. He knew nothing of the fort or what lay beneath it, nor would he ever learn. She may have been indulging herself in physical transports, but she would never transport herself enough to reveal her father's secrets to one outside the family.

Her grandfather's secrets. Her grandfather's grandfather's grandfather's secrets. Not her secrets, of course. They had never been *hers*. And yet this baleful inheritance was all she had. Stuck on this island she had never left. Her mother had told her when she was a child that she might leave one day, and she had painted word-pictures of the London she had herself been born in for her mesmerised daughter, a mighty place of dukes and duchesses, palaces and pleasure-houses, where everyone dressed in Paris fineries and there were dances every night. Her predecessors on the island had come and gone as they pleased. But not her father. He remained, stubbornly and desperately since the death of his wife, his daughter chained to him by unrelenting obligation.

Somewhere between Halley's Mount and the fort, Fernando appeared. He was never far from her, she found, even though he was supposedly busy working in the mine. But her father was ill, she reminded herself. There was probably less work for Fernando when that was the case.

His broken face glared at her, the face which so terrified the children of the island but which she had been seeing since the day she was born. It bore no fears for her, although she found she resented it more and more.

'What? What is wrong with you? Stupid bloody Cannibal.'

He hated her calling him that. It was the name the island children had given to him, years ago. She used to wonder whether he watched them playing their games in the square of James Town, one of them pretending to be him, hiding one hand up a sleeve and making awful slobbering noises as he (it was always a boy) lumbered around trying to catch his play-mates.

'Were you watching us?' she said to him now. 'Were you? You disgusting fiend. You were, weren't you?'

Fernando was no longer glaring. He now looked crestfallen, like the dog she had never been allowed to have. He walked in front of her.

'I see you watching me. I see it. You're disgusting. I hate you!'

She was screaming by now, her previous calm happiness punctured. As they climbed to the fort, she actually found herself sobbing. Fernando made strange noises, perhaps words in his own tongue, perhaps sobs of his own. She pulled the heavy magnet from her bag, the thing she had to carry around with her wherever she went, and opened the door to the fort.

It was so quiet inside. So still. None of the noises she'd come to associate with the fort; the noise of rock falling onto rock, of rock falling into the sea at the bottom of the fissure, the noise of her father shouting at Fernando, the harsh chemical smell from the processing chamber.

The fort felt like it had died while she had been out in the sun enjoying John.

She found herself unable to sob any more. A panic gripped her as she descended, passing through the big central chamber with the fissure cut through it, over the old wooden bridge and into the chambers beyond. Fernando scurried along beside her, very dog-like now, as if he too had detected the strange stillness in the place.

There was a glow coming from the processing chamber, as if the life of the room were not yet extinguished. But when she entered and saw him lying there on his back, on the ground, she saw that the light had lied. There was no life in this room. Only the memory of it, and the bitter stench of almonds.

With a shriek, she rushed to her father's side and took one lifeless hand in hers. Her other hand she laid across his cold brow, recoiling from it as if it had been ice – though she had never seen ice, she had only read about it in the books. And then she laid her own brow on the bed, the top of her head against the still infinite immensity of her father's side, and she wept for the life she had never had and the life that now, at last, was to come.

She would never leave the island, now.

She was watched by the Cannibal, whose eyes spoke only of love and loss.

THE HORTONS GO EXPLORING

The unpleasantness that broke out with Charles the next morning was of a piece with similar disagreements in London. Seale left early to perform some work at the stores, promising to return later in the day and show them around the island. Charles planned to look around James Town while they waited, and had suggested Abigail wait in Seale's house while he did so, 'with a book, perhaps'.

She clapped her hands, once and sharply, and sat down in a chair in Seale's parlour. She felt suddenly as drawn-tight as a drum. She had become furious.

'Husband, sit thee down.' She said *thee* with an acid tone, precisely as she meant to say it. He looked alarmed, almost as if she had raised a hand to him, but he sat down as she had ordered.

'This will end, now, if you please,' she said.

'This?'

'Husband: I am not some sensitive plant that must be preserved from wind and rain. I am not a milk-skinned duchess hidden from the farm-hands. I am a nurse, I am intelligent, and I am made of more robust substance than you give credit for. Look.'

She held out her bare forearms (though not her upper arm, where Rat's bruise lay beneath her sleeve). He looked confused.

'Do you not see?' she demanded.

'See?'

'My skin is brown from the sun. My hair is blonder than it has ever been. I have been changed by this voyage, husband.'

'Abigail, I do not understand you.'

'No, husband, you do not and nor do you attempt to. It is part of a woman's burden to be misunderstood by men. Know this, then: I have sailed halfway around the world with you. Not to escape whatever awaited us in London. I am here because you are here. If either of us is in need of protection, it is not me.'

She stood at this, and turned her back to him at the house's front window.

'Here we are on a rock in the Atlantic, thousands of miles away from home. Is this where you will squirrel me away? Hide me from the bad men? Wrap me in muslin and put me in a box so that none may harm me?'

'But of course I wish to protect you from harm.'

'But what *am I*? Have you considered that? Am I just the woman who cooks you meals and reads her books? Or am I something else? It has not been easy being a woman of my type: too poor to marry well, too educated to sell fish or pick hops or sew dresses or go into service. I became a nurse, but then you came along, and I stopped being a nurse. Or at least I became a wife to a man who needs a nurse.'

'I need a nurse?'

'You need a nurse, you need a confidante, you need a confessor. You are the most frighteningly unhappy man I have ever met, Charles Horton. Only one thing makes you happy, I do believe, and it is myself. So you preserve me from danger, you wrap me in muslin. And this will *stop*, husband.'

She turned to face him again, and felt something surge up within her, as if a poison she had ingested long ago was finally being released into the open air.

'Because never forget, husband, not for one instant, who is looking after whom.'

There.

She understood a new life was being laid out before them. The whale ship had been a voyage from one life to another, as if that great leviathan had been sacrificed for some new conception of themselves.

If I ever return to London, I shall not need Dr Drysdale.

Devils and demons had danced around her head, and now they were silent.

'Well, then, wife,' Charles said, coming towards her. She had troubled him, she saw. 'It seems we have some things to talk about. Perhaps a walk in the sun?'

James Town's single street possessed only a handful of crossings. It ran up the valley, climbing into the interior of the island which, despite the heat of the morning, was once again shrouded in fog – or, perhaps, the peaks were high enough to pierce the clouds.

The climate was still astonishingly pleasant, though breezy. The people out on the street seemed friendly enough, and greeted them with open faces and smiles. They seemed used to strangers.

Abigail wondered as to the island's population; it must run into the hundreds, perhaps even the low thousands. This was the only town, and it was the size of a good-sized village: a few dozen homes, a few hundred residents. The population must, she thought, be swelled significantly by the number of blacks, whose faces were everywhere, all seemingly occupied in some burdensome activity: carrying, cleaning, pulling, sweeping. Some of the Negro men were shirtless, and many of them had vivid white-and-pink scars whipped into their backs.

There were groups of Chinese, too: mainly men, but the occasional small knot of women. She could not guess as to their provenance or purpose, and they took no notice of her or of anyone else. They talked among themselves and moved with single purpose.

Charles said he had little plan other than to find Captain Edgar Burroughs, the new assistant treasurer. He had not asked the Governor for this information – for what would a Royal Society botanist have to do with a new Company bureaucrat?

'But he may know we are here, already,' said Charles. 'I have little doubt that the message has reached Captain Burroughs of our arrival. I half expect the man to make himself known to us directly.'

'We have no idea of the fellow's appearance.'

'No. None at all. He cannot be any more than forty years of age, by my reckoning.'

'He has recently arrived, though. He may still have his London pallor.'

Charles laughed.

'We have lost ours, wife – as you have this morning demonstrated to me.'

There was an idiosyncratic simplicity to the place, one at odds with Charles's stories of unexplained murders, and with the older, murkier story that had been told by Sir Joseph Banks, and which Charles had retold to her in that little cabin on the *Martha*: of Edmond Halley's visit to the island, the strange creature he had found there, the secrets which seemed to go back centuries.

She thought of John Dee's house in Mortlake. She had had time to give Halley's strange tale much thought (when she had not been thinking of Rat, or Drysdale, or lingering with self-indulgent misery on *herself*). She had read something of John Dee and his library, though this reading had only brought confusion. Dee seemed to have a profound understanding and reverence for Euclid's mathematics; indeed, seemed to find mathematics almost the language of God. But he also had a parallel set of beliefs which she found mystifying: that the stars and planets were fixed in their orbits around the Earth, that their influences worked upon humankind through their rays, that there were angels and demons and that mankind could ascend to the Godhead through knowledge and, indeed, through mathematics. And that a man once ascended might live forever.

She looked up at the peaks of St Helena's interior, and remembered Edmund Kean's Prospero casting spells on the stage at Drury Lane, back on that night when this strange narrative began. Had Prospero's island been like this one? Had it had peaks and valleys, streams and rocks, green fields and jagged edges? Did another Ariel ride the winds up there, and was Caliban lurking within the hillside shadows?

'I have been remembering Sir Joseph's odd tale – of John Dee and this island,' said Charles, interrupting her reverie.

'And I was thinking of the play,' she said.

'The play?'

'The Shakespeare we saw. It is a strange coincidence, is it not?'

'Edmond Halley met Caliban, did he?'

Her husband was smiling.

'He met someone,' she said. 'I have read some of Halley's work. He was not a man given to dramatisation.'

'A mystery. One that needs looking into, does it not?'

Now it was her turn to smile.

'A mystery for you, and a mystery for me, husband?'

'It would seem the fairest arrangement.'

'Well then. I shall walk in the steps of Mr Halley, and you shall pursue your killer.'

'We know not how Sir Joseph's story overlaps with the melancholy circumstances of the Johnsons' deaths. But there are secrets here, wife. I believe they are to do with money. Sir Joseph suspects they may be to do with natural philosophy. Let me follow the money. And you follow the science.'

They came to a fine house in front of which sat a giant of a black man, watching the street. He scrambled to his feet when Horton asked him where they might eat some food, and so huge was he that this took some seconds.

'Please, sir,' she said. 'Do not hurry yourself. We do not wish to interrupt you.'

He was confused, and almost scared. He pointed to his mouth and shook his head.

'You cannot speak?'

No, his head shook. He took a medal out from inside his shirt, which hung on a piece of leather around his neck. He bent down so she could read its face.

On one side of the medal the words HONEST DILIGENT FAITHFUL SOBER had been stamped and on the other was a name – HAMLET – and a year of issue, 1805.

'Your name is Hamlet?' she asked, and the giant nodded, almost happy now. She found herself wondering why he didn't speak, and whether his tongue had been removed, and whether that happened before or after 1805.

'Well, Hamlet, is there a tavern down this street? Somewhere we may get some food?'

He nodded, and pointed down the street towards the sea.

'Thank you, Hamlet. Making your acquaintance has been a pleasure.'

And she offered him a curtsy and he looked astonished. She took her husband's arm and they walked on down James Town's main street.

How odd, she thought. She had been thinking of Prospero, but then she had met Hamlet.

'Land or sea?' said Seale, back at the house in the early afternoon.

'Land,' said Charles. 'We have been at sea enough.'

They turned out of Seale's front door, and walked up the valley away from the sea. As the town reached an end, they followed a path, climbing further into the interior. The way became steep, and Abigail had the distinct feeling of walking *into* the island, as if James Town were simply the front entrance to a secret world.

The island was crossed by a central ridge, explained Seale, that ran roughly south-west to north-east. The highest peaks of the island rose from this ridge, and now the morning mist had lifted she could see them clearly, touching the sky. She saw steep brown rock walls plunging vertiginously into green bowls, within which tendrils of fog still stirred like the breath of dragons.

The higher they went, the stronger the wind blew. It was extraordinarily constant, with none of the moist stop-start fecklessness of an English breeze.

'I think of the island as the peak of a mountain,' Seale said, 'for such it must be; a tall mountain which descends down into the depths of the ocean around us. There may be an entire range of mountains beneath us, with this as the tallest peak. But I also imagine a catastrophe here, of a volcanic nature. This may once have been a peak as elegant as any of the famed Alpine mountains, but at some time an explosion tore half of the peak away, and left this behind.'

The conception seemed, to Abigail, a brave but unprovable one. But it had the virtue of explaining the impossible situation of this place, and also the jagged aggression of its topography.

Seale pointed upwards to the south.

'Those are the main peaks of the island: Diana's Peak, Cuckold's Point, Acteon and Halley's Mount.' He moved his finger along the vista, as he named the mountains.

'Halley's Mount is named for the astronomer?' asked Abigail.

'Yes. I believe he visited the island soon after the Company took ownership of it.'

'He had a telescope or some such up there?'

'He did. There is only a small ruin now.'

Seale now pointed to the eastern end of the central ridge.

'On the far side of the ridge there is the flattest part of the island, the nearest it has to a plain. It is called Deadwood. It was once a huge forest, though there are few trees upon it now.'

'What happened to them?'

Seale began walking down the hill, southwards again.

'Mankind happened to them,' he said.

They walked for hours, and for much of the time Abigail was quite exhausted by it, despite the delightful climate, which combined heat and breeze in measures seemingly designed to promote endurance. She and Charles had trouble keeping up with Seale, who bounded from rock to rock like one of the goats which, he said, infested the island despite numerous attempts to kill them off.

'The Portuguese left them when they first came here, and the first English settlers encouraged them also,' said Seale. 'Now they own the island. We are outnumbered by goats, rats and blacks. That at least is the common saying.'

She lost her bearings more than once, and began to use the peaks as a way of regaining them. They came to a glorious confusion of steep mountainsides cascading down to the Atlantic which Seale said was called Sandy Bay. At the edge of some of these peaks Abigail spied impossible pillars of rock, like ancient columns from some uncompleted temple. This, argued Seale, must have been where the calamity happened which blew the top off the island untold aeons ago. 'Imagine,' said Seale, his face lost in an ancient unseen narrative, 'a volcanic explosion so immense as to tear the top of the mountain away and plunge it into the sea. Then came the tides and the wind and the actions of Time, and what must have been a jagged horror was turned into this smooth green landscape.'

Abigail, who thought the landscape was not particularly smooth at all, knew there were blasphemies in Seale's imagined histories. Did not the church argue that the world was barely four thousand years old? How long would time and tide take to wear down jagged volcanoes? Seale's tales of aeons appealed to her more strongly than Biblical narratives.

Half a dozen smart little houses dotted the steep Sandy Bay hillsides, and Seale pointed out one of them.

'That is the residence of Sir William Doveton, the treasurer of the island.'

'Treasurer?' said Charles, catching his breath. 'I should talk to him.'

'Of plants and gardens?'

'It would be a courtesy.'

'And what of those?' said Abigail, changing the subject. She pointed to two of the tall columns of rock, standing like sentinels on their own peaks.

'We call those Lot and Lot's Wife.'

They turned their backs on these columns, as Lot and his wife had so failed to do, and walked eastwards onto a large flat plain.

'Deadwood,' said Seale, and Abigail noted how the dreary old English word sounded mournful on his tongue.

'Have your family been long on St Helena?' she asked.

'Since the first settlement. My ancestor Benjamin Seale had an allotment of land down there' – Seale nodded over his shoulder, to the south, on the other side of the ridge to Deadwood. 'They call it Seale's Flat now; it's at the upper part of Shark's Valley. We no longer farm it.'

He carried on walking. A house he called Longwood sat in the middle of the Deadwood plain, and there were a few dozen small copses of gum trees, but the overall impression was of undressed land, denuded of forest.

'This was all once known as the Great Wood,' said Seale. 'It was almost gone a hundred years ago. They tried replanting it, putting a wall round it, everything. But it was an easy source of firewood. The islanders treated it as a commons, and such was its tragedy.'

From here, up on the plain, she seemed to be standing on a platform above the world. The wind blew in her face from somewhere over there in the south-east, from impossibly distant seas where whales hid from whalers beneath the white mountainous icebergs.

She caught her breath for a moment, and thought herself to be gliding above the world, a London nurse with a good mind, gazing upon the infinite.

MRS HORTON'S ODD MOMENT

The next morning, Charles left early to make his way to see Sir William Doveton, the island treasurer.

Abigail did not mention the prickly feeling she had experienced once again the previous evening, while she washed the dishes and listened to the two men talk in the parlour. She had opened the window onto Seale's little garden – she had been thinking of their first evening in St Helena, when she had seen her reflection in the glass and had felt a moment of profound unease, remembering her sessions with Dr Drysdale.

With the window open she could see into the darkness, and this should have made her more comfortable. Yet that unease persisted. The feeling was vivid that there was someone out there, in the dark, watching this little house. She thought of the whores down by the sea wall, the slave Hamlet, the boys Ken and Hippo. Were they all watchers? Did they all file reports?

She thought she had heard him, then. Heard him breathing out in the dark. But it must surely have been the wind moving in the hills.

She took her time getting dressed the following morning,

allowing Charles to leave early. He asked what her plans would be – and he asked carefully, she was pleased to see, lest his solicitude affront her. She told him she would investigate the churchyard beside Plantation House, the country residence of the Governor. About an hour after Charles had left, she made her own departure, walking back up the valley as they had the previous day.

Plantation House was at the end of the valley in which James Town was set. The tidy little churchyard consisted almost entirely of individual graves and headstones. There were perhaps half a dozen family mausoleums, recording what she supposed to be the oldest families on the island, or at least the ones who had stayed the longest. One of them, she saw, belonged to Seale's family.

She hoisted her little leather satchel over her shoulder, and walked east towards Deadwood plain. It was a walk of almost two hours, and on the way she saw perhaps a dozen whites, all of whom greeted her with the same cheerful lack of embarrassment that had marked their first encounter with Seale. These people expressed a good deal of curiosity as to her presence on St Helena, but it was not of a suspicious kind. The residents of St Helena were used to strangers, it seemed, despite the extraordinary distance of the island from any other human habitation. She wondered at this, and imagined the talk over St Helena tables this evening. 'Saw a woman on her own walking from James Town. Said she was collecting flowers!'

She also saw a number of Chinese as she walked, though these were working away on the ground of the plantations. They looked at her silently as she passed, then chattered to each other, as if she was the victim of a tremendous shared joke. There were no Negroes, and Abigail wondered if they had been supplanted by these Chinese workers. Were the Orientals slaves, then? Or some kind of indentured labour?

At Deadwood she spent some time investigating the treeless, scrubby plain, watched only by some curious goats. It was then that she stumbled upon something of a mystery.

There was a little gut in the middle of the Deadwood plain, not quite a valley and with no stream running down it, although something about the ground at the bottom of the gut suggested it did get particularly wet, presumably at a time of significant rain. She climbed down into the narrow defile in the flat treeless plain, for what she had seen from above was worthy of inspection by a woman with botanical eye.

She was proved right. The gut was, indeed, filled with mulberry trees. She could not count them but there must have been hundreds, crowding the defile like ladies with parasols at a horse race. She walked between them, inspecting various trees closely, noting their long leaves with serrated edges, the male and female catkins, the white fruit, which she picked and tasted. It was sweet but uninteresting. After some thought, she guessed that the tree must be white mulberry, she thought *Morus atropurpurea*, though she was surprised by the colour of the fruit, which was normally purple in the wild and from which the tree got its Latin name. The white fruit was normally only on cultivated plants.

Many of the trees had silkworms on them, which caused her to wonder whether these trees were perhaps native to St Helena, though she had seen nothing like them anywhere else on the island. Had the Chinese she had seen planted these trees, or brought silkworms with them? Was such a thing possible?

The island certainly contained a remarkable hybrid of botanical specimens, a symptom presumably of its fecund climate and its status as a stopping-off point for ships from the Indies, first Portuguese and now British. She snipped a few leaves and fruits from the mulberry trees, and added them to the little bag she used for specimens.

It was pleasantly sheltered in the defile, so she put the specimen bag on the ground and took her other bag, removing from it a flask of water and some bread and cheese acquired in James Town. She sat on the ground at the edge of the trees and ate some lunch. When she had finished she lay down for a while, and drifted into sleep.

She woke suddenly at the sound, she imagined, of someone walking through the trees, but when she sat up there was nothing, only the sound of wind passing through the mulberry leaves. She picked up her lunch bag and walked out of the defile, heading back to James Town.

She was at the edge of the plain when she remembered the specimen bag, and shook her head in irritation with herself. That little nap must have discombobulated her. She turned and walked back to the gut of mulberry trees.

But when she walked down into the trees, she could not find her bag. She spent a half-hour walking around the secluded and dark copse, but every tree looked exactly the same, growing close together as if for comfort against the bleak plain outside the defile. Astounded at her own stupidity, and mourning the little specimen bag with the literal fruits of the day's walk, she gave up and walked back towards James Town.

That evening, Abigail cooked for them again. It had only been three evenings, but already an odd domesticity had descended. Seale's readiness to welcome them into his home was in keeping with the openness of the other islanders she had encountered. They had become used, it seemed, to putting up sailors and other visitors from vessels at anchor off James Town. She thought Seale must be lonely, and filled his life with drink and women and now, perhaps, with the intrigue of a botanical husband and his wife.

Charles and Seale poured themselves drinks, and gazed over an elaborate map that Seale had made of the island: the template, he said, for a planned model he wished to construct.

Once again, she looked out into the dark from the kitchen, though this time she felt no watching presence out there. Or, to be more accurate, her mind did not seem to invent one.

Charles had visited Sir William's house, Mount Pleasant, while Abigail had been exploring, finding mulberries, and losing her specimen bag. He had described Mount Pleasant's situation as 'Cornish, in its way, though sharper, higher and altogether wilder than Cornwall', and the house as having 'a chimney breast which would nestle comfortably in Suffolk or the Cotswolds.' He had a way with description.

Sir William had been at home, and had greeted Charles kindly enough. Charles had given Sir William a flavour of the same story he had told Seale: how he worked for the Royal Society as a botanist. But he had added a new element – that he was a cousin of one Captain Burroughs who, he understood, had recently taken on a new role as assistant treasurer. Assistant, presumably, to Sir William.

Edgar Burroughs had arrived on the island, Sir William told Charles, two weeks before their own arrival. He did not live in James Town, but in a house on the eastern edge of the island, above a place called Prosperous Bay. He had only visited Sir William once, two days after his arrival. Sir William had stated this was not unusual; the assistant treasurer, he told Charles, 'is not responsible to me, but to East India House. I have no dealings with him or his predecessors, and never have had.'

Charles said the old fellow had seemed aggrieved by this, and suspected there had been bad blood between him and

London about it. Indeed, such was his resentment that he seemed to positively welcome any suggestion of impropriety that might attach itself to the assistant treasurer.

'Did Sir William believe your story?' asked Abigail.

'I think he did. I flattered him terribly, called him the most prominent man on St Helena, after the Governor, by virtue of his long years of service to the Company and the island. I fancy he is not used to such talk so far from England.'

'You are turning into a politician, husband,' she had said.

'I do not welcome the development, wife,' he had replied.

So it was that Prosperous Bay was the object under discussion with Seale – though Charles covered his interest beneath the disguise of botanical interest.

'Prosperous Bay?' said Seale, looking down at his map. 'An odd place to site any kind of botanical garden, Horton. No one even lives up there, as far as I know. Other than the Baxters, of course.'

'The Baxters?'

'An old island family. Been here as long as anyone. They live out that way, too. There.'

The two men leaned over the map, and Abigail returned to her cooking. She listened to them murmuring, and tasted the fish stew bubbling over the little fire in the kitchen. It needed a good deal more cooking, so she left it to bubble and returned to the parlour. She stood behind the two men, and looked at the map over their shoulders.

'The abandoned Dutch fort is here,' Seale was saying, pointing to a scribble on the edge of the island. His map was richly detailed and, to Abigail's surprise, magnificently drawn.

'And these?' said Charles, pointing to the map.

'Two batteries: Gregory's and Cox's. They guard the east side of the island, which is where the bulk of shipping appears off the island. You will have gone round Barn Point here, to the north-east of the batteries and the fort, when you arrived. The winds dictate this passage.'

'What else is over there?'

'It is not at all populated; the landscape is the most unwelcoming on the island. Very little grows there. There is a quarry a little inland, and there are two small bays: Turk's Cap, which is virtually impossible to land at, and Prosperous Bay just to the south.'

'Why is it called Prosperous Bay?'

'It was the first place an English ship landed when retaking the island from the Dutch.'

'And the Baxters – which is their house?'

Abigail saw Seale look at her husband. There was clear suspicion in his eyes.

'Here.' Seale pointed to a significantly sized square shape on the map, between Turk's Cap Bay and Prosperous Bay. 'Baxter's Gut, it's called. That's how long they've been there.'

'An impressive house?'

'No, I would not say that. I confess to only having seen it twice, both times from the sea. One could almost assume it abandoned. It must be terribly exposed to the winds.'

'And yet it sees ships arriving. Indeed, is it not the best dwelling on the island for such a purpose?'

Seale frowned at the map.

'Yes. I believe it may be. It is why the Dutch built a fort there.'

Charles leaned into the map again.

'And this?'

Seale looked at where Charles's finger touched the map. It was a point just south of Turk's Cap Bay, about Baxter's Gut.

'Halley's Point? It's said he fell in there and had to be rescued.'

'Who fell in? Edmond Halley?'

'That is what is said.'

'He explored by water, too?'

'Well, that is what is said.'

Charles frowned.

'A lonely point below an abandoned fort,' said Abigail, to no one in particular. 'An odd place to find a stargazer.'

1776: THE YEAR MINA BAXTER'S
SON WAS TAKEN

He came for their son amidst thunder and rain.

The knock sounded on the door of the house soon after dark. Edgar was in bed and, for once, sleeping soundly. Her breasts were sore. He was getting too big to be fed by the breast, though island women often did so well past the age of two.

Did she know, during those first two years, that this night would come?

She opened the door, and there was John. He had come alone. The rain had drenched his hair and face, water dripped down his nose and his oilcloth coat let water fall down onto the floor.

'It's time, Mina.'

He stepped over her threshold, she was pushed back, and it was the first act of violence between them, despite all the arguments of the last two years. When she had fallen pregnant, he had assumed she would come back to England with him, that they would marry and raise the child. Even when she had told him that her future was on the island, he had not raised a hand to her. He had not even raised his voice. He had simply frozen over, like a tray of water in an icehouse. She remembered the warmth of him in her hand. It was like a memory from childhood: warm, unclear, impossibly distant.

He walked through the parlour, dripping water as he went, towards Edgar's room. She went with him, and began to pull back on his arms.

But even then, even while she pulled, she held back. She had known this moment would come. She knew her choices. Go with him. Kill him, or die trying. Or let him take her son.

Even now, those words 'her son' felt misaligned. Not wrong, precisely, but not quite right, as if the wrong planet had appeared in the wrong constellation. Her breasts still ached with the violence of the child's feeding, and there was a bruise on her upper arm where his little hand squeezed her skin tight as he fed, his eyes on hers, determined and hungry. She had looked into those eyes countless times, and on the lonely nights when she and Edgar sat together in this distant house on the eastern tip of the island, the abandoned fort looking over them, on those nights she had tried to find it in herself to love this oddly intense little creature. And, as often as not, she had failed.

What was wrong with her?

She pulled back on John's arms, and casually he stopped, turned, and smashed her away with the back of his hand. A hard, calculated, fierce blow to her face, it knocked her down both with its force, and with its meaning.

Keep away, bitch. You could have been my wife. Instead you have ruined me.

She stayed down on the floor while he went into Edgar's bedroom. She watched the dark square of the opened door, heard his tender words to the child and the child's sleepy wordless responses. Drawers opened and the wardrobe banged, and then John reappeared with Edgar wrapped in a blanket and held within his oilskin coat.

She stood then, propelled by what remained of the maternal instinct in her ravaged breast. The sight of the child looking out at her with its father's eyes was almost too much to bear.

'John, *please.*'

'Come with me, then, Mina. It is not too late. Come with me, tonight, and be my wife. We'll have more like him. We can live with my brother in Seal. We can prosper and be happy.'

His flat, unsmiling face told the lie of his words. He was speaking things he did not feel. A final speech, for form's sake.

Except he was not the only one acting out a role. She was as dishonest as he. She knew, she had always known, that her place was here. Her obligation to her father was too strong, her sense of her family too unyielding, the burden of their history too, too heavy.

And this man and this . . . boy. They were not her family.

How could that be?

She looked at the child's face. It looked back, a slight frown on its chubby brow. Its father's red hair stood untidily from its scalp, threatening to thicken and lengthen as John's had done.

It seemed to smile. Heavens protect her, it seemed to smile.

She looked down at the floor and though no words were spoken, her meaning would haunt the rest of her existence. She heard a curse, the slam of the door, and they were gone.

MRS HORTON ENCOUNTERS A MONSTER

Seale had to report for work the next day in the Company stores, but Charles and Abigail had their own plans. They had discussed them in bed the previous evening, their voices low and urgent while the incessant wind blew outside the window.

Charles had decided he would explore the land over by Prosperous Bay, but it had sounded a bleak place in Seale's telling. Abigail said she would walk up to Halley's Point to find the remains of the astronomer's observatory. She saw Charles's relief that she was not coming with him, which suggested he anticipated some danger from the assistant treasurer, if he was at home. She imagined a table of potential risks in his head, against which he plotted her movements and her exposure to danger. She wondered if he realised quite how transparent he was to her.

They left early, walking into the island together. They separated on a path around a steep defile called the Devil's Punch Bowl on Seale's elaborate map.

'Take care, wife,' he said, and he hugged her to him, an unusual gesture.

'And you, husband,' she replied, and walked away from him, up the path that climbed the hill called Halley's Mount. She looked back once and saw him watching her, standing some twenty yards below, his dark hair blown off his face by the wind. He lifted his hand, turned and walked towards the east. She, in her turn, watched him for a minute or two. *So like our marriage*, she thought. *He watches me and I watch him.*

The mist was low, astonishingly so, such that she walked into it as if climbing up into a cloud. After only a few minutes, the visibility became appalling; she could barely see six feet in front of her. The air was moist on her skin, and her hair began to feel like a damp cloth wrapped around her head. She walked slowly, taking tiny and careful steps, acutely aware of the steep rocky slopes which must fall away to her side, could she but see them.

How was she ever going to find the 150-year-old remains of an observatory in this fog? But the concern was misplaced. Whoever had built this path meant for it to lead directly to Halley's observation point. Perhaps Halley himself had laid it out. After ten minutes of careful going, she saw a low wall at the side of the path, overrun with what she took to be wild pepper. She climbed over the wall, feeling the ground on the other side with her foot as she went.

Inside the wall, the ground was flat, artificially so, and she spied the shapes of half a dozen rocks and manmade stone platforms. It might have been a house, of course, one which had fallen into disrepair. Or it might have been the haunt of an astronomer.

She sat down on one of the rocks, and looked around her into the grey wall of the mist. What an ironic disappointment it was, to sit so, perhaps in the same position as a man who had been charting the stars. Halley gazed across the universe. She could barely see her own feet.

The only sound that penetrated the mist was the wind: constant, almost (but not quite) maddening in its persistence. But then she thought she heard something else, under the wind. The sound of something moving beyond the wall of the observatory, carefully exploring the landscape she could not see.

A goat, perhaps? Or something else?

She held her breath, because the sound she could hear had a purpose to it, and there was a clear moment of terror when she realised this was the case. Had she been followed? Was there someone out there in the mist seeking her out, unable to spy her in the mist just as she was unable to spy him? She swallowed, and the sound of it in her ears was like the rumbling of a reawakened volcano.

The noise continued for a minute that felt like a century. Then it subsided, and all that was left was the sound of the wind, and she was forced to ask if her imagination was once again playing vicious games with her.

Perhaps I shall be revisiting Dr Drysdale after all.

The mist began to loosen. Was it rising, or just dissipating? She wondered about the relativity of observation. How would it look from another peak? She was being revealed to the world. Or was the world being revealed to her? The sun began to pick out the colours of the wall, the rocks, the ground.

After a few minutes, the vista opened out to her, and if there had been any doubt before, it lifted with the sun. This was indeed where Halley had placed his observatory. The mist dissolved like salt in heated water, and she was up above the world. The blue Atlantic Ocean stretched all around, and above it the stupendous vault of the heavens. She felt a single, pure moment of ecstatic awe in the face of Creation, and then she saw her leather satchel.

It was sitting on the low wall over which she had climbed. If it had been there when she'd arrived, she may not have seen it.

But why would it have already been there?

She stood up from her rock, walked over to the wall and picked up the bag. She looked around her to see if the island had an explanation for this rematerialisation. It had nothing to say on the subject.

She opened the bag. She was certain that someone else had rifled through the inside. The specimens from yesterday all seemed to be there, but there was a tidy order to them which she did not remember imposing. She had just stuffed the leaves and shoots and fruits in, planning to order and perhaps categorise them back in James Town. She had not even looked inside while she botanised, but she was sure the order that now persisted inside the bag could not have emerged spontaneously.

A crack of a twig, then, and she looked around sharply. Only the path and the hillside and the spectacle of the view.

'Hello? Is there somebody there?'

Answer came there none. Yet there was a sudden (imagined?) watchfulness to the place, a sense of purpose . . .

'Nonsense.' She spoke the word aloud, as if this would convince her. She would *not* allow her mind to indulge in ridiculous fancy. She knew where such indulgence ended. Madness, visions, fantasies of pursuit.

And yet . . .

She put the satchel over her shoulder. She looked around the remains of the little observatory, seeing only rocks and bricks and flattened ground. She stepped over the wall again, back the way she had come, heading down the hill, but then, on an impulse, she stepped behind a high lonely rock by the side of the path, which had seemingly rolled down from somewhere further up the hill.

She waited, controlling her breathing, listening to the sounds of the island, which were now audible after the lifting of the mist. The wind in the hills, a noise always there. A goat braying some distance away, another goat replying. And, almost beyond the range of hearing, a slow, steady creep along the path from further up the hill. Her breathing became a little ragged, and she forced it to smooth over. She should leave, now. Why this infernal curiosity?

A figure appeared. A man. But when she shrieked and he turned his face towards her, she saw it was not a man at all but some ugly beast: no nose, no ears, and when it raised its arm towards her, no hand either. Its dark skin and almost bald head were covered in evil scars, and its eyes were as dark as caves. It reached out towards her, both arms (there was a hand on the left arm, but it had no thumb), and she was on the point of swinging the satchel at the thing's head to buy herself time to flee when the figure froze, and sniffed the air, and said something which sounded like an angry curse in an incomprehensible tongue, then turned away and ran down the hill.

Abigail stood still for a while, her eyes straining wide, her heart running at a frenzied gallop. After a few minutes, she felt calm enough to look around the edge of her hiding place.

Whatever the thing had been, it had gone. She followed in the same direction, though she would dearly like to have chosen another, and thought of Caliban. It was only then that she remembered Edmond Halley's own encounter with an island ogre – one with no ears, no nose, and a missing hand.

'Did you feel threatened?' was the first question Charles asked, somewhat predictably.

'No,' she replied. 'Not at all. I was scared, of course, but once the initial shock had passed I felt sorry for it.'

'Sorry?'

'Yes. There seemed to be a kind of longing about it. Like it wanted me to approach it – that was why it left my bag behind. And then the way it scurried down the hill . . . I swear, Charles, it was more scared of me than I was of it. It was like some kind of animal.'

They sat in Seale's parlour, waiting for him to return home from the stores. Abigail had made some tea, to which they added fresh goat's milk. The taste of the Company tea with the island milk, which was still new to both of them, was exquisite.

'Can it be, Charles? Can it really be true that this is the same creature Edmond Halley encountered?'

'There may be other explanations.'

'Such as?'

'I do not know. A conspiracy, perhaps, to make us think this is the same man. If indeed it is a man.'

'But why?'

Charles shook his head.

'I do not know, wife.'

'And what of your day?'

'I walked out to the old Dutch fort on the far eastern side of the island.' He described it to her: a plain stone building built during the short Dutch occupation of St Helena. Anything of value – weaponry, or iron of any kind – had long since been removed from the place. The only mystery about the place had been a single locked door, with no external metalwork at all.

'It looked like a large sheet of ancient wood shoved directly into the doorframe. It was impossible to open.'

He had tried getting through that door – had tried shoulders and kicks, smashing it with rocks, forcing the edges with his pocket knife. But all to no avail. The door had remained steadfast, in such a way that strongly suggested to Charles that it was bolted from the inside. But given there was no obvious means of ingress, how could that possibly be?

'You believe someone is hiding something within?'

'It is possible. I walked around the place several times, but then I looked over the cliff face beside the fort, down to the little bay below – we saw it on Seale's map. Prosperous Bay. Is that not a name to conjure with?'

'How so?'

'Abigail, I was a Kent lad and, what is more, I was a north Kent lad.'

He described to her the stretch of coast between Margate and Gravesend, the southern border of the stretch of water where the Thames and the Medway gave up their individual identities to become the North Sea. A coast with numerous beaches and landing places, looked over by little houses, stalked by men carrying torches and lamps, men in oilcloths and hats pushing carts and barrows. Smugglers, all of them, exploiters of the financial gaps which Whitehall ministers were prone to open and close with their incessant fiddling with duties and taxes. Charles had remembered the beaches these illicit men used, and they had something of Prosperous Bay about them. Wild and lonely on the surface, but filled with possibility.

'Did you walk down to it?'

'I tried. I could not find the way. It seemed very much to me that the one path down had been destroyed; there was a defile down which a path might have led, but it was filled with rocks.'

'Then what use can it have as a smuggler's cove?'

'I asked myself the same question, but for different reasons.'

'What were they?'

'Looking down on the bay from the fort, I saw a boat pulled up onto the beach. I found myself wondering who it belonged to.'

1815: THE YEAR IN WHICH
MINA'S SON RETURNED

Mina did not immediately recognise the man from the Company. There had been no warning of his arrival; she had received no visit from the Governor to tell her that East India House was despatching a new man. It had been eighteen months or more since Captain Suttle had taken his wandering eyes and hands back to England. Such a hateful man – even a woman of almost sixty years had not been able to avoid his disgusting glances and leering smiles. He had talked of the females of the island to her, had boasted of his dalliances with various whores, and had seemed to expect her to be excited by it.

Mina had despised him. She had enjoyed the peace since he had left. The work under the fort continued with new efficiency, the Chinese labourers of whom she had once complained now so efficient that output had almost doubled. Suttle had been pleased with the results, but Suttle had also come back, time and time and time again, to the subject of the *Opera*.

She had tried deflecting him or even ignoring him, but Mina

was far too intelligent a woman to pretend to herself that the Company would lose interest in the *Opera*. It was all they cared about. Every missive to her from London mentioned it; Putnam, the new manager of the private trade office who now wrote all this correspondence, begged and cajoled and threatened. She must reveal the *Opera* to them. She had no offspring. Her family was at an end. The reason for keeping the *Opera* secret no longer applied. When she reached death's threshold, there would be no other Baxters to protect and no other Baxters to remember.

But Suttle had failed in his cajoling, and had presumably been recalled. The man had not even said farewell to her. He had simply stopped coming to see her, and after a few weeks of his absence she walked down the hill from her house to his little dwelling and knocked on the door. There was no answer. She had tried the door, and it had opened, and she'd gone inside. The house had been empty. Suttle was gone.

The Governor had confirmed Suttle's departure. She was pleased, but also disconcerted. Previous assistant treasurers had not left until their replacement arrived on the island. Little handover ceremonies had become the norm: Captain Jenkins to Captain Fox, Captain Fox to Captain Campbell, Captain Campbell to Captain Suttle.

A blissful eighteen months followed, until the day he had arrived, knocking on the door of her house one evening as the sun began to sink over Halley's Mount. She had opened the door, and had seen him there, with his new suit and the hat rising from his head and the red hair beneath it being revealed.

No, she had not recognised him, then. But he had stepped into the house without an invitation, she had taken a step back, and she had seen his eyes, and she had known because those eyes had not left her dreams – not really – in the intervening forty years.

'Hello, mother,' Edgar had said.

Back from him, back from him she had stepped, her hand to her mouth and her eyes wide. The baby who had been taken from her, the mouth she had suckled, had turned into a tall, pale man with that shock of red hair. His father's hair. He was as tall as her and his face was broad and almost Slavic, the Dutch inheritance of the Aaksters. He looked powerful. One look into his eyes and she was back, back, back over the years, back to the chair into which she now sank, back looking into his eyes as he fed on her, those eyes which seemed to be full of something old and terrifying.

He closed the door behind himself.

'Mother, I am the new assistant treasurer,' he had said. 'Your family line is, you see, still intact. So we will now begin our lessons. You will teach me the *Opera*, as your father once taught you.'

MRS HORTON AND THE DEVIL

Abigail walked with Seale and her husband down to the harbour wall the next morning, and watched the massive rollers in the ocean with horrid trepidation while the two men made the boat ready. They would be at it for some time, it seemed – Seale admitted that he had not taken the boat out for some time, and it appeared barely seaworthy. Her heart was in her mouth at the thought of her husband rowing out into those waves in a boat which, from here on James Town's wharf, seemed about as robust as a muslin curtain.

'I will leave you to this,' she said to Charles.

'As you wish, wife,' he said, barely glancing at her as he inspected the bottom of Seale's boat, coiling a length of rope between his elbow and fingers as he did so, a task which looked as natural to him as breathing.

Men and boats. She would not try to interject.

The soldiers at the drawbridge waved her back into James Town as if she were an old friend. She had begun to feel comfortable in this strange place – almost at home. The bright sky, the green of the foliage and the brown of the rock, the warm incessant breathing of the wind. She remembered the dark grey skies of Wapping, the smell of shit and piss in the street, the tarry thickness of the air.

She walked back up the main street, and fetched her little leather satchel from the Castle of Otranto, glancing at the map which was still laid out on the table, the map over which the three of them had talked the previous night when Seale returned. He had taken some drink, she could see, so she had made coffee and he had sobered up quickly, and had answered her husband's questions carefully. The two men had a project now – the bay below the old fort – and like all men it was the only connection they needed.

Once more, she walked up the valley towards the interior. There was no mist today, even at the highest peaks, and this as much as anything else lifted the unease she initially felt at walking back up towards Halley's Mount. The creature she had seen was not there.

And, of course, that was the real terror: that she had, indeed, imagined it. That her mind was once again painting pictures of things that did not exist. Charles had made no such suggestion the previous day – but was he just being careful?

The human mind is uncharted, Dr Drysdale had told her. *Your experience at Brooke House demonstrates that fact. It may even be possible to put one man's thoughts into another man's head. The mesmerists believe something like this, do they not?*

They did believe that – and so, clearly, did Dr Drysdale, though he had imagined that *she* had some ability in this direction. Well, he had been wrong, and she had been abused. She would think no more of it. Perhaps she could confront her own imagination up there on Halley's Mount. Is that what Dr Drysdale would suggest?

The path up the mountainside in bright sunlight was a different thing – cosy and rural where yesterday it had been terrible. The dogwood trees cast polite shadows. She picked the occasional flower or leaf: the strange purple bent grass which seemed indigenous to the island; three or four different species of *Aspidium* which she did not immediately recognise; a thick rush which she thought was the same as that used on the roofs of the island, and which she took to be *Fimbristylis textilis;* cherry laurel trees, their leaves smelling slightly of the same almonds Charles had described when he talked of Gay-Lussac's *hydro-cyanic* acid; large *Lobelias* with astonishing white flowers; a stout shrub which she saw in several places, with thick branches, which she confessed herself to be stumped by; a tree which she took to be a kind of laburnum, but of a type she had never seen before. She could not help but feel a stab of excitement at this, even though she knew it was almost impossible that she had come across a new species on an island which the Royal Society had visited so often, albeit looking for myths and not botanical specimens.

She reached the remains of Halley's little observatory, and once again stood watching the blue horizon for a while. No ogres presented themselves. She had been collecting for a good while, so decided to walk east to see if she might catch a glimpse of this abandoned fort. Who knew, she might even see her husband and Seale down in the sea in that untrustworthy boat. She walked quickly. And then there was a moment when she realised that she was probably being followed.

The moment did not consist of any great revelation – she didn't spy a head disappearing behind a rock, didn't hear a careful footstep on the hill behind her – but slowly a dozen or more little signals coalesced into this new realisation: that someone was trailing her, and being very careful about it.

Immediately she imagined the ugly creature of the previous day. Did it wish her ill after all?

A definitive crack of a twig. Her follower had made a

mistake. Whoever it was, they were fifty feet or so behind her, to the south west. She turned around a rocky outcrop – much as she had done the day before – and immediately ducked down and waited. Seconds later, a figure worked his way around the corner, silently and carefully.

It was Ken, the island boy who they'd encountered on their first evening on St Helena. He was alone. No Hippo accompanied him.

'Can I help you?' asked Abigail from her place in the shadow of the rock. The boy yelped, and seemed about to run, but then thought better of it.

'Why, Mrs Horton! What a surprise!'

He smiled his big white-toothed smile, and his charm turned on like an oil lamp.

'You were following me, Ken.'

'Following you? Why no, madam, 'tis a madness to think so!'

'You were. Why?'

'Mrs Horton, you're a suspicious lady, so you are!'

'Ken, I'm warning you . . .'

'Please, Mrs Horton,' said another voice, and a tall man with a shock of red hair emerged from behind the rock. 'It was not Ken who was following you. It was me.'

Seale's boat was an ancient but sturdy thing. Horton imagined it being passed down from Seale to Seale, constantly patched up and added to until the original boat was little more than the idea of a boat, not a single original piece surviving. It might have been as old as the island, this boatish concept. He claimed to have built it himself, but Horton thought there was rather more to it than that.

The ancient thing took some time to prepare. After Abigail left, they were at it for another two hours, though Horton did not begrudge the time. Preparation for sailing allowed him to occupy his hands and the front of his mind in matters of knots and sheets which were as ingrained in his muscles and bones as the memory of the deep orange sand on the beach at Margate. And meanwhile the case churned in the deepest parts of his self, the place from where connections and narratives emerged into the light.

Eventually they were ready, and by now the sea was calm. Seale gave thanks for that. 'The rollers beyond the quay can be murderous,' he said. Horton remembered their arrival, and Abigail's difficulty in getting out of the boat. He remembered the eyes of the men in the boat and the way they rested on his wife.

He wondered if Abigail was safe, and where Edgar Burroughs the assistant treasurer might be. Perhaps he should, after all, have fetched her, brought her with them – but was she safer on this old boat, or on that lonely land? Where was she most at risk? How did he protect his wife from a world which seemed inclined to do her injury? What was the calculus of danger? The unending, unanswerable question.

But now it was too late, they were leaving the wharf, and James Town and its hilltop forts slowly pulled away from them. They bounced and fell through the rollers, and then they were in the calmer and deeper waters beyond. They turned east out of the little bay, the shore on their starboard side, a single sail hoisted by Seale catching the wind with more efficiency than Horton would have ever credited.

'What is that?'

They were approaching Prosperous Bay. Horton pointed at a fissure in the cliff face, a gap through into the island interior, a dry valley which reached its end perhaps a hundred feet into the air. Below it was a huge cave.

'That is Halley's Cave,' says Seale. 'Or so I will call it when

I build my model. It is where he explored in the underwater suit he had constructed.'

He pointed to a single peak in the interior, visible along the fissure in the rock above them.

'That is Halley's Mount,' he said.

Horton looked at the mountain. From up there, Halley had not just been able to see the stars; he'd been able to see down this fissure, and thence out to sea. And he'd decided, it seemed, to explore this particular cave, using this so-called 'underwater suit' of his own devising. Why had Halley come all the way down here?

He pictured it: a ship, anchored off the shore. A boat, let down into the rolling sea and rowed to the beach at Prosperous Bay. A cargo, carried away by that same boat and onto that same ship. An astronomer, high up in the mountains in the dark, watching lights appear off the shoreline rather than gazing at the stars. The stench of illicit activity hung over Prosperous Bay like the nosegay of a Covent Garden beau hunting down a whore.

The bay was now to their larboard; Seale was heaving to before the fissure in the rock, and the cave below it, turning his bow through the south-easterly wind and adjusting his sail so the opposing pressures of sail and wind held them in place. He did this efficiently and well, and Horton could only admire his seamanship. He imagined the mountain dropping away beneath them, down into the depths. Take the sea away, he thought, and this might be a gentle slope leading up to the face of an escarpment, in which there was a gigantic cave below a waterfall. There were, in fact, features just like this in the island's interior.

'We can go no further in?' Horton asked.

Seale looked at him. He had asked few questions about why a botanist needed to see the island from the sea. He seemed to want to ask some questions now, but Horton also saw the man's own interest in their adventure. He wanted to sail in, if only for the thrill of it.

'We can try.' So in they went.

'It is true then, Mrs Horton. You are a botanist. Among a good many other things.'

His words were chilling, even in the warm breeze that came in from the south, over the island at their back. She stood ten feet from him, and even at that distance she could feel how closed off he was, how self-contained. His thick red hair was churned by the wind, but his face and, more to the point, his eyes were dead still.

'You have been watching me?' she asked.

'Of course I have been watching you. I make it my business to watch people like you. And people like your husband. I have been watching both of you for a good long while.'

He had no weapon – no pistol, no knife – that she could see. But then she looked around her, saw the rocks and the steep slopes, and observed that a well-timed shove would be as effective as a knife to the throat. The landscape was the only weapon he needed.

And yet why did she immediately think of murder? What was it about this man that bespoke fierce and immediate danger?

'Sir, you have me at a disadvantage.'

He smiled.

'I do, do I not? Perhaps a good deal more than you might imagine.'

He didn't give his name. His dark suit was impossibly clean, his hands and nails impossibly well groomed. It was as if he'd stepped off Jermyn Street and onto a hillside in the South Atlantic.

'Have you found anything interesting, Mrs Horton?'

He said her name as if he were stabbing her.

'There is much to see of interest on St Helena,' she replied, carefully.

'Isn't there? Of course, a great many of our plants are not indigenous. St Helena has been planted with the seeds of the whole globe, Mrs Horton. We are as it were a microcosm. I believe that is the correct word. From the Greek, yes? *Mikros* meaning small, and *kosmos*, meaning world.'

'You are learned in Greek, sir. But not in manners. You have not seen fit to introduce yourself.'

'No indeed. Let me remedy that. My name is Edgar Burroughs, madam. I am the recently appointed assistant treasurer on St Helena.'

The name, though suspected, still had the capacity to chill.

'You have recently been in London, sir, have you not?'

Why she said this, she did not know. She was scared of what he might do, but she was also angry. The man's impertinence was vicious, and if he had done the things her husband suspected him of doing, he was also the very Devil. Abigail felt a clear pulse of hatred towards this man, an immediate and visceral emotional dislike. It was as if he'd stolen her home from her; which, she supposed, he had.

'You are not in London, now, Mrs Horton,' was all he said. 'And thus you may not benefit from London's protections.'

He looked over to the east of the island.

'Where is your husband, Mrs Horton?'

'I know not.'

'A lie, I am sure. A lying woman. The most common of the species.'

'Sir, you . . .'

'I wish to make your husband an offer,' he said. 'Work for me, live on the island, build a new life. There are worse offers. A house in the sun. Better botanising than is available in Wapping.'

It was a finely calibrated turn in the conversation, and she lost her social balance for a second. He smiled at her – the smile of a torturer picking up a new implement. He had said *Wapping* with the precise care of a surgeon interrogating a cadaver's nervous system.

'This is a kind of Paradise, Mrs Horton. Open to the sky and immaculate in its isolation. So much more pleasing than two rooms near the London Dock.'

God, he knew a frightening amount about them.

'And how would your husband reply?'

'I know not.'

'And I believe you. He is a close one, Charles, is he not?'

'And who are you, to make such offers?'

'Oh, a mere functionary. A guardian of fiduciary matters.'

'You speak for the Governor?'

He smiled, looking at her. His eyes were black buttons, his face long and pinched, his feet cloven inside those beautiful boots.

'No. The Governor speaks for me, my dear.'

'Charles is a good man. The best man I know.'

'And I am a good man too, after my fashion. I preserve the island's secrets, you see. Even when those secrets emerge thousands of miles away.'

'At any cost?'

'At any cost.'

'Including the lives of innocents?'

'No one is innocent, Mrs Horton. Least of all the wife of a Wapping constable who knows more than he lets on, and is privy to secrets he should not be.'

She saw something, then, down in the depths of his face. Something dark and old. It was as if a demon really did exist within those eyes. She wondered if his mother had ever seen it there.

He stepped forward, and for a moment she imagined shoving him, hard, so that his tall black body tumbled, sharp face over cloven hooves, down into the gully below. All it would take would be a step or two.

'Abigail, my dear,' he said, smiling his well-groomed but empty smile. 'We should be friends, not enemies. I am delighted to make your acquaintance, at last.'

'Now, you make somewhat free with my Christian name, sir. It is not welcome.'

'But it is such a good name for you,' he said. 'Pretty, but sturdy. Appropriate, for the wife of a Wapping river constable, would you not say?'

She almost ran, but what would have been the point? He would be upon her in seconds.

'I would like to take a small walk with you,' he said.

'I fear that would not be in my best interests,' she replied.

'On the contrary. I would like to discuss my proposal with you. There will be no harm.'

'Do I have a choice?'

'No, my dear. You do not.'

He walked over to her, and with an impossible smile held out his arm. With a sense of leaping over a precipice, she took it, and together they walked towards the east, away from James Town and towards that eastern point Charles and Seale had become excited by the previous evening.

She wondered if once again she was to be little more than a bargaining chip in a game between men. The bruise on her arm screamed in dull alarm, echoing the shrieks in her head.

The sea was astonishingly clear. He could see the mass of the island declining away beneath them, down into depths he could not possibly fathom.

Something gigantic swam past them in the water, bigger

than a man, fat and slow and incurious. It was a sea-cow slowly making its way away from Seale's boat, like a baronet disturbed at his club by a member of the lower classes. The sight of it calmed him.

He turned his head back to the rocky cliff. For a moment he could not see the opening to the cave; the tide had swept them along a little, shifting the angle such that he could no longer work out where the cave was. They had been pushed southwards, clockwise around the island. The boat was now in front of Prosperous Bay, and he saw the other boat pulled up onto the beach there. 'We need to go back against the current,' he said, and Seale moved the tiller.

Two heads broke the surface and watched them, and he almost cried out in alarm. They had heads and whiskers like dogs, though no ears that he could see, their snouts as slick as oil on the surface of stone. Sea-lions, come to watch the strange sight of humans struggling in their realm. He remembered seeing these creatures when he was on board the *Phoebus*.

The island's rocky sea-face enclosed them as they came close to the cave, passing over a line between light and dark, under the shoulder of the island itself. The mast of the little boat would soon scrape the rock itself, which was turning over the top of them. The current suddenly changed, as if the island was sucking the boat into itself, and Seale hurriedly threw out the anchor behind them.

The rock's surface was ribbed with little seams of strange phosphorescence. This was interesting, but it did not help them move away.

'So deep behind us,' said Seale. 'The anchor is not ... Ah, there it is.'

The cable stiffened as the anchor gripped onto whatever lay below them, and Seale began to haul them out. Looking up into the mouth of the cave, Horton imagined an opening below them. They may have been suspended above a gigantic opening in the side of the island, the top of it just visible above the water's surface as a cave. He looked down at the water, expecting to see nothing but utter, desolate darkness, but instead he saw a bottom, where he least expected there to be one. It looked loose, not compacted like a sea bed or hard like rock, like a rockfall beneath the water, and it fell away steeply into the depths where Seale had nearly lost his anchor.

The idea of the boat hanging above that opening was vivid and terrifying. Where did those sea-lions come from? Were there colonies of creatures down there, waiting for a visitor, hungry and aware and somehow capable of sight in the pitch-blackness?

The current was strong, and Seale made little headway at first, so they remained suspended over that odd rockfall. Is this where Halley had descended in his underwater suit, a stargazer in Neptune's realm? The idea seemed preposterous.

The sea-cow returned, anxious to see its visitors.

Abigail and the devil stood on the windswept point, watching the little boat below bob in the waves. She could see the heads of two creatures swimming in the sea around Seale's boat – perhaps they were seals, too. The boat had emerged from beneath them as if exiting the island itself.

'The brave constable puts himself about, does he not?' said Burroughs, beside her. He turned away from the cliff, pulling her arm gently but with nonetheless indecent force. 'Shall we take some tea at my residence?'

They walked away from the cliff top. The abandoned Dutch fort was above them and to their right. They walked away from it, down a hill and up another, until they came to what looked like a farm on the point opposite the fort. But there were no animals to be seen and nothing was being grown, as far as Abigail could make out. The house itself was well tended, and behind it stood a barn which looked just as cared-for.

Burroughs walked them past the buildings, and after another five minutes' walking they came to another simple dwelling, on its own, in a sort of garden enclosed by a stone wall. Several huge green plants dominated this space, and the smell of them and their morphology led Abigail directly to identification.

'*Cannabis sativa*, Mr Burroughs?' she asked. 'Have you been intoxicating yourself?'

'I am impressed, Abigail,' he replied, opening the front door of the little house as he spoke. There seemed to be about a dozen different locks and keys. 'Yes, those are indeed cannabis plants. The stuff grows like weeds here. My father told me about it. He also introduced me to a delicious way of consuming it. The Indians call it *bhang* – one adds it to milk. It is quite intense.'

The door opened at last.

'Now, if you please.'

She hesitated at the entrance. She felt as if she were going into a mouth. His smile was fixed and devoid of anything. She went inside.

She was very scared, but had, she thought, a clear view of the situation. Burroughs wanted something from her husband. That odd remark about Charles 'discovering secrets' had stayed with her. She was, she supposed, a kind of hostage, but she was only worth anything to Burroughs unharmed. She was in danger, certainly, but perhaps not of an immediate nature.

The house was of a similar size to Seale's – a simple parlour with a kitchen off it, stairs leading up to an upper floor. There was some decoration, most of it appearing to come from India. There were also a great many books.

'What now?' she asked.

He sat down in a chair, crossed his legs and watched her.

'Now, I would like to talk,' he said.

'Perhaps I could make us some tea?' she said, and she saw that he was surprised and pleased. 'The tea here on the island is quite magnificent.'

'Ah yes,' said Burroughs. 'I'm sure Major Seale has an excellent supply. He keeps the stores, after all.'

Again, he had disturbed her. He knew so much about their movements and about their home. He seemed determined that she realise it.

'Your tea is in the kitchen?' she asked.

'Yes. In a jar with a Hindoo motif. I can see it from here.' He pointed into the kitchen, and smiled.

'And the kettle?'

'In the sink. I shall light a fire.'

While he lit the fire, she heard him whistling something tuneless and mildly irritating. Her botanising satchel was still over her shoulder, such that she could reach into it easily enough. She put some leaves into Seale's little kettle, added water, and took it through to the parlour. The fire was already blazing.

'Thank you, Abigail,' he said. He placed the kettle on the fire.

'Do you add milk?' she asked.

'Milk?' he replied. 'In tea? Hmm. I do keep milk, but usually for *bhang*. Well, Abigail, I believe in experiencing new things. I will fetch some milk, and some cups.'

He went into the kitchen, and returned with two cups and a jug of milk, which he set down on a table by the fire.

'Now. Do sit.'

He pointed to a chair, and she sat down. She looked at the kettle, and wondered how long it would take to boil, and whether there would be an odour.

'What will happen now?' she asked.

'What will happen? Nothing will happen. We will wait for your husband.'

'How will he know where to come?'

'He is an *investigator*, is he not? Think of this as a little test for him. The latest of many such tests.'

She did not know what he meant by that.

'May I read a book?' she asked.

'By all means,' he said, waving at the bookshelves in his hand. 'I know how much Abigail Horton relies on her books.'

She shivered as she stood and walked over to the bookcase. The man's knowledge of her was obscene. Her mind raced with anxiety as she pretended to look at the books, their spines blurring into one leather-bound miasma, until a few came into focus.

The selection of books seemed odd. It featured ancient philosophers and mathematicians – Aristotle, Plato, Euclid – but also more esoteric stuff she had not seen before: Roger Bacon, Trimethius, Ramon Gull, Pico della Mirandola – these names tugged at her mind and her memory. And there, another name: Cornelius Agrippa, the man whose name John Dee had evoked.

The kettle boiled, and Burroughs stood up to pour two cups, while she froze with her hands outstretched, frantically sniffing the air for any odd odour. She thought she could smell something. But could he? She heard the sound of liquid going into cups – first the tea, then the milk. Then, the sound of him sitting back down and sipping, carefully, from the hot drink.

On the next shelf, she found a set of works by John Dee: the *Propaedeumata Aphoristica*; the *Monas Hieroglyphica*; the *Mathematicall Preface*. And the rarest of all, the one she had never seen – the *Libri Mysteriorum*.

'This milk idea is excellent,' he said from behind her. 'The goat's milk of the island works wondrously well in *bhang,* too. Will you not sit and drink?'

'I am just perusing your books.'

'Ah, yes. Interesting, are they not?'

'You have some marvellous editions of John Dee's works.'

'Dee! Ha! Yes, indeed.'

She did not understand this strange exclamation. She took a book from the shelf – the *Libri Mysteriorum* – and affected to read it with her back to him, her heart so loud in her chest that she was sure he must be able to hear her tell-tale anxiety. But he said nothing. After a few minutes, he made a small grunting noise, and then there was a crash as he fell sideways onto a table.

She put down the book, and stood and walked over to him. She picked up her satchel from beside the sink and looked at the leaves inside, the remains of the ones she had added to the devil's tea.

'Hmm. Cherry laurel, after all.'

She went to find some rope.

He'd expected to find a cave, an entrance into the island's innards. He'd expected to find a way up inside the hill, a passage which ended, perhaps, at a bolted door inside an abandoned Dutch fort. That was the picture he had constructed in his mind; an internal construction, a repository of secrets and perhaps something more.

He remembered the sight of that loose rock and stone beneath the surface. It had not been the sea bed; it had consisted of larger rocks piled up unknowingly high. A place for sea-lions to scamper in, a place for Royal Society astronomers to lose their footing.

He helped Seale prepare the boat for their return, and they lifted the anchor and stowed it in the stern. Seale turned the bow away from the wind, and raised the sail, and they ran before the south-easterly back around the island. The old abandoned fort slipped away behind one of the island's steep headlands.

He needed to think of another way. That old locked door within the fort had taken on a symbolic weight. Behind it, he had begun to think, was the essential secret of this whole mystery: the reason for the deaths of the Johnsons, and before them the deaths of St Helena's assistant treasurers. It was the motivation he had been unable to uncover. He had sailed halfway around the world, only to stand before a door he could not open.

It seemed to take no time at all to sail back to James Town, and as he helped Seale tie up his boat Horton looked up into the island, up the valley to the peaks beyond. Somewhere in there lurked the new assistant treasurer, the elusive Edgar Burroughs. What was he about? Why did the island have need of this secretive post of assistant treasurer? And why did the holders of the post have to die?

Because they held a secret, he thought. A secret that Emma Johnson discovered. A secret valuable enough to blackmail Captain Suttle with. A secret deep enough to kill her for.

Their rope work finished, they walked back to Seale's house, nodding to the guards at the drawbridge like old friends. He had not been stopped in his investigations by the Governor or any of his militia. For now, his story of investigating the island's flora seemed to be holding. It might hold for some weeks, or a ship from London could arrive this very day with letters from the Company which proved his tale false. He had an unknown schedule to unlock an unseen mystery.

Abigail was not at the Castle when they arrived, and this brought the inevitable stab of fear. Where was she? The afternoon was drawing on, and the shadows of whatever trees

Abigail walked within must be lengthening on the ground. Why would she not stay in one place?

Seale made them tea, adding the delicious goat's milk. Horton stood staring at Seale's map, calculating vectors of visibility and distances between dwellings, trying not to think of Abigail.

She appeared after an hour of this, coming through the door in a hurry, her bonnet dishevelled and her face reddened. Wherever she had walked from she had done so at an incredible clip.

'Husband,' she said. 'I have met your assistant treasurer.'

'What . . .'

'Wait, I must rest.' She sat down in one of Seale's chairs, and Seale went to fetch her water. She sipped it and sat back with her eyes closed for a few moments, steadying herself. Horton saw no injury or sign of struggle. He went to sit next to her, taking her hand.

'I met him up by Halley's Mount,' she said, opening her eyes. 'He took me to a house near the fort, quite a small place near a larger farmhouse.'

'Did he force you to go with him?' asked Horton, his voice tight.

'He did, husband, yes. Oh, he never as much as touched me. But the threat of it was in everything he said.'

He'd known, of course, that this was possible. But now, facing it, he felt a dull helpless anger, and imagined another knife in his hand and Edgar Burroughs laid out on a table before him.

'What did he tell you?'

'He knows all about us, Charles. Where we live. What your work is. He said he had a job for you.'

'A job?'

'Yes. He said he wanted you to work for him. For us to make our future here.'

It was puzzling, this, extremely so. Unexpected and, in its own way, interesting.

'But he let you go?'

She smiled, at that.

'Ah, not quite. I drugged him with cherry laurel leaves, and tied him up.'

Horton turned to Seale, who was standing with a thunderous face in the door to the kitchen.

'You are quite the oddest couple I have ever encountered,' Seale said. 'And I find myself wondering why a botanist needs to poison our assistant treasurer.'

CONSTABLE HORTON AND THE DEVIL

There followed a difficult conversation, in which Horton was forced to abandon their pretence to Seale and take the risk that the man might expose him. The man's reaction surprised him.

'The fort, you say?' he said when Horton had finished. 'I've always thought there was something odd about that place. You'll need a horse.' And without another word he left to secure one. Horton silently prayed their host did not go straight to the Governor.

Abigail wanted to come with him, of course, but he insisted that she stay with Seale, arguing that a carriage would be impossible over such ground and it was too far to walk, and securing two horses would be twice as difficult as securing one. He did not wish to make his way across the island in the gathering dark alone; but he wished to do it with his wife even less.

The horse Seale brought to the door was unimpressive and unimpressed – though he had not had time to visit the Governor, Horton reckoned, and thanked Seale warmly. The horse looked at Horton as if he were an empty bag of feed. Seale gave him an oil lamp, and he wondered if the oil in it had come from the *Martha* – if he had not in fact witnessed its ocean harvesting.

It was now full dark. He rode with one hand on the reins, the other holding the lamp. Its whale-oil burned a corridor through the night, and down the corridor he rode.

It was a distance of four or five miles to the eastern tip of the island, the last third of it bisecting the treeless plain that Seale had called Deadwood. There, surrounded by flat ground over which St Helena's peaks stared seawards, he felt like a flea abandoned in the cosmos. If a dragon had swooped down and carried him away across the Atlantic, he would only have been mildly surprised.

The land rose, and he could see the silhouette of the Dutch fort. He rode past it, and past the big house and barn which Abigail had seen. No light came from either. A few minutes later he came to the assistant treasurer's residence.

This time, there was a light. Burroughs must have escaped Abigail's knots. Horton tied up the horse at a lonely tree some distance away, and walked carefully up to the place. He extinguished the lamp, allowing himself to be folded into the night air.

Burroughs appeared at the door so suddenly that Horton had to throw himself to the ground to avoid being seen, perhaps thirty yards away. The grass was dry, but cold, holding the promise of night-time moisture. This was Horton's first glimpse of the man who, until now, had been only a name, a shadow at the edge of the story.

He stood in the doorframe, lit by the light within. He did not look like a man who had, until recently, been tied to a chair by a woman after drinking a mild poison. He looked like a man under astonishing self-control. He imagined Burroughs standing in that Kent icehouse over the dead bodies of the Johnsons. He imagined him marking their bodies with that device, Dee's Monad. But the question still pertained: why?

The dark-suited devil turned and shut the door behind him. The house stood silent again. Horton could not approach very closely, as there was no cover. But behind the house there were cairns and clusters of rocks. Horton crouched and ran around the house, keeping as much of his attention as he could on the door, in case Burroughs should reappear. He settled down to wait.

It was perhaps another hour, though it felt like eternity. At the end of this first hour, the light in the house went out. Had the assistant treasurer gone to bed? He waited a while longer, just to be sure.

He made his way towards the dark house. He reached its side wall, put his back against it and quickly glanced into a window. There was no light or movement from inside. He worked his way around to the front door at which Burroughs had stood earlier.

He could see the silhouette of the fort from here; it was above him, its edges jagged in the moonlight. From the other side of the fort, the persistent breathing of the sea, in and out of that cave below.

He tried the handle of the front door. It turned. The door gave slightly under his shoulder and then, as if making the decision for him, it opened. He pushed it open, staying as hidden as he could around the edge of the door, pushing it back until it was against the inner wall, squeezing anyone who might be hiding there into an impossibility.

He peeked around the doorframe. The interior was dark and, apparently, empty. He stepped inside.

The air was cold. Burroughs had lit no fire. He could pick out the dim outlines of some furniture in the parlour: two chairs, a desk, a door out to the kitchen. A bookcase lit by a shaft of moonlight from the window.

Slowly, carefully, Horton went through every room of the house, and found nothing. In the surprising light from the moon, he made what investigation he could, and concluded that apart from books and furniture, Burroughs's house was devoid of anything at all. It was even devoid of Burroughs.

He sat in the man's chair, which faced the dead fire and the chimney breast. He stretched out one foot and pushed the rug. For a moment he imagined he saw a trapdoor. But it was no such thing; just a line in the wooden floor, a gap between boards. And how, he asked himself, would Burroughs have returned a rug to cover a trapdoor once he had climbed down inside? He had allowed the night to take over his imagination. It was time to think clearly. Time to head back into James Town, and speak to Seale, and to Abigail, and relocate his rational self.

But where on earth was Edgar Burroughs?

He got up and walked over to the front door of the little house, casting his eyes once more around the place, marking again the strange absence of objects other than furniture and books. All he felt was an emotional vacuum. A building, not a home.

He opened the front door, and a dark blur appeared beside him. An arm settled against his chest and throat, and a sharp point broke the skin on his neck before pausing. A hand gripped his arm and pushed it up behind his back, up impossibly far until the tendons in his shoulder screamed in protest and he cried out.

'Constable Horton, I presume,' said a voice.

She was washing pans again. Her husband was out in the South Atlantic dark, and she was washing pans. Seale had gone out, she suspected to drink. He had said little to her since Charles had left. Perhaps their deception had made him unsure of her. She was alone, staring into the pane of glass which had become her familiar, her own face staring back at her.

Behind that glass, high in the sky, were the stars of the South Atlantic. John Dee believed the 'fixed stars' influenced events on earth; that their size and arrangement in relation to the Earth dictated the strength of their various effects, and that these effects combined with the elements of the Earth – fire, earth, air and water – to create eddies of influence and power. She recognised the nonsense of this, the underlying error – the stars were not fixed, they were in constant movement, not around the Earth but around each other. And yet, what was this but another kind of influence? Did Newton not simply articulate this different kind of action at a distance? Was a distant star even now tugging at her, affecting her decisions, changing her life?

She remembered the way her mind had slipped away from itself. More than a year ago now, it had been. It had been as if there were two Abigails – one acting, the other watching and recording. When she saw her face reflected in the glass of the kitchen window, it felt like she was looking back at herself. There was pity in that watching face, and anxiety, and something like loneliness.

And just like that, she felt alone in the world. She felt the utter absence of children in her life, the signal failure to reproduce herself, to have other eyes and other faces looking back into hers, calling her mother, needing her regard. Abigail Horton had little need for God, for she had found so many explanations for the wonders around her in books and lectures. And yet she wondered at God now, and at why he had denied her children. How did the men of science explain that?

She was angry and frustrated and worried. The fear which had rattled through her while she had undertaken to dose Burroughs with laurel leaves was now, if anything, a positive memory, of a time when she was excited and at least partially mistress of her own immediate future. She had smelled the leaves, and they had smelled of almonds. She had conjectured that they must contain some of the same materials as hydrocyanic acid. In this she had been right. She was clever and well read and imaginative. But now she had been left to wait, again, as all women must eventually wait: for a man to make something happen.

She was very, very tired of waiting.

Horton woke in the dark. He was in an unlit tunnel, and from down at the other end of the tunnel he could hear the sound of the sea.

He sat up, and groaned. He put one hand to his head, and it came away sticky. He had done himself some kind of injury, falling down the stairs from the door. That mysterious bloody door which Burroughs had opened, before he had disappeared.

How long had he been lying here? The blood on his head was sticky but not wet; the wound had congealed, it seemed. A half-hour, perhaps? An hour? He wondered where Burroughs was.

'Edgar Burroughs,' he'd said to the man who had held a knife to his throat outside the assistant treasurer's house.

'Of course. Now, walk. That way. Up to the fort.'

Burroughs's voice had been cultured and educated, the voice of London salons and not South Atlantic hillsides. His grip had been astonishingly firm. The blade had felt cold against his neck, and he could detect a warm trickle alongside it. His skin had been broken, then, by this man whom he still could not see. This man who seemed to be at the centre of every hole in this case.

They had walked up the hill, Horton choosing his steps carefully, Burroughs allowing his own body to adjust to Horton's pace and balance. The pressure on his shoulder had been enormous. As Burroughs pushed his arm up behind his back, it had felt like his internal rigging might snap and pull him down at any second.

It had taken ten minutes to walk up the hill to the fort, past the big quiet farmhouse. The jagged shape of the place in the moonlight had been suitably Gothic. 'Are you going to throw me from the cliff?' he had asked.

'Believe me, I have thought about it,' the reply had come. 'I've asked myself whether it was a very bad idea, bringing you here. She had better be worth it.'

She?

They had walked under the gaping entrance to the fort, its wooden door long taken by the islanders for some purpose of their own. The fort was open to the sky, its roof a distant memory. Horton had heard the waves crashing into Prosperous Bay, over the lid of the point.

Bringing you here, Burroughs had said. *She had better be worth it.*

He had thought of Abigail, because he had thought he was about to die, and he had wondered what she was doing. How late was it? How long had he been waiting outside Burroughs's little cottage? She would be concerned, of course. No. She would be terrified. He had wandered off into the South Atlantic night, and he had not returned. Perhaps, now, he would never return.

They had walked up to the closed door, the infernal door that Horton had tried so many ways to open. With a little shove, Burroughs had pushed Horton's body into the door, squeezing a few more impossible degrees of arc into Horton's agonised arm. Horton had turned his face so his cheek was against the door, trying to ease the pressure on his tortured shoulder.

It had been warm, the wood of the door. Hot, even. As if something had been generating heat from inside. He had listened as Burroughs wrestled with something metallic from within his coat, or perhaps from a bag. Horton had turned his head around the other way, to the side he could detect Burroughs was standing, and he had seen something heavy and metallic being held against the door by his captor. Something that had looked like an iron bar.

He had heard a grinding sound from the far side of the door, as if someone on the inside were unhitching a bolt. Burroughs had moved the iron bar along the door, from outer to inner, and the movement had been matched by the metallic grinding from within. Then Burroughs moved the bar down six inches, and had performed the same procedure, and then quite suddenly the door had squealed open.

Horton had found himself standing before a dark opening. Two or three stone steps, heading down below the fort, had been visible in the moonlight, but other than that the space had presented only darkness. Burroughs still had hold of his arm, and began to push him towards the step, when suddenly there had been something else there, a shape from the outer darkness which had thrown itself at Burroughs with an animal growl. Burroughs had cried out and had released his grip on Horton's arm, and as if waiting for a cue Horton had spun himself around to see what had happened, and had caught only a glimpse of a somebody or something struggling with Burroughs on the ground before his feet gave way beneath him and with a single cry he had fallen back into the exposed entrance and down the stairs. He had managed to soften his body, become a ball almost, as he tumbled down the steps, but then his head had struck a rock at the bottom of the steps and he had lost all consciousness.

But for how long? He put his hand out to stand up, and it grazed something on the ground, something with rough edges. The rock on which he had knocked his head, perhaps. Sitting up – his injured shoulder screaming in pain – he reached out and felt with his hands. He stood up slowly and walked back up the stairs in the dark, and found the door at the top was now closed. He ran his hands all over the door's surface, felt its old wooden immensity, but failed to find anything with which to pull it open. The door continued to be a kind of impossibility, opened as if by magic by an iron bar. So he turned from it, back to the steps down which he had fallen.

It was not quite dark here in the space behind the door. A weak glow came from the bottom of the steps, as if there were a light shining from somewhere within – from the same direction as the sound of the sea. There was only one choice available to him. He began to make his way back down.

The steps were wooden, not stone. They had been built into the rocky cavity beneath the fort. Every step he took was an adventure, and the bottom of the wooden stairs came suddenly and jarringly, the absence of a final step shuddering through his leg. He squatted down in the gloom and felt the ground: soily sand, pretty dry, above a rocky base. He could feel the shape of the passageway around him; it seemed to have been carved by man, its edges relatively smooth. He was reminded of the absence he'd felt beneath his feet while floating at the sea-cave.

He breathed in. He took a step. And then another. And then another.

He walked forward again, hands outstretched. Ahead, something had disturbed the darkness. A yellow light, adding little illumination, such that he could see the shape of the space through which he was walking. He stepped forward with a little more confidence.

After a few more minutes, he put his hands out again to either side, and they touched nothing. Breeze ruffled the end of his hairs, like a memory of the real world. He felt like he was standing in a larger space, and looked above and around him. But the darkness revealed nothing of its dimensions.

'Stop!'

A woman's voice, sudden and loud, echoed around the chamber. A crisp island accent, spoken with real authority. He stopped, unhesitatingly.

'Do not move, constable. Not another step, if you value your safety.'

A light began to glow, and became deeper and stronger, as if its source were approaching him. It emerged from a cavity beside him, some thirty yards to his right, and as it glowed brighter it picked out the shape of the space of the room he was in. With every step, the space grew clearer.

It was enormous, as big as a small church. He saw now that he was standing at the edge of a terrible slit in the floor, its bottom invisible in the darkness. This fissure ran across the far edge of this space. If he had carried on walking he would have fallen straight into the ravine. He took two steps back, an instinctive move of self-preservation. Steadying himself, he looked down into the fissure, but could see nothing in the gloom; the sound of the sea, though, was huge.

Was he looking down into the sea-cave into which he had almost sailed earlier today? He thought he was.

Alongside this fissure ran a series of works which reminded him of the try-works on the deck of the *Martha*. Huge iron pots, almost a dozen of them, stood in a row, some of them leaning out over the fissure. Channels of brick and metal ran from beneath these cauldrons or crucibles or whatever they were. Further along the fissure to his left there was the suggestion of more openings in the walls, leading, perhaps, to other tunnels or cavities beneath the fort. The whole installation looked very old.

A figure had appeared from a space in the wall, carrying an oil lamp. She walked up to him in the gloom: a middle-aged woman, perhaps even old, wearing the clothes of a male worker, trousers and shirt and waistcoat. Her hair was tied up behind her head. She was as tall as him. Horton could not see her eyes in the flickering light, but when the woman spoke, her strong white teeth flashed in the shimmer from the oil lamp.

'I have been waiting for you, constable,' she said, in that forceful yet odd-sounding island accent, English and yet not.

'You have? How did you know who I was, may I ask?'

'Edgar told me all about you.'

'Edgar Burroughs?'

'Aye.'

'And where is Burroughs now? My shoulder would have words with him.'

The woman frowned.

'I know not where he is, constable. He struggled with Fernando, and escaped.'

'He did not follow me into the tunnel.'

'I believe he did not. Fernando removed his key.'

'I saw no key.'

'*In the magnet, God has offered to the eyes of mortals for observation qualities which in other objects he has left for discovery to the subtler research of the mind and a greater investigative industry.*'

'Is that a quotation?'

'It is. From a work by John Dee.'

'Ah. Dr Dee. He seems to have cast a strange shadow over my life, these past months.'

'John Dee's shadow is a long one. It has lain over me for decades. Now, will you come with me, constable? It is time for all to be explained.'

'All?'

'All.'

The warm breeze moved through the cavern, carrying with it the unmistakable smell of bitter almonds.

She picked up a cup from the counter. It was chipped at one edge, and she passed the end of her index finger across the sharp little white wound, feeling it cut into her own skin, and watched with only mild interest as a deep-red drop of her own blood stained the powdery surface.

She put the cup into the sink, and poured some water from a jug over it, and looked up, and shrieked. A face was at the window – an ugly, deformed face. It stared in at her, and muttered some sound from its throat, which she heard as a rasping series of unintelligible noises through the cheap, rippled glass.

It was the ogre from the hillside. Its ugly noseless face stared at her longingly, and then it stepped back and held both arms out in a kind of surrender, a similar gesture to that which it had greeted her with on the hillside. It was a signal made pathetic by the hand missing on its left arm and the thumb missing on its right hand.

It stepped back, away from the window and almost into the darkness. It gestured again with its thumbless right hand; a waving gesture. *Come with me. Come with me.*

She was badly scared. Her heart felt like a rabbit darting about a field surrounded by hounds. But even so, she lifted her hand up and opened the little kitchen window. The creature took another step back, as if signalling that she should trust it not to attack. And this time it spoke recognisably English words.

'Will you come with me?' it said, and its voice was cracked with exhaustion and harsh with an accent she did not recognise.

'Come where?'

'To where your husband is.'

'And where is he?'

'He was with the Company man. Now he is in the fort.'

She frowned at it.

'The Company man? Edgar Burroughs?'

'Yes, yes, the Company man.'

'He sent you?'

'No, no. My mistress sent me. The Company man is not a good man.'

'Who is your mistress?

'Come, come. To the fort.'

'How will we get there? It is dark.'

'You will come on my horse. Come, my mistress said it was time.'

'Time for what?'

'Time for stories.'

Horton followed the woman, as she turned down the opening from which she had emerged and walked down another corridor, similar to the one from which he had come. This one, though, was longer. Taking the fissure and the sound of the sea as his cue, he estimated that they were now walking in parallel to the edge of the island, to the south.

The island had swallowed him up. He walked within it, once more a Jonah – although this time it was St Helena and not East India House that was the leviathan through whose innards he wandered. He had voyaged here chasing a mystery, one which was obscured beneath conspiracy and privilege back in London. He remembered the poor cabin boy on the *Martha*, being forced to climb down into the dead vacancy of the eviscerated sperm whale's head, prodding the cavities of its brain with a sharpened shovel. At least that boy had had a shovel.

The tunnel began to rise, and then the woman's oil lamp picked out another set of wooden stairs fixed into the rock, rising up to yet another black door with no handle and no lock. She pulled an iron bar from a pocket within her dress, and moved it across the door's surface as Burroughs had done, in a series of definite geometric sequences. From within the door he heard metal moving upon metal. And then the door swung open, the woman stepped through, and he followed her.

He emerged into a cellar: a wide space, suggesting a good-sized house above it. It was cool down here, and there were various meat-shapes hung from hooks and the strong smell of curing. There were sacks of grain and boxes of fruit and vegetables. A well-ordered food store.

The woman closed the door, passed her metal bar over it another time, and then turned away. She walked across the cellar, up some more steps, and through an unlocked door. Horton followed her.

'Please, constable, come and wait in the library,' she said, still holding her lamp in the darkened house. 'There is a fire in the kitchen, I shall make us tea.'

She stepped inside. Horton followed her, and entered a room unlike any other he had encountered.

It was finely decorated with dark wooden furniture, which the woman's lamp picked out as she went around the room lighting other lamps. As these fired into life, more detail emerged. The furniture was, indeed, very fine, and some of it looked very old. It was the kind of furniture one might find in a well-ordered townhouse. He had seen nothing like it on St Helena, even in the Governor's office.

And everywhere, there were books: on shelves, piled on tables by the sides of the chairs, tumbling off a writing desk which took up almost the whole of one wall of the room. A hearth with an unlit fire occupied another wall. Looking up, he saw the room was perhaps twenty feet high, and every inch of its surface that was not occupied by the desk or the hearth was covered in books. Hundreds, if not thousands, of books.

He walked over to one of the shelves.

'May I?' he said to the woman, who now stood waiting at the door, despite having promised tea.

'You might perhaps start with that pile of books on my desk,' the woman said. 'There are volumes there which I think may be of interest to you.'

He picked up one of the books from the desk. Its leather

binding was cracked and dangerously dry, its spine rubbed away so there was no writing legible on it. He opened it to the front page, and saw immediately why the woman had pointed him to it. The book was in Latin, of which he had none at all, but it said it had been printed in 'Londini', which he took to be 'London'. A date was given beneath this – 'MDLXVIII' – which he had insufficient tools to decode. The title of the book was *Propaedeumata Aphoristica*, and below it were the words 'IOANNIS DEE, LONDONINENSIS'.

John Dee, of London.

But these signals were, to him, after effects. He knew this book was one of John Dee's, because there at the centre of the frontispiece, on a shield entwined with snakes and what appeared to be the feathers of quills, was the device that had been inked on the chests of the Johnsons. John Dee's device – the Monad.

'These books are all John Dee's?' he said, and the woman smiled.

'It is an interesting question, constable,' she replied. 'These books are indeed mostly John Dee's, though he only wrote a few of them – indeed, the ones in that pile are the ones he wrote. But the rest are his, too.'

She spoke in a mannered, courtly air, like an actor on the stage. As if she had been trained to it, Horton thought.

'I do not understand your meaning.'

'No, I expect you do not.'

She sighed, and it was the sound of someone accepting the end of something.

'My name is Mina Baxter, constable,' she said. 'And this room contains the library of John Dee. My grandfather's grandfather's grandfather stole it from him.'

VIOLENCE

As Abigail rode through the island night with the ogre, St Helena's angular savagery was even more potent, unsoftened by the green bucolic edges of daytime. Peaks cut jagged lines in the moonlit sky, and the lamplight landed every now and again on the demonic eyes of a goat watching them pass.

A fragment of John Dee's words came back to her: *There is such a conjunction of rays from all the fixed stars and planets upon every point of the whole universe at any moment of time that another conjunction which is in every way like it can exist naturally at no other point and at no other time.*

Every moment in time a unique moment, and every point on the map of the cosmos a unique point. Men walked through these conjunctions under an infinity of influence.

And women, of course. Though Dee did not mention women.

They rode east towards the Deadwood plain, and the Moon hung high above them; one of Dee's fixed stars, of course. He had thought much of the Moon. *The Moon is the most powerful governess of moist things: it is the arouser and producer of humidity.* The Sun governed fire, the Moon governed water, tugging at the tides and influencing the hysterics of the mad.

And this was madness: to be galloping across a plain in the South Atlantic with only an ogre for company. This Caliban, this fairy-tale ogre, held the horse's rein in his one good hand, and placed his handless arm behind him and half around Abigail's waist, holding her in place with surprising strength. He smelled of oil and fire and sweat, as if he had stepped out of a furnace. And of almonds. The stench of bitter almonds hung on him like a memory of violence. She had put her trust into him, because he had promised her stories, and was that not always an item of great promise?

They were almost at Deadwood when a shape appeared from within the rocks and shouted something at their horse. The animal reared backwards, throwing her and the ogre. She fell backwards and landed on her shoulder, which then screamed in pain at her, a white-hot spearing agony the like of which she had never felt before, and the nurse in her realised that she had dislocated the joint, and the physician in her knew that the only fix for such an injury would present even more pain.

She tried to stand, but could get no further than her knees before the pain grew too much. Ahead of her she saw two shapes struggling in the moonlight – the ogre, and another. She could hear the ogre growling and shouting, but the other shape made no sound at all. It was taller and altogether calmer than the frenziedly angry ogre, and she anticipated the ending long before it came – a rock raised high in the air, brought down with cold belligerence, and the struggle was over.

She breathed, heavily, trying to control her pain and her fear. There was a harsh sound as the figure dropped the rock with which it had dispatched the ogre, and she watched it stand up straight and rub its face where, presumably, a punch had landed. Then it turned to face her and spoke.

'That was clever, to poison me like that,' it said. 'Some women are too clever for their own good.'

'What will you do with me?' she said.

'Oh, to start with, I might just twist your arm a few times,' said Burroughs. 'But before then, I need to find that horse.'

Mina Baxter told Horton a story.

It was a story that had its roots in the long ago and the now very far away. It was a story of Dutchmen on the make: Amsterdam merchants, an unscrupulous mercenary named Jacobus Aakster (and his wife, Mina Koeman), and the library of the most famous magus in England, John Dee.

Dee's library, an untidy but extraordinary English Alexandria, was said to contain a great secret, though the man himself had become something of an embarrassment, speaking to angels and seeking the perfection of man in the achievement of a celestial magic.

Horton heard the words *the perfection of man* and his eyes passed over the books in the library in which they sat. She had still not made him any tea.

These Dutch merchants paid Aakster to steal Dee's library, or at least to steal that part of it that would most likely contain this great secret. But the merchants were outdone by another Dutchman on the make: Aakster himself. Word had reached other men of Aakster's interest in Dee, and he was approached by, of all things, a Jewish merchant from Portugal. This man told him of a certain manuscript which he had bought from a rogue Janissary which he had then sold on to John Dee. He called this text the *Opera*. It was said to have been written by an ancient Persian named Jābir ibn Hayyān.

When Mina Baxter said the name of this thinker, it sounded to Horton like she was clearing her throat, so he asked her to say it again.

'The name doesn't matter,' she said. 'The Europeans called him Geber.'

Geber was an alchemist; some said he was the *original* alchemist. To Dee and men like him, he was a giant of the obscure science they wallowed in. To find an unknown text by him would have excited Dee beyond understanding.

But there was a problem – the text of the book was in Arabic. And Dee had no Arabic. The Arab works he owned were Latin translations. But if what the Janissary had told the old Portuguese Jew was true, the contents of the *Opera* were such that he could not rely on any translator to keep them secret. Dee was trapped inside his own secret stories, unable to exploit whatever lay inside the old book.

It was one of those strange coincidences from which stories grow. For Jacobus Aakster, a man of several parts, had been captured as a young man by pirates off the Barbary coast. He had served five years as a slave, before escaping. During that time he had become a mercenary. And he had also learned Arabic.

So, on the night of the raid, he found the book. He read the first page or two, while the morons he had hired rampaged through Dee's library. He realised, instantly, what the book was about. Out on the river his wife Mina was waiting with a boat, just in case. It turned out it was needed. Aakster left with Mina, and disappeared.

This modern Mina, Mina Baxter, told the story easily, as if she had been rehearsing all her life for the moment she had an audience.

Jacobus Aakster disappeared for three years. During those years the merchants paid experts to pore over Dee's stolen books. They grew exceedingly knowledgeable on the influences of the stars and the mystical properties of mathematics – none of which they cared a jot about. None of what they learned could be turned into the one thing the merchants really did care for: money. Even Dee's thoughts on navigation were either old hat or pure tat.

At which point, Aakster returned. He introduced himself to the merchants again, who expressed their fury at his disappearance. He silenced them, though, by simply stating the substance of the book he had stolen from Dee's library. That shut them up. They asked to see the book. He told them he had destroyed it. They grew angry.

Then he told them he had memorised the book's contents.

It took a while for the implications of this to sink in. If the book contained the secrets he claimed, then it might be worth money. More money than it was possible even to quite imagine. But if no copy existed (and the merchants certainly didn't know of one), the only way to turn that theory into cash was via the mechanism of Jacobus Aakster's memory.

'Prove it,' demanded the merchants. So Aakster did, with the help of some alchemical apparatus and some unusual ingredients. One of the men appointed to help him with the process ended up dying, succumbing to a strange substance which turned from liquid to gas at dangerously low temperatures and which smelled of bitter almonds. They worked in an icehouse deep in the flat Dutch countryside, its temperature kept low by the North Sea waters. This particular worker had not been as careful as he needed to be.

But the test was successful. And thus Aakster's request was agreed to, without delay. What was needed was a distant place, one where Aakster could go about his business undisturbed. At least, this was the requirement Aakster demanded. He wanted to be far from Holland, far from Europe, far from prying eyes and glittering temptations. He would establish a new dynasty, and he knew the place for it. He had discovered it during those three years of investigation.

So he and Mina Koeman had set sail for St Helena on a vessel bound for the Dutch East Indies. They set up home there, out on the eastern lip of the island, and put the processes outlined in the *Opera* into action. Aakster also demanded that the other books stolen from Dee's library be handed to him, though it was never clear why. The merchants were happy to hand the books over. Aakster had taken the only one that mattered, and now it existed only as recollections in the canny fellow's head.

Jacobus and Mina were immediately successful. And they continued to be successful for another twenty years. Merchants came and went. Some of them demanded that Aakster increase production, or move his manufactory to another location, perhaps on the southern tip of Africa. But Aakster refused. He had made a comfortable life for himself, and he knew he could defend his position in St Helena. He could see the ships as they arrived, and with the help of an ugly little Portuguese beast who lived on the island he carved out a great manufactory beneath the fort and his home.

During their time on the island Mina Koeman gave birth to two sons: Carl and Jacob. The family travelled to and from Europe, indulging themselves in the shops of Amsterdam and Antwerp, but always returning to their island refuge. But on one of these European jaunts their son Carl was intercepted by representatives of the merchants and tortured, desperate as they were for the secret. But Carl had not learned the *Opera*; that had been Jacob's role. Carl returned to St Helena quite out of his wits, driven utterly mad by the labour of the merchants.

When Aakster learned of his son Carl's fate, he grew angry and threatened to end production, at which point the merchants panicked and apologised, and proposed an almost Imperial deal. Aakster's other son Jacob would marry one of their own daughters, Claudia van Denburg, and Aakster would be given a significant stake in the merchants' new venture: the Verenigde Oostindische Compagnie, or Dutch East India Company.

Years passed, things changed. The English forced the Dutch from St Helena during a moment when the Dutch government had been casting avaricious eyes on the southern African coast. The Dutch merchants had never formalised their ownership of St Helena; it was the property of the Dutch government, not the new VOC, and that government had no idea what the Aaksters were about. So a great prize slipped from the merchants' grasp, and they were annoyed – particularly as their rivals in London, the East India Company of England, had been the ones to seize this lucrative little asset.

Did the London East India Company know what they had in St Helena? Perhaps – it might even have encouraged them to persuade the English authorities to seize the island from the Dutch in the first place. And they realised soon enough when they discovered this Dutch family of murky provenance. Old Jacobus was dead by this time, and his son Jacob was not long for the world of men, either. Carl also still lived, but was destroyed by his imagination and by the books in the library which Aakster had assembled from the remnants of that stolen from Mortlake. Carl started to believe himself to be John Dee himself, his soul occupied by the undying power of the old magus.

But Jacob's wife Claudia, the daughter of great merchants and a woman of considerable parts, handled negotiations with the new owners of the island, the East India Company. A new way of trading was established. The Aaksters would continue their work and continue their shopping, though in London rather than Antwerp. They reported to a secret committee back in London. They changed their names. The only child of

Jacob and Claudia, Cornelius, would henceforth carry the surname Baxter.

And so the little business continued. Elder sons took over from fathers, each of them learning the *Opera* by heart; other siblings were sent back to England to quietly thrive on substantial but not exotic dowries and bequests. The Honourable East India Company kept the secret to itself; the profits from St Helena preserved the good health of its accounts in the leanest years, when the Indians turned up their noses at heavy English woollens and the Company was forced to fall back onto violence, extortion and taxation to keep the fiscal wheels turning.

The family may have taken an English name, but it still proceeded with Dutch care. Cornelius Baxter handed the reins of the operation to Edwin, who handed them to Frederick, who handed them to Gilbert. All the time, the Company pressed for expansion of the project, for a new facility to be opened somewhere else. But the Baxters resisted. They knew where such a move would end. It would end with the destruction of their family.

But then, disaster. Gilbert's wife died giving birth to a son. He was left on the island with no wife, and no male heir. He was left with only a daughter. She was named after Jacobus Aakster's canny wife: Mina. She never married, but that is not the same as saying the line ended.

The pain in Abigail's shoulder was like nothing she had ever experienced. She tried to keep her arm still and wondered about fashioning some kind of sling, but Burroughs gave her no time, returning with the ogre's horse within minutes and yanking her by her good arm with such gleeful violence that she feared her good shoulder would also dislocate itself.

She screamed out, and Burroughs laughed at her. He laughed a lot as they rode back to the fort, talking as they went.

'Did you read any of the books in Johnson's house, Abigail?' he said, his arms reaching around her to the reins, his breath warm on her neck.

'The books?'

'The *Mathematicall Preface*, perhaps. That is the volume with the most to say to a sceptic such as yourself.'

'I read it.'

'And what did Abigail Horton's fine mind make of it?'

'Please, my shoulder.'

He shifted his weight slightly behind her, and the movement felt obscene to her. But the pain in her shoulder lessened somewhat.

'I found all of Dee's writings to be misguided,' she said, her voice pulled tight by the agony. 'He appeared a very intelligent man misguided by his trust in fallacious authorities.'

'Ah, yes. It is well put. He took the cosmos to be Aristotle's, when in fact it was Galileo's. But he never met Galileo. I made the same mistake.'

'You? You believed Dee's writings? His talk of angels?'

'I did. I believed it all. I was schooled by those books. I grew up alone in my uncle's house in Kent, surrounded by a fac-simile of Dee's library.'

'A facsimile?'

'My uncle believed Dee's secret – the secret your husband came here to uncover – was not in *one* book but in *all* the books. So he acquired copies of all of them. He reconstructed Dee's library, and I read the books. I learned my Latin and my Greek and even my Arabic. By the time I was twenty-five I was, in my way, a facsimile of John Dee.'

'That must have been extraordinary.'

'It was. I believed I saw the universe as it truly was. I was obsessed with that Monad. Dee believed it held the entirety of the cosmos in its design.'

'You must explain that to me.'

'One day, Abigail. When you and I are embarked on our project.'

'Our project?'

The secret your husband came here to uncover, he had said.

'I must speak to your husband first. It is only right.'

'What happened to you?'

'Enlightenment happened to me, Abigail. Or, to be more accurate, *the* Enlightenment happened to me. In one singular year, I read Galileo, and Halley, and Kepler, and Herschel, and every edition of the *Philosophical Transactions* since the Royal Society's first meeting. I saw the cosmos for what it was. A vast predictable mechanism. I turned away from magic, and I embraced the Machine. I put away childish things, and I drowned my books.'

'Yet you read your Shakespeare.'

'My dear woman,' he said, as the silhouette of the fort rose above them and he climbed down from the horse. 'I read *everything.*'

And with that, he pulled her from the horse and carried her down into the tunnels below. She imagined his cloven feet as they made their way down and within, her shoulder lashing its pain through her whole body.

Eventually they came to a deep fissure at the bottom of which she could hear the sea. He lashed her to one of six massive cauldrons which lined the fissure, and by carefully positioning herself as he did so she managed to line her arm and shoulder up in such a way that Burroughs's rope held her shoulder in place. An accidental sling, which did nothing but turn knives of pain into needles, but it was better than nothing.

And then, the worst thing of all. Then he stood to leave.

'Leave me a light,' she said, desperately.

'You have no need of one,' he replied. 'What do you expect to do? Read?'

He laughed, again, and he left. With the light. His laughter resounded off the rock walls, and the glow of his torch receded, and then she was in darkness. Complete, solid darkness, of the kind that seems to fill your nostrils and slither down your throat. The only sound that of her breathing and the breathing of the ocean, below.

As Mina Baxter told her tale Horton remembered himself back into the Drury Lane Theatre, to where this strange story had began, watching Prospero cast his spells over another island. Mina Baxter was a mesmerising storyteller – as mesmerising, to a man of Horton's deliberate mind, as Shakespeare himself.

He looked up, despite himself, to the roof of the library in which they were sitting, and he half expected to see a hole up there. On the other side of that hole, he would catch a glimpse of the candles of the Drury Lane Theatre swaying in their chandeliers. He would see Prospero peeking over the edge of the hole to look down at him, his staff in his hand and his magical eyes blazing. He might even see himself high up in the gallery, enchanted.

And what would Prospero make of this?

He did not know when Shakespeare wrote his play. But he imagined it might have been from the same glittering decades that had witnessed the life of John Dee. Had Shakespeare met Dee? Was Prospero a homage to a Mortlake reality?

And what on earth could be called 'reality' in a world where this story could unfold?

The library of an Elizabethan magus, hidden on a lump of rock in the South Atlantic, on an island nobody even considered. A forgotten magic.

His mind had been prepared for what Mina Baxter had told

him. It had been softened to these mysteries by the puzzles he had already seen these past four years. It was as if John Dee himself had appeared to him, the old wizard of Mortlake, the natural philosopher who wanted to be something more, who wanted to consort with the celestial. The man who did not drown his books.

But this was not the story he had voyaged here to tell. This was a tale of Ratcliffe Highway murders and slaughtered Company treasurers. On the face of it, a simple murder mystery. One for which he had still not been able to locate a motive.

Mina Baxter had finished her tale – or rather, she had stopped it, and was looking at him expectantly. He had expected a confession. It was not apparently forthcoming.

'But none of this really happened like that, did it?' he said. Mina frowned. 'This is the story you made up. The *Opera* contained the essential secret, did it not? Dee's secret. The way to become one with God. The route to eternal life. Your name is Koeman, not Baxter. You are more than two hundred years old. Your husband Jacobus – what happened to him? An accident? Does the potion not work in such cases?'

She opened her mouth, and closed it again. She looked almost amused. Then she turned and picked up a small wooden box, and walked over to him. She put it on his lap, and stood over him.

'I think, sir, that you are labouring under a misapprehension,' she said.

He turned the key on the box, and its lid popped open. He gazed at the lump of gold within. He took it out. It was about the size of a duck egg, but had none of an egg's graceful design. It would have been ugly if its warm yellow gleam did not speak so immediately of wealth and artifice, of immense mirrored rooms and imperial crowns and clustered burial chambers. Of a world built upon its unreactive beauty.

Gold. Enough gold to buy a ship, probably. Held in his hand.

She may have lost consciousness for a while, but it was nearly impossible to tell in this dark cave with only the ocean to speak to her. She had little sense of how long she'd been there. But after an unknown time, she heard a different sound, other than the ocean's breath and her own.

Another breath. Somewhere out there in the darkness, a ragged breath, and the sound of something scratching on the wall. The click of boot nails on rock. And then the sense that whatever was making the noise had emerged into the same cavern as her.

A sniffing sound.

A grunt that could perhaps be a growl.

She took a chance, then.

'Fernando?'

She had not used the name before. She remembered it only from what Seale had told her. But the name brought another grunt, and the shuffling started again. And the sniffing. And it came closer.

'Fernando? I am here.'

The agony in her shoulder was so enormous that the terror she felt was a little thing, a side-issue, one to be barely concerned about. Even when the creature in the dark – *Fernando, please, let it be Fernando* – leaned in to her and sniffed and then ran one dry finger over her skin, her terror remained less than her pain.

'Fernando, I need to get out of here. My shoulder is injured.'

Another grunt, and then the thing spoke.

'*He killed me,*' it said.

'But you are alive. Can you help me?'

'*Alive. Yes. Always alive. Always.*'

She felt its hand sense its way along the line of the rope to where the knots where. Then the feeling of the hand went away, and within seconds the hard coldness of a knife was slicing through the rope. The support for her shoulder fell away suddenly, and she cried out, and the creature in the dark moaned.

'He went down the other tunnel,' she said. 'Not the one we came down.'

Fernando's remaining hand took hers, and he pulled her to her feet. Then he held her hand.

'Don't let go,' he said. 'I know the way, even in darkness.'

'What are we going to do?' she asked.

'Make a big noise,' he said.

'You made this?' he asked her, holding the gold in his hand. It was heavy and it was cold.

'Of course I didn't make it. I am not God.'

'Then where does it come from?'

'It comes from the same place all gold comes from.' And she looked around her. 'It comes from the rock within the Earth. She hides it as best she can, but some of us may find it, if we have the tools to look.'

'There is gold in this rock?'

'There is. A good deal of it. But it is almost impossible to extract using traditional means. Gold runs through the veins of the Earth, but in most places the veins are so thin as to be unreachable. Therein, and therein alone, lies the alchemy, constable. A process Geber discovered in Persia, a thousand years ago, transported to this island.'

'And what does this process involve?'

'Constable, have you not been paying attention? It is my secret. It is the secret that keeps me alive and this place – this island – protected. I have memorised Geber's process, and I will not pass it on.'

'But you have no children,' said Horton. 'The sequence will end with you.'

'Aye,' said Mina, flatly. 'That it will.'

'So it ends here?'

'That is my wish, yes.'

'And what do you plan to do?'

She looked up at the ceiling, and smiled. An oddly young smile, as if she were remembering a pleasant childhood dream.

'I will leave this island,' she said, still looking up. 'I will fly away.'

'The Company may not permit it.'

She looked at him then, the warm smile replaced with something firmer, and he saw the steel in her.

'I have my own means of transport.'

'Miss Baxter, your secret here on St Helena has come at a price. The price of a number of lives. I believe those lives were taken by the man who now watches over you, here on the island. This Edgar Burroughs.'

'Ah yes. Edgar.'

Something about the way she said the name arrested him.

'What is your relationship with Burroughs?'

She turned away.

'He represents my employer.'

It was only a half-answer, but she gave him no time to ponder it.

'Were they poisoned, these people in England?' she asked.

'I believe so.'

'There is a ... substance that is part of the *Opera* process. Its Latin name would be something like *Aqua interitus* – the water of destruction.'

'If I am correct, a French chemist has isolated it. He calls it hydro-cyanic acid.'

'I have not kept up with such developments.'

'It smells of almonds, I take it? And must be preserved in cold conditions?'

'It does smell of almonds. Yes. And we make it and store it deep in the caverns underground, where a chamber is kept cold for the purpose. Some have died over the years, if they have not been careful.'

'Edgar Burroughs left London soon after the last killings. And he lived on an estate with an icehouse. I believe he killed people with this poison, and masked his involvement. But he also marked the bodies with a sigil.'

'A sigil?'

'Yes. John Dee's Monad.'

She spun round, and seemed inexplicably angry and upset.

'What are you saying?'

'That Burroughs killed people to keep your secret, on behalf of the Company.'

'That is . . . no. That is impossible.'

'Why do you say that?'

'Because she is my mother,' said Burroughs, stepping into the library. 'And does a mother not defend her son?'

The ogre carried her along a tunnel in the dark. Abigail had no conception as to how he knew his way. He carried no lamp. But his steps were sure, and when her head faintly grazed a rock and she cried out the ogre stopped.

'Sorry! Sorry!' it breathed – he *breathed*, his *name is Fernando* – he breathed, and she felt the stump of his wrist touch her face. 'Did I hurt you?'

'No, Fernando, no. I thought I would hurt my head. On the wall.'

'Ah.' He began walking again, more slowly this time.

The pain in her shoulder had turned into an ugly ache with the occasional pierce of a knife under her skin, and she thought of childbirth again. Why so many thoughts of that? Was that pain really worse than this?

Eventually, the tunnel began to rise, and soon they reached some wooden steps, ones she thought she recognised from when Burroughs had brought her down here. Fernando carried her up the steps.

'Down. Must put you down for a moment.'

'All right.'

He placed her gently on the step, but even that soft change in movement caused her to cry out.

'Sorry! Sorry!'

He moved in the dark, and she heard the sound of iron on wood, the grating of some internal mechanism, and the door she could not see opened wide and the warm St Helena air blew through it. She saw stars and the glint of a near-full moon.

'Pick you up. Last time.'

'Yes.'

She gritted her teeth and he put his arms around her and lifted, ever so gently, but the pain was so enormous that she shrieked. He didn't say anything. He began to run, out through the door and into the night.

Once more, she was running across St Helena, carried this time not by a horse but by an ogre, a relic of some past whose existence she could not account for. He ran for several minutes, until they came to a barn which sat next to a house. She could see lights in the house. Was Charles inside?

Fernando opened the barn door, and carried her in. He placed her down gently against a pile of some stiff fibrous material. She whimpered gently, but then managed to move herself into a position where her shoulder became acutely uncomfortable rather than agonising. Fernando moved away, then returned with a lit oil lamp. She saw his face emerge from the gloom, a sad gargoyle walking out of her childhood night-mares to save her from the present.

'I will go now.'

'You are leaving me?'

'Someone will come for you.'

'Charles? Where is Charles?'

'There will be a bang. Soon.'

He placed the oil lamp down beside her, and she sat in a warm sphere of light. He stood at its edge.

'Fernando. What are you?'

His ugly face turned into the dark.

'I am a coward.'

He walked away.

'You should know, Horton, that your wife is in considerable pain,' said Burroughs. He carried no weapon, not even a sword, and Horton considered rushing at him, but Burroughs looked at him and said: 'Do as you are told and I may tell you where she is.'

Burroughs walked over to his mother and hugged her. Mina Baxter's eyes widened in surprise and her arms stiffened at her shoulders. Burroughs placed his nose into the side of her neck and inhaled deeply, then let her go.

'You smell like a dried-out tree stump,' he said, stepping away. Then he turned and sat in the chair opposite Horton.

'So,' said Burroughs. 'Waterman-Constable Charles Horton. I have waited a good while to speak to you. We were sorely interrupted by my mother's beast when we first met.'

'My wife is safe?'

'She is, within constrained limits. She has a badly injured shoulder, and is in great quantities of pain. She wept when I carried her, and begged for her life. We talked of the cosmos. She has no access to food or water where I have left her, but

I'm sure she can survive a day or two, though in considerable distress, certainly. Her prospects rest entirely on this conversation.'

'What do you want?'

'I shall answer a question with a question. What do you know?'

'I know that somebody – probably you – has killed the most recent assistant treasurers to St Helena. The last two men to be killed were called Suttle and Campbell, and I believe you killed them, probably with poison derived from whatever process is being used to take gold from the rocks of this island, a process this woman here has only just told me of. You then took them to the icehouse in the grounds of Robert Burroughs, alderman of the City of London and Proprietor of the East India Company. Robert Burroughs is, I believe, a relative of yours.'

'He is. My father was his brother. He died soon after we returned to England, and I was made a ward of my uncle.'

'So, I assume these former assistant treasurers were killed to keep St Helena's secret, though the circumstances were somewhat different to the earlier murders. Captain Thomas Jenkins was the first man you killed, some fifteen years ago; he was with a whore, and was a noted attendant at London's gaming tables. I assume he endangered the Company's secret in some way, and had to be got rid of. His killer left a strange mark on a dead whore – a mark I believe to be the Monad of John Dee.'

'Good, yes. Very good.'

'Two years later, Captain Robert Fox was pulled dead from the Thames. He was the subject of some scandal involving impropriety with small boys. And thus, he must have presented a problem for those keeping all this secret.'

'Yes. Fox was an inveterate interferer with small boys. He was no loss.'

'But there was no Monad on his body.'

'Well, there might have been, of course. The river could have washed it away. But no, I had moved on from such arcane plodding by then. I was growing up. John Dee's cosmology held no more appeal for me.'

'And yet, you returned to the Monads.'

'We shall come to that. Pray continue, Constable Horton.'

'Nothing happened for more than a decade. But Benjamin Johnson discovered St Helena's secret. He told his wife, and his wife began to send blackmail letters to Captain Suttle, a man she had known previously. Suttle spoke about this to the Company, and it was agreed he too was a great risk to the secret. By extension, the other surviving assistant treasurer, Captain Campbell, was a risk. They needed to be got rid of. So did the Johnsons.'

'Excellent, yes. There was panic at East India House. But not entirely because of the Suttle situation. There was much talk, you see, of St Helena being removed from Company control; of its becoming a Crown territory, for a great purpose. Even if it remained a Company holding, the role of the island would change.'

'Change? To what?'

'It matters little. The Company needs to address this situation. This little operation is coming to an end. The activities of my mother need to be relocated, as they should have been done decades ago. To another Company location, perhaps India. It needs to pass the operation of the facility over to a trusted individual, one with no ties to England – indeed, one with no prospects at all of advancement in England. And at the same time it needs to ensure that any knowledge of this secret which falls outside the very small circle of initiates within the Company is wiped from the map. Which brings us to you, Constable Horton.'

'You were sent here to discover your mother's secret.'

'Hardly. She is not going to tell *me*, constable. She hates me, I think. I asked as soon as I arrived, just in case her approaching death would scrape up some residue of maternal love in her desiccated breast. But there was none. She means to die with the secret still locked inside her head. Unless someone else can persuade her to divulge it. Or someone else can discover it another way.'

Burroughs grinned demonically. And, like that, Horton saw it all, for the first time.

'The Monad on the bodies of the Johnsons – you left them there for me to find.'

'Indeed, yes.'

'The book with the pages torn out of it. Johnson knew nothing of John Dee, did he? You planned to hook me on your snare.'

'Not just you, constable.'

'The Royal Society. Sir Joseph Banks. You knew they would seek my help, would send me here. You knew they believed Dee had discovered the secret to eternal life. The Company need not be involved. And then there is Putnam. Your dupe.'

'A dupe? No indeed. Feel no sympathy for him. He engineered the tableau on the Ratcliffe Highway.'

'You killed the Johnsons, and left them in the icehouse.'

'Yes.'

'And he removed them, carried them to Wapping. He injured them with the maul. All that – it was to attract *my* attention.'

'Yes!'

'And what of Amy Beavis?'

'Amy who?'

'She was killed. She took Captain Suttle's letters from Johnson's house.'

'Ah. Unfortunate. Putnam was supposed to remove the

letters. I suppose he had to kill her to get them back. Perhaps she was blackmailing him?'

'But I do not understand – if you wanted me here, why poison me?'

'*Poison* you, constable? Who on earth poisoned you?'

'I suspect the Company. Unless . . . unless they don't know what you're really up to. You plan to take over this little operation. Your uncle. Even he doesn't know. The Company saw me as a threat, and needed me silenced. They must have tried to make it look like the same killer despatched me as killed the Johnsons.'

Horton thought.

'And Putnam – he knew nothing of this elaborate charade to get me here. He saw the Monad on Benjamin Johnson, and tried to rub it off.'

Burroughs breathed air out through his nose. He looked troubled. But then his face cleared.

'You are correct. Putnam only knew of the plan to silence the Johnsons and hide their true murderer. This other little scheme is entirely my own. I imagined that the combination of John Dee and a great secret would be enough to tempt you here. And here you are. They failed to stop you. It was a lucky chance, perhaps, that you avoided death. Perhaps the gods are on my side. Perhaps Dee himself is watching over us.'

'You plan to take over from your mother?'

Burroughs leaned forward, and Horton saw he was holding one of John Dee's volumes before him, like a Bible.

'Have you ever heard of David Ricardo, constable?'

'No.'

'I expected as much. Ricardo is a kind of natural philosopher of money. He is to the Bank of England as your Sir Joseph Banks is to botany. Some time ago he wrote an essay in the *Morning Chronicle* saying the English currency had been debased by the suspension of cash payments in 1797. Does that mean anything to you?'

The year did, of course. The year of the Nore Mutiny. Of hardship in England and renewed warfare in Europe. Of the rise of Bonaparte and the newfound confidence of the French. Oh yes. 1797 meant a great deal to Charles Norton.

But *suspension of cash payments* did not. He shook his head.

'Well, if I were to give you a silver shilling or a gold guinea, we would both understand that the value of the coin I was giving you was essentially the value of the metal it was made of, as declared by the Mint. But what of *paper* money? In what is that value vested? Well, in its potential convertibility; in the fact that the Bank will, if asked, change that paper money for the equivalent value in gold from its own reserves. Or at least that used to be the case; until 1797. In that year, the Bank began to refuse converting notes into gold. Since then, the value of our paper money has been entirely notional and, since we can print as much of it as we like, that value has been degraded. This is Ricardo's argument. We need, he says, to start linking the value of our paper money to the value of gold. Which means we'll need more gold. A lot more gold.'

Burroughs's eyes twinkled.

'You see what is at stake here, constable? It comes from the ground. It comes out of the rock. It flows through the veins of the Earth before it is transmuted into the lifeblood of our Empire. Gold. And here, I have the means to extract as much of the stuff as I like.'

He put down the book.

'Or rather, I almost do. This stupid little secret, held entirely in that woman's head, is holding the entire Empire to ransom.'

'And you believe I can discover it?'

'Oh, no, constable. Not *you*. The little woman, currently

tied up in agony at an unspecified location. She's the reason I brought you here.'

'Abigail?'

'My uncle is a patron of St Luke's Asylum for Lunatics. It is one of his good works. Earlier this year I met an interesting man at one of the events the asylum holds for its patrons. He was a man called Drysdale, and he had an unfortunate thirst for liquor. Somewhat in his cups, he told me about an interesting case he was working on. A case of a woman who could make others do as she wished with only the power of her mind. He called her a *mesmerist*. A woman who had been in a madhouse in Hackney just last year. A woman called Abigail Horton.'

Mina Baxter was staring at her son, her fingers scrabbling on the cloth of the trousers she wore.

'My mother won't tell me her secrets, Constable Horton. But she will tell Abigail. She won't be able to stop herself.'

You're wrong. You've got it wrong. Horton had only a second to grip onto the extent of Burroughs's scheme – the extortion of an Empire, and the exploitation of his own wife – but then the air sucked itself out of the room, accompanied by a hellish bang, and suddenly the room was full of smoke and screaming.

Horton's ears no longer seemed to operate. He was lying face down – had he dived for the floor, or been thrown there? Heavy rocks lay across his back and his arms; he was virtually buried in them.

Slowly he moved his hands down his sides, put them either side of his chest, and began to layer himself up. The rocks fell from his back as he rose.

No. Not rocks. Books.

Smoke and paper filled the air, the contents of John Dee's

library merging with the destroyed remnants of Mina Baxter's house to form a new kind of gas, one that was thick with detritus and derivations born of the building and the books. It filled his lungs and coated his skin.

In front of him, a four-legged monster struggled to lift itself from the floor, with its four arms and two heads. It rose and fell, rolled and struggled, and spat and cursed and bit, a horrible chimera whitened by dust and paper.

But again his distorted senses were mistaken. It was not a monster. It was two men, struggling with each other. The gargoyle and the assistant treasurer rolled around in the destroyed library, while Horton screamed out one repeated question that he could barely hear himself.

'*Where is she? Where is she?*'

He stepped towards the struggling men, almost tripping over a long body lying, like him, face down on the floor under a pile of exploded volumes. He bent down and removed some books from the body, and saw the side of Mina Baxter's face lying there, a trickle of blood coming from her ear.

His hearing was beginning to work again, as if he were swimming up from the depths of the waters in the cave below them. He could hear the struggles of the men fighting nearby. And he could hear his own voice shouting that question over and over again. He stumbled towards the men.

'I *killed* you!' said an angry but desperate voice. 'I killed you not three hours ago!'

Horton lifted his head, in time to see Burroughs pin the gargoyle to the floor and straddle his chest. The assistant treasurer took something silver and sharp from his jacket, and Horton threw himself at him, his head connecting with the side of Burroughs's face with an alien crunch and his weight sending the man sprawling.

Horton felt around on the floor beside him, and he picked

up a heavy volume, its cover half-blown away but its spine still intact, and with a yell smashed the book down into Burroughs's face, over and over and over again. The white dust which had settled onto the destroyed pages on the floor became spattered with red. He would not remember how many times he brought that volume down.

After a while, he stopped, and got to his feet, and so did the gargoyle. They looked down at the shapes on the floor: Mina Baxter, and her terrible offspring. Burroughs's face was no longer a face. It was a red circle of horror, a gigantic full stop in a room full of sentences.

'Where is she?' Horton said again, and the gargoyle turned its ugly face to his.

'Come with me.'

They left the room. The hallway outside was, if anything, even more destroyed; it must have been here that the gargoyle left the explosive. The ceiling had been opened to the sky in one or two places, the front door to the house was no longer there.

Outside, the gargoyle pointed to the barn beside the house. A light was glowing from within. Without waiting, Horton ran across to it, and found her.

'Charles,' she said, her arm held in an awful shape, her voice as thin as the paper in one of Dee's ravaged volumes. For a moment he could not breathe, so great was his horror and anger, and when he moved to put his arms around her and she cried out in pain, it seemed like a commentary on their marriage. But he found a way to hold her that did not cause her pain, and for a good while that was more than enough.

'Fernando saved me,' she said.

'Fernando?'

'The ogre.'

He looked up to thank this Fernando, but the gargoyle – or

ogre, as Abigail called him – had gone. How long had he been sitting here with Abigail? A year, or a minute? Puzzled, he gently unfolded himself from his wife, and stood up to look around.

'See, Charles? See what she has been making?'

A gigantic blanket covered the floor. No, not a blanket. A sheet of silk, held down by rocks, its components sewn together by hand, covered almost the whole floor of the barn.

'The mulberry trees, Charles. Remember, I discovered them?'

I will leave this island, she had said. *I will fly away.*

I have my own means of transport.

In the far corner of the barn, he could see the shape of an enormous wicker box, as big as a horse. Was that what she had intended to travel in?

A thought occurred to him.

'I must check inside the house.'

'Charles, don't. It may be dangerous.'

'I must. I shall only be a moment.'

He walked back to the house, through the space where the door had been and down the exposed corridor. Paper still fluttered in the warm night air. His hearing had returned, and there was a great pain in his head. He may have been injured.

He went into the library. Burroughs's body was where he had left it, half-submerged beneath the volumes he had made such a study of. But Mina Baxter's body was gone.

THE HORTONS LEAVE THE ISLAND

The island's doctor came to reset her shoulder and it was as agonisingly awful as she had envisaged, with none of the immediate relief she had seen in the eyes of other patients with dislocated joints.

'How long has it been like this?' the doctor asked, and she made up some story about falling down a defile. He tutted, and told her there had been a lot of damage, though she doubted greatly whether he knew what this might mean. What it meant for her, just now, was pain, and a good deal of it. She lay in Seale's bed while her husband sought Mina Baxter, sometimes with Seale, sometimes without him.

The man who had injured her, Edgar Burroughs, was dead. Charles told her what had happened to him, though she felt he left out the more sanguinary details. The simple fact was that Charles had killed him. She wondered at how little she was chilled by this, but then remembered her own temptation up on the hillside. One did not kill demons; one simply exorcised them.

Charles tried, with difficulty, to explain the secret which Burroughs had sought to protect. She knew of no part of natural philosophy – none whatsoever – which could explain the process which the Baxters had used to extract gold from the rock of St Helena. But she thought she could at least imagine it.

'The rock would have to be mined,' she said, as her husband sipped water after a morning scouring the island's hidden places. 'I assume that whatever the substance is that Mina was using reacted with the gold in the rock, somehow, and allowed for it to be reconstituted in some way. But gold does not react with any substance I know of.'

'There was definitely a mine,' said Charles. 'We found workings, and explosives. Indeed, the explosives the gargoyle used.'

'He was called Fernando, Charles,' she reminded him.

The Governor had become involved, of course. There were Chinese workers attached to the mine, and when they discovered Seale and Charles poking around in the caves beneath the mine, word got back.

'We are to leave on the first available ship,' said Charles. 'The Governor seems very minded to see the back of us sooner rather than later.'

'But what of the Company? Won't they react to this?'

Are we in danger? That was the unspoken question. She watched Charles ponder it.

'I do not know, wife,' he said, eventually. 'When we return to London . . . a good many things may have changed. Harriott may no longer be well enough to work. Graham, too. My word, they might not even be alive. We will have to talk of the future.' He smiled, weakly. 'When you are well.'

It was the first time she sensed they might not return at all. She changed the subject.

'Alchemy was about more than gold, you know,' she said.

'Indeed?' he said. He was looking at Seale's map.

'Gold is the purest metal – the purest state of matter. But

alchemists believed there was a pure state of *being*, also. A state for mankind to aspire to. To be at one with God, and to live forever. Some alchemists believed that you could reach this state if you drank liquid gold.'

Was that Fernando's secret? Was the ogre the face of God? The thought was unfathomable and unspeakable. Watching Charles gaze at Seale's map reminded her of Halley's maps, the ones showing the lines of magnetic variation and the way they bent over the surface of the Earth. Were these lines of magnetic force actually images of something invisible, a field of magnetism enclosing the Earth, acting at a distance?

She wondered if the *Opera* had remained hidden for so long because, in most places and at most times, its recipes for gold extraction had failed to work. She wondered if there was something different about St Helena – some confluence of magnetism, some expression of the inner workings of the Earth – which might explain Fernando Lopez and the endless stream of gold which had poured out of this island and had, in some way, sustained an Empire.

That door with no lock, worked by magnetism. Indistinguishable from magic, if you did not see the mechanism. Was there a lesson there?

Her husband had been up at Mina Baxter's house, and had, he said, discovered another of those strange doors. He had tried to use the same magnetised rod as had worked the door of the fort, but to no avail.

'A different lock?' said Seale.

'Perhaps,' said Horton. 'Or a different mechanism entirely.'

'Another secret, then.'

'Perhaps.' He smiled at Abigail. 'They have found us a ship. She sails tomorrow.'

But to where, thought Abigail, does she sail?

'Will you find her?' she asked Charles, and he looked up at

this. He was happier to discuss investigations than he was listening to scientific speculations.

'I think not,' he replied.

He had been searching for days, but from the start he knew he would never find Mina Baxter. She had disappeared so utterly on the night of the explosion, along with her strange ogre, that he found himself wondering if she'd uncovered other secrets in John Dee's library – the secret to walking down into the Earth, for example.

On the morning of their departure he was woken at first light by a soldier carrying a note from the Governor, a carefully worded little missive which said more than it seemed. It was a politician's letter, designed to be read by others than those to whom it was addressed.

Horton – I have in the last day received orders which will change forever the nature of this island. I do think that the eyes of the World will be on this place. I am not at liberty to reveal these matters, and in any case it would be unbecoming to discuss them with a constable. I will simply take this opportunity to say that the militia will shortly take hold of Miss Baxter's farm and outbuildings. I request that you supply Mr Seale with any keys or devices necessary to gain ingress to the various facilities. This is a matter for the Company and for the government of St Helena. If any discoveries are made which impinge on the Crown's settlement on the island, they will be made known and dealt with in the appropriate manner.

You will today leave the island aboard the whaler Bala. The Council of the island acknowledges your work in discovering this matter. We trust the sensitivities regarding the private affairs of this island and its inhabitants will receive due regard from you and your superiors in whichever report you decide to file.

Governor Colonel M Wilks

He had known the Governor wanted them gone, but this sudden urgency was odd. There had been rumours for days of great events, though what these events were nobody knew. He left the note with Abigail and said he would be back by lunchtime.

First, he went to the barn where he had found Abigail on that terrible night. In daylight it was a trim, well-cared-for place, and inside it had lost some of its secrets. The vast puddle of silk had gone, as had the big basket which, he suspected, had been designed to hang beneath it. The pile of material where Abigail had been sitting turned out to be rattan, presumably taken from East India ships where it had been used as ballast. He found this interesting. Mina had presumably used the rattan to make the basket.

Next, he walked up to the fort, where the door which had befuddled him for so long stood open, and he stood before it for a long while. He had perhaps four hours, and in his pocket was a ball of string.

He tied the string to an old screw in the doorframe, and jammed the door open with a heavy rock. He walked inside and turned up the oil lamp he had brought with him. Then, down he went, walking into the Leviathan a final time.

He walked down dozens of tunnels and several different staircases, doubling back on himself time and time again, using the string to keep contact with the strange door above him. He found a wooden bridge across the crevasse within the cave, and discovered another set of steps built into the rock on the far side. These went all the way down to the level of the sea, and gave out onto a little beach. The same little beach he had seen from the sea when he had gone out with Seale.

There had been a boat on this beach, the last time he saw it. There was no boat now.

He thought of Jacobus Aakster, that old Dutch mercenary

who had tricked a cabal of Dutch merchants and whose family had, ever since, held a great trading company to ransom. Mina had learned a good few things from him, after all. The art of misdirection, for example.

If he looked further, he suspected he would find the remains of a fire somewhere up near the barn – a fire which had consumed the silk and the basket from the barn. Mina Baxter had flown away in her balloon, the wizard's final apprentice flying into the sky as she had dreamed of doing. Except, he believed, she had done nothing of the sort. He spent some time on that little beach searching the horizon, but could see nothing.

Over that horizon was London. Soon, the things he had discovered here would come to light there. He had fled the East India Company's clutches, and now he had discovered the Company's ultimate secret. Alderman Burroughs, Magistrate Markland, even Home Secretary Sidmouth. Would they welcome Constable Horton with open arms?

Finally, a question to which he knew the answer.

Some time later, he was walking down the town's single street when a great boom of cannon resounded through the air. Seale stepped out of his front door to look down to the sea, and turned to Horton as he walked up.

'I have never heard such a racket,' said Seale.

'I should be surprised if you had,' said Horton. 'That was a 15-gun salute.'

'How on earth do you know that?'

'I was a Navy lieutenant.'

'And what does it signify?'

'It rather suggests an admiral has arrived in St Helena.'

That 15-gun salute was an emphatic full stop to the Governor's odd letter. Horton itched to get down to the wharf, now, and found himself hovering around his wife as she made their luggage ready for the voyage, her arm in the carefully engineered cotton sling.

'Husband, make yourself useful, and wait outside,' said Abigail, so outside he went, and encountered a familiar face scurrying down to the sea.

'Ken!' he exclaimed, grabbing the boy by the arm as he hurried by. Ken's gigantic and slow friend Hippo came to a halt at the same time, as if they were connected by an invisible spring.

'Here, now, let go of me, constable,' said Ken, outraged. 'I've got important business down in the town.'

'Important business watching ships and fleecing new arrivals, I'll wager,' said Horton.

'Now, then, what do you mean by that? An affront, that is. An affront to my dignity.'

'I wanted to discuss Edgar Burroughs with you, Ken.'

At the mention of this name, Ken's body went loose and Horton was able to let him go. The boy's face looked miserable.

'He made me point out your missus to him, constable. He was a forceful character.'

'Tell me a bit about him.'

'I don't know anything about him. Company man, he is. Big fellow.'

Horton noted the boy's use of the present tense. Word had not got out, then.

'His character?'

'You mean, what is he like?'

'Yes.'

'Oh, I don't know. Keeps himself to himself.'

'And what about the Cannibal?'

'The Cannibal? Who you been talking to?'

'Have you seen him?'

'Of course I haven't bleeding seen him! He's a fairy story, isn't he? Something to scare the kids with to get them to behave.'

'I seen him.'

They were the first words Hippo had spoken, and the lad looked as surprised by them as Horton and Ken were.

'I seen him up at Deadwood.' Hippo gazed back up the valley, into the heart of the island. 'He saw me and he ran off. He only had one hand. And no ears.'

And then Ken grabbed his friend's hand and yanked him away, and the two of them set off down to the wharf.

'Ready, husband?' said Abigail, appearing at the door of the Castle of Otranto.

'Ready, wife.'

Seale came out behind Abigail, carrying her bag.

'I shall be your packhorse, my friends,' he said, and winked at Abigail, and Horton saw that his remarkable wife winked back.

There was a great scurrying in the square behind the sea-wall. St Helena's population could not run to a crowd, but it was doing its best now. A mighty ship had arrived, it seemed, one which would bring paying customers.

A man was waiting for them by the drawbridge. He looked entirely out of place in this sun-kissed square, his thick beard and heavy body speaking of frozen seas and ice-clad spars.

'Horton?' he said, and when Horton nodded he nodded back and would not speak again until they were approaching Tenerife, weeks from now. Horton, Abigail and Seale followed him out through the wall and over the drawbridge.

There were five ships out in the James Town roads. One was obviously a whaler, and under normal circumstances it would draw the eye by its ugliness alone. But today it was competing with a creature of a different stripe – a ship of the line, third-rate and elegantly lethal, every one of its lines speaking of war and glory. She was ringed by three other vessels, all frigates – a small fleet sent, presumably, from England. But for what purpose Horton could not imagine.

A longboat was making its way from the warship, and a large group of islanders had gathered on the wharf near the point it was to tie up. At their front Horton could see the Governor, Colonel Wilks, his face fixed on the longboat. The seaman from the *Bala* stopped and waited patiently for the longboat to arrive, presumably used to biding his time when he had to.

A few minutes later a rope was thrown to the wharf from the boat and tied fast. A man stepped up onto the steps. He was an admiral, a creature Horton had not laid eyes on since the Nore Mutiny, an elegant peacock of a fellow whose dress uniform glittered with prestige and made everything on the wharf seem suddenly drab and austere.

'Admiral Cockburn, I presume,' said Colonel Wilks.

'Governor Wilks,' replied the Admiral, as if he were talking to a shopkeeper. He looked at the crowd of people that now surrounded him on the wharf. 'Perhaps we can retire to somewhere more discreet?'

'Of course. Follow me, sir.'

The crowd parted, and the Admiral and the Governor made their way along the wharf and into the town. Cockburn glanced at Horton and his whaler companion briefly and saw only two specks of humanity for whom he had no time. The man from the whaler continued his interrupted walk down the wharf, picking his way through the crowd which was beginning to disperse.

'Horton, goodbye,' said Seale. 'It has been an interesting experience making your acquaintance. I trust, though, we shall not meet again.'

'My thanks to you, Seale. You have aided us greatly. I wish you well.'

Abigail squeezed Seale's arm and leaned up to kiss his cheek; he smiled delightedly, and he hugged her to him, scandalously and delightfully.

Then they were in the whaler's boat, rowing away from the island. Seale waved to them from the wharf, and some in the crowd looked at them as if they might be part of the excitement of the Admiral's party. But no, they were a dull affair compared to the Naval masque being played out in the roads.

'I wonder why they are here,' said Abigail.

'Yes. It is extraordinary for an admiral to arrive with such a small fleet. Unless he is bringing something to the island.'

He looked at the warship, and noted a small figure in a bicorne hat standing on the forecastle gazing intently at St Helena. It turned its head towards him, and raised one hand in greeting, and Horton, despite himself, raised a hand in return.

'You look pensive, husband,' Abigail asked, and he noticed her hand was holding his, and squeezing gently.

'Doubtless I do,' he replied. 'Where would you have us sail to, wife?'

He felt the lump of gold in his pocket. The lump Mina had shown him in the little wooden case. The lump he had put in his own pocket while Edgar Burroughs told his tale.

Enough to buy a ship. Probably.

Abigail looked at the horizon as her husband had done.

'West?' she suggested.

She almost didn't make it. She had prepared this little voyage for years, but Horton had nearly discovered her in the days after the explosion and the death of her son. But then the little barque had appeared off Prosperous Bay and had made the agreed signal, and the plans she had put in place to escape as soon as her son had been taken from her moved smoothly into effect.

She and Fernando burned the silk and the balloon basket – not without a twinge of sadness on her part. She would never fly up to the clouds now, but flight of a different kind was required. The smoke from the fire was still visible as they rowed the boat from Prosperous Bay and out to the barque.

They sailed away. Francesco died after only three days, and it had been terrible to see. The further from St Helena they voyaged, the more he aged, his skin drying and his body shrivelling as if he had been placed inside a gigantic oven, as if every bit of moisture inside him was being burned away.

She tried feeding him and giving him water, but it was no good. He ate and drank what he could, but still he continued to wither. Whatever had kept him alive for so long was disappearing. The minute St Helena slipped below the horizon behind him, his death began. He began to mutter in his own language, words that she did not understand which sounded ragged and bitter, and when his death came it was like a wind had become a breeze which had finally stilled, leaving only silence.

She cried, not just for Fernando but for herself, for this baleful inheritance, for the knowledge locked inside her head which was both a curse and a lifeline. She wrapped his body in some silk left over from her balloon. She weighed him down with some of the gold she had brought with her. It seemed a small price to pay for his companionship. She pushed him over the side. The dozen men who crewed the boat muttered beneath their breaths and crossed themselves and felt relieved that they no longer carried an ogre.

The barque sailed east towards Africa, despite the prevailing winds. She sailed for a week, until the master spied land and the barque anchored off a beautiful beach. Mina paid the master and his crew in gold, and they piled provisions into the boat which she had brought from Prosperous Bay, and she rowed up to the beach alone.

The land here was flat and unpromising, but she had heard there was gold in the land beyond. She had enough to keep her alive until she found it.

AUTHOR'S NOTE

As in my previous books, *The Detective and the Devil* contains a mix of fact and fiction. Those who are interested in what is real and what is not should read the following.

The cyanide method of gold extraction is now widely used in the gold mining industry, but it was not invented until 1887 by John Stewart MacArthur, Robert Forrest and William Forrest.

The alchemist Jābir ibn Hayyān did write about gold, as he wrote about a great many things, but he did not know about cyanide.

The history of the discovery of cyanide as described in the book is based on true events.

There is not and never has been, to my knowledge, a gold mine on St Helena. Other than that, the history of the island's discovery and its ownership in the story is drawn from fact. The story of Fernando Lopez's exile on the island is also true – up to the point at which it isn't.

Edmond Halley did visit St Helena as described within for the purposes of making a star chart and to observe the transit of Mercury (which creates its own little alchemical echo, Mercury being 'quicksilver', a substance alchemists believed had arcane properties).

He also drew a chart of lines of magnetic variation based on his own observations. The line of zero variation does indeed pass close to St Helena before heading north-west and crossing Florida, a fact which readers of my first book *The English Monster* may find resonant.

John Dee did live in a house at Mortlake, and his library was ransacked, though I give the ransacking mob an intent they cannot have had.

I also have taken the liberty of having Dee's house still standing in 1815, a fact I have been unable to confirm and which, I am sure, must be said to be entirely made up.

I also have no evidence that the Royal Society did indeed think Dee had found the source of eternal life, nor do I think the Society has any particular interest in that subject (though I'm sure if they did, they would keep it to themselves).

Charles Lamb did work as a clerk for the East India Company, and was known to take drink to settle his stammer. His sister did suffer the mental disturbances I describe herein, and her poor mother was a victim of them.

My thanks to Sophia Tobin, Goldsmiths librarian and novelist, and to Rupert Baker at the Royal Society Library. I should also like to take this opportunity to particularly thank my editor at Simon & Schuster, Jo Dickinson, and my agent, Sam Copeland. This book is dedicated to my brothers at a particular time of crisis and care, and to my wife Louise, who can read me like a book.